SIXTEEN SHILLINGS AND TUPPENCE HA'PENNY

After the horror and darkness of the Second World War, Tabby spends her formative years in a large East End family and blossoms from being a typical teenager to an independent woman who makes her own choices which include establishing a happy marriage and having children. Tabby's knowledge and understanding of the English language had increased by leaps and bounds and she welcomed the change, but did not lose her Cockney dialect. Why should she? It was her heritage from aeons of ancestors. With hardships interspersed with humour, this true to life story is guaranteed to warm your soul.

SIXTEEN SHILLINGS AND TUPPENCE HA'PENNY

Sixteen Shillings And Tuppence Ha'Penny

by

Violet Frederick Foot

Magna Large Print Books
Long Preston, North Yorkshire,
BD23 4ND, England.

British Library Cataloguing in Publication Data.

Foot, Violet Frederick
    Sixteen shillings and tuppence ha'penny.

    A catalogue record of this book is
    available from the British Library

    ISBN   0-7505-1952-5

First published in Great Britain in 2001 by Minerva Press

Copyright © Violet Frederick Foot 2001

Cover illustration © Len Thurston by arrangement with
P.W.A. International.

The moral right of the author has been asserted

Published in Large Print 2003 by arrangement with
Mrs Violet Foot

Magna Large Print is an imprint of Library Magna Books Ltd.

Printed and bound in Great Britain by
T.J. (International) Ltd., Cornwall, PL28 8RW

*For my late husband Frederick George,
our sons, James and Robert and grandchildren,
Wesley, Matthew, Christopher, Ashley and
Charlotte, with much love.*

This book is dedicated to the Memory of my deeply loved, late husband, Frederick George Foot, who was a fountain of diverse knowledge and wisdom – without his faith and encouragement I would not now be the woman I am. He passed away on 17 March 1991. His loving smile and good nature will remain with me for ever.

Violet Frederick Foot
Norfolk, 2000

Acknowledgements

Staff at King's Lynn Reference Library for verifying tobacco coupons and facts and figures on housing, wages and pensions.

Nationwide Building Society, King's Lynn and Downham Market who are most helpful and courteous with faxes and information at all times.

My siblings, Emmie Oler, Matilda Edwards, Eileen Paratt and Doreen Morgan, my brother-in-law Harry Edwards, my niece Joan Middleton, my daughters-in-law Barbara Foot and Caroline Foot for their faith in my ability.

Friends scattered nationwide, from co-ed halcyon days of our youth who have helped me to enjoy life again.

Jennifer Rye, Jean Sellers, Shirley Old, Colin and Rosalia Robb, Alfred and Gwen Frith, Ronald Sutton, Ena Parkes, David Chaplow, Donald Brown, David Moulding, Valerie Aston, Cyrilla Hall, Eleanor Herd, Anne Davies, and anyone I have inadvertently omitted, thank you one and all. Anne reminded me she's a few months older! Jean for her charming un-posed snapshot of me. Life is grand once again. God bless you all.

Chapter One

With a light hop and skip – and another hop –
Tabitha Braithewaite fairly skimmed along the
pavements; her narrow feet looking incongruous
at the end of pathetically thin legs – like those of
one of Lowry's matchstick paintings! Her feet
were clothed in pristine white socks, falling
concertina fashion round bony ankles. Their
spindly appearance semi-permanently mottled in
various shades of mauve did not exactly add to
her charms. Neither did it detract from them!

Her mother, Jean, had repeatedly warned her
about the danger of sitting too close to the fire in
winter. The coal fire was the only form of heating
in the houses; only the rich had central heating.

Tabby had turned a deaf ear to her mother's
warnings, she didn't care – as long as she was
warm.

'You'll be sorry young lady, when you grow up
– mark my words.' Tabby heeded not, water off a
duck's back. Warmth was of paramount importance – on account of her thin body and limbs,
she hugged the fire all the more. Years of living
most of the time in air raid shelters – theirs and
other people's, 'out the back garden' – had not
given her a head start in life. Hence her thinness
and wan features and the poor skinny limbs. But
she was perfectly healthy, wiry and as an added
bonus, a most cheerful and pleasant child – with

not an enemy to her name.

'You'll have legs like an old woman when you grow up Tabby!' said her mother.

Tabitha – Tabby to most people – who knew her around the six streets where she'd lived all her young life, knew quite well what her mother meant. The *old women* had a tendency to sit almost on top of their fires with their dumpy legs splayed apart, revelling in the warmth; savouring the delicious heat reaching their private parts. Their bloomers (or drawers) guarding their honour, were fleecy inside and smooth outside. The long legs of the bloomers reached down to their knees. It was no small wonder that the heated fleeciness (from hugging the fires) often gave a certain odour from nameless women – especially the few who were not over-careful in their personal hygiene.

Even down at Kent whilst hop-picking – ah glorious days – the old dears couldn't tear themselves away from the crackling, flaming faggot fires. After a hard day's graft, picking the fat hops, they couldn't wait to push their stools as near as possible. The stain of the hops on their hands – for they were most industrious pickers – added to the aroma.

When the faggots subsided, the men and boys threw on heavy logs of wood. The old dears told them what *lovely boys* they were and pushed their seats a bit closer to the logs!

There they sat for hours of an evening – warming their private parts with just the firelight for company; telling their stories and regaling their memories which were handed down by word-of-mouth from family to family – generations of them had made the yearly exodus to the hop fields.

In summertime they wore their silk bloomers, but hopping mornings and nights were chilly – the fleecy ones became *de rigueur*. The silk bloomers were Directoire – same sizes and same lengths as the fleecy ones. Both kinds were universally known as '…-stoppers' in working class circles.

Crumbs! If I called bloomers …-stoppers my mum'd wash me mouf aht wiv carbolic soap! Anyway, as Tabby comfortingly told herself, she'd no intention of wearing bloomers when she grew up. No blinkin' fear!

Her mother wore them and judging by the neighbours' washing flapping on their clothes lines, so did most of them. Her mother was in good company.

Up to recently, Tabby's world had mainly encompassed the block of six streets with a few handy shops up the top – round the next turning just off one of the streets. Only they weren't named streets, they were roads.

She'd lived at 48 Granite Road since she was born – well, since she was about four years old actually (been born in Bethnal Green hadn't she). She knew her way around the streets blindfolded. They all did in the six years of blackouts! Near the shops, just a wee bit further along the main road, was situated the local pub – The King's Oak – her father's favourite watering hole. Not that he drank too much.

There were plenty of pubs but this was the

nearest to 48. They always referred to their house as 48. Her father enjoyed a good game of 'arrers' (darts) with his mates in a convivial atmosphere. They didn't have to worry about driving home afterwards – none of them owned cars! Who did?

The off-licence was situated at the end of the pub, with its own entrance and counter, away from the male *hoi polloi*. Tabby was used to running errands to the off-licence for all and sundry; collecting the full bottles of their favourite tipple and then taking the empties back. It was a lucrative trade for her. She was paid a tanner at the end of the week – from her regulars. Shopping errands were also her forte. Didn't stand much of a competition from others of her ilk – did she? Not until they came back from evacuation. However, Tabitha Braithewaite had already built up her clientele – she continued to be in demand, even without her monopoly during the war years! The tanners and the few coppers she picked up from returning certain bottles all added up. She'd even managed to invest in her own private national savings stamps book; buying stamps regularly and sticking them into her savings book. She loved spending almost as much as she loved saving! She paid for her *luxuries* with the coppers obtained from occasional extra errands – not from her regular sources! Mainly spent on the movies – the American word had crept into the English language! The Americans arrived in 1942 taking the breath away from the female population! Every American was from Hollywood! 'How about me taking you to the movies tonight,

18

Honey?' Their opening gambit became almost as familiar as the opening lines in the Book of Genesis!

'In the beginning...!'

The women were fascinated with the Yanks but the men were not! They'd quickly labelled the GIs – 'overpaid, oversexed, over here.' A British private got fourteen shillings a week, his American equivalent was paid £3.8s.9d. (70p and £3.45 approximately). Even Tabby was not averse to asking them 'got any gum chum'? They never refused. Americans were the soul of generosity ... it took them awhile to realise people 'passed round their cigarette packets'! 'They're dead smart in their uniforms,' said Tabby to nobody in particular. 'I wonder if I'll marry an American? Mum said I might.' It was every mother's dream to have a rich American son-in-law. The food parcels were the attraction. Made a change from the boring spam, corned beef, and other scarce wartime rations.

The British boys conscripted into the armed forces to 'take the King's shilling' had sadly depleted the six streets of eligible young men. It made her eyes water when she thought of some of her favourites who'd never ask her to 'Run and get me a pint, Tabby', ever again. Her mum said they were asleep in foreign countries, with a white cross on their graves.

Tabby recalled reading a poem by Seigfried Sassoon from the First World War ... she thought of those white crosses whenever she thought of the poem.

Tabby had thought quite a lot lately about the

war and God and the dead boys! Her mind was being stretched by a good teacher at school. She certainly thought more deeply.

'Yeah! The Americans were nice blokes, smashing drawling voices, easy access to luxurious goodies, especially nylons. Her mum had said some women would sell their soul for a pair of nylons. I don't think I'd sell my soul! 'Ow would I go to 'eaven if I did? The food, that was different!'

'Yer 'ave ter 'ave food to stay alive. Yeah! The Yanks were okay. Nice of 'em ter come and 'elp us fight the Huns, it were – Dad sed we'd been fighting on our own for three years. He said it was a Godsend the Americans came and 'elped us ... they're all right I like 'em!'

Her mother had heard her talking to herself. 'Yer'll get yer knickers in a twist talking to yerself Tabby, you are a one!' Jean linked her arm into Tabby's. 'Wot yer on abaht, me li'le cock sparrer?'

'Oh! I do love the American films Mum. It's so different from our lives. It makes yer feel like yer livin' in a dream.'

'Yer ain't the only one Tabby – we all think that. Hollywood must be a wonderful place to live in. But I'm not sure all the Americans over here are from Hollywood! And I'm not sure they've all got the "ear of a producer" who can get the girls into the films. That's men sweet talkin' Tabby, they don't mean wot they say, most men don't, lovey.

'Yer'll larn one day. I 'opes yer get a good bloke one day, lovey. A good bloke is worth 'is weight in gold.'

'Me teacher said the films 'is an escape route Mum.'

'She's right, lovey, she's right, we all need escape routes in our lives, that's wot makes the world go round.'

All this and more was going through Tabby's busy mind. Jumping the hopscotches made yer think – yer were on your own for a while. Her teacher told her, 'You need solitude to think Tabitha. Just let your mind roam free – it's a wonderful rejuvenator.' Tabby wasn't quite sure what a rejuvenator was – she couldn't remember meeting one. She wondered what a rejuvenator looked like. Would he look like the Americans? She made a mental note to ask her teacher to tell her a bit more about rejuvenators. They didn't have a dictionary at home. Anyway she couldn't spell it, so how could she look it up?

She'd thanked her mum for 'telling me things' and run off blissfully, serenely, to spend some of her coppers on one of her favourites – sherbert dabs. She poked the little straw provided through one of the corner triangles. Greedily, she sucked hard, and choked. Coughing and spluttering, a passer-by kindly thwacked her between her shoulder blades. Feeling a bit ashamed at her own greediness she'd run off with a stammered thank you. A few minutes later, a glutton for punishment, she was sucking and spluttering on her way back to the sweet shop. A handful of gobstoppers with their tangent aniseed flavour was her next weekly buy. Moving the gobstopper from cheek to cheek she resembled a chipmunk. If you'd told her, she wouldn't have known what it was, she hadn't seen a hamster let alone a chipmunk; anyway, the latter was American. Her world was the six streets, some bomb sites (now she was older) and the garden out the back of the house; that only ever had rabbits and chickens, the former for the stew pot any day now, the latter after their egg-laying ended, would become roasts for Sunday.

The liquorice ritual – one of Tabby's favourites – was not her agenda this week. She'd buy that next week. Long black 'shoelaces' – slowly dropped into the mouth. The trick was to tilt your head back. Oh, that was fun. Your tongue would be black. 'It's about time you started growing up a bit more, Tabby.' Jean had been annoyed to see her black tongue.

'Perhaps I am gettin' too old fer likker-riss? Suppose I'd better start growin' up. I'm two years older than Esmeralda. Still, it was fun chasing each other with our black tongues stuck out like Maoris. Like those on the films last week.'

You could always find a hopscotch drawn on the pavements. You could tell whose it was by the way it was drawn. 'This must be Janet's. She never could draw a straight line, not even in geography. Come to that, yer don't draw many straight lines in geography, it's nearly all angles.' She picked up a smooth hop-scotch stone from the gutter. 'Janet leaves this on her window cill. Someone must've forgotten to put it back. Perhaps their mum called them home.' She expertly flicked the stone along the pavement. She was good at this game, it landed in a square. With a hop and a straddle and another hop, balancing now she twisted round, picked up the stone and made it back to base. Huh! It's easy!

She looked around, not even a lace curtain twitching. Must be eating their dinner.

Laughing exultantly she went on her way.

'Make sure yer ain't out of earshot Tabby, or yer'll feel my 'and on yer backside.'

She was old enough now, thought Tabby. Twelve she was. Even her father had said she was older now. 'If I didn't care abaht yer I wouldn't worry abaht yer,' said her mother.

The funny things grown-ups say? Even the five year olds went to school, there and back on their own or with friends. If their mums were out after school they could get indoors with the string key hanging behind the letterbox. Every house in the six streets had a 'string key'. If you were very short, your mum left a piece of wood or a brick for you to stand on. It was easy to open the door and let yourself in then.

Some families left their doors permanently open on the latch all day, you just pushed it open.

A heady, balmy day; it was a wonderful world. A few tandem cyclists passed her by – she waved; they waved back – bunches of bluebells hanging from their back saddles. Drooping already, they'd be dead by tomorrow. Bluebells never lasted long, once picked. Such a shame!

Tabby had left the streets far behind – she was out in open land, a small area nearby. Her happy carolling, arms flung wide, her body weaving along in a ragged line seemed to have an airborne movement of its very own. Face uplifted to the sky, she spun around like a top – the air passed through her stretched-out fingers. Oh! It's a wonderful, wonderful world! She wished she was down Kent, hop-picking – the highlight of their year. The annual 'Hopping' excursions – a few weeks in real country air; she loved the Hopping song:

When yer go down 'oppin' –
Knock at number one,
See old Mother Riley banging on her drum.
With an ee-ie-o-ee-ie-o
Eee – ie – eee – ie – ohhhh!

When the man went round measuring the bushels of hops, a few times a day, he entered the figures in his book and in a little tally book in her mother's name (Mother kept it in her bag). They'd draw the money at the end of the season. If the mothers were short of ready cash they could have a bit of it to tide them over until their husbands were down with their week's wages. Some husbands spent the whole of the hopping season with their wives.

Our luvvly 'ops.
Our luvvly 'ops.
When the measurer 'ee comes round –
Pick 'em up, pick 'em up
Orff the ground.
When 'ee starts ter measure –
'Ee don't know when ter stop.
Aye aye!
Jump in the bin –
And take the blinkin' lot!

Her head twisted all ways; good, nobody was in sight! If she'd sworn, somebody might have heard her – and if it got back to her mother, Jean, it would mean a mouthwash of carbolic soap. She could almost taste it in her mouth. Ugh!

In wartime, huge posters said, 'Careless talk costs lives!' That fear was ingrained in her subconscious mind. She wasn't exactly scared of ghosts – but listeners. Nah! nobody 'ere. All hell would break loose if she was caught swearing. If there was one thing her mother didn't like it was swearing in children. Hard for them not to – all the adults swore; profanity was their 'best friend'!

Henry Braithewaite once made Tabby laugh. He'd been to The King's Oak – the blokes must have used every swear word invented and added a few choice ones of their own making! 'I was fit to burst wiv laughter,' chortled her father. 'A young Sally-Anne lass (Salvation Army) was standing mutely behind them, with her collecting box. Was her face red – poor lass! Yer could've warmed yer 'ands by it! Wiv 'er collectin' box in one hand and the *War Cry* newspapers in the uvver. Wot me old dad used to call "a figure of propriety". She really were. Obviously her first night in a pub. A coin clinked in 'er box, she thanked the giver loudly. Oh my word! The Sally-Anne – she froze: the lads 'ad 'eard 'er! Spun round they did. Were their faces red! Nearly as red as 'ers. Turned their pockets out they did. Oh my and "sweet Fanny Adams"! All their loose change. Even got the landlord to change their pound notes to 'alf crowns. Yerse! They did. The rest of us were nigh-on wetting ourselves. Couldn't stop laughing, we couldn't. Filled her collecting box to the brim they did. Must've been the first time a Sally-Anne lady got 'er collectin' box full on 'er first pub duty c'lectshun!'

'Wot did the Sally-Anne do, Dad?'

'Blimey gal! Wot did she do? I'll tell yer! Smiled sweetly, thanked them prettily and stuffed a copy of *War Cry* into their 'ands, that's wot she dun!'

Tabby enjoyed the *War Cry*, her mother always brought it home for her – from their pub night out. And a packet of crisps – she loved searching for the blue bag with the twist of salt, it was usually somewhere in the middle!

Running off to tell her mates the story, her mother had called out, 'Remember, me li'tle Rosebud, no swearing or else–'

'A mouf-ful of carbolic soap,' Tabby finished for her getting out of earshot first; she could really run when the need arose.

Admittedly Jean and Henry Braithewaite were her parents. She hardly ever saw the latter – except at meal times. Either 'at work or 'down the Union' were the glib explanations. Mind you in the war he could be found at the ARP base. He'd failed his medical – something to do with his chest, and the number of young children. At The King's Oak he spent quite a bit of time – playin' arrers or shove ha'penny with stakes of thruppeny bits, purloined from Jean's Christmas hoard, in the old biscuit tin! Or, even worse! He was *somewhere else*. 'Mind yer own business Tabby,' her mother had said to her on many occasions. 'Mind yer own business.'

It was a dead cert her older sisters were more in the 'know' than Tabby. Jean was well loved by her children, family and neighbours. Help anybody she would. A good clean, well-respected woman of the six streets. If somebody gave her a load of cast-off dresses for her children, Jean had always insisted on giving them half a crown. It behove her conscience – she'd paid for them.

Enjoying her quiet reflections, Tabby was amazed with all the things tumbling pell-mell through her brain. That must've been wot me teacher sed – gives yer time ter think!

The Plimsolls fad – now that was an auspicious occasion in the six streets. Their mothers being movie fans of Hollywood, they'd fallen in love with the tan and white bobby-soxer lace-up shoes, with thick white laces. All the college girls wore them and some of the boys – in Hollywood movies. Unobtainable in early post-war Britain the mothers had hit on white plimsolls newly available. Wanting the best for their youngsters, all the children over ten years of age suddenly found themselves the proud possessors of white plimsolls. Needless to report, the shoe shops did a roaring trade in white plimsolls and tins of white blanco.

'Yer spit on a bit of rag, rub it in the blanco then over yer plimsolls. Put 'em outside on the wringer in the yard until they're dry. Keep nice and white, they will.' They looked pristine white, until you walked in them, and that cracked the blanco! Never mind, plimsolls were now cleaned twice-a-day. A popular excuse now – 'I can't come out 'til my plimsolls are dry.'

Tabby voiced her thoughts about plimsolls in their streets. She got short shrift. 'Wot's wrong wiv our streets, we keep 'em clean don't we? Throw buckets of water over our part of the pavement don't we? Every morning, regular, we scrub with our yard brooms. Could eat orff our pavements, yer could.'

True! Hopscotches apart, the pavements were clean. Women took pride in their clean fronts, wouldn't be seen with a dirty frontage. From their gates down to the gutter the soapy water was swilled. Brushing the gutter emptied the water into the nearest drain. Disinfectant was liberally used. 'And if that don't kill the germs I don't know what will?'

Plimsoll fever hit the streets like a rash! Even school dinner hours at home meant whitening plimsolls.

'I'm waiting for me plimsolls' became a catchphrase – an excuse. Like Tommy Handley's ITMA Radio Show, thought Tabby. His office cleaner always aid, 'Can I do yer now, Mr 'Andley?' Catchphrases had been proliferate in the war – on the radio and in the armed forces. Jack Warner's was 'Mind My Bike'. If you were courting and one of you was noticeably shorter than the other, you were called the 'long and the short of it'. After Ethel Revnell and Gracie West on the radio shows.

Tabby plumped to the ground to 'fix' her socks – always falling down they were. Just needed a tug and a sharp twist to remedy it. Her dad had been very disparaging in his remarks one day, referring to the thinness of her legs and long feet.

'They'd be shameful on a leg o' lamb on the Sunday dinner table. No meat on 'em!'

Shrugging her pathetically thin shoulders, she'd muttered *sotto voce*, 'I'll show 'im some day, yes I will. Mum said I'll be beautiful one day. Then I'll throw it back in his face. Oh, yes I will!'

Her words were tossed away like fluttering leaves on the breeze blowing up. How she longed for the day she could leave off silly white socks. An everlasting annoyance with their slipping habit. She dreamed of nylons. Real nylons. Her mother was still painting her legs with gravy browning powder. Except on best occasions her one precious pair, bought on the black market for twelve shillings (60p). Oh! Expensive they were. Shops sold out quickly – like gold dust were nylons. Unless you knew an American. They seemed to have no problem getting nylons – real ones! Lisle stockings were available of course, they could be, and were, darned repeatedly. Little cards of several shades of darning thread were kept in handbags, for running repairs. The latest craze was to pluck a long hair from your head or somebody elses! It was great for do-it-yourself invisible mending on nylons. Better still, if you laddered one, you could go to a shop called the Invisible Menders, or even a dry-cleaning shop. They were so skilled, you couldn't find the repair. It was best to roll your nylons down round your ankles inside the house, then pull them up when you went out. Everybody did that.

On your last day at school you wore socks. The next day, because you were fourteen, you went into stockings. You were an adult. There was no in-between! Tabby was going to be unlucky. Little did she know it. School leaving age was going up to fifteen! There was to be much resentment and anger amongst those who just missed leaving at fourteen. You could wear pan-stick make-up, lipstick and spit-on black mascara when you left school. Until then you could put lipstick on during the interval at the 'movies'. Girls crammed into the lavatories to make-up! It was corsets which were worrying Tabby.

'Will I 'ave ter wear stays like yer mum?' Choking with laughter – the picture conjured up of thin little Tabby wearing long whalebone stays had her in paroxysm! Jean couldn't imagine it. 'Why they'd 'ave taken Tabby for a walk up the street on their own they would! She's that thin,' she'd told her friend, Maisie. 'My Tabby would be lost in whalebone stays.'

Attempting to allay her daughter's fears she'd said, 'Of course not sweetheart. You'll wear a lightweight girdle with two bones in it. Or one of them new rubberised roll-ons!'

'Roll-ons!' Tabby voiced her horror at the new invention. Her sisters locked themselves into the bathroom for hours trying to wriggle into the blessed things – torture instruments: chastity belts. They'd emerge victorious hardly daring to breathe. Any superfluous stomach fat would now be automatically juxtapositioned into a roll of fat round their waists! Didn't make sense.

A lovely day, yes! Tabby's little grey cells were working overtime. She'd thought so hard lately – all this business of growing up it was the brave new world now, a land 'fit for heroes'. Austerity was still very much in evidence. The Labour Government was building simply thousands of prefabs (prefabricated low-level houses): made of wood and asbestos; very comfortable, and self-contained – very popular! There was some talk now about a Festival of Britain, just talk, at the moment. It was going to be in London, of course. Things were changing.

One hundred and twenty-five thousand prefabs and half-a-million new houses were planned, or had been built. Her teacher had said, 'Tabby, Rome was not built in a day.' She didn't want to go to Rome – goodness knows what her teacher meant! Bombed, derelict houses had thousands upon thousands of squatters – even good empty council homes! People had to live somewhere.

Weddings were so much in vogue they were fast becoming commonplace. Neighbours still crowded outside houses to see the virgin-white brides! Tabby had been a bridesmaid so often – to her sisters and friends and neighbours – she reckoned she could expertly take the marriage service herself! That made her father laugh. He broke into song, 'Why am I always the bridesmaid and never the blushing bride?'

In Europe the American GIs were marrying six hundred girls a month! Half of all USA servicemen were now married overseas. 'Give a man a sense of being boss, they do – American women don't!' That was what the Yanks said! In Britain, about two hundred and fifty girls a month married Americans. Dead cert they would send food parcels home to their families in Britain – and clothes. Badly needed!

31

There was talk now of self-service shops. Somebody had been to one somewhere! Jean thought it would be a good idea; no more queuing in several different queues at Sainsburys, Home & Colonial and Liptons! Self-service had not materialised their way yet.

February 1947, the winter was severe – the coldest in living memory, some people said! 'Cold enough to freeze the brass balls off a monkey,' said her father.

'Mind yer language Henry,' said Jean. Henry looked askance, 'I only said brass balls!'

'Well don't! The war's over, I want Tabby and Benjie to learn good language!'

'Well I'll be blowed!' He'd slammed out of the house. Two million people couldn't go to work for a few days that winter – fuel shortages; transport difficulties; electricity was cut off for hours during the daytime! Most people gave up and went back to bed!

National Health Service stamp money was rising just under three bob (shillings) a week, (or 15p) now. The NHS had started in 1948 – cradle to grave care! Butter, marge, fats and cheese, condensed and dried milk were all still on ration. The meat ration was about sixpence-worth a week per person. Jean managed to make do with bones – Benjie liked the marrow from the marrow bones.

A man's weekly wage was not much above five pounds, depending on his job. Working hours in factories were still 'long'. Tabby's uncle, an engineer, worked from 7.30 a.m. to 6 p.m., Monday to Friday, and Saturdays were half days for blue-collar workers, finishing at dinner time. Most men went to the football matches. Tabby had been with her dad but wasn't over-keen standing there watching some men run after a silly ball.

The King hadn't been very well. King George was very much loved and respected, so was his wife, Queen Elizabeth. They felt they were one of their own because, when the palace was bombed, the King said, 'Now I can look the people of the East End in the eye.' They'd got something in common.

The newsreels were a source of interest to Tabby. There was always so much to see at the movies with Gaumont British News and Pathé News. She only ever saw the Royal Family on the newsreels or listened on the radio to the King's speech at Christmas time. After the final film finished they played the national anthem. *Everybody* stood up. They all stood to attention singing the national anthem with the music very loud and the Royal Standard fluttering on the screen.

Nobody would have dreamt of doing otherwise. It was respect, wasn't it? Her mother told her, 'You always had to "respect respect".' Whatever that meant?

Mulling over these things Tabby felt her brain was fast becoming overloaded. It seemed simpler – life did – in the war. Not so many changes – for the better, it would seem. Time would tell! They still had the string key behind the letterbox. They had a radiogram now in the best room – the room was kept locked. 'So it doesn't get dirty,' Jean had said. 'Nice to have one tidy room in the house.' Records were popular, but the piano was still Tabby's favourite – she loved piano music.

'What a change from war! Life I mean! Are yer listenin' God? I 'spects yer are. My RE teacher said yer everywhere! I wonder how yer manage that God?

'Sorry! It would be rude to ask yer God. I'm doin' me best ter understand about everything but sometimes me poor brain is baffled! Baffled! That's a new word I learnt last week, God. Sounds nice don't it? Yer don't mind me chatterin' on, do yer God? I do say me prayers every night. Me mum sed so! Wot me mum sez I 'ave ter do, don't I? I'd like ter thank yer fer baby Benjie. We all love 'im. He luvs us! Yer know abaht me prayers and Benjie already, don't yer God? Yer knows everything! I duzzn't understand prop'ly abaht the war, God? Such terrible things 'appened. I've seen the newsreels at the pictures – movies the Yanks call them. Them poor people in the concentration camps, God. Where were yer then God? I 'ope yer duzzn't think I'm rude askin' that? Don't tell me mum – carbolic mouf wash, yer see. Don't like that! I know yer a lovin' God, the Bible sez so. But where were yer when those people needed yer, God? Why? Me RE teacher sez yer 'ave ter let peoples find their own ways in life, 'cos yer give 'em freedom of thought. I can understand that a bit, but where does the evil and pain and suffering bit come into it? Those terrible things done in Europe? Those people loved yer God, just like I do. Maybe they loved yer a bit more than me? Prob'ly! But yer still ain't answered me question! P'raps I ain't old enough ter know yet, dear God? I can't know everything can I? Anyway I guess these poor people know the answers now. They're wiv yer in paradise. Like the bloke on the cross next to Jesus. He asked yer son to remember 'im and yer son told 'im "terday yer will be wiv me in Paradise." That was a luvverly thing to say, God. I think yer Jesus is luvverly. Nice of yer to send 'im from 'eaven ter 'elp us. Pity 'ee didn't come again and help us to stop that evil in Europe. I'm glad I'm British, God. We're nice people. But I'm sure there's nice people in Europe as well. Me mum allus sez it takes all sorts to make a world! Well God, I thinks that's all I've got ter say ter yer for now. I'll see yer when I say me bedtime prayers ternight. I'm teaching our Benjie, "When I lay me down ter sleep, I beg thee Lord my soul to keep, when in the morning light I wake, help me the path of love to take, for Jesus Christ's sake, Amen" Benjie can't talk much yet. But if I keep tellin' 'im every night he'll larn it, won't he? Benjie can say me name now – and he's got a lot of teef. And he loves bread soldiers wiv a runny egg. I get the egg from the 'en coop fer him, every mornin'. Sometimes they've not 'ardened com-pletely and they feel a bit rubbery – the shells I mean. That's my fault, God. I'm too impatient, I don't give the 'ens time ter finish laying their clutch. That's what me mum sez! Well! Goodbye, God. Have a nice day in 'eaven. I'm 'avin a nice day on Earth. Yer know that, yer can see me!'

Tabby felt a bit better after talking to God. Somehow, being on her own made her feel nearer to him.

Born in London, Bethnal Green, Tabby had relatives all over the East End. When she was a toddler, her parents had moved to Dagenham, the six streets were surrounded by fields. Then! Pushing her in her pram Jean had taken her children potato-picking and pea-picking in the fields. Sometimes they went to fields a bit further on – by the owner's lorries.

What with hop-picking in Kent and strawberry-picking and gooseberry-picking at Wisbech, Tabby had a bit of a country upbringing.

War had broken out in September 1939 – the Germans had defied the West and marched into Poland. Britain declared themselves at war with Germany and all that it represented. The second time. The first time was the Great War, millions were killed in 1914-1918. Nobody ever thought the Germans would rise again! But they did – in 1933, a house painter and other odd jobs man named Schnickelgrüber called himself Adolf Hitler and the rot set in! By 1939 we were at war!

Tabby fervently hoped there would never be another World War. Seeing the suffering on the newsreels she'd cried her eyes out. So did millions of other film-goers. God hadn't answered all her questions about that. Maybe He would, when she was older. They'd got the United Nations now. Europe could learn to be friendly with lots of countries, and avoid war.

Men had returned from National Service in droves, about thirty thousand a month; then sixty thousand a month. All had new demob suits, they did! Still in uniform of a different kind.

'Never seen so many men, Mum; they had an

"aura" about them in uniform. They duzzn't look the same now. There's no "aura".'

Jean's mouth gaped, she'd eyed her clever daughter incredulously. 'An *aura?* Wot's that when it's at 'ome? Goodness child, you've been coming aht wiv some newfangled words lately.'

'Their appearances, Mum – it gave them status. Now they look – well, just y' know – ordinary. 'Eard me farver say it!'

'Sometimes little ears 'ear too much. Better not let yer farver know yer been earwiggin' his talking!'

'Yer wont tell, will yer, Mum?'

'Course I won't, stoopid! That's wot yer say ter Esmeralda, ain't it? Yerse! I was earwiggin' yer! Yer ain't the only one likes earwiggin'! Our Gertie is the best earwigger of 'em all! Where d'ya fink I gets orl me information from? I jist told yer – Gertie's a crackin' earwigger. Yer wanna know somefink. Ask our Gertie. She'll know – if she duzzn't, it'd surprise me! She'll find out fer yer, a great earwigger our Gertie! That's how come she's so knowledgeable. She ain't clever like youse Tabby, but her *gleanings* make 'er know a lot. Your cleverness is from books. Our Gertie's from what yer Grandpa used ter call the "school of life"! Sometimes the best school of all!'

The school of life – that's a nice one. Tabby tucked it away amongst her little grey cells! Might come in useful one day. You never did know.

She'd walked quite a way now and was near a landmine site, whatever? Its initial starkness had given way to softness, provided by grass and other fauna and – in springtime – beautiful buddleia bushes with their glorious racemes of closely packed star-like flowers. The bushes were white, lavender, or deep purple or pink, but the reddish ones were dominant. Mallow bushes with their arching branches of glory had also taken root, from seeds blown by the wind or dropped by birds. Indeed, overnight, bombed or landmine sites (landmine site in Dagenham, bombed sites in London) everywhere you went, had become small fertile oases, gifts from God. That's what Tabby secretly called them, gifts from God. They cheered people no end.

I'm going ter grow them in me own garden some day, she'd promised herself. It had never crossed her mind she might never have a garden of her own – she took it for granted. Her own house and garden were what she was planning. Saving towards it, wasn't she – with her National Savings stamp book!

'Hope springs eternal in the human breast, Tabby.' That's what her teacher, Miss Brink, had said, 'hope springs eternal.' Tabby wasn't exactly dumb! She'd already worked out that hope would need money to boost it!

Flying her kite high! Nobody she personally knew in the six streets owned their house. They were private landlord. She'd heard her parents discussing that the other night. Earwigging again! They said something about buying a house at such and such a price… Tabby's eyelids drooped then … as she slid off to sleep she caught the words 'sitting tenants'! Tucked away in the little grey cells she would 'keep it in mind'.

She'd had to laugh! Gertie's husband had told

them about finding bombed houses in London still with their lavatories intact. Their occupants blown to smithereens, but not the lavs! Some wag had commented, 'If we'd all used the air raid shelters as lavs we'd 'ave been saved!' The irony was not lost on the company he was keeping. They'd sighed and softly told him to shut up. 'Yer couldn't laugh at such terrible things as families blown ter smithereens.'

Jean had gently said, 'There but for the Grace of God...' They all knew what she meant. The Braithewaites had been a lucky family – all intact, they'd not been flattened by bombs.

Tabby'd learnt a valuable lesson in life. Some things you just cannot joke about. It was called *bad taste*.

True! A landmine had dropped near them and their windows with the sticking paper criss-crossed on them, had been blown out and doors had become a bit drunk! Jean had crossed herself and said, 'Somebody up there is taking care of the Braithewaites, thank you, Lord.'

Having turned the magic age of twelve some time ago and 'seeing' every month, she didn't go to the bombed sites so often (they were mostly in the East End where her relatives were). 'Yer'll 'ave ter stop yer climbing and clambering around now, Tabby. Keep yer skirts discreet!'

'Don't wash yer 'air when yer 'seein' – not that week. Don't go swimmin'. Keep aht of the rain. Keep yer feet dry! Yer'll catch yer deaf of cold iffen yer do, yer deaf o' cold, mark my words. Yer a woman now, a Beginning Woman.'

Not understanding Tabby had mulled it over

and over again. It's not as if I want ter *see* every month! Unfortunately, her mother had ear-wigged that! So she'd given her a sharp clip round the ear'ole. Wasn't 'avin' any daughter of hers talkin' like that, was she?'

'Now look 'ere Tabitha Braithewaite. Yer growin' into a woman. Whether yer like it or not duzzn't matter. Yer goin' ter see *every munf* re'glar or I'll want ter know the reason why.' Her ominous tone boded no good for Tabby if she dared forget! 'Until yer in yer change or 'avin' any babies yer goin' to ter see every munf. Yer sure as 'ell ain't in yer change an' yer sure as 'ell ain't 'avin' any babies – yet. I can tell yer my fine lady!' Tabby'd gulped hard, not understanding it all.

'Unmarried daughters don't 'ave no babies out of wedlock in our 'ouse. D'yer 'ear me? I'm warnin' yer jist warnin' yer. None of youse is bringin' shame on our 'ouse!'

Wanting to know what the 'change' was she'd put it to her mother – in trepidation – it sounded awful! Would she change into somebody else? Why wouldn't she see when she was 'avin' a baby? Assuming she would someday?

'Ask no questions 'ear no lies
Ever seen a donkey doin' up 'is flies?
Flies are nuisance I mustn't tell–
Or I will break the fairy spell.'

quoted Jean. 'Yer just not old enuff ter know some things Tabby. All in good time girl, all in good time. Yer'll go ter work in a few years, yer'll meet somebody, get married, and 'ave a baby every year like me. That's the picture more or less Tabby!'

She'll never tell me where babies come from – even if I ask her, 'n' I daren't ask her *that*. Tabby heaved a sigh!

It had been *more* rather than *less* of babies in her mother's life. Fourteen children, all alive, thirteen girls, one boy! She was still under forty! Her mother's voice had dropped to a whisper. 'It's the *change* which women fear the most Tabby, the *change*. The bogeyman in every woman's life, my own mother used to say, the *change* drives some women mad! Supposed ter be even worse than 'avin a baby. At least yer 'ave sumfink ter show fer the pain when yer 'ave a baby. I never regretted 'avin' any of youse lot!'

Startled, Tabby'd kept shtum! Couldn't be any worse pain than having a baby? Heard her friend's mother screaming blue murder hadn't she. Just before she dropped it! Whoosh! Tabby – earwiggin' – had run for dear life! Back to the familiarity of her own home, shaken to the core! There and then her mind was made up. If dropping a baby was such terrible pain she didn't fancy having any! Later the same day she'd gone back with her mother. Ostensibly to put a silver half-a-crown (22½p) into the baby's hand for good luck. Whose luck, hers or the baby's – nobody informed her. She'd have to ask Gertie who'd been around babies all her life. She was the eldest of the family. The baby looked beautiful, the mother was clean and smiling in her bed, freshly made up! Some things were a puzzle in life!

The episode passed into history as far as Tabby was concerned. Her mother, however, hadn't finished by a long chalk! She never did, once she got her teeth into something.

'Jist thank yer lucky stars, lovey, yer only seein'. The rest will come soon enuff! We women don't arf go through it, I can tell yer lovey. Wot wiv seein' every month, babies, the milk, the change – a woman 'as a 'ard row to hoe!'

Tabby still said nowt. She thought seein' was bad enough. She thought men had it hard. They *had* to go away overseas and fight wars up at the front line, dying in their millions!

'I'd rather be a woman than a man, never mind the milk! Nor the seein' nor the change. Goin' ter war must be worse than the change or childbirth. In her 'umble opinion, anyway. She guessed her mother was referring to breast milk from her bosoms. Her baby brother's cornucopia of milk and honey. He loved it!

'Esmee! I wonder jist 'ow a woman 'as a baby jist by 'avin' a gold ring put on her finger, on the left hand – it's the right hand in Europe. Me uncle told me that. Had ter be different didn't they – them Europeans! Wonder why, it's the same God innit?'

Esmee looked at her friend. Tabby'd told her a bit about what her mother had lectured her on. Didn't make sense!

'It's called culture and customs Tabby, even I know that, and I'm two years younger than yer!'

'Wot I mean ter say is–'

'Yer duzzn't mean anyfink, Tabby. 'Cos yer

don't know any more abaht 'avin' babies than meself. See!'

'I don't know anyfink at all abaht 'avin' babies! Not really, yer see!' Her face broke into a mocking sneer.

'I'll 'ave yer know, Miss Esmeralda Toffeenose, I've got me a good brain. Can fink fer meself, can't I?'

'Ow can yer brain fink of summat yer brain duzzn't know abaht? *We* duzzn't know 'ow a woman gets a baby, do we, stoopid!'

'Jist let me fink, Esmee, think 'ard yerself, I'm thinkin' 'ard!'

Plopped down on Esmee's doorstep, face cupped in her hands, elbows resting on scraggy knees, she beetled her brows in concentration.

'I know! I know what it is, Esmee! The man stands next to the woman – the bride – in church. He puts the gold ring on her finger. The wedding march wheezes out on the organ ... I know it all orff by 'eart. Been a bridesmaid ain't I?'

'Seven times, at the last count!'

'All right, seven times, so I know it all don't I?'

'And?'

'It's the confetti, Esmee. Yeah! That's it. The confetti! Stands ter reason, dunnit? The confetti.'

''Ave yer lorst yer marbles, Tabitha Braithewaite?'

'Course I ain't, stoopid. The more confetti they have thrown at 'em, then the more babies they 'ave. I jist told yer – stands ter reason, dunnit? It must be the confetti! Me mum allus sez a weddin' ain't a wedding wiv aht the confetti! It's the confetti – soppy date! Why didn't I think of that afore? Clever ain't I?'

Esmee's raised eyebrows, lost beneath her long fringe, now relaxed again. Twisting her head, she gazed at Tabby.

Tabby was jubilant, 'Wiv aht the confetti, Esmee, a woman's barren.'

'Wot the 'eck is barren? D'ya mean burrow as in bunny rabbits?'

'Nah! Stoopid! Our Gertie told me. Barren means a woman can't bear children.'

'Yer mean ter say a woman don't like children, 'cos she can't bear 'em?'

'Nah! Wake up, Esmee – 'ere am I searchin' me poor addled brains ter 'elp yer more – addled brains which yer ain't got, stoopid! Sometimes words sound the same but mean diff'rent things. Anyway burrows sounds different to barren. It means a woman can't carry babies inside 'er!'

'Well! I wouldn't mind bein' barren then. I bet there's a lot of women wouldn't mind either? None of that frighteningly terrible, horrific birthing pains! But, it's not makin' sense Tabby. All women 'ave got two arms like youse an' me. See! They can carry babies. That's what God gives muvvers two arms for!'

Standing up, hands on hips Tabby faced her muddled friend. 'There's a lot of fings yer don't know Esmee. I'm not sure I should be tellin' yer orl this? Yer only nine years old.'

'Oh, go on, Tabby, be a sport, anyways yer can't count! I've had me tenf birthday. Yer only two years older 'n' me. Anyway, I'm yer bestest friend!'

'Yer won't be much longer if yer don't keep yer

trap shut, and listen! My dad's aunt was barren. She niver 'ad any children at all. No! Not one! And she niver lost any either. Me mum sez me dad's aunt niver 'ad any confetti at 'er wedding! There yer are – see! It must be the confetti! Clever clogs ain't I?'

Not fully persuaded by her friend's rhetoric, Esmee wanted to know how a baby knew if it was going to be born a boy baby or a girl baby?

Not to be outdone, Tabby had a ready answer to that!

'Pooh! I jist told yer – yer soppy date! It's the confetti, didn't I?'

Esmee's tiny mind, clouded with doubt, had to admit Tabby was correct. It must be the confetti!

'Y'see Esmee, the confetti its allus pink and white, innit? God works out how many blues and how many pinks land on the 'appy couple's 'eads? He works aht how many boys and how many girls – from that. Simple ain't it?'

Dumbfounded; perplexed by her bosom friend's logic, Esmee remained trenchant in her disbelief.

'Orl right then. The confetti! I can't fink of anyfink else. How does God know which to send first – a boy or a girl? Come ter that, 'ow abaht twins and triplets? How does God work that out, Miss Clever Cloggs Braithewaite?'

'I ain't God. He knows best! Our RE teacher sed, "With God – all things are possible." So there's yer answer, Miss Toffeenose!'

Bit between her teeth, Esmee hung on grimly. 'How did God send three sets of twins ter me eldest sister ... me mum reckons it's a record!

''Er 'usband were away fightin' in the war! Some women's husbands hadn't been 'ome fer years. So 'ow d'yer work that one out?'

'I can't tell yer everything Esmeralda – only what me brain in me bacon bonce knows!' Her thin shoulders shrugged expressively. 'Our RE teachers says we have ter rely on the Lord to answer some of our questions. I ain't as clever as God, I told yer. Anyway, God must be busy answering millions and millions of questions now the war is over. Lots of people want answers, don't they? We'll jist 'ave ter take our turn in God's queue. He'll tell us one day when he's not so busy. Poor bloke must be run off 'is feet! I'm just Tabby and yer just Esmee. Our mums don't tell us nuffink! We 'ave ter find aht fer ourselves. I mean ter say, I niver knew abaht seein' did I? Nah! Thought I'd cut meself, didn't I? I told yer, I couldn't find where I'd cut meself. Had ter tell me mum, didn't I? All I could do? Had blood, didn't I? I hadn't 'ad blood in me knickers afore. Strange! Me mum was ever so nice! She took me into the best room and I said "I've got blood in me knickers, Mum, and I can't find where I've cut meself!" Nice she were! Dead scared I was ter tell 'er. Fought the bleedin' meant I woz dyin', didn't I? S'funny! She never took a swipe at me, soiling me clean white knickers. Never even gave me a fourpenny-one she didn't! She jist told me what to do abaht it, and said, "Yer growin' into a woman now, Tabitha. You're a *Beginning Woman*"!'

Esmee's eyes were as round as saucers. She'd heard this story many times before. It had lost nothing in the telling – still made her catch her breath – her friend was a little bleeder now!

'Yer sees wot I means, don't yer, Esmee? I *knows* yer me bestest friend; but yer ain't a Beginning Woman like me, are yer?'

'Can't see yer a woman meself, Tabby, yer still go ter school, don't yer?'

'Yer a right one, Esmee! Enough ter try the patience of Matthew, Mark, Luke and John! That's wot me farver allus sez. He never goes ter church, so I dunno wot 'ee knows abaht the saints? I'm sure! I'm a Beginning Woman, yer ain't.'

Esmee shrieked with laughter. 'Come on Tabby – wot's a Beginning Woman, really?'

Esmee's lack of respect for her superior knowledge was grating on Tabby's nerves. 'It's a young girl who's jist beginning ter turn into a Woman – see? Like an apprentice boy. He starts training but 'ee ain't a man 'til 'ee finishes 'is apprenticeship and is twenty-one. Then he gets a man's wage. Takes some of 'em seven years! They leave school at fourteen don't they, Beginning Men – I'm a Beginning Woman.'

'Yeah! But they don't bleed do they?'

'Yes they do, starts shavin' 'n' cuts themselves, don't they? Shave every day of their life, they do!'

Esmee's brain, not quite up to all this muddlesome talk, called it a day!

Tabby pointed out some girls who had babies before marriage had shotgun weddings. She didn't quite know how God worked that out, either. Her RE teacher told her 'All things come from God and of His own do we give Him.' Anyway, her mother said 'there's many a vessel with leaks, nobody is perfect.'

'Don't yer dare ask me any more, Esmee. 'Cos I ain't sure I know or understand prop'ly meself. I tell yer wot though! Can't understand why I can't 'ave me barf when I'm seein'? Me mum says I'd better not, it's too dangerous when yer seein! Won't even let me wash me hair she won't!'

'It must be the blood,' tittered Esmee. 'P'raps it does something terrible to yer if yer get wet? P'raps yer mum is too frightened ter tel yer?'

She eyed Esmee warily. Both young girls were mystified, but neither would admit it.

'Okay, Miss Clever Clogs, 'as yer mum told yer?'

'Nah! Was goin' ter ask me sisters I was, cross me 'eart, 'ope ter die! I ain't got the courage. Mum'd slit me tongue if I kept askin' questions abaht seein'. Said I'm too young ter know!'

'Yer are!'

'It's good of yer to explain things ter me Tabby ... I won't be frightened when I do start seein' – I'll know, won't I? 'Cos yer kindly showed me the blood in yer knickers ... don't let me mum know will yer? She doesn't know I know everything, she thinks I only know the word seein'. She sed ladies don't talk abaht them sort of fings. Ladies secrets – yer mustn't let men know!'

'Huh! Stoopid! I won't tell yer mum! She'd tell my mum I'd told yer! That would be a carbolic mouf wash fer me! I ain't that daft, Esmee!' She chuckled, 'Me sisters call it Eve's curse 'cos of Adam and Eve!'

Esmee's head nodded energetically.

'And! Esmee, guess what?'

'Wot?'

'I even 'eard one of me sisters tell 'er latest boyfriend ... y'know the Flash Harry one, (I 'eard Mum call 'im that) the spiv bloke – she was tellin' me dad! His name's Charlie. Really ... Mum told Dad several times, "He's a Flash Harry if I ever did see one, Henry!" ... anyway I 'eard me sister (I was earwiggin' – I'll cop it if me mum finds out, so keep yer mouf shut). "I can't go swimmin' wiv yer Charlie," and he hit the roof! Yer should've 'eard 'im, 's'wonder the whole of the six streets never 'eard 'im! Me sister kept tellin' 'im to shush! "Why not? Yer me girl ain't yer everyone knows we're walking aht tergevver! Why can't yer go swimming wiv me?" And ... I 'eard 'er whisper to 'im.' Esmee listened with bated breath ... '"I can't go Charlie, I've got Eve's curse this week!" And Charlie burst out laughing. That upset me sister! Charlie shouted out "Oh! Yer've got yer manhole covers on 'ave yer? Why didn't yer say so? Silly bitch...! I thought yer were goin' orff of me!" Then I 'ear 'em kissin', he's a noisy kisser. You should've 'eard 'im! And he said, 'Orl right babe, wait until the manhole covers come orff!"'

All agog, Esmee looked suitably impressed – revelations to (shock) add to her gleanings of knowledge.

'But 'ow can she tell that there Charlie to wait until Eve's curse is gone? Your mum said...'

'I know! I know! D'yer think I ain't been puzzled abaht that! Me mum told me wiv 'er own lips – I swear it Esmee – I swear it. She did 'n' all! She said, seein' stays wiv yer fer the rest of yer life

49

until yer change. And that – I can't tell yer that, don't wanna frighten yer, do I!'

Esmee pleaded to be told the rest. Tabby was not to be swayed. 'Nah! Can't tell yer. Too terrible. Best yer don't know. Anyway, I don't really understand it all meself to be quite 'onest wiv yer!'

Looking at her *bestest friend* admiringly, Esmee knew what her mother said that 'Tabby's got 'er principles and she sticks to 'em.' Having no concrete idea of what principles were Esmee didn't mention it to Tabby. 'At least yer honest, Tabitha Braithewaite!'

'Course I am – well – most of the time! It were nice of yer ter share yer packet of sherbet dabs wiv me, but the straw was soggy! I'll do the same fer yer some day. My English teacher sez:

This above all things–
To thine ownself be true:
Thou can'st not then–
Be false to any man

I'm not sure if I r'cllcts it prop'ly – it's sumfink like that, anyway.'

'Crumbs and Custards Tabby! Who sed that? Wot's it mean? Yer ain't arf clever – yer really are!'

'Shakespeare, I fink? Didn't yer know that? Neither did I – troof ter tell!'

Reminding her friend she hadn't yet started at the big school she gazed at her adoringly. Tabby was happy to bathe in childish adulation. 'Me mum sez yer 'ave ter be ever so–'

'Old,' obliged Tabby, cutting in.

50

'I woz jist gonna say that! Why d'ya 'ave ter snatch words from mc brcff? Go on Tabby, go on!'

Getting back to the subject which still bothered the two children Tabby told Esmee about next door – old Mrs Davies. 'She's ever so old, ever so! Last munf she were forty-five! If that ain't old I dunno wot is. I mean ter say – forty-five! Perish the thought! I were earwiggin' agin – I 'eard her tell me mum she were in the early change. Me mum was shocked. Guess yer got ter expect fings wiv old people. Now that is old, ain't it?'

Her head nodding fast and furiously like a nodding doll, Esmee didn't dare to interrupt the flow of earwiggin! Not she! Apparently Tabby's sister told her when yer forty-five yer old, when yer sixty-five, yer dead. The government likes that – yer pension is small but they don't 'ave ter pay so much to yer widow. The two discussed what it must be like to die at sixty-five. Concluding most men died at sixty-five or after about three months of retirement. 'Me mum were talkin' abaht old Mr Davies and Mr Sparrow of Willsmore Road. Yer knows them!'

Esmee certainly did. Old men, aged sixty-five. Both died within three months of retirement. Workmates had bought them a mantle clock each. Tabby couldn't fathom what they'd want with a new clock. 'Now them clocks is ticking and they ain't! Must be awful ter fight in wars, work 'ard all yer life, with no reward but a clock. Three months later yer in yer coffin! Me mum said it "were a merciful relief," sorry, release! 'Cos their pensions weren't enough ter feed their

51

chickens, let alone themselves and their wives! Me mum sed it were private pensions. Me dad reckons the government is going ter 'ave better pensions for everybody. Gotta pay fer it they have. Stamp money me dad sez!

'I don't think it's the same stamps as me National Savings stamp book. I don't understand some fings. Anyway, old Davies and Sparrow is dead. Buried by Jack's Funeral Parlour. But me, no buts! A boo'ful send orff they did. Mr Davies did! Went round on the knocker wiv me mum, didn't I? C'llected from all the six streets – a fortune, as Mum sed. Enuff fer the wreath and a bit fer 'is wife. Somebody else c'llected for Mr Sparrow, 'is funr'lls next week. Sorry, I meant Mr Davies was buried by Jack's Parlour: Mr Sparrow ain't gone under yet. Old Davies'll be pushing up the daisies a bit before Mr Sparrow … buried first weren't 'ee! Fer Mr Davies we c'llected three pahnds, fourteen shillings, and free farvings. 'Elped me mum ter count it, I did. Turned the tin upside down on the table. My! Yer should've seen the fortune! Half crowns, florins, shillings, tanners, thrupenny bits, ha'pennies, pennies, farthings. Would've done yer 'eart good ter see people's generosity. I counted it carefully – gettin' good at arithmetic I am. We paid *sixteen shillings and tuppence ha-penny* fer the wreath. Beautiful! Red, white and blue flowers it were. Patriotic man was old Mr Davies; older than 'is wife. Patriotic she said 'ee were. Loved the flowers. Made 'er cry. 'Ad a little Union Jack on the coffin. It was 'is pride and joy. 'Ee were in the Great War – the First World War, 'ee were! Yer gotta 'ave respect fer people like that!'

'Know, don't I? Was there, weren't I? 'Ow come the women don't always die at sixty-five like men seem to?'

'Search me, Esmee? Mabye 'cos we 'ave the curse. Get fresh blood every month! Men don't! Their blood must be very old! Stale blood – ugh! Now yer knows why Dracula wanted young women. Fresh blood yer see. Needed it ter stay young and alive. Didn't 'ee?'

She was hanging on to every word of her learned friend. Esmee had a gem of her own. 'I 'eard me dad – I woz earwiggin', yer ain't the only one who can earwig, Tabby – he were telling me mum, "If our Herbert don't lay orff the crumpets it'll be the deaf of 'im!"'

Suitably shocked was Tabby. 'Wot a terrible fing ter say abaht yer 'Erbert? D'ya fink 'ee ain't got enuff money ter buy fresh crumpets from the baker's shop?'

'Nah? Me dad said our 'Erbert's got too much money … and too many crumpets! Must be overeating I reckon all them crumpets, oh, me poor bruvver, me poor 'Erbert.'

'We shouldn't be talking like this Esmee … it's dismal morbid talk. D'ya like that word morbid – 's a new one I've learnt! I were earwiggin' Aunty Maisie, yer muvver and my mum. Yer muvver says "It won't be long now before my Esmeralda starts 'er seein', she's growing into a big girl now." Nah! I ain't sed nuffink ter yer mum or mine. Don't want my mum ter know wot we talk abaht do I?'

'Thanks, Tabby, thanks!'

'Yer welcome. Now, spit on me 'and, and I'll spit on yourn. Rub our 'ands tergevver like this. Say after me. Ter deaf as wimmin' we pledge ourselves, lightning tear our tongues from our moufs. We will never tell!'

Staggering backwards, an astonished Esmee blinked rapidly: 'I've got to say orl that?'

'Yerse! Don't be lily-livered! It's the code of honour of the girls who're seein'. Us in the six streets. "Daughters of Eve" is wot we calls ourseln'.'

'I ain't seein',' interpolated Esmee.

'Like Aunty Maisie sed yer gettin' a big girl! Yer prob'ly will soon. At least yer'll be prepared for it – I weren't!'

Chapter Two

Her weekly strolls became a habit – she felt rejuvenated with her new-found solitude; giving her time to dwell on times past, in comparison with the brave new world of post-war Britain. Every day it seemingly changed for the better; including her own personal life. Life became more exciting, pleasurable, hopeful. Today, Tabby had traversed quite a distance from the six streets, in a roundabout direction past the forbidden sewage way! What the eye doesn't' see … thought Tabby! It were a smashing 'at me mum made me for the VE Party down our street in May 1945. It was shaped like a crown; trimmed with cotton wool and little black bits presumably in imitation of ermine fur! What a party they'd had! Three months later they had another big street party for VJ day. Long trestle tables down the length of their street, covered with best white tablecloths of precious sheets. Her mother and the neighbours made a celebration feast fit for a king!

It was the street lights and the house lights, blazing and twinkling; making the dark streets of the enforced blackout years so lit up – they literally turned night into day. Upstairs and downstairs lights in each house were kept switched on – all the night long until daylight the following morning. Front doors were wide open – all night too! It seemed the party would never end – because nobody wanted it to! They had six long dark years of war to forget and by heck, celebrate they did! The music, impromptu acting, singing, knees up – like only Cockneys know how! 'Knees up Mother Brown' wheezed from accordions or tinkled on pianos – which had literally been manhandled into the street; the conga line, in and out of the houses and back again; the sheer happiness generated by people who'd come through hell to heaven. Church bells pealed incessantly; the *ringers* being fortified by a drop of the hard stuff! You had to be there to appreciate the party to end all parties! Evil was vanquished, laughter prevailed.

The post-war years had seen an immense change in Tabby. Her knowledge, assimilation, understanding of the English Language – the King's English – had increased by leaps and bounds. The little grey cells in her bacon bonce made skilful use of it. She welcomed the change but did not lose her cockney dialect and vernacular – why should she? They were part of her rich heritage from aeons of ancestors. She used them mainly at home or with mates. She revelled in *proper* English for its beauty and diversity. Her mind had been stretched by good teachers. Many had been commissioned or non-commissioned officers in His Majesty's armed forces. At school, discipline was the order of the day. It bred respect in the children's perception of their elders. Order and sanity reigned supreme in post-war classrooms. The war had bred patience and a better understanding of their fellow men amongst the demobbed teachers. Women had changed – they were no longer content to be mere chattels. They outnumbered the men!

Tabby was looking forward to the day when she could go dancing at the Palais. She was growing into a fine young woman. Her limbs and body had taken on a fullness matched by her plumper face. Most food was still rationed. Several foods were more easily available. Her mother's soups – their mainstay in the war, apart from stewed rabbit or roast chicken – were now supplemented by other dishes. Jean was experimenting with Bakewell tart, bacon turnovers and corned beef rissoles! Seasonal vegetables from their bigger back garden – the air raid shelter had gone – meant Tabby was getting a more healthy and varied diet.

Henry, her father, no longer taunted her with sarcastic remarks about her thin legs!

Tabby was staying at school a bit longer. Jean had been persuaded to permit her to take a secretarial course at school. 'The world will always want typists and secretaries, yer see, Henry!' Not that her father was interested!

'Nah! Yer can't go wiv yer sisters lovey. There ain't much of yer. Yere'd git crushed in the crowds!' Jean had never said a truer word! VE celebrations – her sisters were up the West End all night! Crushed? Paddling in the fountains at Trafalgar Square. 'Orl lit up it were, Tabby, all lit up!'

The radio newscaster said even the little

Princesses, Elizabeth and Margaret Rose, went outside to mix with the crowds, waving to the King and Queen at Buckingham Palace! Tabby didn't know if that was true! Her sisters got home the next day, tired, dirty, dishevelled, their adrenaline keeping them on their feet! Jean had laughingly packed them off to bed 'ter sleep it orff'.

The spivs and the black market did a roaring trade – suddenly seeming to have access to scarce foodstuffs.

Tabby had gone to the movies with her mother to watch the newsreels of the celebrations. It was duplicated in August for the forgotten army – VJ day.

The war over, rations were cut! To share with the liberated countries of Europe who were literally starving. The Huns had used a 'scorched earth' policy when they retreated in their hundreds of thousands. Cooking fat was cut from two ounces to one ounce; bacon from four ounces to three ounces. Soap was cut by one eighth. Fortunately, fish and fruit had become more plentiful.

The Braithewaites had managed to survive the war intact. 'The luck of the draw,' said Henry. 'Providence,' said Jean.

'Well, we're better off now,' murmured Tabby, scuffing one shoe by dragging it deliberately along the grass verge. From a wayside shrub, she plucked a few dull green leaves, and chewed them thoughtfully. The locals called the leaves, bread and cheese – she meant to find out what the shrub really was, one day. 'The road to hell is paved with good intention', had been part of yesterday's English lesson ... she had good intentions ...but!

Poor Mr Churchill – lost the election, and was no longer the Prime Minister. They always called him Mr – not Churchill – like some people.

'Yer gotta 'ave respect fer people in high office,' said Jean.

'Mr Churchill seemed one of us – a great man,' said her father. 'Led the country ter victory, didn't 'ee? Even when France surrendered to the Germans, Mr Churchill vowed, "We will never surrender..." he was adamant we'd never surrender! Mr Churchill inspired the peoples of the occupied countries and elsewhere, almost as much as he did the British. We all felt great hope with Mr Churchill; a magnificent warrior and warlord. And now what has happened? After all he's done fer us the electorate has replaced him with nice Mr Atlee of the Labour Party.' Tabby knew nothing about politics – but she thought it was a crying shame and shouldn't have been allowed. For the umpteenth time she thought how could the people do that to such a mighty warrior? She'd asked her father ... he'd said she would understand when she was older!

That had been in 1945, the electorate had wanted a change – hopefully for the better. Traditionally, the men had told their womenfolk who they were to vote for in elections. But things had, and were, changing. Oh yes! Women were determined to be legal chattels no longer! They said, 'We'll vote for who we want!' Tabby had been to young to properly understand in 1945.

However, reading the daily newspapers, listening to the radio, and having her mind stretched by good teachers, Tabby, slowly but surely, had become quite proficient about the electorate and the three main parties: Labour, Conservative, Liberal. From her teachers she'd learnt that the Liberals had once been a great power. With the people wanting prosperity and their rights in a land fit for heroes, it seemed that politics had become a one-horse race. Personally, Tabby felt she had no allegiance either way. She would continue to listen and bide her time, until she got the vote! She didn't mention politics at home much. Her father didn't like the way she dissected the status quo! 'Keep yer foughts to yerself in this 'ouse, my young lady. This is a Labour household – see!'

'Who sez so?' asked her indignant older sisters.

'I sez so an' don't yer fergit it! Youse girls'll toe the line – or else!'

'Give over 'Enry, give over man. Women can fink fer themselves nowadays.' Jean glared at her husband.

'Oh yerse…?' Oo sez so? I'm still the 'ead of this 'ouse an' wot I sez – goes. Don't yer niver fergit it!'

Muttering angrily, his daughters left the house – anywhere to get away for a bit. 'Dad's out of the ark,' said one.

'Orl blokes is the same,' said another.

'Fink the little women 'ave ter wipe their backsides for 'em!' Sally said. 'They'll larn one day, yer'll see, they'll larn!' Jean's second eldest daughter was absolutely fuming which had

60

surprised Tabby. She'd not thought her sisters took any notice of what Father said, nor realised how strongly they had their own views. Wonders would never cease!

The Braithewaites were mad on music, so was ninety-nine per cent of the British population – it had kept them going through the long dark years of the horrors of war. Miss Brink, Tabby's classroom teacher, had once said, 'Music is the opium of the masses!' She never did say where that came from. Every Saturday the Braithewaite girls pooled some of their hard-earned wages to purchase the latest recording available at the gramophone shop. The records broke easily – very easily! One Saturday morning, coming home on a crowded bus with Johnny Ray's 'Cry' record in a brown paper carrier bag, with its cord handles, that is just what happened!

'All aboard, all aboard, hold tight there, go on then, squeeze yerselves on, git up them stairs.'

'They're standing up there, mate!'

'An' they're bloody standin' down 'ere 'n' all! Oy, youse lot, move on dahn, move on dahn, 'old tight!' He rang the bell. The bus lurched forward, shuddered, and stopped.

''Fraid yer'll 'ave ter git off some of yer! Sorry, maties, sorry!'

Too late, the carrier bag was the first casualty! 'Crack!'

'Aw! Bloody shame! Yer've broken the lass's record!'

'I ain't broken it! Come on, maties, bloody bus won't start, 's'too 'eavy, innit. Oy youse lot upstairs. No standin' upstairs, come on dahn, if

61

me inspector gets on I'll lose me bloody job. 'Ow will I feed me kids then? Come on maties, only let youse on out of the goodness of me 'eart, didn't I?'

'We'll get off!' chorused the Braithewaite girls. ''Ave to, won't we. A broken record's no good to our muvver. Do 'er nut she will. Wot time's the next bus?'

'Gawd knows – I don't. Come on … a few more of yer – orff yer get. Thanks, maties, thanks, 'old tight there – 'ol' tight! Thank Gawd, we're off! Move along, tickets, tickets!'

Tabby's oldest sisters had worked up London in the war. Every weekday their lunch hour was taken in the National Gallery, where Myra Hess gave splendid musical recitations. Thousands could remember her concert recitals. 'The opium of the masses indeed!'

One morning, after a particularly heavy rainstorm – and the heavens above seemed intent on punishing them all, for some unknown reason – Tabby and her mates arrived at school, rain-sodden, bedraggled, like drowned rats. Not possessing a single raincoat between them, nor even an umbrella – although the school was but a spit from the six streets, it was far enough to get sodden. Shaking their wet hair, lank or tousled, in imitation of a dog – it didn't help their tempers any; the God almighty crashes of thunder and the forked lightning had not exactly been conducive to a good night's sleep.

Sitting cross-legged on the polished floor of the hall for the morning pep talk from the head-mistress – then standing for morning prayers, they dutifully intoned 'I will lift up mine eyes to the hills from whence cometh my help...' and the hymn, 'Now thank we all our God'. They'd eyed each other askance, breaking into fits of giggles which were quickly smothered and suppressed, for the headmistress's gimlet eye was enough to quench a roaring fire at five hundred paces! Then they filed into their classroom with its row of Butler sinks (used in cookery classes). They were confronted by their classroom teacher, Miss Brink who with tears in her eyes, admonished them for moaning over their wetness when other people in the world had more pressing problems to contend with. Mouths agape, confronted with a popular teacher whose usually soft, well modulated voice was raised so loudly to make herself heard over the buzz of their chatter and banter – they dutifully shut up clam-like, and sat down behind their ink-stained desks wondering what had wrought such a change in her. They did not have long to wait. Rapping a ruler sharply on her desk, to command their sole attention, she read aloud from a newspaper in front of her.

'Children! You will, I am sure, feel as sympathetic as myself to know the official figures of the homeless in Europe!' Heads turned questioningly and a soft murmuring of conversation arose. With a few more sharp taps of her ruler, Miss Brink ordered them to shut up and listen! 'There are eleven million homeless in Europe; they are cold, wet, hungry, destitute; a multitude which, at the end of the war, was literally starving due to the German's scorched-earth policy. A destitute army of people with nowhere to go. Not knowing where they are going to; not knowing where the next meal is coming from. Or even if they're going to have a next meal! The women and children prey to rape or murder or both! Children with no families – hope almost non-existent – fear – the survival of the fittest! And, in China, there are some forty-three million Chinese refugees who fled from the advancing Japanese! And you, children, you come from your nice warm beds, from loving families to a warm, clean school environment and you spend your time feeling sorry for yourselves! Just because you got soaking wet and didn't have a good night's sleep due to the storm! Children! You should be ashamed of yourselves!'

Her bright, eagle eyes slowly wandered from child to child, and they held their heads downwards feeling ashamed – just as she intended them to be!

Confronted with such heart-rending statistics, what could they do? They'd often seen *that* on the newsreels, Pathé or British Gaumont Newsreels at the movies. It had bothered young Tabby – her puzzled brain had no answer. She was a compassionate child.

Afterwards, when she'd told her mother, her mother had reiterated 'Yer can't take everybody's troubles and woes on yer own shoulders, lovey. We c'n only do so much. We can't perform miracles, only the good Lord God can do that!'

'I know, I know, Miss Brink sez it's the Lord's prerogative – it's still terrible, Mum. And Miss Brink sez the word *terrible* must be the most over-used word since 1939! What d'ya reckon Mum?'

'She's prob'ly right I suppose. I ain't' brainy like yer Miss Brink. Twenty years or so before 1939 that was a very overused word then. Terrible! World War I – the Great War was *terrible* – worse even. A catastrophe of *terrible* proportions that are hardly bearable for many many women. Why d'ya fink there are so many old maids around, Tabby?'

'Yer means spinsters, Mum? Because nobody wanted to marry them, I suppose?'

'That's where yer wrong, lovey. *Spinsters* because their sweethearts were killed going *over the top* to crass orders – to be mowed down within seconds! We lost the flowers of our youth then. That was a *terrible 'terrible'* Tabby.' Tabby's eyes were round as saucers; she bit her bottom lip uneasily.

'I didn't know about that, Mum!'

'Like I sed, lovey, yer can't know everything – not at yer age; still got the birth marks on yer back yer 'ave; too young ter know it all! I 'eard there's some country villages in Britain which lost almost all of its young men! Brothers, cousins, schoolfriends – the whole lot! Nah! I'm not makin' it up, lovey. *Flowers of our youth they were, poor boys.'* She wiped tears from her eyes with the corner of her wrap-around apron which had blue flowers printed amidst green leaves, made of cotton – called an overall actually, because it was worn over the outer clothes and fastened with tape carried round to the back, and again to the front. It was sleeveless. All the mothers wore them! 'Yerse! Twenty years it were from 1918 after Armistice Day to 1939. The *never again* vociferous voices have been proved wrong! *All war is terrible. Tabby,* an' don't let anybody tell yer otherwise, lovey. Hundreds of thousands of men were killed – for what – before they'd hardly learnt ter shave themselves. Mere boys, some still had the bum fluff on their chins when they valiantly took the King's shilling!' She sniffed heartily. 'Always makes me cry. My friend's youngest went ter Souf Wales. Real 'appy she were in Wales; didn't wanna come 'ome again did she?' Having heard that story many times over, Tabby hugged her mother; she'd an aroma of Sunlight soap about her where she'd been washing some of Benjie's clothes that morning. It pervaded the whole house giving it a fresh fragrance, most appealingly.

The kitchen of the house at Granite Road was not much bigger than a double cupboard. There was a moveable pantry which her daughters had clubbed together to buy for her after the war. It was modern, it even had a pull-out table from beneath the drop flap of the daily foods section, where the most used basics were kept; margarine, butter (when they could get it), jam, bowl of sugar, milk jug, all conveniently to hand. Tabby was not quite sure of the width of the kitchen, she'd never measured it, but she'd hazard a good guess, no more than five feet wide, and the same length. To pass by someone you had to literally squeeze against them! Crockery was kept in the bottom cupboards: with everything else needed for meals or cooking purposes, kept in the double fronted cupboard above the drop-flap section. Very compact, neat and tidy, it'd caught Jean's eye one day, at Andrews store. She felt like a queen with it in her tiny kitchen. There was just room for the gas stove, with its rack above which held the everyday dinner plates and warmed them. Next to it was the old Butler sink. Jean found it useful and refused to get rid of it. All her girls had had baths in it when very young! Benjie was still having his baths in it!

Jean had tiled the walls halfway herself getting fed up of waiting for Henry to do it – and she'd managed to save for a new kitchen carpet. It made the kitchen warmer! And it was no problem to roll it up, hang it over the clothes line and brush it down with the hand brush. When she felt like it, she gave it a good *thwack* with the broom. The kitchen was her territory – the rest of the house was seen to by her girls! From the kitchen to the back yard (garden) with the old-fashioned, cast-iron mangle underneath its cover of a sheet of tarpaulin – her feet never got wet because Henry had made a concrete patch. In-between showers of rain, Jean rushed out to mangle her washing! It was wonderful for sheets provided they were well-folded, they came out looking pressed – hung out to dry on a windy day they never needed ironing. Nobody who had a mangle ever thought of ironing sheets!

Tabby's world had been a sort of cosy world apart from the hazards of war time and the rationing, and the shortage of decent clothing. Being the youngest then, she'd been quite fussed over by her family.

When the street's children returned from evacuation 'her cup runneth over' with plenty of mates. True, she wasn't streetwise like them – lots of them were cocky and blasé, and the six streets had never been noisier. But that was preferable to the wailing of the air raid siren and the all clear siren, which induced fear into their hearts.

The spotlessly clean fish and chip shop up the Fiddlers – with its tiled walls, staff in crisp white overalls or aprons – was as much a part of their lives as breathing. On the way home from the movies the night air was redolent with the tantalising aroma of cod and chips, or skate and chips, or if you were really hard-up, a ha'penny worth of crackling – the crispy bits left in the sizzling fat, after the fish was removed from it … it was a feast fit for a King.

Apart from visiting *family* – and that wasn't very often – Tabby had never gone anywhere apart from shopping at Green Lanes or Romford. They'd not exactly been encouraged to travel – evocative war posters were everywhere… 'Is *your* journey really necessary?' Other posters warned you to be careful because you never knew who was *listening*. Then there was the caricature drawing of Mr Chad, with his long nose, peeping over a brick wall; the words 'wot no?' was written on the wall, which gave great scope to waggish sayings like, 'Wot no beer' or Wot no fags'!

Tabby had taken to heart the Squander Bug posters and became an avid saver of National Savings stamps with the extortion of the squander bug'll get yer if yer don't watch out! The habit was to stay with her all her life.

Her mother dressed in her second best rig-out had gone off to visit her favourite daughter,

Gertie, who was expecting again – having suffered a few miscarriages possibly due to food shortages in the war. The whole family were feeling anxious about this pregnancy. Donning her hat – made by Gertie who could turn her hand to practically anything – Jean had admonished Tabby not to go too far away on her walk: 'I'll only be round the corner at our Gertie's … mind 'ow yer go and behave yourself.' Gertie did indeed live but a stone's throw away, but all women liked an excuse to dress up, so Jean wore her second best when she visited her Gertie's!

So many thoughts darted hither and thither like mad fireflies through Tabby's brain that she felt she ought to – or could – write a book! And she tucked the idea away nice and neatly amongst the little grey cells of her bacon bonce. Gazing around her, noting the freshly grown grasses, wild flowers, and dock leaves, with their inevitable accompaniment of stinging nettles – find a stinging nettle and there'd always be dock leaves in the vicinity – rubbed on a sting from a nettle, nature's cure and prescription. She found such a diversity of flora over near the sewage bank walk, she was teaching herself to sketch them. Untutored she might be with a pencil, but her walks had brought familiarity with her surroundings that she made quite passable sketches, from memory. Vaguely she wondered if she should learn *real drawing* for pleasure? Nibbling a long plant stalk from a huge clump of grass – it never occurred to her it could be poisonous, fortunately it wasn't, it grew just past the stinging nettles and dock leaves. She permitted her little grey cells to ponder anew on the possibility of becoming an artist deciding that was another moot point, she found another niche amongst the little grey cells, and it was quickly dismissed from her immediate thoughts.

That was the beauty of solitary strolls, one could think, walk, stop or anything. Anyway, apart from hop-picking and fruit-picking, it was the nearest she ever got to the country, and she'd never been to the seaside at all!

Eventually her circular route would bring her to the main road, then past her school, some shops, the cinema and back to Granite Road of the six streets. She revelled now in being a member of the Tank Trap Gang, with the older children, having *aged* enough to leave the young 'uns behind – that chapter of her life was over. The TTG turned out to be a motley assortment of eleven to fourteen year olds – who hung around on the tank traps, which were the edifices of solid concrete placed with the sole purpose of hindering the Hun should he – heaven forbid – land on the British mainland. If the council buildings were bombed, the council would use their school as base.

On her infrequent visits to the East End of London with her mother, Tabby'd gone visiting various relatives, and had taken the opportunity to go out to play with her cousins. That was really something – the bombed-out sites! You never knew what treasures you would find. Holes and craters full of rainwater, made spiffing jumping games! Too bad if you missed – you got sopping wet! Tabby had found the East End bomb sites to be one of her favourite playgrounds. She'd found plenty of adjectives to describe them in her English essays. Miss Brink was truly astounded how young Tabitha Braithewaite had metamorphosed almost overnight. Nobody was more surprised than the 'child'.

Somehow a little window opened up amongst Tabby's little grey cells in her bacon bonce; all was revealed – magical! From being bottom in English, she shot to the top! Nobody could fathom why. It just happened. Her teacher called it a miracle, her mother said, 'It's the hand of God!'

From being lukewarm, Tabby now found herself eager for English lessons! Hitherto, unable to vent her feelings descriptively she'd fallen back on common basic Anglo-Saxon English – unfortunately relegated down the centuries to become obscene words. Jean naturally had objected strongly to swearing even though Tabby's life had been surrounded by people who used such language as regularly as they breathed! Tabby's swearing had been her Achilles' heel for as long as she could remember.

'How lucidly she writes, how coherently, how descriptive – what a miracle in one of such tender years!' Miss Brink ran out of adjectives describing Tabby's make-over.

'I'd put our Tabby up against Churchill or Atlee, any day of the week,' hooted Henry, her father. 'Got the gift of the gab she has!' He even solicited her aid when unable to understand a sentence or word in the newspapers.

On this happy day, with thoughts tumbling higgledy-piggledy, she mulled them over in her ever-fertile bacon bonce. Tabby licked her sticky lips, she should have wiped her mouth over – it was all sticky with cod liver oil and malt. Her mother had given her an extra big dollop from the big, brown, glass jar. What with a share of Benjie's bottle of concentrated orange juice, very cheap from the health centre, locally, her mother had ensured that her youngest daughter was getting vitamins and everything else necessary to fill her out. It had worked too. No longer spindly legged she was fast becoming a *bonny lass.* Initially, her thinness had been put down to the fact that she was the youngest of thirteen girls. Her dad termed her the *runt of the litter.* But, from out of nowhere Jean had conceived again! No runt of the litter this time. A *boy!* There was such rejoicing the whole family was ecstatic, not least Henry. He had a son at last.

Thirteen disappointments and now Benjie. He was no runt either, not Benjie – he weighed in at nearly ten pounds! He was as plump and cuddly as Tabby had been thin and weakly.

'Loquacious, nauseous, circumstances, parallel, pedantic.' Tabby was enjoying rolling some newly-discovered words around in her mouth. She liked the taste of them!

In her best schoolmarmish voice, mimicking Miss Brink, she announced, to thin air, 'Words make the world go round, children; dialects add spiciness – but there is a time and place for everything. In school and at work you use the *King's English.*' Tabby peered round guiltily – she needn't have bothered, there was nobody within earshot. 'Remember children, there is a place for dialects and a place for the King's English. The language which we have given to the world! Never belittle a person's dialect, it is their heritage. Dialects add a richness to life; without them, it would be a grey world – a very grey world. Now, run along children, don't forget your homework!'

'I'm getting good at Miss Brink's voice,' giggled Tabby.

She was almost word-perfect in her imitation. Mimicry – that's the word; I'm a good mimic. And she was.

She passed the boiler suit factory; the hooter tooted and the girls streamed back to their sewing machines. Even the war hadn't stopped production. Whatever uniforms they were machining then were made-up at top speed. A landmine did some damage to the factory; the next day the girls were back at work dead on time! The British with their indomitable spirit were a byword. Indomitable – a lovely juicy word which she'd recently learned.

Central to Tabby's life now were three main things.

1. She was a Beginning Woman.
2. English had become a doddle.
3. Graduation to the TTG.

Her teacher and headmistress felt it was such a

73

shame – a few years earlier Tabby might have got into Grammar School.

But a few years earlier she'd been hopeless at English! Anyway at Grammar School you Matriculated and had to pass several core subjects to actually Matriculate. Tabby was not much good at any anything else, apart from sewing.

Esmeralda's mother was suitably impressed with Tabby's new knowledge. 'Helps my Esmeralda, does your Tabby.'

'I fink me 'meralda will be clever like Tabby. She's learnin' fast. Shame yer Tabby never went to the Grammar School! Made fer life they are iffen they goes ter grammar, s'fact!'

Jean had nodded, taking another sip of tea. 'It's a bloody cryin' shame. Blame Parliament meself, yerse, I blame Parliament. Yerse I do Maisie. Gotta blame somebody ain't yer? Bleedin' politicians! Makes all them laws, them do, I can tell yer. We folk don't 'ave a leg ter stand on. Nah! we don't!'

Her friend agreed. 'I were only sayin' ter me Reg the 'uvver day. I woz yer know, yerse I woz.'

'Wot did yer Reg say, go on, tell us!'

'My Reg! I sez to 'im I sez … all loike yer jist sed abaht politicians … an' wot did my Reg say?' Maisie took another sip of hot tea, paused to draw breath. 'My Reg? Whatd'yer fink the bleeder sed? Cross me 'eart, 'ope ter die. My Reg? Glared at me, yerse 'ee did. Sed ter shut me bloody trap! Sed… "Wot do wimmin know abaht Parl'ment or anyfink else fer that matter … only fit fer babies and 'ousework!" Didn't say that when the bleedin' war was on, did they? Oh no!

Oh no, I tell yer Jean…'

'Bloody cheek of yer Reg! Wimmin worked at home, in the factories, on the ack-ack-guns, slaving in munitions, still had ter cook the b … their meals whenever they were on leave. Driving ambulances, making barrage balloons, make-do-and-mend wiv clo's. In the navy, airforce and everything else. Not to mention the ruddy Land Army doing men's farming jobs. Expecting us to entertain them in bed and 'ave babies. Bloody cheek! I'd like ter give yer Reg a piece of me mind I would, Maisie!'

Taking another sip of tea, Maisie burst out laughing. 'Don't worry, ducks, gave 'im a piece of me own mind, didn't I!'

'The blokes 're tryin' ter turn the clocks back, Maisie. Want women as chattels like before the war! I know, legally we're chattels but it'll change, it'll change, yer'll see.'

'Mind yer Jean, they've got a thing abaht jobs, the women want ter keep their jobs and the men don't like it. A man's got 'is pride, yer see. He's the traditional breadwinner. Gotta bring a few quid a week 'ome, ain't 'ee? Duzzn't feel like a man iffen 'ee can't support 'is family!'

'Yeah, gotta pay the rent, ain't 'ee? I 'eard the council rents is going up ter nearly two quid a week. That's a helluva lot fer a workin' man. Luckily ours are private. Private landlord I mean – all of the six streets.'

It was also true that many of the men's jobs had disappeared. New ways, new demands, changes, changes, changes! Some firms had been totally obliterated by bombing or landmines. Mentally, materially and physically, the war had taken its toll on the people.

'Maisie, wot some men and wimmin went through, don't bear thinkin' abaht!'

''S true, 's fact. We woz lucky in the six streets.'

Maisie's aunt had lost her whole family! Up the East End of London, bombed out of one shelter, they'd rushed to a neighbour's. Direct hit! Never found a piece of them or the neighbour!

'Ain't got nobody on earth 'cept me – I'm an in-law! She were stayin' overnight wiv me, missed the last bus 'ome. Must've been fate. Didn't know 'til she got 'ome, did she? Just a bleedin' big crater where her house had been. The neighbour's was even worse. ARP bloke sed it were one of the biggest craters they'd ever seen! Said they never knew nuffink! Direct 'it! Hitler and his bleedin' bombs. I'd 'ave Schnickel-grübered 'im iffen I'd got 'old of him! Beautiful 'ome she 'ad. Her own; bought and paid fer weren't it? Cost 'er 'usband five hundred pounds afore the war. A lot of money that!'

Jean whistled incredulously. 'Five 'undred knicker? I ain't ever seen money like that!'

'Me neither, cash 'er husband paid fer it. I know, 'cos he were Reg's third cousin, once removed! His dad died and left him a shop in the country. Aunt wouldn't live anywhere except London, born and bred there she were. So he sold the shop for seven hundred pounds and bought the house for five hundred pounds! She lost the lot. Always been generous to us, she had. Told her she could squeeze in wiv us iffen she wants ter? But she's taken up wiv a spiv bloke.

That's 'oo I got me nylons from. D'yer like 'em?'
She stuck her nylon clad legs out for Jean's
approval.

'Bloody 'eck! Smashin' ain't they! Yer can see
thems Yank's nylons, Maisie. Lucky bleeder ain't
yer? I 'as ter keep me one pair for best, still usin'
gravy browning, I am. Our Tabby draws the line
up the back fer me! Me one good pair are in and
out of the invisible menders so often, they take
themselves there and back now!'

'Oh! Aunty Maisie!' Tabby had let herself in
with the string key. 'I fought yer were at our
Gertie's house?'

'She 'ad her mother-in-law there, can't stand
the woman! Bumped into Maisie on me way
back. Just 'avin' a cuppa we are. Wotcha been up
ter, lovey?'

'Me! Nuffink, Mum, nuffink! Wot makes yer
say that?'

'Yer kissed me. Yer don't do that often now!'

'Growin' up ain't I! Just practising me kissing.'

'Whattd'ya mean? Yer been practising on them
boys our Tabby? Yer'll 'ave a shotgun wedding
iffen yer goes kissin' boys!'

Maisie sniggered.

Tabby blushed brick red, then white.

'Come on, Tabby, weren't born yesterday, was
I? C'mon aht wiv it!'

'Ginger kisses the girls, French kissin', puts 'is
tongue down their throats, 'ee does yer know.'

'Oh he duz duz 'ee? Mind yer don't go French
kissin'! Yer dad'll tan yer backside wiv 'is belt. An'
that ain't a threat or a warning – it's a promise!
'Ave yer guts fer garters 'ee will – yer father.'

'I wouldn't let Ginger Morley kiss me, Mum. Wot d'ya take me for?'

Maisie tittered again.

Tabby looked daggers at her. 'I wouldn't kiss 'im, I might catch sumfink from 'im!'

Maise was in hysterics now: 'Yere'd 'ave caught sumfink orlright, Tabby.'

'An' iffen yer 'ad, our Tabby. I'd 'ave killed yer ... and ... iffen I didn't, yer father would've.' Jean's tea choked in her throat; she was laughing as heartily as Maisie.

Tabby's eyebrows beetled together across the bridge of her nose. Grown-ups could be so peculiar she wondered what they meant? Obviously, they didn't mean to enlighten her little grey cells. She'd 'ave ter *ask me sisters!*

'Yeah, lovey, ask Gertie, she'll tell yer?' Tabby shrugged, funny yer parents love yer one minute and tell yer off the next. She fastened the buttons which were popping open on the bodice of her shrunken blue velvet dress: a hand-me-down! Material was still scarce. Washed so frequently the rich colour was more grey than blue now.

None of her schoolfriends were dressed much better. From the ragbag, same as her. Why couldn't they have lovely clothes like the college girls in the Hollywood movies? Her friend's (not Esmee) sister had gone to America; she was a GI bride. Sent back loads of food and clothing parcels she did. Best dressed girl in the class was Jessie. She'd got a Teddy-Bear coat, with a dress of pink with yellow butterflies all over it. Her parents had got gold watches. Lovely food they received! Every week they had two or three

78

parcels. America must be the *Valhalla*, thought Tabby. Things were improving in Britain, but not to that extent! She'd sighed and wished, not for the first time, that her sisters had married Yanks. Not all of them, but at least one. Thinking of the nylon stockings Jean had secretly hoped that too!

The buttons had popped again. Sighing, Tabby fastened them. Her growing bosom was fast becoming a source of embarrassment! Her *sweeties* her father called them. He was so insensitive to people's feelings! The liberty bodices were no longer a part of her apparel. She'd given up trying to work out how they got the nomenclature *liberty*. With their abundance of little rubber buttons and their fleecy-side-to-the-skin – anything more unlike liberty – well! Though admittedly warm in winter. There was nothing suitable for young boys and girls over the age of twelve in Britain. You were either a child or an adult! There was no in-between status! Unlike the Yankee movies – teenagers had not been invented in Britain!

Her mother's breasts had no support other than the rigid whaleboned corset and her vest. The older girls wore pinkish cotton hammocks with no support – called brassieres. She felt sorry for girls who had very heavy breasts – especially after childbirth! Tabby was perplexed by seein' – well it had nearly frightened the living daylights out of her. Why couldn't somebody have prepared her for it? Nobody had sat her down and said 'Tabby this is what is going to happen to you as you grow older.' She'd grumbled to Esmee. ''Ow's a girl ter know *what's what* and

79

when's when, iffen nobody tells us nuffink. It ain't fair, it really ain't! I'm not a magician, can't tell meself can I?'

Esmee had sympathised, but had no answers. Jean was not impervious to her daughter's feelings. Nobody had told *her* when she was growing up, she'd not told her daughters either! Ignorance was bliss! Jean didn't read books; rarely looked at the newspapers. Anyway, newspapers and magazines didn't tell young girls things!

Thousands of young boys went to war pig-ignorant about the other sex, and about sixty per cent were illiterate or semi-illiterate. They came back – if they came back – as men. It had been a brutal baptism of fire for the boys.

Tabby's sister Sally was one of the first daughters to be married. At the factory, they'd stitched pieces of cloth over her best coat and stitched the arms together!

On her way home, one of her mates ran after her. Junie had been married three weeks previously. 'It's all right, Sally, don't be frightened – nothing 'appens on yer wedding night! Yer too tired, yer jist go ter sleep! It ain't nuffink ter be frightened of.'

'Thanks, Junie, I'll remember that tomorrow. Dead scared I am, I dunno wot ter expect? Me mum sed wait 'n' see, same as she 'ad ter!'

She'd told Gertie, married just before her – a few months after the wedding. The same thing had happened to Gertie! And Gertie'd sed, 'Mum reckons ignorance is bliss, Sally! Iffen yer don't know nuffink then yer can't get into trouble. That's wot our Mum thinks!'

Henry was taking great pride in his back garden. Suddenly, the gardening bug had got him! The yard became our garden overnight. 'Like Capability Brown,' said Henry.

Jean's shrieks of laughter had made poor Benjie jump! He didn't know what his mum was laughing at – but he joined in! 'It's a wot, Henry Braithewaite?'

'A Capability Brown, don't see anyfink funny in that? Me garden's like Capability Brown.'

'Yer jist sed that ijjit, 'oo's 'ee?'

'Blimey, missus, ain't yer pig-ignorant? Did rich folk's landscaping – is what 'ee did. Capability Brown! Yer knows them there big estates – I don't rightly know which ones, but they were big like Hampton Court or Windsor Castle not sayin' they were them am I, but big places like them; vast lands – he landscaped 'em. As I jist sed I dunno which big places, I'm jist givin' yer some ideas in yer noddle of the size of the lands he landscaped. Didn't know I'm a bit edicated did yer, me old Dutch?'

He bussed his wife heartily on the cheek. She pulled away sharply; one thing led to another – she didn't want no more babies, not every year. Not her, she wanted to be part and parcel of this new land fit for heroes, to go out, wear make-up, new clothes, nice ones, not maternity smocks, to go dancing – like in the Hollywood movies. She'd dreamed so long, and she was determined not to keep having babies! She'd done her best for King and Country to help repopulate the world. She fancied the camaraderie of working in a factory with her daughters. They were always telling her of the laughs they had. She'd be able to pick up gossip and make new mates. It would be a fresh start in life. She imagined herself singing along during workers' playtime music in the factories. Meanwhile her smashing baby boy – an accident he'd been, but a godsend now – he needed her. She loved him to bits, and adored singing to him, jiggling him on her knees.

Her Gertie had offered to take care of Benjie; she loved him almost as much as her mother did. His fair, curly hair, cherubic face with his Kirk Douglas dimple – he was a delightful baby. Very good too! From birth he'd always slept at nights, and played happily all day. He walked early, pulling himself up against furniture, Jean was still feeding him herself; over a year she'd been feeding him. Her breasts were full of rich creamy milk, and there seemed no end to it. Benjie did love his mother's breasts! He was going to be weaned on to solids now, he hadn't actually bitten her yet, but, he had three front teeth and the beginnings of five other teeth meant it wouldn't be long before he did. She'd run her finger over his little gums, yes the five teeth were nearly ready to break through. Benjie thought it was a new game and bit her finger – gently, 'Yer little rascal you!'

Henry had been dead set against his wife going out to work. But visibly brightened when she mentioned it might mean more beer money for him, until she mentioned night work, he hit the roof! 'Yer c'n sleep on yer own Henry Braithe-

waite. Done me duty ter King 'n' Country I 'ave.
Fourteen children – done me duty I 'ave!' Henry
had slammed out muttering about the Union.
Half an hour later he was back with a few bottles
of beer.

'Well, me old Dutch, iffen yer works nights,
don't expect me ter warm yer bed for yer! I'll git
me oats somewhere else!'

Jean was incandescent with rage and she spat
out, 'Oats! The bloody oats yer've sown Henry
Braithewaite, must've covered several fertile acres
these past years. Not ter mention the bumper
'arvests – somewhere not far from the six streets!

'Oh yes! Don't think I don't know, do yer? ARP
duty; the Union. Yer needn't shake yer 'ead at me
'Enry Braithewaite. I could take yer round some
of the back streets where yer oats were green and
fertile! But them were different times, them were
the war years … but, I'll tell yer this much 'Enry
with an "H"! Iffen yer scatterin' of oats turns into
more sprogs now, yer'll niver get back into my
bed … 'Enry with an 'aitch! Now give us a kiss,
yer goose! Yer wanna tie a knot in yer wotsit!'

He went white with fright; he hadn't thought
Jean knew! Somehow Jean didn't think Henry's
arrers would hit the bull's eye at The King's Oak
darts match that night!

Henry'd stopped at the door of his latest amour
several streets away and warned her he'd be
kicked out of the house if her latest sprog was his!

Up the spout his paramour certainly was; she
couldn't actually be sure if it was Henry's or that
of several blokes who enjoyed her warm convivial
hospitality. With the tenth child due any day she

didn't fancy letting Henry know that! She specially favoured Henry; he was *expert* in bed – with great staying power. Mabel also liked Jean. She was oblivious that Jean might know Henry shared her bed! Mabel was a good woman in other ways, and a smashing mother to her happy brood.

'A good woman needs a man, Maisie, she's clean she is.'

Jean had regularly passed on hand-me-downs to Mabel for her children. She felt extra sorry for her because she'd lost her husband at sea; a mine blew up his tanker! Henry was like the Yanks, 'Oversexed, overpaid, over here!' Maisie could never figure out why Jean was so understanding!

Maisie said the Americans were overpaid, oversexed and over here only because they were thousands of miles from home – away from the normal sanity of their homes with everything in abundance. And they didn't know if they would live or die? Anyway, the way Maisie saw it was, 'They're men yer see, they've gotta 'ave it: 'ow do we know 'oo our blokes are with in Europe. Works both ways yer see! God made men different from women, Jean!'

Both Maisie and Jean found it quaint – the questions Tabby'd been asking about French kissing. They told her it was the way people kissed in France. 'That's why it's called French kissing, lovely.'

Tabby wasn't going to be fooled with that blithe explanation. She scuffed the toe of one shoe down the other leg, slowly, deliberately. 'Nah!

's'not true! Me friend Arfur's sister French kisses – he's American! Her friend French kisses an' he's Italian!'

''Eaven's above, Tabby. We ain't edicated like youse! 'Ow do we know all the answers? Yer put me brain in a spin. Why can't yer jist "grow up" same as orl the other girls? They don't ask questions like youse, they don't. Go and bother Gertie, she'll know orl the answers. Go on, afore I swipes yer one!'

Tabby'd fled before she'd finished speaking, slamming the front door after her. The window frame rattled alarmingly. 'A few more slams like that from our Tabby and she'll finish orff what 'Itler's bombs and landmines didn't!'

Aunty Maisie was nice and Tabby liked her. She was not her real aunt. In the six streets you had lots of aunts and uncles. Then if your families fell out, they weren't your aunts and uncles any more! When you made up they were your aunts and uncles again! The world of the grown-ups was so confusing to young minds!

Tabby felt really cross, she couldn't make out why grown-ups went all round the Mulberry Bush and back! 'It doesn't make sense, it doesn't make sense!' She liked the sentence and repeated it several times to herself.

'Wot duzzn't make sense? Who 'er yer talkin' to Tabby?'

Tabby jumped guiltily! Esmeralda was waiting on the corner of the road, holding a piece of old clothes line which she'd found on a bomb site ages ago. *They won't need it any more,* said Esmeralda. 'They've pegged their last!' She'd

85

rolled around laughing at her own wit.

'It's not nice ter think or speak like that, Esmee. Just becos they were bombed ter smithereens.'

Esmee had choked off her laughter, pretending to look grave. Tabby hadn't finished with her insensitive friend. 'Just 'cos they didn't die naturally in their beds ... yer should be ashamed of yerself, Esmeralda Toffeenose.'

Tabby had seen a dead body – once! She'd gone a bit too far from the six streets, to a bit of a rundown area which was a surprise to her, she'd thought all the streets round their way would be clean like the six streets! The door of a decrepit house was wide open. Thinking the house was empty, she'd listened carefully; hearing no sound and, being in a cantankerous mood, she'd decided to be daring and adventurous, and dared herself to enter the house. You don't stop to think when you're young. Slinking through the open doorway, brushing her shoulders against the badly peeling stanchions she sidled along the gloomy dark passageway.

With her back to the wall and her arms out-splayed on either side of her body she hastily wrinkled her nose to the obnoxious aroma of old boiled cabbage cooked with bicarbonate of soda! Her eyes quickly adjusted themselves to the gloominess of the long narrow passageway and she observed the peeling Lincrusta on the lower half of the walls. Prob'ly been there hundreds of years, thought Tabby. She liked Lincrusta, her father painted theirs bright yellow every year, before Christmas. Stealthily she crept nearer to the staircase confronting her and, with arms still spreadeagled on the wall, she dared herself to inch her way up the stairs to the top – her feverish thoughts switched to *The Hound of the Baskervilles* by Conan Doyle; her recent English lesson – hoping the hound wasn't up the stairs! A shiver trembled silkily up and down her spine; the hairs on her arms stood on end and she felt all goose-pimply. Inch by inch she mounted the staircase, following the threadbare eighteen-inches-wide carpet runner with its loose stair-rods ... the encircling gloominess failed to disguise that it could have done with a good scrub. Reaching the stairwell, she paused. Frightened, but with her adrenaline now flowing freely in the excitement of the moment, she paused to listen carefully. Her ears were strained for the merest sound, however slight. Then there was a sound from the door of the front bedroom, where it was hanging *hopefully* on clapped-out hinges. It was a heavy shuffling noise. Tabby's blood ran cold! Ghosts! Her common sense told her that ghosts didn't have feet. Her friend Arfur had told her that. She furtively peaked inside the room. It was bathed in weak sunlight, filtering hesitantly through filthy net curtains, sham blinds – with their string tassels of indeterminate shade, hung from the tops of the grime-encrusted windows. It was a large room, running across the front of the house. The customary two sash windows were inveigled by the determined efforts of the weak sunlight to penetrate half-heartedly in motes and flooding spasms through the unwashed panes of glass – tentatively on the threshold of giving up its effort as a bad job.

An enormous blowsy looking woman was standing there, in the act of placing a penny on each eyelid of a comatose body which was lying on none too clean bedding. The spasmodic victory of the shafts of sunlight temporarily invading the gloom of the bedroom gave an *aura* to the poor threadbare clothing of the corpse which was claiming the woman's attention.

Three of the brass knobs of the black cast-iron bed were intact; the fourth rested upside down on the rickety, wicker bedside cabinet.

Tabby couldn't stop herself, a shrill high squeak – almost strangulated in its intensity – emitted from her fear-dried throat! Apart from the movies, it was the first dead body which she had *actually seen.*

Breathing heavily with rasping gasps, the fat woman spun round. Seeing nobbut a child – which she later told her equally obese husband – she raised a short stubby forefinger shushingly to her sensuous, heavily-lipsticked mouth. '*Shush! Shush!*'

She needn't have bothered for Tabby now resembled a frozen marble statue!

With great difficulty, the man's stiff arms were now being folded across his chest. He'd obviously been dead quite some time. Taking a clean, folded sheet from a bag, the fat woman laid it gently over the corpse. She crossed herself piously and bowed in a form of benediction and to Tabby, shooing her down the staircase. Once downstairs, her harsh voice grated 'Who're yer? What d'yer want?'

'Nuffink! I'm Tabby from the six streets. I'm

every so sorry – I didn't know, I mean, I saw the door open, thought the house was empty! I didn't 'ear anyfink 'til I got up them there stairs, honest I didn't. Cross me 'eart, 'ope ter die!'

Resting her hands on her ample hips, the woman sniffed suspiciously. The child didn't look like a liar, she were nobbut a child. Thin as a garden rake! 'So! Me young leddy, yer fought yer'd 'ave a nose did yer? Too bad, ain't nuffink worth takin', there ain't. Wot there was – I've already got it, ain't I? Yer see, Mr Jameson the dead geezer up the "apples and pears" – found 'im dead, I did! Yerse! Deader 'n a doornail! 'Ad no family alive, poor soul. Promised 'im when 'is time came, I'd lay 'im aht good and proper, an' put them there pennies on 'is eyeballs. Yer 'ave ter do that, keeps their eyelids shut, yer see!'

The woman wasn't going to let Tabby know that she'd given her a fright. Oh no! She'd thought at first it was the ghost of Mr Jameson's deceased wife! But she wasn't going to let on to a child! Least said, soonest mended, was her motto.

Tabby took a huge gulp of air and swallowed hard. 'Will 'ee 'ave a prop'r fun'rl wiv the glass cage and the black 'orses wiv their black fevvers on their 'eads? We're 'avin' a fun'rl down our streets! Wiv orl the trimmings, me mum sed.'

The woman chuckled good-naturedly. 'Lord bless yer child!' There was nothing for her to fear from this wisp of a tiny mite. Starting to fill out by the looks of her, but probably been a bag of bones before, you could always tell.

Patting her own ample hips complacently, she

smiled self-consciously. Men liked their women like her – well upholstered. Size didn't bother her, even rationing hadn't bothered her – plenty available if yer were in the know on the black market!

'Yer larnin' ain't yer, lovey. Ah well! Sooner yer larn the be'er. Yerse! Mr Jameson is 'avin' orl the trimmings, as yer put it – get 'is insurance book I 'ave. An' a letter ter *prove* ter the insurance man. The man from the Pru will be 'ere soon. Oh yerse! Sent one of me own chillun round 'is 'ouse fer 'im, I 'ave. Lives near us he duz, knows us orl duz the man from the Pru; all good neighbours we are from these parts. Yer see I used ter clean for Mr Jameson and give 'im a bit of a bite – paid me 'ee did. Lovely man! Went strange 'ee did, past few munfs! Yerse, 'ee did. Wouldn't open the door to anyone. He jist gave up on livin'! Can't say as I blamed 'im poor man! 'E'll 'ave a fair bit of a send orff; me an' me neighbours'll git a bite tergevver … 'avin' a real *old-fashioned wake* fer 'im we are. Yerse! A good send orff – roight yer know! Which is more 'n yer can say abaht his fam'ly … got blown up years ago, they did!'

She crossed herself again – very fervently. 'God Bless their 'umble souls!' She fingered a Rosary round her none too clean neck! 'Holy Mary, Saints be praised! Jesus and Mary – rest their poor 'umble 'earts in peace! Geezer upstairs – Mr Jameson – 'ee were away fightin' fer King and Country yer see, lovey. Yerse, 'ee were! Can't r'cllct exactly where, didn't talk abaht it much 'ee didn't. Them that really were in the thick of it, like ter fergit yer see! Ter'bl memories some of

90

'em 'ad – and still 'ave, the Saints preserve them. Heroes – they orl were bloody 'eroes, 'n' duzzn't anybody tells me diff'rnt either. Orl bloody 'eroes, they were. Iffen it wurn't fer them young 'ns 'oo went overseas as boys 'n' came back men – those which did come back! 'Eroes, iffen it wurn't fer them, we'd 'ave been slaves now – to that Boche over there! Our boys, orl of 'em! Some muvvers' babies they'd been once – yerse – some muvvers' babies.' She surreptitiously scrubbed at the corner of her eyes with the edge of her floral apron. 'Makes me cry lovey, it do, it do. Me own sons were there. Praise be the Lord! Sent 'em back ter me and their farver! Mr Jameson – 'ee were at D-Day, 1944, that were a fact: went over in one of them *glider things,* 'ee did 'n' orl. 'Is mates, poor souls, jist boys they were, jist boys, makes me blood run cold ter think of it! Weighted down by their gear they were, *drownded* in the cold water! Niver 'ad a chance, poor lads, jist sank 'n' drownded! Mr Jameson – sensitive soul 'ee were – sed some niver got ter land, niver fired a shot!' Still cried for 'is mates 'ee did, still cried! Yerse! Men cry, lovey! Yerse! Saw it orl they did! Fought in Anzio, Sicily, Salerno, orl them places 'n' more, me own sons an' me nephews! Terrible it were! Mr Jameson saw lots of *deafs* 'ee did. Then came 'ome ter more deafs! Went missin' 'ee did. Couldn't be traced. Some'ow 'ee got home again. 'N' fer wot? I'll tell yer wot fer – came 'ome didn't 'ee? Been missin' in one of them prisoner-of-war camps! Like a skeleton 'ee were. Yerse! Youse niver seed nuffink like it! Yerse! But 'ee were lucky – some blokes 'ad years 'n' years in prison camps! Ask anybody in the streets, they'll tell yer! Cried a lot 'ee did! Nerves! Orl shot ter pieces they were! Were bowed down wiv memories of terrible things *he seed* on D-Day and in the camp. Couln't eat prop'ly niver agin. Yer jist saw the poor man. Thin, like a skeleton. Wouldn't open the door – I tried ter give 'im me soups, nourish'n' me soups are – liked 'em afore but last two months I daresay 'ee niver ate *nuffink*. I could lift 'im wiv me own 'ands!' Hastily she again crossed herself fervently.

Tabby followed suit, her mother was always dinning into her brain: 'Yer gotta 'ave respect fer the dead Tabby, it'll be yer own turn someday!'

Now that Tabby's initial fears had been allayed, the woman looked in a more kindly light. Obviously her bark was worse than her bite.

'We 'adn't 'eard nuffink since the uvver day! Kept callin' an' listenin' at the letterbox I did. Then I sez ter me Bobby – me 'usband – I'm goin' ter let meself in! So I did. Got in wiv 'is string key, didn't I? "Mr Jameson," I called aht, "it's me, Mrs Baker, next door. Are yer orl roight? Loike a bit o' broth ter sup, would yer?" No reply there wasn't. Found 'im as dead as a dodo on the floor I did.'

Tabby mentally wondered what a dodo was?

'Lifts 'im onto the bed I did – light as a fevver he were. Knocks on the wall an' me youngest comes runnin' in – told 'im ter run an' git the doctor, I did! Doctor MacFaddie, 'ee knows me – allus layin' dead bodies out fer 'im I am, round our streets. People trust me yer see. Doctor – 'ee comes runnin' – like, sees poor Mr Jameson's been dead some time. He were blue orl over, heart attack and blood clot. *Frombosis* is wot doctor called it. *Yerse!*

'Lorst 'is fam'ly as I were tellin' yer – terrible shock ter 'im when 'ee comes 'ome from the war! Turned aht 'ees fam'ly were stayin' wiv 'is sister over Peckham Rye way – somewhere like that. I did 'ear tell. A doodlebug got 'em! Blew them orl ter smithereens – niver found a little bit of 'em! Yerse! – that's the troof, as God's me witness. Them blinkin' doodlebugs ... no warning .... they jist cut aht all of a sudden, no sound, suddenly, an' yer niver knew where the bomb – the doodlebug – would drop, until it 'it yer, then it were too late: St Peter were orl ready takin' them by the 'ands an' leadin' them through the Pearly Gates! Them buzz bombs and doodlebugs scared the livin' daylights out of orl of us. Yer 'eard them comin' then it were absolute silence and yer prayed it weren't yer turn! Orl of 'is fam'ly gorn! He weren't old Mr Jameson, nah! I knows 'ee looked old. Went white overnight, 'ee did. Terrible shock, poor man – ter come 'ome from 'ell and finds yer fam'ly is in 'eaven' – gave orl of us a shock when 'ee turned up! He'd been posted missing – presumed dead! We orl rallied round 'im. The 'ouse had been locked up pending tracing of relatives! Oh yerse! That's wot neighbours is fer, lovey. Iffen yer got good neighbours, orls right in yer world, lovey. Yerse! He were only in 'is late thirties ... they do say yer shouldn't grieve fer them that's gorn ... it's them that's left behind yer should grieve fer. 'S'fact, lovey. Yerse! Then 'ee gits anuvver shock ... in walks 'is dead sister's 'usband ... 'ee were reported killed in action! Nobody'd 'eard from 'im or 'is mates fer years. After VJ Day in August 1945 'ee were discovered barely alive in a Japanese prisoner-of-war camp! Japs got 'im an' 'is mates when they were fightin' aht in Burma. My God, lovey! God fergive me fer takin' 'is name in vain: Georgie Boy 'ee were called. Georgie Boy I seed more meat on a leg o' lamb after it's been eaten. Georgie Boy went to 'is old 'ome – the authorities found 'is 'ouse wasn't there – the old doodlebug took it, I jist told yer. They contacted Mr Jameson 'is bruvver-in-law, now 'is only livin' relative! Mr Jameson took one look at Georgie Boy and had a *nervous break-down!* On top of 'is own troubles and dreadful memories 'ee now had to look after 'is bruvver-in-law! Yer niver in yer life see two such shattered men! Cruel it were! Well, yerse, yerse! So Georgie Boy come ter live 'ere wiv Mr Jameson. Niver bovvered a soul they didn't. The Red Lion – every night, sat in the corner wiv one pint of beer each. Niver spoke, jist sat an' sat! Pub closed fer the night – they went 'ome, an' that's 'ow they lived, those brave men ... *in a land fit fer 'eroes* is wot the nobs allus sed abaht Britain!' She cleared her throat noisily and so did Tabby.

'Georgie Boy! He were crossin' the road last year, he'd gone a bit funny in the 'ead from the brutality of the prisoner-of-war camp. Got knocked down by a tram 'ee did. *Instant deaf,* the coroner sed. Poor Mr Jameson. It were the last straw for 'im poor man!

'Been in a Japanese prisoner-of-war camp, had

94

Georgie Boy. Yerse! 'ee worked on that there *deaf railway*, didn't 'e? Suffered 'ee did, yerse, 'ee did, as God's me witness – would I lie ter yer? Abaht sumfink so terrible? Yerse! 'Ow 'ee suffered! Beriberi – wot ever that is … 'n' dysentery … an' Lord knows wot else besides. It do fair make me cry it do. Yerse! Went ter war a chubby young lad, came back an old man – a livin' walkin' skeleton! Lorst orl 'is 'air, 'ee did, niver grew again it didn't! Poor, poor laddie. I 'spects 'is deaf woz a merciful relief fer 'im, poor tormented soul!' She wiped her streaming eyes again with her apron. 'Wiv 'is fam'ly now, 'ee 'is, the Lord God be praised. I reckon Georgie Boy were waitin' wiv St Peter ter take Mr Jameson froo the Pearly Gates. Luvverlee innit – orl tergevver agin? Mr Jameson – 'ee 'ad such a luverlee smile on 'is face when I laid 'im out good and proper like. Wiv the Lord and 'is fam'ly 'ee surely is!'

She sighed heavily, and Tabby nodded her head in vigorous assent. She knew what the woman was referring to – the death railway. She'd seen it on the Gaumont British News at the movies – everybody had! Most of the cinema audience had jumped to their feet shaking their fists at the screen and *vowing never, never again*. It had quite frightened Tabby – the ensuing furore during the screening of the released prisoners from the Japanese prisoner-of-war camps; cinema audiences were not known for jumping to their feet and shouting in anger. It just wasn't British – laugher and catcalls during some films or newsreels and even shrill whistles of approval at certain delectable film stars!

95

'Mr Jameson – 'ee jist let fings go after 'ee lorst Georgie Boy. Niver cleaned or cooked fer 'isself agin. I did me Christian best 'til 'ee became wot they call a recluse. Proud 'ee were – wouldn't let anyone from council 'elp 'im. Well, lovey, we'll make sure Mr Jameson's fam'ly up in 'eaven knows 'ee 'as a right good send orff.'

Tabby felt her own eyes prickling with tears at this sorry tragedy; as young as she was she was able to realise that poor Georgie Boy, and poor Mr Jameson were just two of literally thousands of human tragedies in the aftermath of the horrendous Second World War.

'Yer gotta respects the dead, lovey. Yer better git yerself 'orff 'ome or yer ma'll tan yer 'ide fer yer. Bye, lovey!'

Having already reached the same conclusion at the mention of her mother, Tabby mumbled a brief 'tara fer now' and hared off home. She had to get home before her mother was back from Green Lanes, shopping at Sainsburys! She'd gone all the way there just to get the sausages which her father liked! He wouldn't eat any others! Tabby had been delegated to clean dust and polish her parents' bedroom. And she hadn't! Not fancying another backhander from her mother, her feet hardly touched the ground. She was cognisant that her mother – as much as they loved each other – could pack a real wallop when she liked!

Puffing heavily, she stood on tiptoe to feel for the string key just behind the letterbox. 'Thank God for the gift of *fleetness* of foot – another saying of her teacher's! Hastily filling the kettle from the tap she shoved it onto the gas-ring and struck a match, so it burst into flames. Grabbing dusters and polish and a hand broom from the cupboard under the sink (which her dad had made), her feet took the stairs two at a time ... a lick and a promise left the bedroom superficially clean, which she hoped would pass muster, she jumped down the staircase three steps at a time; expertly – born of long practice! Lighting the grill, she swiftly cut some doorsteps of bread – her mother was partial to a few slices of toast with her cuppa cha. For once, she remembered to wet the teapot with scalding hot water before emptying it and placing three teaspoons of tea – Horniman's – into the pot and then filling it with scalding hot water from the kettle before it went off the boil!

Her mother insisted on the repetitive rigmarole – so did other mothers. Tabby herself couldn't see what difference it made – whether the teapot was wetted or not; however, hers was not to argue why – hers was but to do or die!

Opening the front door as if on cue – for Tabby had timed the fresh tea spot on – Jean sniffed appreciatively. Her Tabby was a good girl – little did she but know!

'Well done, lovey, perfect timing – ohhh – me arms is killing me, Benjie's a dead weight when 'ee's asleep. Luckily someone gave me their seat on the bus. Ohh! Me poor bunions. Wish they'd make a pram small enough ter take on the bus ... next time I take Benjie I'll put 'im in 'is big pram 'n' I'll walk there and back! Give us a kiss, lovey. 'Ad a nice day 'ave yer? Blimey yer should've seen the queues at Sainsburys! It were the same at Home & Colonial and Liptons! Orl the world an' 'is wife were out shoppin' terday! Orl wimmin – no men actually! 'ere – take 'is lordship – wake up Benjie, go to yer sister!'

Benjie slowly opened his sleepy eyes, giving a seraphic grin; only half awake, he let Tabby take him from his mother. Then he yawned and fell fast asleep again: Tabby rocked him gently.

'Yer better take 'is 'at and coat off, lovey, I bet 'ee's wet hisself! He's a bleedin' wee-wee-wee-er is our Benjie, bless 'im. Everybody made a fuss of him! The shopkeepers gave 'im biscuits ter eat – look at the mess orl down the front of 'is coat! Let 'im pick 'is own few biscuits they did – from the tins.

'He got more kisses from the ladies than a girl gets on 'er wedding night. Our little Benjie's going ter be a lady-killer, yer'll see!'

Tabby smiled secretly glad that her mother's attention was diverted from *Tabby's day out*, to the condition of Benjie's coat sprinkled with sugary biscuit crumbs – and her pride in his wooing of the ladies!

Probably Tabby knew she would tell her mother a little of what had happened to her – but not everything; she didn't want a thick ear'ole, did she? Because that's what she would get if her mother knew she had entered somebody else's house – uninvited – and, even worse, a total stranger's house and a dead one into the bargain!

Chapter Three

'Tabby! Tabby! ... I'm speakin' to yer!'

'Sorry, Esme – me mind was wool gatherin', like.'

'What d'ya mean wool gatherin? I ain't 'eard that afore.'

'It means me mind's miles away, dunnit. Thinkin' orl sorts of things, I am! That's wot it means stoopid!'

''Ow that's got anyfink ter do wiv gatherin' wool – I dunno.'

'Me Uncle Reg – yer know – Aunty Maisie's 'usband, he allus sez "Maisie's wool gatherin' agin'!"'

Slow of mind, Esmee pondered that for a moment. 'Oh yeah! Wot wer yer thinkin'? Yer can tell me, Tabby, I'm yer *bestest* friend.'

'Knows that, dun I – stoopid! Yer younger than me though – yer ain't started *seein'* yet. Not growing into a woman yet – like me. No, yer ain't.'

Esmee, quite indignant, spluttered, 'Yer can't add up for toffee nuts, Tabitha Braithewaite. I'm only two years younger 'n yer! Anyways I wishes I woz a woman like yer – wiv yer *seein'* an' yer *bosoms.* It must be the bees knees, now yer growin' into a real woman! Wot's it like, Tabby? *Seein'* – is it nice?'

'Nice! Nah! It bloomin' well isn't! I ain't got no

99

choice 'n' neither will you when yer turn comes round! Me muvver sez it goes on almost for ever and ever ... every munf, every year of yer life. Well nearly! An' yer bosoms 'urt: 'cos yerve got growin' pains ... me muvver calls it *growin' pains!* Me, I calls it purgatory! One day yer dresses fit yer orlright, next day, they don't ... or yer butt'ns pops opens 'cos there ain't enuff room any more fer yer *growin' lemons* ... sometimes yer bodices *rip!* I wonder when me lemons'll stop growin'?'

'When yer big enuff I guess! I'd like to grow *my* lemons!' Esmee self-consciously smoothed her hands over her obviously flattish chest. 'I ain't even started me pebbles yet! Still flat they are. Litt'l peas they start as – that's wot Ginger told me – yerse!'

Tabby rounded on her: 'Yer'll get yer lemons soon enuff after yer *peas.* 'Ére! Wot were yer doin' near Ginger? Yer wozzn't lettin' 'im French kiss yer, were ya? Yer ain't started yer seein' yet – yer keeps away from Ginger!'

Esmee laughed knowingly. 'Nah! I wouldn't let 'im. Told 'im I 'ad ter tell me best friend, Tabby first, didn't I, 'cos she's a *nearly woman!* Ginger laughed ever so nasty – 'ee did'n all! Yer knows 'ow he does: yer know wot 'ee sez, Tabby?'

'Nah – go on tell us.'

''Ee sez...' Esmee crept closer and whispered in her ear. '"Yer'll orl be wimmin by the time I've finished wiv yer orl – yerse yer will!"'

Tabby, suitably shocked exploded: 'The litt'l stinker!'

''Ee ain't so litt'l, Tabby! Me sister, Lucy – she were talkin' to a friend of 'ers who gets around a

100

bit and ... 'ear ... yerse I did ... I 'eard 'er say ... *"Ginger's got a whopper!"* That's wot she sez – cross me 'eart and 'opes ter die! And Lucy sed she once tied a pink ribb'n round Ginger's whopper! D'ya fink she meant Ginger's ears? They duz seems ter stick out a bit, don' they?'

Tabby flushed scarlet, to the roots of her ears. She knew very well what Ginger's whopper was. He'd tried to force her hand onto the front of his trousers. To feel his whopper. It had given her the fright of her life! She'd screamed blue murder and ran off – she didn't want to touch it, whatever it was! Tabby wasn't sure quite what she'd catch from touching Ginger's whopper, but she wasn't taking any chances. She knew there'd be hell to pay if her mother found out!

Her bosom friend's span of attention not being one of her greatest assets, her airy-fairy mind had already forgotten Ginger's whopper. Her mind was now on skipping! That's why she'd brought the old piece of clothes line, wasn't it? ''Ere Tabby, got us a new skippin' rhyme I 'ave!'

''Ave yer?' asked Tabby. Jolly glad to change the subject – anything but Ginger's whopper would be a welcome relief from her confused thoughts!

'Yeah! Let's go 'n' get some more girls – race yer to the uvver road.'

'Race yer – race yer. Yer better be fast Esmee!' Wide grins splitting their happy young faces from ear-to-ear, they raced like the winds of March; up one road, down another and round the corner of Granite Road – without let or hindrance from cars or bicycles, not even a hand cart or the ragman's pony and cart were to be seen! Apart

101

from the *sentinel* gas lamps there were no barriers in the six streets. Nobody owned cars – yet! Only the doctor – who valued his little black Ford with its tiny rear window – possessed such a luxury.

The midwife, often seen in the six streets, rode a bicycle with her wicker basket in front of the handlebars. There were some children in the six streets who naïvely assumed the midwife brought their mother's new babies in her wicker basket! Even the costermonger and the Sunday morning fishmonger – cockle 'n' whelks man – were not mechanised. Pushing or pulling their big *barrers* they were a regular and welcome sight down the six streets. Sunday high tea wouldn't 'ave been the same without cockles, shrimps and winkles along with meat paste sandwiches or cucumber sandwiches, or even mustard and cress and butter – best butter! Butter was usually kept for Sunday tea and visitors. Most people had Sunday visitors. It was great fun removing the black bit from the winkles with a pin – a dressmaker's pin – and sticking it on the cheek or cheeks, à-la-Margaret Lockwood who was famed for her beauty spot and sultry beauty.

The children of the six streets found them smashing places to play. If they were too noisy outside their own house their mother shooed them off to play outside somebody else's house. And vice versa! It was common to hear the shout, 'Oy youse lot – go 'n' play down yer own ends.'

Roller skating was one of Tabby's greatest joys. Her skates had been handed down in the family; easy to alter the size with a special key. Strapped on to her shoes or plimsolls she whizzed up and down the streets and round corners at high speed. Most of her mates could skate like her. Except Esmee, who for some unknown reason did not take kindly to skating, preferring skipping and whip and top. Esmee adored colouring her tops with chalks and whipping them so fast, they turned into a glorious rainbow of all the colours of the spectrum. Whips and tops and skipping ropes were the mainstay of games in their immediate environment. They could either be bought from the shop or handmade with screw-on tops from old Tizer bottles. The war had taught everybody how to improvise on most things, so that improvisation had become a way of life and you were not looked down upon for improvising in any way.

The old piece of clothes line was Esmee's pride and joy. It was a good skipping length and she'd found it – it was treasure. Her dad always asserted *finders-keepers, girl.*

As they sped down the streets, they'd yelled out their mates names. 'Effie, Molly, Clarice – skipping, skipping, come on out, orl in tergevver girls, come on out!'

Like the Pied Piper of Hamelin enticing the children to follow him, girls of all sizes and shapes and heights wrenched their front doors open and fled after Tabby and Esmee! The more the merrier was their motto when it came to real good skipping games. If they didn't know enough skipping rhymes they ingeniously made them up as they skipped! Or, they went round other places poaching their skipping rhymes!

'Oi! It's our skippin' rhyme! Clear orff! We

fought of it first. Clear orff – or we'll get our dad out after yer.'

'Yer can't 'ee's at work, ha! Ha! Ha!'

Then there'd be name-calling, trying to out-shout one another.

'Sticks 'n' stones may break me bones – names'll never 'urt me! When I'm in me grave yer'll be sorry that yer 'urt me!'

Mollie and Effie volunteered to be the first 'turners' and took their stance, each on opposite pavements, with the long clothes line strung across the road. Slowly they swung the rope in a wide arc. Into the rope jumped Clarice, one of the best and very nimble skippers.

Her voice in a high-pitched tone carried a fair distance.

'There's somebody under the bed,
'I don't know 'oo it is
I feels so shockin' nervous–
I calls me Esmee in:
Esmee lights the candle–
Esmee light's the gas–
Run out, run out
There's somebody under the bed!'

Into the rope jumped Esme, and Clarice exited smartly.

Watching from her front window, Jean let her thoughts flow through her head like waves. The children's innocent enjoyment of their simple games always touched a chord in her heart. 'Enjoy your childhood,' she murmured *sotto voce*. Jean sighed heavily, it wouldn't be long now

104

before her Tabby became a real woman. What a shame young girls had to grow up so quickly! At school one day, an adult the next! She sighed, and glanced down at baby Benjie nestling blissfully in her arms. Fast asleep his little pink mouth was still firmly sucking her nipple, from where he'd been happily guzzling from his mother's cornucopia of plenty! His chubby little hands, with their fascinating tiny fingernails, were clutching at her breast as if he never intended to let go – ever! Jean's milk was rich and nutritious, and, she'd fed all of her babies for over a year. Benjie looked fair set to be no exception!

Jean was looking forward to becoming a grandmother. Gertie, their eldest was expecting. It would be good to have another baby around the house. Her family loved babies! Their first grandchild could expect to be smothered with love! Even though life had seemed to consist of queuing for food and washing dirty nappies on the glass rubbing board she told herself re-peatedly that it had been worth it!

'Us Braithewaites 've been a lucky family – we've come intact through war and childbirth!' Although she was speaking softly to herself, her voice caused Benjie to stir in his sleep. She removed her nipple from his moist lips, tucked her breast away and rocked him gently, crooning soothingly. He lapsed back into sound slumber.

Jean smiled and deposited a gentle kiss on his damp curly hair. Benjie'd had his morning bath in the Butler sink. He loved a bath, and had taken to it like a duck to water.

'Yes,' she murmured, 'our friends have lost their

relatives – too many to cry for, but with a few minor exceptions the Braithewaites have been lucky!' Sometimes she felt almost guilty at admitting her immediate family had survived especially when chatting to mothers who had lost one, two or even three sons! She went out of her way to be extra kind and gentle to those mothers thinking, if I'd had sons and not girls – there, but for the Grace of God goeth I! It was even harder speaking to friends and neighbours whose husbands had been called up – they'd never seen them again since the day they'd left home to go overseas – their last weekend passes had been so welcome yet a bitter-sweet welcome, for they knew that within hours they'd be on their way! Jean had felt for them – and had cried too! Yes her Henry had been lucky – graded (3) on his call up medical! But he'd found it hard going into the pubs and in public – he wasn't in uniform like other men! Then he'd become an ARP man and the situation was a bit better after that! He was doing his duty in the ARP! (Air Raid Pre-cautions).

She dropped another soft kiss onto Benjie's head. He smelt gorgeous. Such a sweet-tempered child. She called him her little angel!

'Hi, love, are yer in?' It was Maisie letting herself in with the key-on-a-string.

'I were jist watching the kiddies skipping, Maisie. Thinkin' I was, thinkin' 'ard about yer Esmee and my Tabby – some day soon they won't be children any more, and they'll have gorgeous babies like our Benjie – God willing. Hope they get good blokes! A good husband makes orl the difference to a woman's life.'

'Yer can say that again, lovey, iffen yer wants ter. Yer right yer are, Jean, youse 'it the nail on the 'ead. Long may they enjoy their innocence!'

Jean laughed gently, careful not to awaken her sleeping son – the family's pride and joy: 'I 'opes me lit'l' angel 'ere gets hisself a lovely lit'l' wife some day!'

Her little angel's hand had found her breast again – she'd left her buttons open, forgetting to fasten them. He lazily opened one eye and dug his nails into her soft flesh. 'Ouch, yer stinker!' His eyelid dropped again and he relaxed his grip – he'd heard his precious mother's voice. All was right – in his little world everybody loved him.

Chapter Four

Blinking reluctantly, Tabby opened her sticky eyes; she always got sleep in her eyes, nobody quite knew why. It was just one of those things. She'd long stopped worrying about it.

She shared the cosy bedroom with her sisters – well four of them. Except for herself it was now empty. Her sisters had been up with the lark off to their daily grind to earn their morsel of bread. But Tabby didn't have to get up early today. Surprise, surprise, she'd been told last night she could have a lie-in today! It wasn't Sunday or her sisters would still be snuggled up in bed with her ... in the big double bed. Another sister would have been in the single bed in the same room. For some reason or other the schools were not open today! In the playground yesterday the news had been met with a rousing cheer! Esmee had told her the schools were shut because of polling day.

Tabby couldn't care less what they were closed for – it meant a whole day's freedom. She lay there dithering and dathering over what to do on such an auspicious unexpected day's freedom. Should she go to the public lending library and borrow another Enid Blyton book? They were rather young for her more advanced reading ability, but she did enjoy reading out aloud to her mother and Benjie ... who was growing up so fast he left the family spellbound! Most of the Enid Blyton books she'd read from cover to cover, but they never lost their magic in the re-reading.

Tabby sighed, and stretched slowly and languorously, kicking her legs free all over the bed. It wasn't often one could do that in a shared bed where she slept with her older sisters, for all the world like a family of dormice curled up for the long winter hibernation!

She wiggled her toes in happy anticipation of the day about to unfold. Shall I keep a look out of the window to see the hearse and black horses pass by, in all its magnificence? There'd been another death in the six streets. Today, it was Mrs Taylor's funeral! She was being interred in the same grave with her long-departed husband. She was *ever so old,* thought Tabby. Nearly seventy! Died of a heart attack, apparently. She'd been in the garden feeding her precious chickens and she'd dropped like a stone! Her head went right into the enamel pail of chicken feed and mash – made from old potato peelings boiled up and mashed together with some powdered chicken food for her laying hens. She lived alone and nobody had seen it happen. Fortunately, when her next door neighbour got back from a shopping trip she'd gone out into her garden to fetch in her clean, dry washing. My word, what a shock she got! The hens next door were squawking like mad and running all over the garden, and the rooster had got free and was strutting his stuff!

With great presence of mind, the neighbour had rushed round to Mrs Taylor's front door, let herself in with the latch key hanging from the perennial string behind the letter box, and rushed frantically through the house into the back garden, just in time to shoo the rooster off the top of poor Mrs Taylor's half-submerged head! He didn't take kindly to being removed unceremoniously from his new domain! But the good neighbour grabbed the yard broom which she'd had the presence of mind to take with her and swiftly shooed the rooster and his harem back into their chicken run. Once safely behind the chicken wire she locked them in by the simple expedient of wedging a piece of wood expertly through the catch. She'd automatically collected the eggs first – well, *food was food,* wasn't it!

The doctor, alerted by several helpful youngsters who'd run hell for leather to his surgery; congregating in a panting mass of humanity all trying to talk at once, had diagnosed a massive heart attack and death had been instantaneous – she wouldn't have known a thing. Everyone put it down to the strain of the war years.

That very same night, Jean had chattered away, trying to tell Henry about poor Mrs Taylor, the rooster and the bran mash, and her head in the pail. Henry was busily, noisily, masticating his supper alone. He'd come home late, hadn't volunteered an explanation and Jean hadn't bothered to ask him – she was too full of the drama of poor Mrs Taylor, the rooster, the squawking chickens and the pail of bran mash, with Mrs Taylor's head partly submerged in it!

Spluttering indignantly, almost choking and

belching very loudly Henry had expostulated 'D'ya mind woman! I'm eating kidneys, ain't I? Don't try to put a bloke off his grub – will yer?'

Jean didn't take much notice – just continued chattering like she always did. Her own father had likened his daughter's chattering to a clock which never ran down! He'd waggishly warned Henry, when he requested, civilly, Jean's hand in marriage. 'She's like a train steaming along without stopping.'

Still hurtling along verbally, Jean spoke pityingly of poor Mrs Taylor. 'It were her heart love; the war I reckons – never got over 'er 'usband's death, did she? Poor old soul. Doctor MacFaddie said 'er heart were old and worn out! Still, I mean ter say! Orl of us 'ad ter put up with the war – one way or another. We survived – it were stressful, not just for poor Mrs Taylor.'

Henry's eyebrows beetled and furrowed; he grimaced at her, but said nothing. He licked his gravy off his plate with enormous enjoyment and great gusto; his fat tongue flicked expertly all round the plate, then across it, until the plate was as clean as a whistle.

'I wish yer wouldn't do that, Henry! It's not very nice yer know – yer not settin' a good example to the children. I allus keeps tellin' yer, but yer don't take much notice! Wastin' me breff I am!'

'Well, don't then. Keep yer mouf shut!' He glared fumingly at his wife. 'Been lickin' me plate orl me life, ain't I? Had to, when I was a boy. We didn't get much solids on *our* plates – jist plenty of gravy. Can't yer stop yer witterin', Jean? Can't

111

a man eat his victuals in peace in his own house? Wiv aht dead bodies bein' shovelled willy-nilly down 'is gullet – along wiv devilled kidneys? I licks me plate ter show yer me appreciation, love – of yer good cooking!'

His wife's disdainful, very audible sniff was indicative of having heard that one before.

'I appreciates yer appreciation of me cooking Henry Braithewaite. However, I'm glad none of our children 'ave picked up yer disgustin' 'abit!'

Henry grinned disarmingly, he was well aware that his wife never stayed on that subject for too long: it was just force of habit on her part, when she couldn't think of anything else to rail about.

A twinkle of devilment gleamed from his eyes. 'Maybe our little Benjie will take after 'is old Dad? He *'is* the only boy in a 'ouse of females. Yeah! Maybe our Benjie'll be like me? Look at the way 'ee laps up yer breast milk – always squeezing yer titties 'ee is – anybody'd think the little tyke were starving.'

'Over me dead body, Henry Braithewaite, over me dead body. Our Benjie is going to grow up ter be a gentleman going ter work in something like a bank or an important office. So there – Henry Braithewaite, 'Enry wiv an "H"!'

'Nah, nah, nah! Love, only white collar workers work in banks and offices. We're blue collar workers round 'ere, love. Folks'd fink our Benjie were a snob if 'ee worked in a bank or an office. We're workin' class folk, Jean, Labour, not Conservative, not Liberal either. Good old Labour!'

'Yer might be Labour, Henry, an' I ain't sayin' nuffin' to yer, but, there's folks of the six streets who 'ave *crossed the floor* they 'ave – yerse, they 'ave, since the war. Don't ask me wot I am 'cos I ain't tellin' yer, Henry with an "H".'

Henry banged his fist thunderingly on the table, making his plate leap several times. 'Yer'll vote Labour the same as me, Jean, or else! Orl the blokes' wives vote how they tells them to. Why should yer be different?'

Hands on hips Jean leant forward tauntingly. 'Or else wot? Things 'ave changed now, Henry. Us women 'ave got our sights set 'igher. Mark my words, Henry, times is a changin' and wimmin is changin' the most. Wimmin know wot it is ter 'ave fat wage packets now – their own wages that don't get lorst on the beer or the dogs or the horses or cards ... afore they've even seen it! Yerse, Henry, the workin' class wimmin is a changin' and it's fer the better 'n' all! I aim ter see that our Tabby gets a foot on the ladder and then our Benjie – or me name ain't Jean Braithewaite.'

Henry couldn't believe his ears; he hawked and spat into his spotless white hankie.

Jean prided herself on her white washing, her whites were always sparkling, pristine – she boiled them in the old copper.

Wiping his nose, Henry said, 'Yer barmy girl, yer barmy ... the workin' class will always be workin' class, mark my words, wife! Anyhow I've got ter go to the Union now!'

Jean threw her head back and laughed heartily. 'The Union! Ha ha! That's a laugh – the third time this week. I thoughts yer only paid yer Union subs once a mumf? Getting' greedy for their money are they? The Union!'

'Er well! I told me mates I'd meet 'em fer a game of arrers – after *they've* paid their Union subs!' He shuffled his feet and shifted uneasily in is chair – peering lopsidedly at his wife. It was a nervous habit of his.

'Yere'd better go then, 'adn't yer, don't want ter keep them waitin', do yer? Maybe they've got other fish ter fry?'

Henry left the house quickly, grabbing his bike from by the front door!

Jean yelled after him – 'I 'opes yer gits a puncture 'Enry Braithewaite – I 'opes yer gits a bad flat tyre! Nah, make that two flat tyres!'

Tabby'd finished the washing up and said, 'Yer won't die like Mrs Taylor, will yer, Mum?'

Patting her daughter's cheek gently Jean had laughed softly. 'Lord Bless yer child, the things yer come out wiv! I sometimes wonder wot goes on inside that lit'l' 'ead of yourn? I really do, lovey. Me, die like Mrs Taylor? She were *only* seventy! Me grandma lived ter eighty-seven and me granddad ter ninety-seven!'

Now, that was something Tabby hadn't known! Her mouth gaped open and she stared in amazement and shock at her mother!

''Ow can a man live ter ninety-seven, Mum? That's *terribly, terribly,* old. Like Moses in the *Bible*. Our religious teacher told us Moses lived even more years than yer granddad!' She shook her head in puzzlement. 'The *Bible* sez, "Three score years n' ten' fer a man," Mum!'

'I can prove it to yer, lovey, got yer great-grandfather's birth certificate ain't I? Go an' git

114

me the tin box from upstairs in my bedroom!'

Tabby knew what she meant – it was the tin box in which all the family documents were kept. She'd never read the contents of the box. For six long dark years it had rested ensconced just inside the air raid shelter – for safety. If they'd been blown to smithereens by a bomb or landmine or buzz bomb or even a doddlebug the authorities would know all about them and how many there were in the family. They'd know how many people to search for. It was a very, very *important* box – the key to their existence! Everyone was well aware that a direct hit – barring a miracle – would most certainly have been the end of the Braithewaites at 48 Granite Road. And baby Benjie wouldn't have been born!

It was strange, but very true to say – a family cat or dog often survived a direct hit even if nobody else did!

As she raced up the stairs – two at a time – Tabby felt the importance of this auspicious occasion. She knew where the box was hidden with its grubby piece of old knicker elastic to keep the bulging lid shut tightly. Jean had refused to put a clean piece of elastic on it after the war, contending that it would be unlucky!

'That litt'l bit of elastic kept us alive in the war.' Tabby couldn't see the logic of a piece of 'lastic keeping them alive – neither could anybody else; Jean, however, was very superstitious about the bit of 'lastic and remained adamant it would stay there for ever!

Some time ago, Jean had promoted her youngest daughter as the official cleaner of the main bedroom – her and Henry's – when he was there! All of her daughters at some time in their lives had been promoted to that honour. Tabby'd had a good nose around and found the secret drawer in her parents' dressing table; but she'd never had the courage to open the tin! The knicker 'lastic stood guardian of the contents – and there was no way that Tabby could persuade herself to remove the 'lastic.

In wartime, Tabby'd been too young to take any notice of certain cards and telegrams. She'd been aware of the telegraph boys in their smart suits and tiny hats bowling along on their bikes. If the boy was whistling cheerily it was taken as an omen of good news … if he wasn't whistling…! The word then went round the streets faster than a Hun's bullet!

Then the women (who were at home) stood silently at their front doors or gates, wringing their hands or wiping them nervously on the corners of their wraparound cotton floral pinnies, silently dreading if the boy was making a beeline to their house. Their daily lives revolved around *dread* and *fearfulness;* never knowing if a bomb or landmine was going to target their house but, the telegrams were the most feared of all – they tied their guts into knots. Most families dreaded the *no reply* telegram with its doom-laden words, tersely informing them their husband or sons had been reported MISSING OR PRESUMED DEAD OR KILLED IN ACTION!

The combined heartfelt sighs of relief – collective relief was so tangible – the babble of good-natured chatter which followed could almost be *seen* … it showed on their faces. At times like that it had been important to have good neighbours.

Jean removed the 'lastic which seemed grubby and smelt of the old demolished air raid shelter. Bewitched, Tabby's eyes never left it, when Jean opened it with a flourish .. it put Tabby in mind of Pandora's box wondering just what would be revealed to her young eyes.

'Here y'are, love. Look! My grandfather's birth certificate – I got this copy from Somerset House up London.' (Now kept at St Catherine's House at the Aldwych.)

'Here's the marriage certificate – twenty one years old he was. Yer weren't a man until yer were twenty-one. Couldn't get a man's wage until twenty-one. 'Ad ter wait 'n' till 'ee passed his "apprenticeship" yer see. Doesn't make sense do it – they could die for their King and Country – and they sadly did – but they were still boys 'ntil twenty-one years old! I allus say that were crackers. But then, I don't make the laws of this country! It's them there pol'shuns duz that, innit?'

Tabby held her tongue – thinking she might learn a bit more that way.

Her mother held up a flimsy yellowing piece of paper. 'Look! My grandmother's death certificate: *died of malnutrition* and *pneumonia,* she did. Just stopped eating – no reason for it – but she did it. P'raps she felt she was nearing her time to pass over. Who knows? Malnutrition it were – malnutrition.'

Her feverish thoughts doing some quick mental

arithmetic Tabby held her tongue.

'Yer great-grandmother – no, I mean yer grandmother – now she died in her eighty-eighth year – just passed her eighty-seventh she had. Yer grandfather – he died in his ninety-eighth year … a few more munfs and he'd reached it – but he didn't! Them's very old ages, lovey, very old they were – yerse!'

Like Brer Rabbit and the Tar Baby, Tabby said *nowt*.

Jean rummaged out a few more family certificates and some black-edged cards displaying *sympathy* in silver lettering – bereavement cards. Apparently they were the only kind that people sent to funerals!

Packing everything neatly back into the box until it had its customary bulge; protesting at being so squashed and replaced the knicker 'lastic round the tin once more, Jean gave it to Tabby to take back upstairs.

And that was Tabby's first real introduction to family affairs – proper!

'Tabitha Braithewaite – are yer awake?'

'Yes, Mrs Braithewaite – I'm on me way down now.'

Tabby and Jean always bantered with Tabby calling her mother, Mrs Braithewaite. 'I'm jist getting' dressed, Mum.'

'Fetch our Benjie out of 'is cot will yer, lovey? Bring 'im down wiv yer – startin' 'im on solids I am, this morning. 'Is first solid breakfast. No more milk fer 'is breakfast terday. Got more teef 'ee 'as – the litt'l bugger – bit me 'ee did!'

Tabby, like everybody else, slept in her under-wear – vest and knickers, sometimes her liberty bodices too.

Only she didn't wear liberty bodices now. Her mother said her lemons were growing too fast, it would restrict them! Tabby was of the personal opinion that her growing lemons were a dratted nuisance. It was only men who seemed to love bosoms. The other day she'd heard her sisters squeal, as their boyfriends grabbed and squeezed their full ripe bosoms during their last goodnight kiss on the doorstep. 'Let's 'ave a feel of yer tits,' was what they'd said!

Whilst on the subject of lemons or bosoms, or *breasts* – the latter was a daring word, never uttered in the presence of their parents – Tabby thought about babies; babies loved tits! Benjie loved tits, he called them his Mum-Mum's 'its!'

'Saucy beggar,' Jean had laughingly said.

Benjie loved tits – full of an unrestricted flow of scrumptious thick creamy milk, they were. Her little brother Benjie had unerringly found his way to them the moment Jean first held him in her arms after giving rapturous birth to her one-and-only longed-for son. Could find his way to them blindfolded could Benjie.

'Oh, Benjie, you're soaked!' Benjie chuckled as his sister lifted him from his cot. He'd been standing waiting for her and excitedly jabbed his dummy into her mouth. 'Oh, you nasty little stinker, I don't want yer dummy! Throw it away, Benjie. Nasty old dummy, throw it away! Lifting him high not bothering to drop the rails (they had to be tied now), or Benjie let them down

119

himself. He was smart, was Benjie. He'd taken notice when the family dropped the sides of his cot. He was expert at it. His soggy, rancid, odorous nappy fell into a heap round his ankles. Tabby lifting him higher – the nappy fell to the floor. Benjie crowed it was a relief to lose his nappy! He loved his 'abs' she was always around. Breakfast, dinner, tea, supper – 'abs' was there. He saw more of her than his other sisters who went out to work. She threw him playfully above her head. Catching – she threw again. Benjie's joyful screams reached Jean's ears. She smiled. She knew Benjie loved his sister fervently. He loved everyone really. Life was a game to Benjie. With fourteen females to spoil him!

'Oh ohhh! Benjie! I could eat yer all up!' Tabby squeezed him, and he fair cackled with laughter, waving his dummy triumphantly. 'Nasty old dummy! Tabby throw it away for Benjie!'

'No, no, no, 'abs', no, no, 'abs'.'

'All right, not this time, I love yer Benjie bunna-bunna I luvs yer.'

His mouth tried to playfully bite her cheek.

'Ouch! Ouch! Leave off, Benjie! Ouch! – he's got more teef! Mum was right. Show us yer toofy-pegs, Benjie!'

He obliged, opening his mouth wide, chortling, made a lightening grab for her pigtail, stuffing it into his mouth.

She jerked her head away. 'Oh, Benjie, bunna – wunna – bad boy Benjie, bad boy.' He stopped smiling – looked crestfallen. She gave him a big kiss. 'It's all right, Benjie not bad boy, Benjie, lovely boy, 'ab-ab' loves her Benjie.' An angelic, seraphic smile broke loose on his face. His chubby hands patted her cheeks lovingly.

'Could any baby be more beautiful than Benjie?' asked Tabby aloud. Benjie shook his head energetically. He'd understood. A bit of a smart Alec was Benjie!

'Pooh – yer do stink pet ... the ammonia in yer wee-wee! It's terrible pet, terrible.'

'Tebb'l! Tebb'l,' copied Benjie obligingly.

'Mum!' screamed Tabby. 'Benjie's said a new word!'

'Come on yer litt'l stinker. Breakfast! No Mum-Mum's 'its fer breakfast. Benjie big boy now. Benjie 'ave real breakfast.'

Downstairs she handed her brother over to Jean. 'He's soaking wet, Mum, and his bedding.'

Jean playfully smacked her baby's rump gently. 'Ohh! Benjie, son, who's wet 'is drawers?'

'D'ors!' chattered Benjie, 'd'ors, d'ors!'

'Did year 'ear that Tabby, he just sed anuvver word. Ohh! Wot a clever boy our Benjie is! Give Mummy big kiss!'

He tangled his fingers in her hair. 'Ouch! Yer can stop that afore yer start, fancy pants. Naughty!'

'He don't like bein' called naughty, Mum. He did that ter me – didn't yer, yer little wee-wee-stinker. Pooh! He's terribly wet, Mum. Why does he do such a lot of wee-wee?'

'Yer were the same – weren't she, Benjie? Yerse she was. Give Mummy a big kiss, ohhh that's a whopper!'

Benjie wriggled free holding his arms out to his big sister. 'Dab – Dabs!'

121

Tabby squealed excitedly. She cupped his face in her hands and kissed him. He blew raspberries at her.

'Mummy 'eard that, Benjie, what a big boy yer are no, take yer thievin' 'ands away! No! No Mum-Mum's 'its for Benjie's breakfast! Look at the beggar would you? Opened all my buttons 'ee did! Here Tabs hold 'im a minute!'

Benjie's astonished little mouth began to pucker alarmingly – a sure sign he was going to howl! He wanted his creamy breakfast: 'is Mum-Mum's 'its. It had been his cornucopia since the day he was born.

Tabby tossed him playfully into the air which brought smiles and chuckles to his face once again; his delighted shrieks of pleasure filled the house! He rarely cried anyway. He was so well loved and pampered he didn't need to cry!

Jean wrinkled her nose delicately. 'It ain't no good, Tabby; 'ee don't 'arf pong. Puttin' me off me own breakfast it is Keep 'old of him a minute – just a second – I'll run some warm water into the sink. Take 'is "pyjie" jacket orff, where's the bottoms?'

Dried, renappied, dressed, Benjie tucked into the freshly-hatched, boiled egg, from his father's hens – dipping his soldiers of bread enthusiastically, he found it a vast and likeable improvement on his Mum-Mum's 'its!

'Like a duck ter water, ain't it, yer precious littl'l scallywag!' Benjie grinned, bright yellow yolk trickling from his full mouth.

'His three front teeth, Tabby – bit me 'ee did – yesterday when I was giving him me tits. The

122

sooner 'ee's on solids, the better'll be for me I c'n tell yer, won't it Benjie?' Benjie carried on masticating the buttered soldiers. He was well in his element this morning, too busy to talk!

'He's got another four *nearly through*, Mum, I ran me finger round 'is gums yesterday. Ain't yer, Benjie?' Her only reply from the happy little rascal was half an egg-soaked soldier, waved victoriously. As much as he loved his 'ab, 'abs, he was far too busy to speak to her!

Happily scoffing away, his face literally smothered in egg yolk, Benjie fed his face as well as his mouth, being in such a hurry to cram everything in all at once. Well! He had an excuse, didn't he? It was his *first solids breakfast;* an important day in his young life. He made no objections when Jean ran a wet flannel over his *mush,* he had another bite at that too! He hung on grimly for a few seconds, until Jean exchanged it for a bottle of weak tea, with lots of milk and sugar … the latter a luxury in itself. Ohh! What a day Benjie was having, he'd found nothing wrong with this breakfast! His teeth gnawed at the bottle's teat, chuckling strongly, he was too full up to drink it all.

His mother thanked her lucky stars it was not her nipples which Benjie was gnawing gleefully. She could always buy him a new teat but she couldn't replace her own nipples.

With a superhuman effort, Benjie had now managed to drink the tea, he held up the empty bottle and looked perplexed.

Empty! But his Mum-Mum's 'its were never empty! He shook the bottle and looked at Jean puzzled, 'Bot-bot gorn, orl gorn!'

Jean was amazed, 'Say that again to Mummy, darling, say it again.'

'Bot-bot orl gorn, orl gorn way,' obliged Benjie.

'D'ya 'ear that, Tabby, said a sentence 'ee did, didn't yer, Mum-Mum's little precious, well done, Benjie.'

He cocked his head on one side and gave a beatific grin. He was certainly a forward child, he'd had enough sisters to teach him things. His mother felt that if he carried on so well, like this, he'd be at school as soon as he was out of his pram!

'Can I go to the lib'ry for anuvver Enid Blyton book, Mum?'

'Yeah! D'ya wanna take litt'l egg-face wiv yer ter give me a break?'

She couldn't take a pram into a library. If she carried him and left the pram outside Benjie would start laughing, chuckling and crowing – he'd rip the books to shreds! There was a large notice in the Library – SILENCE PLEASE! Admittedly Benjie couldn't read the notice but that would be no excuse. If she dared ask to take the pram inside – at her peril, the wheels would mark the shiny parquet flooring!

The little stinker would have to go shopping with his mother. He liked shopping anyway. People made a fuss of him and he could show off his new teeth! With no fridge or freezer (and Jean didn't know anybody who had!) the food had to be bought fresh every day. Meat, butter, anything which might go off quickly. Milk was delivered to the doorstep. In hot weather it had to be stood in a bowl of cold water in the scullery (kitchenette). Butter and fat could be kept in an old biscuit tin, buried in a shallow hole in the garden.

His mother was trying to clean his eggy, sticky moush! Benjie was capitalising on a *fun breakfast*, his teeth had sunk into the flannel. He held on to it grimly. He was killing himself laughing! Jean's relief that he'd eaten his first all-solids breakfast without rancour had put her into a good mood. The fly in the ointment was the corner butcher shop. The butcher was a nice enough bloke but a bit of a pain in the neck. Seemingly knowing everybody's business. A proper old washer-woman was what Jean termed him. He was an obliging bloke, a few extra meaty bones for a nourishing soup was no problem! He loved babies and Benjie charmed him out of the trees.

Chapter Five

Time passed by – as it always does; the maxim that time and tide wait for no man was never truer than in the Braithewaite household. Tabby had come to terms with her changing body. She'd grown a good foot taller and plumped out in all the *right* places. Her *lemons* no longer warranted the nomenclature; they were now *breasts;* very full, very rounded, like two big coconuts. Glory be! Some of her friends who hadn't filled out so well actually envied Tabitha Braithewaite her new look mature bosoms! Her appearance was very luscious and bonny.

Tabby likened herself to the changing of the seasons or the *changes after the war* because, as she wryly admitted to her best friend Esmee, 'everything changes.'

Esmee, of course, wanted to know why.

Tabby didn't have a concrete answer – she told her to read Ecclesiastes, Chapter III, which begins:

To every thing there is a season, and a time to every purpose under the heaven…

and goes on to say that–

A time to love and a time to hate; a time of war and a time of peace…

One of their teachers had read that out at morning assembly a long time ago and it had stuck in Tabitha's bacon bonce where she'd stored it away amongst the little grey cells.

It helped to make more sense of the world at large – for her. She hoped Esmee would read Ecclesiastes, Chapter III because sometimes it was difficult to explain certain things to her best friend Esmee and she felt obliged to try because she *was* her best friend. What other good reason did she need?

It was her eldest sister, Gertie, who suggested she call her bulging bosom – her bust, which all the older girls and women called it. 'Yer might as well, Tabby, now ya wearing a hammock for two!' In other words a non-supportive brassiere in that dreadful pinky beige hue with the non-stretch straps that left a permanent dent in her young shoulders, just like her sisters' shoulders! Obviously the deeper the indentations were, it was because of having an extremely heavy bust – no structured uplift!

Her mother was proud of how her youngest daughter had filled out just as she'd predicted to Henry years ago. She gave credit for the metamorphosis to the cod liver oil and malt mixture which she'd religiously shovelled down Tabby's throat as soon as she was old enough: she'd only recently stopped insisting upon it!

Tabby herself gave approbation for her mother's filling stews – they were filling and nourishing.

Henry, her father, put it down to a growing young woman and said it was only natural for girls to have big breasts – it showed they were sexy, didn't it?

Tabby had fled from the house in acute embarrassment it was too much for her sensitive little mind to absorb such crudeness of banter about *her* body, it was *her* body not theirs – the mocking banter upset her.

Jean had turned in fury to her hapless husband who wanted to know what all the fuss was abaht? Couldn't he tell his own daughter, the seed of his loins, that she'd got a smashing pair of knockers?

His wife told him to wash his mouth out with carbolic soap. 'Yer knows yer upset our Tabby: sensitive she is, poor littl' soul. Yer should fink before yer talks 'enry with an "H"!'

Henry was adamant that he meant no harm – he loved his Tabby. 'I were just paying me littl' daughter a compliment – and, furthermore, she'll be getting compliments from the older lads soon – likes big knockers, them do.'

His attempt to explain himself then upset the Sually twins because, unfortunately they both had smallish breasts yet were full grown women, older than their sister, Tabby.

Oh my! With the Sually twins moaning about his choice of *figure of speech* and his wife railing at him for upsetting the twins and Tabby – that put the kibosh on it for Henry! He stormed out of the house in a huff, yelling, 'It's coming to something when a man can't express his own opinions in his own house!'

His wife had sarcastically retorted. 'It's eight o'clock, don't yer think yer'd better get orff down the Union, Henry Braithewaite?'

'Went last night, didn't I? Well blast it. Blast yer all – yer can all go to hang fer orl I care – blast the lot of yer!'

Jean had merely shrugged at his outburst, and, when Doris pointed out that Union meetings were only once a fortnight, her mother shut her up, saying, 'If yer Dad sez he's going ter the Union – then 'oo's ter say he ain't? Wot the eye don't see, the 'eart don't grieve! Yer Dad's gorn ter the Union, Doris, now pour me out anuvver hot cuppa cha and 'old yer tongue! Now stop snivellin' youse twins, can't all have big busts!'

Truth to tell, even young Esmee – two years younger than Tabby now had a beautiful bosom, looking older than her actual age, with a figure to reinforce the notion. Like Tabby – Esmee's mother Maisie had kept her well fed with cod liver oil and malt and some of the orange juice – the concentrated kind which had miraculously come to hand.

Nobody said to fatten-up like a pig any more, the British Isles had become Americanised with the Yank's sayings: it was to fatten-up like a turkey for Thanksgiving now. Around a quarter of a million or more Americans had been in Britain during the war and, as could be expected many had either married British girls or were courting them and it stood to reason that their quaint American expressions and words were offloaded to the population as a whole – the host nation. In 1946, when the special ships took the GI brides to the United States of America – their new homeland – to be reunited with their husbands, it wasn't long after that the families left behind began to receive regular parcels of clothes, foods and presents – many things still unobtainable in post-war Britain that were looked upon as luxuries.

Maisie said, 'They're oversexed, overpaid and over here, them GIs.'

'Nah, Maisie, when all's said and done, they're just lads, a very long way from home with lifestyles far removed from ours.'

'Guess yer right – yerve 'it it on the nail, Jean. Me 'usband, Reg 'ee orl ways sez we owe the Americans a lot – we do. Damned good brave fighters them were!'

'Yeah! I agree wiv that. Poor lads, long way from their 'omes, their comforts, and never knowing if they would ever see their old mums again!'

Jean and Maisie's girls had not married Americans – they didn't even marry Scots, Welsh or Irish; they married English fellas. Which, although just a coincidence, had chuffed Henry greatly. Secretly Jean and Maisie had half-hoped for a Yank for a son-in-law; their daughters had gone jiving with them, and they'd brought them home – but the ones they liked had been in the same outfits and gone off to war together and were lost in battle. It had been a terrible shock for the two families as they'd genuinely liked the lads; even if they did call jam jelly! After that they couldn't bear to get too closely attached to the Americans, just in case the same thing happened again, they couldn't have coped!

Jean wasn't bothered really whom her girls married – just as long as they found *good* husbands. It wasn't easy to divorce, it was terribly expensive – someone said *fifteen thousand* pounds. But that was a fortune so Jean never knew if it was true or not. Going by the newspapers, if you wanted to divorce, you had to hire a detective and prove adultery! In working-class circles a woman separated or divorced was looked down upon – in the same manner as if they gave birth to a child out of wedlock. People avoided them or walked past them with their heads down.

Jean nudged her friend saucily. 'Yer knows wot I means: youse ain't the litt'l innocent Maisie – got seven of yer own yer 'ave! If yer Reg hadn't been out wiv the Army in them there war days I reckons youse've 'ad anuvver seven – like me. Still, yer've got plenty of time ain't yer, yer only thirty-five. Yer jist wait until yer Reg gets 'is strenff back it'll be wham, bang, fank yer mam – yer won't know wot's 'it yer!'

Maisie didn't even blush let alone flutter an eyelid! She never hid her light under a bushel, no, not Maisie! She visibly preened herself and patted her ample bosom complacently. 'I do know 'ow ter keep a man – sorry my man 'appy – even iffen I sez so meself!'

'Ohh! Ohhh! That's a dig at me innit? Jist 'cos my 'Enry wiv an "H!" scatters 'is spare seeds over nearby acres! 'Ee's still wiv me ain't 'ee? Sometimes yer 'ave ter turn a blind eye! Highly sexed me 'Enry wiv an "H" is. Heavily sexed! *Real* men – like my Henry are all the same. Want it served up on a plate – in a variety of various dishes.'

Maisie nodded in agreement. She knew Henry

131

thought the world of his wife – she was often pregnant within a year to eighteen months and always appeared to be pregnant again as soon as the latest baby was on solids. And Henry, well, Henry! He could no more be celibate than fly to the moon. Seems he always had to have it! Always hunting for a bit of skirt on the side! The women of the six streets knew it – some a bit more than others! But nothing was said to Jean – they liked her too much to tattle about that. It was the unwritten code of the six streets and they never let slip a word. But Jean wasn't daft, she knew!

Maisie had her own secrets anyhow – and entertained quite a number of obliging fellas during the long dark war years. With Reg absent overseas, what was a sexy woman to do in-between her husband's furloughs? Maisie was a part-time barmaid at The Kings Oak pub. Enough said! Even Henry, husband of her very best friend, Jean, had made saucy overtures to her – she'd slapped him down good and proper she had!

Tabby, of course, knew nothing of all this, and that, and the other! She did know her dad went down the Union quite a bit. She didn't want to marry somebody like her dad. Nor anybody like that horrible Ginger Morley and his *fabled whopper!*

Her mind had grown faster to maturity than her body and she had privately set her sights higher than that.

Her mother looked at her lovingly this morning, the first solids breakfast day for Benjie; it was an auspicious day, to say the least. She nursed hopes that her Tabby would go higher in the world, because Tabby was a bit different from her other daughters – but she couldn't quite put a finger on it!

Cheerfully Tabby had taken herself off, it was a pleasant, balmy day. She liked getting out and about – a bit further from the six streets. Gertie had given her a nice green crepe dress, Gertie had only worn it twice – somebody had handed it down to her; it was a bit pre-war in style but had a good cut and didn't quite show its age! It fitted Tabby to a T, and, as she sauntered along the six streets, she held her head high and felt quite a lady. She was dangling her home-made drawstring *Dorothy bag* and it felt nice and heavy with her bit of money clinking loosely – nine big pennies to spend; well, six actually, the other three were for her bus fare. She felt as rich as Croesus – but she had no idea who he was; nevertheless, that's how the saying went and that's how she felt, on her way to the Number 23 bus stop.

Curtains twitched significantly as she passed by, and the women gossiping at their gates gave a warm smile or cheery flap of their hands, which made Tabby feel ever so grown-up. So she reciprocated in kind. There were half-open or fully-open front doors; nobody at home – the woman of the house had popped round the corner to the oil shop which sold paraffin and hardware, fire wood, tin openers and Oxos, just about everything for the home – but *not fresh food*. It sold Oxo cubes for a farthing or two. Tabby couldn't rightly remember how much Oxo cubes were right now, her mother had quite a tinful of them. Jean always picked up a few when out shopping, whether she needed them or not. It meant she always had them to hand. The family enjoyed a hot cup of Oxo with chunks of bread in it – for a late-night 'treat'.

The women didn't always pop round to the oil shop – they also popped round the bakers or to the tobacconist for twenty Woodbines.

'Going out, young Tabby?' asked Mrs Brown, strolling out to her front gate; she'd seen Tabby from her window – she liked to keep a 'friendly eye' on the young ones, as she lumped them all together regardless of age. 'Hope yer enjoys yerself?'

Tabby smiled, walked past, turned and waved at her; she smiled in return and flapped her podgy hand.

Tabby didn't mind the neighbours, they were just being caring – any child knew they could knock on any door if their own Mum was out and they were in need or in trouble. *Help one – help 'em all* was the motto of the streets.

She sprinted for the 25 bus just rounding the corner, and made it by the skin of her teeth. 'Phew!' said Tabby. She was finding it harder to run with bosoms than without!

The conductor's lopsided grin widened, he knew Tabby's family well, played darts with her father. 'On yer own, Tabby?'

'Yeah, I'm more grown-up now, nearly a woman, so I can go shopping up Green Lanes on me own. Mum said it's all right.'

He surreptitiously handed her a ticket, taken

134

from the coloured display in his clipboard, different colours for different bus fares. He clipped it neatly and refused her money ... and winked at her.

Tabby had a good browse around the shops, especially Woolworth's and British Home Stores, her favourites. They sold a variety of merchandise ... she didn't have the means to buy the things which she would like to have purchased – never mind, *browsing* was good fun.

It was the in thing to say to your friend or a boyfriend, if you had one, 'Meet me in Woolworth's down the Lanes' or 'I'll see yer outside the Home Stores' (British Home Stores).

If you were going to the cinema down the Lanes, it was common to meet your boyfriend in the evening; loads of young blokes could be seen (by street lighting) pacing up and down, puffing furiously at their Woodbines or stamping one out under the heel of their very polished shoes. They usually had their hair slicked down with Brylcreem; best shirts ironed carefully, sometimes stiff starched collars – nearly choking them. The early evening, when light was just fading, was a charismatic time.

If a young girl hadn't got round to taking a boyfriend home to meet her parents then he usually met her off the bus at the nearest stop to the cinema. She would usually have another girl with her who would be blind-dated with a friend of her new boyfriend. Girls didn't go to the pictures on their own.

'Can I help you, miss?'

Tabby jumped guiltily! Why she didn't know,

not having anything particular to feel guilty about. She'd been so deeply engrossed eyeing-up the merchandise tantalisingly displayed all along the long counters. There were several of them with gangways in-between which the sales girls paced ready to be of service. Tabby always felt in deep awe of the Woolworth's girls, looking so smart in their uniforms – you were *somebody* if you worked at Woolworth's!

Tabby tentatively held up a sachet of shampoo powder; she was determined to have one – her hair was usually washed with ordinary soap.

'This is a special offer, madam, two for the price of one – with a fragrant hyacinth smell.'

'I'll take it please, lady.' Tabby made sure she was extra polite, she was a nearly woman after all!

'I bet your boyfriend will love the smell in your hair.'

'Haven't got a boyfriend, lady.'

'Oh sorry! Pretty girl like you should have one! Would you like half-a-yard of hair ribbon to tie back your curls! Another special offer this week – what colour would you like?'

'Well, just half-a-yard of bright yellow, please, and I'll have this little packet of clips for me mum, please, lady.'

'Right, that comes to sixpence please, madam.'

Tabby felt elated with her treasures – even excited at the thought of washing her hair with real shampoo powder. She knew how to mix it in a cup – her sisters used shampoo powders. But she hesitated. 'Are you sure it's kosher because it is a special offer?'

The Woolworth's girl displayed a sparkling

white set of pearly teeth when she smiled. 'It certainly is *kosher*, I use it myself, and I've got nice hair haven't I? Anyway, we are an American firm, we sell the best, madam.'

Tabby knew that the word kosher was the one which the Jewish pawnbroker used; it was one of his favourite words. She'd been into his shop with an older sister who'd gone there to redeem a pledge on a ring. So if the girl said it was kosher then it must be all right – kind Mr Isaacs wouldn't use the word kosher if it wasn't something good.

The sales girl looked round furtively. 'Phew! No sign of the dragon – must be at her tea break. Like to chat for a bit ... the supervisor's not around for awhile?'

'Okay!'

'You look like a nice girl, you're awfully pretty, have you left school yet?'

'Nah!'

'I hope you get a boyfriend soon, bet you do when you wear that yellow ribbon. It'll attract the boys – you'll see. Me! I used to go out on my own like you but I'm nearly sixteen now so I've got a regular boyfriend. Taking me to the Odeon tonight ... we saw *Jamaica Inn* last week. It was smashing! We're going to see *The Man in Grey* tonight – always sit upstairs in the back row we do – *ever so romantic* it is.'

Tabby's eyes were like saucers, she'd heard her sisters giggling together about the back rows in the cinema, up and downstairs. So she gathered it must be romantic!

'Not that I saw much of *Jamaica Inn* though –

my new boyfriend is like an octopus.' She giggled and blushed beetroot. 'His hands are everywhere – and kisses me to bits, I have to be careful that my mum doesn't see the love bites! Know what? I couldn't tell you what *Jamaica Inn* was about if I tried – and I bet my boyfriend couldn't either!'

Tabby's eyes blinked rapidly: this was confusing. 'But you just told me it's a smashing film?'

'Everybody says it is – so I told my mum it is! My boyfriend is taking me up London to a posh cinema next month, I can hardly wait – he gets his extra bonus in his wage packet then. He's earning good money,' she lowered her voice confidentially – £4.5s.6d is what he earns, with overtime!' Tabby's eyebrows shot up alarmingly, that was a big wage packet for a young lad to be earning. She asked how old the boyfriend, was, and it wasn't a boy after all it was a man!

'He's twenty-two this year, he's finished his apprenticeship – he likes to be a flash Harry and spend his money on me.'

Tabby's little grey cells were seething with curiosity. She wondered what the boyfriend got back in return?

'Have you got any sisters?'

'Course I have,' said Tabby proudly, 'there's thirteen of us girls, and we've got three sets of twins – yerse – we 'ave yer know Dora and Peggy and Sue and Sally and Ivy and Daisy, and now we've got a baby brother, Benjamin – well call 'im Benjie. Ohhh! He's luvverly, but he do wee a lot.'

'Blimey! Your mum must be a bit of all right!

Fourteen children – are they all alive, did you lose any in the war?'

'No! Me mum's luvverly, she's a bit of all right, I guess. I 'eard her tell me Aunty Maisie, me dad's got a lot of spare seeds! Don't know what she means but that's wot she said.'

The Woolworth's girl choked suddenly!

'Have you swallowed something?' asked Tabby innocently.

'No – just some air went down the wrong way. You seem a bit innocent … not putting it on are you?'

'Putting wot on?' asked Tabby ingenuously.

'Never mind, never mind – you've got a lot to learn, still you are a bit younger than me! Are your family all alive?'

'You jist asked me that didn't yer – of course they're all alive! The lucky Braithewaites they call us round the six streets, and I'm Tabitha, Tabby for short!'

'Lucky! I should say you are, I lost my dad at Alamein! My mum still cries for him, it's terrible, really terrible!'

Uttering some tut-tutting of sympathy Tabby gazed in pity at the crestfallen face of the salesgirl and thought of her own father. Henry, she'd never seen much of him, always out he was – somewhere, but he was still her father and he was still alive.

'My mum had a lovely boyfriend. I called him Dad but she lost him too! Got blown to smithereens – he was on a minesweeper.'

Poor girl, Tabby felt struck dumb by such a tragic story. One lost at Alamein and one lost on a minesweeper. It was almost more than she could bear to hear, and this was meant to be a happy day for herself!

Turned out that the Woolworth's girl was an only child, but, she had three male cousins who were looking out for nice girls to marry.

Tabby assured her of the niceness of the Braithewaite girls, but said 'Gertie's married, and a few others, and some are walking out seriously or engaged.'

Acting on impulse, Tabby asked if the cousins would like to play cards one night round her house; they only played for coppers – friendly games! Her mother, Jean, liked meeting new people. 'They'll get a warm welcome,' said Tabby enthusiastically. Well, she seemed a nice girl and Tabby needed some more new brothers-in-laws. There'd be more room in the bed for herself!

'Don't like playing cards meself, but me sisters and parents love it. The air's always blue with smoke, everybody smokes, I don't. I'm not going to when I'm really grown up either,' proclaimed Tabby wrinkling her pert little nose in disgust.

The three cousins smoked, loved cards, were very sociable (they enjoyed being sociable in the armed forces) – and were honestly wife-hunting!

Leaving instructions and her name and address on a piece of paper, Tabby left the salesgirl to pass on the *open invitation* to her cousins. Number 48 Granite Road – the girl wrote down in a neat rounded handwriting, she stuffed it into her overall pocket. Her name was Joan.

'Cheerio,' they said to each other. Tabby spent some time browsing around the rest of Woolworth's and the other shops down Green Lanes. She gazed at the engagement rings in the Feitelson's Jewellery shop and wondered if she'd ever have one of her own some day? The trays of rings were just above a gorgeous selection of powder compacts. Everybody used them, they were a bit beyond her pocket at the moment but, one day…

Trailing back to the bus stop she reflected that her mum would certainly be pleased to have some new life in the house – especially of a masculine nature!

She managed to catch the same bus conductor on the return route so she travelled free again.

Chapter Six

The Braithewaites had returned en masse from the hop fields in Kent. Hop-picking was their annual working holiday where they felt as free as the wind and revelled in the primitiveness of their housing conditions; the Braithewaites being such a large family and seemingly growing even larger with the new son-in-laws and steady boyfriends ... had the dubious privilege of three huts for accommodation. Very cramped, but they were outside in the open most of the time. What with their faggot fires, freezing cold water from the communal taps (also out in the open), a fair distance from the huts ... muddy wellies with sock tops turned over them, it was a real family affair.

The evenings, drawing in were pleasurable with songs round the open fires, the crackling blazing faggots giving way to huge logs, about five feet long.

Even Benjie, now a sturdy toddler, helped in the hop fields, picking hops into an upturned open umbrella. It was handy for Benjie to use, and handy when it rained. He thought hopping was a lovely game. His mother sat him on an old blanket and he picked away quite happily – leaving Jean free to do her share of picking the plump hops into the hop bin.

Hopping down in Kent was *it* – the highlight of

their year, and everybody else's; the working class's holiday – the hop fields of Kent.

In years to come the smell of fresh straw was to remind Tabby of hop-picking. The farmers left bales of it inside each hut, and the women stuffed pillowcases and mattress ticks with the sweet-smelling straw; the men went to get the faggots and wood all stacked ready for them in a hollow behind the huts at the bottom of the hill. The filled ticks and pillow cases laid on the slatted, shelving bed in each hut were lovely and comfortable. Sheets and blankets topped them.

Some of the men wangled time off from work or went down at weekends. They went further afield hunting rabbits for the stew pots and scrumping for the big apples called *hopping apples* which, at the end of the season, were taken back home to blighty to be used for scrumptious apple pies during the autumn and early winter. Hopping apples seemed to have a fragrance all of their very own, especially when they'd been inside the sacks for several weeks.

Half walking and half skipping along the six streets, Tabby was enjoying herself, lilting, 'We're going hopping, hopping, hopping – even though they'd just come back! It was still fresh in her young mind ... being a nearly woman the thought fleetingly stirred in her little grey cells that she would soon be too old to go *scarping* alone, like she was!

She thought of the night of the cousins as Jean called it. It had been a bit of a landmark in their family, to say the least! Such excitement before-

143

hand, with the unmarried sisters pushing, shoving and elbowing their way to the big mirror over the mantelpiece. Such a prinking and titivating! Horrible red lipsticks making jammy cupid-bow mouths, tons of loose face powder being puffed here, there and everywhere which made Henry feel fit to choke, so he went to The King's Oak for fresh air but he was no better off there, the smoke curling upwards was like a blinding fog, he had to push his way through.

Hair was teased into waves and curls, Mirror mirror on the wall, thought Tabby watching her sisters and their judicious puff-puffing of their powder puffs, making little Benjie cough violently and sneeze; he thought it was a new game – great fun.

The girls always used the downstairs mantle mirror to fix their make-up; the only other one was in the front room where Jean kept the clean washing and therefore kept it locked! There was no clean washing in there tonight – the room was prepared for company! 'If the card games were a *sociable dud* then they could have a sing-song round the old Joanna,' averred Jean to her excited daughters.

The three male cousins turned out to be perfect gentlemen. Wonderfully sporting, Benjie adored them – they fed him sweets, so he would, wouldn't he?

Jean reckoned Henry would toddle back sooner or later, but she wasn't worried – he could go to the Union after the pub if he wanted to, or he could come back and have a game of cards. It was up to Henry, she wasn't bothered. Henry

144

could be a real pain sometimes, even though she loved him!

The long war years of camaraderie meant nobody was self-conscious for long with the evening's guests. They declined Jean's offer of hot tea and opted, from force of habit for *brown* ale. Suddenly it seemed that thousands of pairs of willing hands appeared from nowhere – all anxious to pour out the bottles of ale for the guests! Jean shook her head in bewilderment and gave up – left it to her conniving romantic offspring! She sat Benjie on her lap and settled for the evening as a spectator. The air was soon blue with smoke, and Jean hadn't realised just how coquettish her daughters could be!

Her sixteen year old Hettie, at an impressionable age, eagerly poured the brown ale into the expertly tilted glass, giving it a good head. She handed it to Eddie, tall, broad shouldered, he'd been a pilot in the RAF ... Hettie felt her heart racing and the attraction was obviously mutual!

His brother called Billy Boy had been in the Army – one of the Desert Rats – a little bit younger than Eddie. Hettie was all of a dither, not sure if the younger brother was the best one for her, or the older one!

The other brother, Horace, had been in the Royal Navy – a Petty Officer. He was showing his pictures (photos) to Margo, who was coming up for eighteen. When he shook hands with her and held on to it, she had raised no objections. She rather wished he was still in his naval uniform, he looked so handsome in the photographs. Uniforms gave added allure to women!

Attempting to politely defuse the romantic atmosphere a trifle, Jean asked Eddie, 'Been demobbed long?'

'Yes, Mrs Braithewaite, all of us several months' ago within weeks of each other. Our Mum weren't half pleased she got us all back safe and sound, even though she has all our dirty socks to scrub now!'

It was blatantly obvious to Jean that they were experienced men of the world, even though still in their late twenties. The young boys grew up overnight in the armed forces. She prayed fervently for her young romantically-minded daughters to be able to handle the situation. She needn't have worried – before the night was out, it was obvious the cousins were absolutely splendid, honourable chaps – at least whilst she was there to chaperone her daughters!

Hettie mentioned there were thirteen girls – Joan had forgotten to tell them how many just in case it frightened them away. Well, thirteen...! 'You don't look old enough for so many children, Mrs Braithewaite,' riposted Eddie gallantly.

Proudly she rattled off the names and ages of her numerous offspring with Benjie trying to say them with her – he got the usual hugs and claps and kisses for trying!

'Well done, Benjie, well done!' His cherubic face and tousled curls, with his cheeky grin almost splitting his face in half – well who wouldn't love Benjie? Absolutely adorable and a saucy little rascal, and he knew it, oh yes he did, Benjie knew it all right!

'You've met our Tabitha haven't you?'

'No!' assured Horace. 'It was our cousin Joan who met her – in Woolworth's.'

'Silly me!' simpered Jean coyly. 'Right! Here goes for wot it's worth! Tabby sitting on the stool – almost 14, Hettie next to her is coming up to 16, Esther is 17, Margo 18, Lottie 19, Jenny 20, Sue and Sally, the third set of twins, are 21, Dora and Peggy the second set of twins are coming up to 23, Ivy and Daisy my first set of twins are 24. Lastly, our Gertie, she's expecting her second child – she lost the first one, I'm afraid. As you see they are not all married. A few are here tonight, a few more will be in later, and the rest are out with their boyfriends going steady. Obviously, this young rascal here is our Benjie – the only boy; you can guess how spoilt he is!' She pretended to bite a lump out of Benjie and he squealed with laughter. 'Yer should've been in bed hours ago you litt'l stinker!'

'No!' said Benjie adamantly. 'No, no, no, Benjie good boy, Benjie is. Mum-Mum naughty – naughty.'

'He doesn't seem a bit spoilt, Mrs Braithewaite, seems a lovely, loveable little chap to me.' Eddie winked at Benjie, and made him burst out laughing.

'Me name's Jean, lovey, not Mrs Braithewaite!' Eddie gave her one of his quick flashing smiles, guaranteed to charm the birds off the trees and nodded appreciatively.

Tabby sat and watched. They played 'Pontoon' and 'Penny-in-the-kitty' – many tedious hours in the air raid shelter had been whiled away with the cards. Card playing had become the norm in most households; but, only for pennies if women participated – or even for matchsticks. It was the smoke which bothered Tabby: the air was blue with it during card games. Her sisters pooh-poohed her fussiness. 'A little bit of smoke, won't 'arm yer – Miss Fuss Pot!'

Tabby spoke the truth, though little did she know it with her riposte, 'You'll be sorry one day, that you ever smoked.'

Her sisters and parents had fallen about laughing fit to burst. Everybody smoked – what did a child know about it?

Her father choked on his own laughter, coming up for air – he chuckled derisively. Even Mr Churchill smoked bloomin' big cigars, 'ee wouldn't if it was 'armful, would 'ee? The great man 'imself – our heroic war time leader – one of the wisest men going – yer never see him on the picture newsreels wiv aht 'is cigars. His face was suffused with laughter at his youngest daughter's prophesy. 'Oh! Grow up Tabby! All the armed forces smoke and the government puts tobacco coupons* at the back-end of pensioners' pension books. Wouldn't do that if smoking were 'armful would they? Nah! The Ministry of Pensions would stop them, wouldn't they, girls!'

Her sisters had chorused, 'Yeah! Yeah! Anyway wot abaht the glamorous Hollywood film stars – smoke don't they? Look at Bogart, always

*Hugh Dalton, when he was Britain's Chancellor of the Exchequer, introduced tobacco coupons for old age pensioners in his 1947 Budget. They were discontinued in 1958.

smoking. Don't do 'im no 'arm does it?'

Tabby could see the logic of their kind of wisdom, yet she remained unconvinced and vowed she herself would never smoke. And she never ever did.

Benjie was oblivious to everything except the fantastic smoke rings Horace was blowing for his delight. 'Yer, a lovely lad, son, he really is Mrs ... er ... I mean, sorry, Jean!'

Jean acknowledged his compliment, for Benjie was the apple of her eye and she remarked tauntingly, 'I know, but he's a stinky little wee-er, ain't ya, Benjie?'

Benjie laughed fit to burst and crowed, 'Wee-wee-wee-er!' Jean laughed with him, he had a really infectious laugh – a saucy laugh, 'Yer c'n say that again – yer should smell 'is nappy of a mornin' – my word 'ee *still wears one ter bed* – just in case – sort of – yer know! Ammonia! Fairly makes yer eyes blink and water, duzzn't it, Tabby?' Her daughter nodded vigorously and affirmatively.

'Yeah. When 'ee were very young and me mum were bathin' 'im – 'ee did a-a – stream, like a fountain, right smack into me mum's gob, didn't 'ee, Mum?'

'Yeah! Not 'arf 'ee didn't – the little bugger!'

'Litt'l bugger,' copied Benjie obligingly, once more.

'Oy! Oy! Who's been teaching the baby to swear – I ain't 'avin' that – 'ee ain't old enough.'

'It's you, Mum,' giggled Hettie, 'yer always callin' 'im that, 'n' 'ee copies everythin' yer say, it ain't us, it's youse.'

149

Jean's face dropped solemnly. ''Ave ter wotch me words with 'im won't I?' She tickled Benjie under the arms, and had him rolling on the floor.

'No! Mum-Mum, naughty Mum-Mum!'

Eddie, Billy Boy and Horace – a few pints under their belts, cheered, clapping enthusiastically, roaring… 'Well done, old son, yer a chip off the old block – a real man!'

Mockingly indignant Jean cackled, 'Oy, youse lot! Don't yer encourage the litt'l bleeder!'

'Litt'l bleeder!' obliged Benjamin disarmingly! 'Fuz pot, 'abs, fuz pot.'

Sally cautioned her mother, 'There yer see Mum – yer'll 'ave ter watch yer language now wiv His Master's Voice!'

The last three words clicked in Benjie's brain. He toddled over to the pile of gramophone records and pointed blithely at them, ''is Marterz-voyz.'

'Well I'll be damned,' said his mother. 'He means the litt'l dog and loudspeaker on the label of the records! Yer looks iffen yer goin' ter be a smart a…' she bit her tongue sharply. 'I'll have ter watch me mouf wiv yer, Benjie, won't I?'

'Wash yer mouf,' said Benjie obligingly.

Being the centre of attraction suited him down to the ground. The atmosphere was convivial; plenty to eat and sup, warm, pretty female company, the three men felt almost as happy as Benjie!

Horace chuckled him under the chin… 'You'll be our next Prime Minister one day little laddy, you're a grand lad, and a smart one. Our Mum'd love you – had five boys she did.'

150

Several pairs of eyes focussed Horace's way, it was Jean who voiced the words. 'Where are the other two?'

The three men were silent, it was Billy Boy who spoke. 'Six feet under – but we don't know where. Unknown grave with lots of their mates! Our Mum ain't got over it yet!'

Jean stared at their guests, and could have bit her tongue out. 'I'm so sorry, I didn't know!'

''S all right, Jean! It was some years ago – they were smashin' blokes, even though they were our brothers. They really were smashin' blokes. Mum's hair went white overnight!'

'I'm so very, very, sorry, makes me ashamed that we all survived – your poor Mum, I am sorry! Tabby – fetch those sandwiches in, the cheese ones, like a bit of cheese do yer lads?'

'Certainly do, Jean, I'm famished,' said Eddie. 'Men can always find room for a cheese sandwich! Don't want to eat you out of house and home though.'

'That's orl right, me lads, anyfink fer 'is Majesty's late armed forces. Our Gertie is off cheese at the moment ... she's expectin' – the first free munfs, orl she craved were cheese and pickled onions – now she's fed up wiv that an' gorn orn to chips wiv bread and jam! Ugh. We've got her cheeses!'

'Women!' said the male company!

Tabby privately thought her brother could become the Prime Minister one day! Well! The war was over and the government said *Britain would be a land fit for heroes* and all the men had been heroes in the war, hadn't they? Tabby had become an avid reader of the daily newspaper; with her new knowledge of language she'd have preferred a more upmarket daily rag – but her father chose the newspapers in their house. According to the dailies, with Labour in power it was the *people's land* now; shed enough blood and guts for it, hadn't they, not to mention tears! Lord knows there were very few families who didn't have a tragic story to relate, some worse than others. But, now they were free – free to work and get a decent wage packet at the end of the week; free to smoke, drink, be merry and bright, half-day working on Saturdays for the blue collar class – and to the football grounds at West Ham in the afternoon to support the Hammers in their distinctive maroon and blue strip.

No more pitch-black nights, bumping into people; no more black-out curtains and 'Oy! Put out that light!' Light streamed from windows these days, the streets lights were lit at dusk and there was hardly a house in the six streets which didn't have its own piano – the old Joanna – even if nobody could play it properly with music – they could tickle the ivories and play by ear! New records sold out as fast as they came onto the market; everybody had a radiogram now; you were posh once you had your own radiogram – polished it lovingly every day. The men complained to their wives – the radiogram got more loving care than they did! Records and sheet music sold out faster than you could say Jack Robinson.

No more nasty telegrams: 'Missing – presumed

killed in action' – whatever.

The new era after the war was exciting – the forelock tugging era had gone but the cloth caps were side-by-side with the trilbys. Hospitals were crowded, chock-a-block with *Britain's Bonny Babies* and the midwives were working at full stretch on home deliveries down the six streets. After the initial novelty wore off, the figure on the bike with her wicker basket became just part of the scenery. It was rare not to see a back garden with an endless line of terry towelling nappies flapping white in the wind – a bonny sight, like a full rigged and sheeted sailing ship, blowing along in all its glory ... in full, glorious sail. Men who'd gone to sea during the war or were shipped abroad – landlubbers – never wanted to see any kind of ship again; well not for a long time!

Pram shops did roaring trades, and could scarcely cope with the demand. Every new mother wanted a big, brand new, shining coach-built pram – the favourite colour was maroon or navy, with sparkling chrome wheel guards. You just left a deposit on your chosen pram at the pram shop. If, unfortunately the baby was lost or stillborn, the pram shop gave you your money back, without quibbling. New mothers didn't like to temp fate by getting the pram home before the baby was birthed.

The weddings! My, the weddings! The actual year in which the war ended was a record year for weddings – seemed like all the world and his wife was having, or going to, weddings! No wondered there was a boom in babies. Tabby and Jean loved weddings and went to see as many as they could.

Weddings and babies were like a fever – running helter-skelter through the fertile population; you could bet your bottom dollar, if there was a wedding down a street, all the neighbours from roundabout would turn up outside your front gate to watch the new virgin bride leaving the house in her wedding dress – with many Ohhhhs and Ahhhhhss! 'Oh don't she look lovely – bless yer sweetheart *keep yer legs close tergevver tonight* and hope fer the best!'

Telling her mother about the three men cousins had been no ordeal for Tabby, she knew her mother would welcome them with, if not open arms, in a friendly fashion. And the card night was a roaring success. Tabby preened herself and felt a beautiful warm heady glow – her sisters were so grateful to Tabby. She cheerfully accepted the monetary largesse bestowed upon her as extra pocket money and revelled in being called Miss Cupid!

She was mystified when her mother said it was comical the day she told her about the three cousins, one in the Army one in the Navy and one in the Airforce. 'Why're yer laffin', Mum? Ouch Benjie – stop tugging me 'air, I'll play wiv yer in a minute.'

'Because lovey, three of my daughters are going to be ravished by the Army the Navy and the Airforce – at that card game or my name's not Jean Braithewaite.'

'Oh, Mum, I'm sure they're nice blokes, Joan said they were ever so nice.' And it proved right, they were.

Tabby assured Benjie she loved him to bits but

handed him to his mother to sit on her lap. Growing fast and getting heavier every day was little Benjie – his Mum-Mum's stews, loved them he did. Sitting at the table Tabby and Jean had a good old chinwag – with Jean mindful of her language in earshot of her mimic of a son! 'Oh! He's a right little rascal our Benjie – yer goin' ter break lots of 'earts some day with your twinkling eyes and long dark lashes ... have you ever seen such long eyelashes on a boy, Tabby? Yer've got a nerve, Tabitha Braithewaite, unloading the King's Army, Navy and Airforce on yer sisters, wivout warnings. Not that they'll mind – oh no ... it'll be–'

'Mirror, mirror on the wall...' said Tabby, finishing the sentence for her. 'Anyway yer've got it wrong – it's the Navy, the Army and the Air-force: not the other way round! Our teacher told us the Navy is the Senior Service – yer know that! It's on the front of Player's cigarettes ain't it. Senior Service they calls 'em. King Alfred had the first Navy, didn't 'ee?'

'Dunno! Did 'ee? Yer orlways 'as ter 'ave the last word don't yer, Tabby!'

'It's a cryin' shame yer never got ter Grammar school, our Tabby. A great big cryin' shame! Your Miss Brink telled me yer English is nearly as good as hers! Lappin' it up like a kitten wiv a saucer of milk, is wot yer Miss Brink, yer English teacher told me!'

Ambling along, sometimes executing little skipping steps and other times merely dawdling, many thoughts were tumbling through the little grey cells of Tabby's brain … higgledy-piggledy – it made her think of one of Benjie's favourite nursery rhymes:

Higgledy-piggledy
My fat hen.
She lays eggs for
gentlemen.
Sometimes nine
Sometimes ten
Higgledy-piggledy –
My fat hen.

Observing the crudely chalked hopscotches on the pavements she was passing along her mind's eye saw them in a higgledy-piggledy form! There she was off again… English lessons were certainly stretching her mind, enabling her to think more clearly and accurately with her greater range of vocabulary. Why! Just think of all the words in any dictionary! It was mind boggling! The fabled penny had definitely dropped for Tabby, making her realise how education would take her up higher away from the six streets. She didn't think that in any sort of *snobbish manner*, but, she felt there must be more to life than the six streets, her present encompassing world – after all those terrible years of war and strict rationing of practically everything. As young as she was, a nearly woman, she realised that a good education with her knowledge of the King's English, would enable her to help educate her own children one day. Miss Brink had said 'educate a mother and you educate a family.'

Miss Brink also mentioned 'education is the master key for the working class children.' She loved Miss Brink, lavender and lace is what the children called her strict but kind. She had provided a rock of stability for the children.

'Yer orlways knows where yer are wiv Miss Brink' was what they attested to – out of earshot.

'Yer can arsk 'er anyfinks yer like an' she'll tell yer.'

Like Miss Mitchell, the headmistress, Miss Brink had never married. 'Once upon a time there was a war, Tabby,' Miss Mitchell had said. Enough said, thought Tabby pityingly.

Jean liked both Miss Brink and Miss Mitchell – in fact the whole of the six streets did, children and adults.

'Let me see – that's Lucy's 'opscotch squares, 'n' that one is Lena's. I bet the next one along is Jessie's. Why! Yer can practically tell where kids lived by the shape and size of their own 'opscotches! Aren't I the clever one? I wonder if anyone else has fathomed that out?'

She clapped her hand excitedly – pleased with her own reasoning – now that's a nice word on the lips – *fathomed,* it's wonderful knowing orl these new words. Orl I needs now is a nice boyfriend 'oo' finks like me!

Tabby had long ago stopped swearing – *didn't need to now* – did she? With her command of English language she could pick and choose more descriptive words. *Crumbs 'n' custard* or *sausages* pronounced very emphatically were the lowest she permitted herself to descend to these days. Much better that those horrid overused and

157

worn out four letter expletives!

'I'm getting really good with words,' said Tabby out aloud 'really good! Maybe I could be another Conan Doyle and write mystery books … write about a female Sherlock Holmes!

'I could call meself *Shirley Holmes* – I mean the heroine, not the hero, Sherlock Holmes. After you, my dear Miss Watson, no after you, my dear Miss Holmes!' she bowed deferentially to a mythical duo.

'An arfter youse, Miss Tabitha Braithewaite!'

Totally engrossed in her imaginary role playing of make-believe, Tabby jumped, as if a bee had stung her! She knew whose hateful voice that was! Audibly sniffing, she swung round slowly and majestically. 'Oh! It's you Ginger – look what the cat brought 'ome. What d'ya want?'

'Who were yer talkin' to, Tabby?'

'Meself, stoopid. Then nobody can answer me back What d'ya want Ginger? 'Op it faggot face, no, Carrot Tops. 'Op it. Vamoosh! Skedaddle! Sling yer 'ook!'

Everybody called Ginger names – he just grinned fatuously, water off a duck's back to him, wasn't it! Assuming what he hoped was the classic Humphrey Bogart style, he hunched his shoulders inside his too tight jacket and drawled menacingly… 'Yer gotta 'and it ter me kid,' growlingly pretending to turn up his coat collar like Bogart's famous raincoat scenes. 'Yeah! We're goin' ter git along jist fine – me an' you – baby!'

For the millionth time Tabby wondered why Ginger kept pestering *her*, of all people. There were umpteen girls far prettier – and some willing – than herself!

Ginger, like all males on the prowl, with their inflated egos, thought himself irresistible to women and Tabby was a *nearly woman*. The more she fended him off and rejected his overtures, the more determined he became to overcome them – and have her surrender to him; he longed to ravish her and have her drooling over Ginger's Big Whopper!

She stared at him. She stared at his over-fat tummy. Liked his food did Ginger, his mother had her job cut out feeding his gargantuan appetite. Food coupons only went so far. Ginger didn't do too badly for food, streetwise he was – knew quite a few black marketeers, did Ginger! Ohhh yes!

In Tabby's considered opinion, Ginger was the pits. Seemingly to think himself the cock-o'-the-walk where females were concerned – young and old. Females were females … and nobody could convince Ginger otherwise!

Only one year older than Tabby, Ginger was a most promiscuous laddie. He'd grown into a man well before his chronological, corresponding age. There was many a wartime love-starved woman who could vouch for that. Come to that, there were always a few Gingers knocking around in the world.

His *spiv uncle* encouraged him in his ways and obtained a great kick whenever Ginger regaled to him the nitty-gritty of his turgid conquests. Ginger was even bigger than his uncle – in every way! The latter, unfortunately was a weedy, seedy, unsavoury-looking character. Never as successful as his lascivious nephew however, he regularly greased Ginger's ever outstretched palm with a crackling ten-bob note!

In the Uncle's 'umble opinion his pernicious, smarmy nephew's female exploits were more entertaining than *certain looks* from under the counter in the seedy parts of London's Soho precincts! Oh yes, not 'arf! He got quite a *titillation* from Ginger – oh yes – which he, in turn, passed on to the blokes at work ... earning himself a free flow of pints of Guinness, Brown Ale, and some chasers of Rum – when they met at The King's Oak. Basking in the notoriety of being quite a lad with the boys at the pub, he didn't tell them it was Ginger's conquests, did he? He made it appear that he had done this, that and the other – not his more successful nephew. Not to mention having touched this, that and the other. He never let on it was Ginger and not himself, ohhh no! A couple of chasers down his throat to oil his vocal chords and he could belt out the bawdiest songs with the rest of the lads at The King's Oak Public Rooms...

I saw it, I saw it – I put mine before it...
and the 'airs on me d... – d... stood up like
   barbed wire!

A few more brown ales and he was well into–

'I wish I was single agin,
I wish I was single agin
I wish I was single–

160

My pockets would jingle–
I wish I was single agin.

Then a few more chasers and he couldn't stop
for the life of him – in fact the whole congregation in the pub were yelling with him–

I married anuvver agin–
I married anuvver old 'en–
I married anuvver–
'Oo turned out a b...
And now I'm the farver of ten!

The publican – mine host was carried along
enthusiastically – and joined in with his rich
baritone–

Now orl youse young men that 'ave wives
Now orl youse young men 'oo 'ave wives,
Stick to the first–
For the second's the worst–
An you'll wish yer were single agin.

To say Tabby was annoyed, was to say the least –
she never did like Ginger and especially now,
when she was on one of her *happy solitary walks.*
She snapped sharply, 'Scram, Ginger, I don't
want anybody ter see me walkin' wiv youse! They
might get the wrong idea. So scram or I'll
scream!'
   Hastily she glanced round again – she'd somehow wandered off the beaten track well away
from the safety of the six streets.
   'Nah! Yer wouldn't do that, Tabby – yer a nice

161

girl .. me muvver orlways sez yer a nice girl.' Knew how to wheedle and cajole did Ginger ... had lots of experience with women hadn't he! And with girls! Oh yes, ohhh yes! Ginger *thought* he knew what's what and when's when – or did he?

He'd just appealed to Tabby's vanity – a girl liked to know she was praised by other mothers!

It stopped Tabby in her tracks – wheeling round – keeping a fair distance, she faced him. You never knew with Ginger! Had very long arms and big strong hands had Ginger – once been an amateur schoolboy boxer, he had until he put on too much weight – through over indulgence in food and ale!

'Did yer mum really say that abaht me, Ginger?'

He nodded his head slowly and cunningly. 'M, Tabs!'

'And let me tell you once 'n' fer orl – me name is Tabitha, it's only Tabs to me friends! Yer ain't me friend!'

Ginger crossed his chest dramatically, leering in what he fondly hoped was a real Bogart look! Obsessed with Bogart was Ginger – saw every one of his films. 'Cross me chest, 'opes ter die – now, would *I* lie to yer? Miss Tabitha Braithewaite, me mum said I should get a nice girl like Tabitha – fer walkin' out prop'ly!' He bowed and smirked.

Her eyes shot upwards – the eyebrows lost beneath her fringe. 'Iffin' yer thinks that yer c'n charm me wiv yer smart talk, Ginger – yer've got anuvver fink comin'! She was so cross she lapsed back into the vernacular of the six streets. And Ginger had noticed it too.

His frown brought his flaming red bushy eyebrows into close contact with his rather bulbous nose – it'd been broken twice and matched to a T his cauliflower ears.

'Yer don't talk like that ter me mum, Tabitha Braithewaite. Yer speaks good 'n' proper to 'er, that's why she orlways says yer a smart girl, Tabby.'

But Tabby was not to be deceived by all this *flummery* chatter from Ginger. Ohhh no! Not Tabby. This was one female who was not going to end up at his feet, flat on her back, ohhh no! 'Yer muvver 'appears ter be a nice woman, 'ow she come ter giv birf ter someone rotten ter the core likes youse I nivver did know. I likes yer Muvver – but I don't likes 'er son – you Ginger. I ain't nivver like yer an' I ain't niver goin' to eiver! Ohh! I know 'ow yer sniggers wiv the uvver guttersnipes round by the lavs. Yer'll be leavin' school soon – an' it can't come too early or too soon fer some of us good girls. Yer disgustin' yer are – yer reeeellly are! And! As fer that mealy-mouthed cross-eyed worm of an Uncle of yourn – iffin' 'ee bothers me agin I'll set me dad on 'im!'

Ginger's guffaws at Tabitha's indignant tirade caused the buttons on his trousers to visibly pop open from the enormous strain of his girth – his belly wobbled for all it was worth! The trousers had been made for somebody less ample than him and it showed – frighteningly! Ginger's *whopper* looked set to be let loose!

163

He bellowed like a trumpeting elephant and Tabby clapped her hands over her ears. 'At the Union yer Dad is. Orlways at the Union – haw-haw-haw.'

Incandescent with rage, Tabby's tongue lashed him good and proper. She wasn't having anybody laughing about any member of her family – not even if it was just her father she was laughing about. Her little grey cells speedily admitted her father deserved to be laughed at – for everybody knew the Union fees and meetings were *not* every week – let alone three or four times a week on the trot!

'I jist told yer, an' don't yer let me 'ave ter tell yer agin – Ginger Carrot Top Ginger!' She broke into her poshest voice. 'And, furthermore, young man, I would deem it agreeable if you were to stop pestering a young lady such as myself!'

'Blimey!' shouted Ginger. 'With brass knobs on – and the same to you, Miss Tabitha Braithe-waite!'

From vernacular to posh speech and her spleen spitting forth such a tirade had flummoxed Ginger good and proper!

Tabby, having got rid of her anger, now reverted back to the street vernacular – reverting to kind. 'Blimey ain't got nuffink ter do wiv it, Ginger, jist a few 'ome troofs. I've got good English I 'ave when I wants ter use it. Don't see why I should waste me learnin' on a cheeky bugger of a Lothario or Lochinvar like youse. Ohhh yerse! I knows orl abaht yer. Ohhh yerse I do. I knows wot yer gits up to wiv those silly girls down the back alleys 'atween the 'ouses. An' over the sewer banks – yerse orl us good girls knows wot Ginger is like, Ginger Morley, and I ain't stoopid. Walk out wiv yourse? I'd rarver walk out wiv the devil 'imself! Provided 'ee leaves 'is horns at home!'

Ginger was whooping and chortling now and his sides were aching with laughing so energetically, only one more button to pop on his trousers and Tabitha Braithewaite would get a good front view of his whopper whether she liked it or not! Oh! She was a real lass! A sizzler of a lass. 'Ohhh my word, yer a bonny Cockney girl, our Tabs – a bloke could do worsen yer, I can tell youse. Ohhh yerse!'

'I don't want yer ter tell me anyfhink an' I don't want yer walkin' alongside of me … I woz enjoying me walk … so scarper, muck face … yer've got the 'ide of a rhinoceros.'

'Yer can't stop me! Got as much right as youse, Tabs. The ground duzzn't belong to youse, it belongs ter nobody. I c'n walk along 'o' yer iffen I wants ter an' yer can't stop me. It's a free country – won the war didn't we?'

Hands on hips Tabby faced her adversary. 'Shame yer weren't old enuff ter be called up for the forces – old 'itler'd 'ave kept yer as 'is bodyguard. Then it would've been good riddance ter bad rubbish, I sez! No! It 'ad ter be the nice blokes which went ter fight and didn't come back – should've been youse. Right! That's that then – I ain't 'avin' yer walk wiv *me!*'

Like a whirlwind, Tabby spun round and scarpered as if the *Hounds of the Baskervilles* had been swiftly on her heels along with Ginger, she knew which she would have preferred – and it wouldn't 've been Ginger and his fabled whopper!

Shrugging, Ginger grinned and plodded on – his flies wide open and his pants bulging ominously. He knew his portly frame wouldn't get him along at anywhere near Tabby's speed. She could run like a hare – bosoms or no bosoms – when the need arose.

His words followed her on the breeze. 'Anuvver day, Tabitha Braithewaite, anuvver day. Yer won't be so stuck up someday an' yer'll come ter me wi open arms!'

'Like hell!' said Tabby. Her head flung back she shouted for all she was worth. 'Never in a million, trillion years, Ginger Morley … an' yer ain't no Humphrey Bogart … 'ee nivver 'ad freckles nor ginger 'air nor cauliflower ears 'n' a twice broken nose, so there!' With a very un-ladylike action Tabby stopped dead in her tracks and stuck her tongue out as far as it would go, then she fled until she was out of his sight!

Poor old Ginger. What a nasty leveller for a Romeo of such magnificent proportions: he vainly tried to refasten his fly buttons – he looked round hastily but nobody was in sight. He didn't want to be had up for indecent exposure, his mum would literally kill him. Fortunately nobody had witnessed the tirades and altercation between the two young antagonists.

Puffing heavily, Tabby pulled the string through the letter box. 'I'm home, Mum, I'm home! That beastly Ginger Morley's been pestering me agin. He's horrible, Mum, really horrible.' She flung her arms around her mother's neck, Benjie sitting on her lap slobbered his sweet little mouth against his sister's cheeks. 'Don't cry 'abs – Benjie luv youse!'

'Ohhh Benjie, Bunna-Bunna I 'opes yer nivver grows up like Ginger Morley.' Benjie smothered her face with his warm sympathetic kisses, 'abs-abs? Wot ma-er, don't cry!'

'Tabby – you're like a runaway express train thundering down the tracks in all directions – here, 'old Benjie, I'll make yer a strong cuppa an' yer c'n tell me 'n' Benjie orl abaht it!'

'Yer started ter speak good English then, Mum!'

'Yerse! I know! Pickin' it up from youse ain't I!'

Chapter Seven

It wasn't for want of trying, Tabby repeatedly told herself; scurrying home hungrily from the baker's shop, the fresh aroma of newly baked bread exuding from the brown paper carrier bag. No! It most assuredly wasn't from want of trying. She licked her sticky lips appreciatively – the baker always favoured her with a free iced bun.

From *want of trying*, that was a nice phrase on the mouth; she was becoming very skilful with her usage of various words and phrases. She liked the three words – *letters, let us,* and *lettuce.* Spoken quite quickly, she often managed to confuse people with them – which was a right laugh. Of course, in context, one could easily distinguish them. Coincidentally if they were mouthed with no sound at times, it was impossible to distinguish the three words. It's strange how some words actually look what they mean!

Miss Brink loved words and, by patient diligence, she had conveyed that love to Tabby and a few more receptive students.

'For instance, children, consider the word *sneer* or *sneeringly,* note how your nose wrinkles a trifle nastily? That's what is meant by looking what they mean? Or try *regretfully,* your face and manner seem regretful, don't they?'

'Miss Brink's a one,' said Tabby out aloud. 'Knows some smashing words, she does. I especially liked "it is quite quiet here in this quiet white room" – alliteration, she called it!' She smiled a slow smile which gradually crept, in a curved arc, across her face. She, Tabitha Braithewaite had never ever thought that some day words and their good usage would be accepted by her little grey cells, nourished and stored for future use!

Henry Braithewaite's mouth had dropped open in sheer surprise at some of the fine words his Tabby came out with. This better educated Tabitha was a new turn-up for the books in his not-so-humble opinion. None of his other twelve daughters had been bookish and he queried it one day with his wife.

Jean was proud and protective of her thirteenth daughter and told Henry he should be proud too: it was an understandable thirst for knowledge – Tabby's teacher had said those very same words to Jean, who had stored them in her memory to use verbatim!

'How can it be understandable?' asked Henry perplexedly. 'I don't understand why our Tabby's suddenly got this thirst for knowledge. If she ain't careful she'll become a bookworm and a blue-stocking!'

Jean snorted. 'Huh! 'Enry with an "H", blue stockings went out with the ark – this is modern times – it ain't the bloomin' 1800s!'

Quick off the mark for once, Henry rounded on Jean and asked her what she knew about it. He pointed out again that the other daughters were not bookish and doin' all right. 'I means ter say, love, we ain't got a lot of books in our 'ouse, an'

I don't know anybody 'oo 'as, so where does our Tabby get this thirst fer books – who from?'

His wife explained all over again, for the third time running, that her teacher, Miss Brink, had been the instigator of Tabby's interest in English and general knowledge. And she introduced her to the public library. Happy as a lark our Tabby's been since then, yer must've noticed it, Henry? "Like a lark soaring inter the sky" is 'ow she put it! Now ain't that boo'ful, Henry? Our litt'l Tabby like a lark? Pity the uvver girls didn't learn a bit more, you and me could've learnt from them by now.'

Henry looked poleaxed! He mentioned forcefully that education's all right fer boys, yerse. But why bother fer girls? They got married had a baby every year – or near enough; did the washing and shopping, put a hot meal on the table for a man after a hard day's graft, and, in his opinion, what else was there for women? They shouldn't be taking jobs from men, once they were married. 'I, myself left school at twelve, didn't I? Got on orl right, didn't I? Orlways 'ad a job, ain't I? Always brought wages 'ome every week, ain't I?'

His wife admitted to the latter but not the former: 'Fings is diffr'nt now, Henry – it were diffr'nt fer the working class when youse and me were young. But the war has changed everything – like the Great War changed fings too. People's setting their sights 'igher now; duzzn't wanna fink of orl the 'ard work, sorrow, inconvenience of the war years woz orl fer nuffink! Yer can't turn the clock back, the people won't 'ave it; the men

170

give six years of their lives, didn't they? Ain't going ter be pushed around by bosses now they ain't Well maybe a bit, but not in the same old grovellin' way. And girls is getting' their rights more now – they ain't prepared ter be skivvies 'n' chattel any longer. Before the war, yerse! But women know their *true werff* now. Served in the armed forces – served everywhere women did, on the farms, in the 'ospitals – everywhere. Got up at dawn ter queue fer the day's rations – or there'd be no evening meal – then they went on to the factories ter do long hours of shift work! I dunno where this country'd have been wiv aht the women ter keep it tickin' over!'

Jean swiftly pointed out that before the war a man went to work, came home, ate his grub, read his paper, listened to the radio or went down the pubs or the dogs or horse racing or football. Certainly the woman listened to the radio but she still had to scrub the kids, pack them off to bed, and iron clothes and darn socks endlessly – the darning mushroom was always to hand in her work box along with the darning needle and thread.

Henry had no concrete answer other than, 'That's wot I'm trying ter say, Jean, let a bloke 'ave 'is say will ya? Take yerself fer instance, iffen yer wants ter work in the factories, why, yer'd 'ave ter do orl wot yer jist sed and work a shift! It'd kill yer girl – it'd kill yer!'

Sighing heavily, exasperatedly Jean shook her head sideways. 'Yer'll niver learn will yer – wimmin did it – like I jist sed orl froo six years of war and horror and upheaval. Sometimes niver knowing if they'd see their kids agin in the evening or morning – a doodlebug could've got 'em or even the women. That were a real harsh lesson of life, Henry! Me, been stuck at 'ome orl me married life, ain't I? Where've I been? Wot've I don wiv me life? Go on then, man, tell me.'

Drawing himself up to his full five feet three inches he uttered the time immortal working class phrase, '*Yer knows wot I means girl!*'

'Don't ya girl me! Miss Brink says an investment in knowledge pays the 'ighest interest.'

Henry permitted himself a derisive snort or two.

'Huh! Huh! Benjamin Franklin!'

'What'd ya mean, wotch jist sed – Benjamin Franklin?'

'Benjamin Franklin 'ee woz the geezer 'oo sed that! Told yer before didn't I, *edicated I am!* Orl right yer niver asked before so I nivver told yer, did I? Me granmuvver on me muvver's side – she were like wot yer jist sed, edicated – fond of words 'n' phrases like our Tabby – and proverbs! Oh yerse, oh yerse! Orlways sed that she did – *educate a woman and you educate a family.* How abaht that fer posh speakin', c'n do it like Tabby, I kin, yerse, iffen I won ter!'

Jean thought hard; she recalled Henry's mother used to use a lot of nice sayings and thought to ask her how she – a woman – knew them all? In those days it was considered rude to ask too many questions of one's elders.

Henry was in his element now, got the upper hand – at last – well for a while, and he was determined to make the most of it! He rubbed his hands gleefully, pointing out to his surprised wife that *that* was probably where Tabby got her ability from, handed down from brain to brain from his maternal family line; Miss Brink had merely been the key which unlocked Tabby's mind, the ability was already there! Henry was quite cock-a-hoop now, wait until he told the blokes down at The King's Oak tonight!

Jean had burst out laughing at the drollness of Henry's outburst and asked how had it bypassed his brain then?

''Ow do I bloody well know! Me Aunt Aggie, who got killed when I were abaht fifteen, she were edicated ... me grandmuvver's pride an' joy she were!'

'Well! Henry Braitheweaite – married orl these long years and yer nivver told me – yer louse!'

'Nivver 'arrssked me did yer, love?' He cackled triumphantly, 'She were me great Aunt Aggie, actually. They orlways said it skipped a generation each time and only carried on down the female line – me great-grandmother and 'er mother an' orl that, picked bits up from the edicated ones – orlways female yerse. Now yer know why it didn't rub orff on me much, an' it won't on Benjie eiver!'

'Yerse it will rub off on Benjie – our Tabby's teaching him lots of things. 'Ee luvs larnin', duz our Benjie. Just fink 'Enry yer could've been an edicated man – if yer'd been a female. But then yer wouldn't 'ave been a man would yer? It gets curioser and curioser – that's wot Alice sed.'

Henry grunted. 'Alice 'oo, when she's at 'ome?'

'Tabby were readin' *Alice in Wonderland* and

Alice froo the lookin' glass ter our Benjie. 'Ee jist luvs it when our Tabby reads ter 'im, 'ee really do.'

The mention of his pride and joy, his only son, caused Henry to sit bolt upright in his chair. It made a man feel powerfully good to have a son, especially after thirteen girls!

'I'd like ter see me son as a bookworm – maybe make somefink of 'imself – maybe become an MP? Or even Prime Minister? Yer nivver do know, yerse – yer nivver do know!'

'That's not impossible 'Enry ... the working class're on their way up, be ownin' their own homes 'n' all that; well, I means ter say, some duz orl ready – but most don't – lorst their 'omes in the blitz didn't they, an' most workin' class nivver earned enuff afore the war, did they? Of course, some of us'll 'ave ter be at the bottom of the 'eap – that's life I'm afraid. But where there's life and a good job with a decent wage, there's 'ope fer us, yerse – ain' there 'Enry? Our Benjie'd make a smashin' MP. I c'n jist picture 'im now wiv 'is blonde curls standin' up makin' 'is maiden speech, an' us sitting upstairs in the Strangers Gallery at the House of Commons listening to 'im. I'd be so proud – yerse! Wot a fevver in our caps that'd be fer us Braithewaites!' Henry's head was nodding vigorously – maybe there was something in this education lark, after all. If it led to his only son ... *legitimate* ... becoming Prime Minister! The Right Honourable Benjamin Frederick George Braithewaite. Who was to say he couldn't be? The humble backwoodsman – Abraham Lincoln became President of the

174

United States of America? Jean was correct. The world had changed – for the better. Henry envisioned himself in the pub; 'Meet Henry Braithewaite – the father of our esteemed Prime Minister! Ohhh! Yes! Henry's fanciful vision suited him a treat – there would surely be free pints in it for himself!

Three times a week Tabby visited the library – she'd become a voracious and avid reader. At school she'd learnt typing and shorthand skills; it was encouragement all the way for Tabitha Braithewaite who looked fair set to break the mould – the working class mould – or was she? Time would tell; life seemed full of changes. Women's fashions had become prettily feminine with Christian Dior's Fashion House promoting the New Look – almost ankle length (some were ankle length – a few a trifle higher) – which permeated down from the exclusive fashion houses to the ordinary female population, who took to it like a duck to water. Suddenly young ladies were no longer lovely legs – they were hidden, much to the chagrin of red-blooded males! Waists were tight, busts hitched as high as they would comfortably go – and a trim ankle elicited many an admiring wolf-whistle from the building site workers! Heels were high contributing to the swaying walk of the lassies. What the men couldn't actually see gave forth to fantasising!

From the drab service-coloured uniforms, the young sparks blossomed into fancy Edwardian-style clothes with long jackets and loafers' on their feet. The short-back-and-sides and a singe,

175

became longish hair, well greased, with upstanding quiffs at the front. The young lads stood on the street corners frequently combing their locks or sauntering along in gangs swaying proudly and swankily for all the world to see them – the new peacocks! Strutting their stuff was the in-phrase. After the drab war years, it was a real tonic to witness so much colour and novelty of styles.

Ladies wore pert little hats with silly bits of veiling or cartwheel concoctions – feminine and flattering. Nylon see-through gloves in the colours of the rainbow; stockings edged in lace of lilac and other pastels. A well-dressed working girl almost never went on a date or somewhere special without her gloves. Half slips – petticoats – were froths of tulle, making their new look dresses stand out like ballroom dancers at the ballroom dancing competitions. The fullness of the dresses served to emphasise the waistlines, making them look even smaller. Tabby and her mates lapped it up like a cat with a saucer of milk.

A long talk with Jean and Henry'd had to accept change; he could no longer completely rule the roost with his daughters; he acquiesced – partly. The rich desperately appealed for servants using slightly less offensive names! His twins, Dora and Peggy, expressed point blankly their objections to such menial work.

'Who wants to wait on Lady Muck after orl we've been through in the war? Not blinkin' likely – they can "shove it up their jumper" – we ain't goin' ter be no blinkin' servants. Earning good money in the factories with mates, or in offices, is beter than waitin' 'and an' foot on someone – jist 'cos they've got a lot of brass.'

Poor Henry – had to change didn't he? Couldn't beat thirteen females, could he? A man wasn't quite a man in his own house now. But he wasn't going to give in to them hook, line and sinker – oh no. The younger girls still had to be indoors by ten at night – or else! Unless he gave them special permission. He never went to bed until they were in at night.

Lost in her own thoughts, Tabby'd no idea of all the discussions by her parents, but, she noticed her dad no longer objected to her library books. Wonders of wonders, he now permitted her to read the Sunday papers! She was elated – some good novels were serialised in the Sundays. Her dad had several papers on Sundays – not just one – so she was doubly happy and joyful; only costing a few coppers each, in broadsheet form – it was a victory! Henry spent Sunday mornings, elbows on table reading – mouthing the words visibly in an unintelligible murmur. Once he popped off to The King's Oak Tabby was free to read them, making sure she creased each page correctly or meet her father's wrath!

She was scurrying along a bit faster now – all the thoughts tumbling, being sorted and sifted, by the little grey cells. The slight breeze now threatened to turn into a mini gale – a real south-westerly and, inevitably she collided with some-body else. He'd appeared from nowhere and like herself was not actually looking where he was going. Apologising, but not looking at him, she increased her speed – with panic setting in – she'd automatically thought it was Ginger! She made haste to put a distance between them. But it wasn't Ginger! Heavens be praised. No! It was a tall fair-haired lad – a few years older than Tabby – maybe four or five – a nearly man, like Tabby was a nearly woman. Their heads had smashed together and poor Tabby reeled like a drunken person as she staggered along from him! Being made of sterner stuff and having a thicker skull he recovered his senses quicker than Tabby. Besides, as it turned out, he was built on rugger-lines, used to rugger-scrums and could take hard knocks!

'Ouch! That hurt didn't it? Sorry, ever so sorry. I just wasn't looking where I was going, I had my head turned sideways from the wind; it's coming from a south-westerly direction – and it looks like we're in for it!'

'Yes, it was the wind, but much more my fault actually – wasn't looking where I was going, was I?' She liked the voice; she liked the body even better – with a face atop it akin to the one she'd often dreamed of – what she'd like to have in a steady boyfriend! Her thoughts instantly made her cheeks suffuse from pink to scarlet and back again. Had she been aware how attractive she now looked she'd have blushed some more! She looked most appealingly attractive.

'Are you all right, miss?'

'Uh-uh! Pardon?'

'I only asked if you're okay, miss ... er ... I ... didn't catch your name,' he said hopefully.

''Cos I didn't give it to yer, did I?'

178

He grinned rakishly. His face lit up into an infectious smile, displaying a perfect set of film star-teeth. She wondered which toothpowder he used. He could warm the cockles of her heart any time he liked! He lowered his face to hers solicitously, Tabby was ready to swoon – move over Clark Gable.

Tabby thought quickly, here she'd been strolling along, minding her own business, permitting the little grey cells to have a field day and repeating to herself *it wasn't for the want of trying* that she'd not got a steady boyfriend to walk out with, and wow! Smack, bang, wallop – fate had delivered Mr Right – even if he had almost cracked her head!

She knew it! She knew it! Rooted to the spot, her legs like jelly – her blood turned to water – and pistons at full speed in her bacon bonce. 'Gosh!' she uttered with great feeling. The voice – its huskiness – it thrilled her to the marrow; blowing in and out of her tiny perfect ears, setting the *hammer anvil* and *stirrup* into quick motion, oscillating his melodious tones via the cochlea to her brain which instantly became the custodians, *for ever!*

'I'm Freddy – and you are...?'

'That's the second time you've asked me.'

It was his turn to blush scarlet... 'Er ... I ... didn't ... we ... know ... I mean ... I didn't mean to imply ... that you had ... or ... that ... you ... were...!'

'Yer didn't mean ter 'urt me and yer didn't mean I had given yer me name. Okay? That's all right. I'm Tabby.'

179

'Sorry, really sorry, I didn't mean to sound so crass. I thought you hadn't heard me; can I walk you home?'

Cupid's arrow had penetrated her heart and her knees started to buckle, whether from the arrow or the close proximity of his head bent solicitously she didn't know – nor cared. Time stood still – Cupid was poised with a second arrow – it wasn't needed – his shaft had struck dead centre, it couldn't have been a truer aim. How utterly kind fate could be. Ohhh! Her mind conjured up the immortal words of Mae West, 'Come up and see me sometime.' She extended her limp right hand to be engulfed by his man-sized paw and happily returned to earth. 'Yes! It didn't 'arf 'urt; got a bump already – I have yer know!'

Flesh to flesh – his warm grasp precipitated nerves zinging up her arms; not quite what Faraday had in mind, but an electric shock, nevertheless! Reluctantly he released her hand even more reluctantly, Tabby withdrew it! Privately she swore blind that she would never wash it again – at least not until the warmth of his pressure had worn off! Rubbing her head, where an egg-sized bump was trying hard to increase its girth, to no avail, he became most attentive and seemed to know what he was doing. Tabby didn't, but was content to let him touch it gently.

'You must have a thin skull, Tabby, may I call you, Tabby?'

Tabby's eyes were limpid pools, she murmured in a strangulated voice, 'Of course you can, Freddy.'

Freddy nodded his head sagaciously, 'Not too bad – my rugby mates get worse cracks and come out of it unscathed. They do say men have thicker skulls than women. You're only a young girl – it's probably a very fragile one!'

Indignantly Tabby drew herself up tall – she was the smallest of the Braithewaite girls. 'Nearly five feet I am! And I'm not that young – be leaving school, I will, soon.'

There he went again, laughing huskily – sent shivers up and down her spine! He chuckled, he saw what effect he was having on her feelings and from sheer male devilment he persevered. Out came the brilliant white teeth once more – bright enough to eclipse the sun thought Tabby tremulously. His voice lowered a fraction,

'It wasn't your fault, dear! Oh, really – please don't blush, I won't eat you!'

'I'm not your dear, I'm me! I know you won't eat me – but I must get home with the bread or Benjie won't have his fingers for breakfast.' She added lamely, 'Likes fingers wiv 'is eggs does our Benjie.'

But he was determined not to lose her now he had found her: perforce he inveigled her to tell him who Benjie was.

Oh crumbs! thought Tabby swiftly, this is beginning to get like a Regency novel. Obviously, the young man was well educated; that'd been obvious the first time he spoke. There was nothing for it – he didn't look like he was going to buzz off! Not that she wanted him too, either.

Tabby spoke in her best English – 'Would you like to come home and meet my mother and

Benjie – my little brother?'

He nodded eagerly, 'Will your mother mind?'

Would her mother mind – Tabby was astonished that anybody could think that her mother would mind her taking home such an obviously eligible boy ...well ... young man! Let's not split hairs! Especially this one; head and shoulders over other eligible boys and acolytes and enemies. Not that Tabby had many of the latter! Most people liked her. Apart from Ginger – but he liked her even thought she didn't like him. He certainly didn't perceive himself as Tabby's enemy and would have been hurt to know she felt that way about him!

But after the latest Ginger episode, Ginger had decided she was his enemy and he'd declared war on Tabitha Braithewaite. Ginger could be a nasty adversary when he wanted to be – all because Tabitha Braithewaite wouldn't allow him *certain favours* – to put it delicately. She'd refused him point blank when he'd offered – yes, he'd deigned to offer her – the art of French kissing – he'd offer to teach her and who better, for he revelled in the knowledge that he was the champion in that art. Or so he deluded himself!

It was Tabby's turn to smile, it split her face open ear-to-ear and her tiny chuckle was music to Freddy's love-smitten heart. For smitten it was for poor Freddy. 'My mum keeps open house and anybody'll tell you that. Her name's Jean, she simply adores people – except (she added under her breath), Ginger Morley.' It was all right – Freddy never caught the last bit, the wind tore it from her and it disappeared in thin air.

A happy Freddy assured her he would take Tabby's word for it, and could he carry the loaf of bread for her?

'I'm not that weak – you know! I *can* carry a loaf of bread.'

'Did I say you couldn't? What a girl you are for putting words of your own into another person's mouth!'

'Like what? I only said I could carry a loaf of bread for myself.'

'I know you did. But it is *gentlemanly* to carry a lady's parcels or packages for her!'

Tabby stood stock-still, her eyebrow disappeared once more under her windswept fringe. She'd never heard that one before. 'Pull the other leg, Freddy!'

'No! Honestly – you said yourself that you're near school-leaving age ... so ... you must ... be *nearly a lady!*'

She eyed him obliquely, her fluttering eyelashes like a Red Admiral butterfly, hovering over a buddleia bush. Thick, long and curled upwards, almost as beautiful as Benjie's. She asked Freddy if he'd been reading the Brontë novels. Smilingly he chuckled unaffectedly, and Tabby's heart flipped a double somersault. 'My sister is a Georgette Heyer fan – she reads bits to me sometimes, for the sake of a bit of discussion. No! I don't read them – nor the Brontë novels – perish the thought. Anna's quite a bookworm – likes to discuss them with someone, usually me! At the moment she's into poetry and *The Lady of Shalott* ... and don't ask me about *that!* I do read of course, mysteries, and all that – especially Agatha

183

Christie's books.'

Tabby sighed, she could have listened to him all day! 'You are forgiven,' she said magnanimously – for all the world as if she was the Lady of Shallot. And she passed the carrier bag and loaf to him.

'Come on, Tabby, hold tight.' The wind whipped his trouser legs round his ankle, 'this old wind is starting to gnash his teeth and bite, we must be in for a big gale! Hang on to my arm, there's a good girl!'

'I am a good girl,' shouted Tabby as the wind ripped at them, her arm tucked into Freddy's they faced the weather together ... head on! Freddy was made of tough stock and, head down, he charged along as if he was in the middle of the rugger field. Whoosh went the wind! Getting into its element it howled and screamed like a banshee and Tabby felt quite alarmed. Freddy, gripping her with all his strength laughed out loud, but the stormy wind wasn't having that. It blew into his open mouth – all but choking him in its suddenness. He gritted his teeth and a chuckle rose from behind them. No wind was going to get the better of Freddy, especially not in front of a lady. Tabby was pulling her skirt down with her free hand, and Freddy's wide bottomed trousers – flares they called them – ballooned out making Tabby giggle uncontrollably causing Freddy to ask what she was giggling about. Tears of laughter streaming down her face, stinging in the wind, she shouted above the roar of the pushing shovin' wind. 'Your wide trousers! Your flares! Me dad's got a pair of pre-war ones

… wider'n yours. He calls them his Oxford bags!'

'Well these were my dad's! Come back into fashion they have.'

Reaching the six streets he turned to her. 'What road and what number is your palace, Princess?'

'It ain't a palace … I mean, it isn't a palace.'

'Ah! No, Tabby, you mean, *'it is not a palace'*.'

'Don't you start!' grinned Tabby squeezing his arm. Oh but she was enjoying herself – this physical contact with Freddy! 'Granite Road, 48. Benjie'll be glad to have his fingers and my mum'll think I've left home.' Fumbling for the string key, it was pulled back inside and the door opened – by Jean.

'Goodness, Tabby! Where have you been? Benjie won't eat his egg without his fingers and now it's stone cold! Where have you been? My goodness – that wind – quickly get inside girl and I'll shut the door. Was there ever such a strong wind as that? Hope the chimney pot don't blow down!'

'Mum, this is my friend, Freddy, here give Mum the bread, Freddy.'

'Okay, lovey! Come in, take him through, Tabby. I'll make another fresh pot and a boil a fresh egg for Benjie. Fortunately the hens laid two this mornin'.'

Benjie was most indignant, 'ab-abs – naughty girl, Benjie wait fer soldiers – eggie orl cold!'

'Sorry pet, Mum-Mum's boiling another egg for you. 'Ere give us a kiss. Mmmm! That's lovely. This is ab-abs' friend, Benjie. Say hello to Freddy.'

'Ulooo-Veddy, ulooo. You like soldiers?'

185

Freddy was entranced with the child. 'I most certainly do. I won't eat my egg without soldiers.'

Benjie chuckled, 'Benjie likes Veddy, ab-abs. Nice man.'

'Friends,' exulted Freddy, chucking Benjie under his chin. Her mother was bowled over with Freddy – just as Tabby knew she would be. Good-looking, well-spoken, smartly dressed with a smile to break any mother's heart. Jean couldn't have wished for a nicer walking out friend for her daughter. No! Jean mentally contrasted Freddy against the likes of Ginger Morley – there was no contest. Freddy was every inch the young gentleman. Admittedly, her daughter was young, but it was quite common for young girls to have a walking out friend of the opposite sex, near to or just after they left school. They usually ended marrying having grown up together. By the time they married between 17 – 19 they were used to each other's faults and failings so they were not a problem by the time the knot was tied.

Jean knew that even Henry wouldn't fault this prospective husband for her daughter. Admittedly they'd just met – but they were meant for each other – Jean could feel it in her *water!*

Chapter Eight

Everything in her garden was flourishing nicely when Tabby celebrated her fifteenth birthday. Jean had knitted her a blue and white bikini swimming costume with a blue sailing boat on the bottom right half of the trunks. She'd unravelled an old jumper into skeins; washed them, and pegged them out to dry to remove the crinkling. Her sister Norah gave her an old knitting pattern from an even older boxful – she hoarded them! Nora was an indefatigable knitter – her tongue keeping pace with their fast clacking. You could hear her needles and her tongue a mile away! Nora had knitted a tam-o'-shanter with matching gloves, edged in Fair Isle; Nora was a nonpareil when it came to Fair Isle knitting on four needles. The three sets of Braithewaite twins had knitted jumpers – six altogether, so Tabby wouldn't have to rely so much on hand-me-downs which were usually faded and shrunken from repeated washings.

Gertie, the eldest of the Braithewaite girls, had thoughtfully provided her with a red lipstick, not too red for a young girl! Another sister gave her Pan-stik – which Freddy was going to rue, – most of it would end up on the shoulder pads of his best, *made-to-measure suit* when Tabby cuddled up to him at the movies. Ignorance was bliss – he didn't yet know that!

Freddy's gift to her was a glorious string of pearls. 'They're not real Tabby – I'll buy you some real ones someday, you see if I don't!'

Tabby'd kissed him, told him they were gorgeous and she didn't want a real set of pearls. Anyhow they looked real, so who was to know the difference? Freddy said he did!

Freddy was an extremely tactile man and found it difficult to keep his hands off Tabby, and constantly cuddled and kissed her. Not that Tabby raised any objections – she took it in her stride as a *nearly woman!* Just as Jean had predicted years ago, Tabby's figure had filled out, she'd become curvaceous with a hint of plumpness, yet retaining quite a small waist. Her breasts were full, high and as Henry put it, enough to excite any red-blooded male. With her plumpish face and good, natural colouring, Freddy was of the opinion that Tabby didn't need make-up … she was still in the bloom of youth. But he held his tongue. From his sister he'd learnt how exciting it was for a young girl to leave school and officially start wearing make-up.

Jean was more than just proud of her daughters – and her son – she often remarked on their beauty to Henry and he'd had to admit she was spot on!

'Our Tabby is going places with Freddy – you mark my words!'

'She's only jist fifteen, Jean, anyhow, what'd ya mean "going places"?'

'Henry! It's not jist me talkin' – everybody sez wot a smart couple they is. Young Freddy's got 'is 'ead screwed on all right.'

188

He had to admit his wife was right – as usual! It rankled with Henry, she never praised him, like she did Freddy. He didn't stop to reason that his wife *didn't have much to praise him* for. He was always at the Union or The King's Oak; she wasn't daft, she could put two and two together!

Henry felt further hurt because Freddy was still but a young lad, nearly eighteen but not getting a man's wage until twenty-one. That was the status quo and the law of the land. Could Henry perhaps be a little ... nay ... a trifle ... jealous of the young fellow? Jean knew he was and she pointed out that it was not just her speaking, it was everybody who met him, as he had his head screwed on all right. She'd just told him that, hadn't she? Why do women have to repeat themselves? Because men *don't listen,* his wife had said. Anyway it didn't matter what Henry thought – the young couple were invited here, there, and everywhere, being well-liked and respected. 'And iffen yer don't work fer respect 'Enry Braithewaite – yer duzzn't get it!'

Nowadays, the Braithewaites, with so many wage packets coming in were reasonably comfortable. Henry was a good worker – when he could tear himself from certain clandestine affairs; obviously, his wife now knew more than he'd thought she did! But she appeared to love him – warts 'n' all!

One of Jean's favourite maxim's was 'the mills of God grind slowly...!'

Proud of his female brood was Henry; especially of Tabby and *her education.* Tabby's boyfriend receiving such accolades from his wife did upset him though – jealousy; it was many years since she'd praised him! Yes, jealous he was! If he hadn't been so busy sowing extensive fertile acres with his seeds, then things might have been different!

Peevishly he pointed out Freddy's age, nearly eighteen – not yet a man with a man's wage! He wouldn't get that until he had turned twenty-one; obligatory status quo – *the law of the land – affirmed Henry majestically.* It did seem daft – a boy could die for his country at eighteen, many did, but could not be a man until he was twenty-one! With no legal rights until twenty-one in relation to property and other things – couldn't even vote!

Ah well! The trouble with Henry was he didn't actually quite know how to *gracefully extricate himself* from the tangle of his *bits on the side!* Many a better man than him had faced the same problems – all down the ages!

Money rolled into the Braithewaites – men were disgruntled at women working taking their jobs; women had become accustomed to their own good wage packets – it went into their purses not into the Publican's till or on number 6 dog at Walthamstow race track!

Jobs were available – fairly easy to go from one job to another, the Labour exchange offered you three jobs. You went for an interview for the first two – if you declined the jobs, then there was no alternative, you had to take the third job: or stay in your present job 'til you got yourself another job.

Within nine months of demobbed men, pregnant women were to be seen *everywhere!* It was like the plague! They'd become blasé and cocky at 'avin the missus wiv *one in the oven.* The women talked of nothing but babies because it was right under their noses wherever they went. 'When's youse 'avin' yourn?', 'When's it due to drop?', 'I'm 'avin' mine the day afore youse – see yer in the 'ospital'! For all the world as if going on the same cruise! Ten days was the norm for women who had their babies in hospital. It was a good rest and a bit of a holiday – many friendships were forged that way. The terry towelling manufacturer's and nappy businesses had their work cut out – to supply the obvious demand!

Freddy was improving himself. He'd successfully attended classes in bought ledger work – having confided his secret ambition to own his *own* shop to Tabby. Britain was a nation of shopkeepers and he wanted to join the ranks.

Lauding his ambition – ready to go along with it, Tabby quietly had reservations about him making it!

'The world's our oyster, Tabby! People want pretty clothes and nice merchandise. The factories are on the move – people've had enough of make-do-and-mend. We've got to get our foot in the door, love – jump on to the bandwagon, before it rolls too far without us!'

Freddy was aiming high and had youth on his side: Tabby skilled in typing and shorthand, had nevertheless, decided to work in a clothing factory, *'To get my hand in,'* she'd said to Freddy. They would be selling clothing in their shop one day, amongst other things, it would be good

191

experience to *see* how things were made. Freddy kissed her. 'You'll be a wife worth having, love – I'm so proud of you.'

Tabby positively glowed – it was grand to have ambition and to be doing something about it. '*Great trees from little acorns grow*,' Miss Brink had said!

Freddy was an extremely passionate and tactile young man. Tabby was aware that she'd probably have a *bun in the oven* on their honeymoon. She was, however, determined it wouldn't be every eighteen months to two years like Jean. There was family planning and the Marie Stopes clinic...! She hadn't broached the subject with Jean – one just didn't! Her mother actually enjoyed her pregnancies – if she'd been unaware of Henry's prolific seeding elsewhere, she'd most possibly have had another thirteen children by now, given Henry's passion and lack of self control! Jean was still of childbearing age – even now!

Sex wasn't openly on the library shelves, or on the bookstalls – not the nice sex ... the other sex was in seedy places and under the counter! The nearest to it was limp biology classes at school – that was the extent of sexual knowledge available! She'd tried to discuss it with Freddy – *try* was the word, hesitantly at first, finding it very painful to broach the subject. Cheerfully Freddy said, 'We'll see about *that* when the time comes!' which didn't exactly boost Tabby's ego – nor enlighten her! Freddy was set to be like other blokes when it came to babies ... *hit-and-miss!*

Still it was early days – she'd not long had her

birthday. Freddy wanted the wedding to be as soon as possible near to his twenty-first birthday.

Women of the six streets told Tabby to 'ave yer babes wen yer as young as yer can, Tabby – yer'll drop 'em easier – yer more supple when yer young. Nodding sagely, pretending to understand Tabby felt quite nervous; a girl at work had told her about the clinic and the Dutch Cap. Tabby was darned sure she didn't understand that!

Her friend had a droll anecdote to relate, her husband, newly demobbed, said, 'Blimey girl! I didn't fight the Jerries jist ter come 'ome 'n' find me darlin' wife has either got a 'eadache tonight or she's got her manhole covers (periods) – blow me down – it's the bloomin' raincoat now (Dutch cap)!'

'It works, Tabby – the Dutch cap, I mean! 'ee gits 'is dues regular, wivart' me 'avin' a "bun in the oven" every nine months, regular! I love kids, but I wanna furnish our new prefab first; me money 'elps pay the hire purchase payments. Jist got a new free-piece-soot (three piece suite), we 'ave. Cor yer should see it! Sort of pinkish-floral – 'ee wanted black 'imitation lever – I wasn't 'avin' none of that, woz I? No bloomin' fear – 'ad enuff of blinkin' black didn't we – wiv the hellish blackouts and the drab blackout curtains. "I'll tell yer wot, mate!" I sez to 'im I sez, "I ain't wearin' black and I ain't 'avin' black furniture in our prefab," I sez. "Black furniture in our 'ouse an' yer'll carry me out in me box!" Cor, Tabby! Kin yer believe it? A luvverly new prefab – like a bungalow it is – real luvverly – own front and

193

back garden ... an' 'ee ruddy well wants black furniture! "No way," I sez ter 'im, "no way!"'

'Then wot?'

'Then wot I did, I 'ad an 'eadache every night fer a week didn't I!'

Tabby couldn't stop laughing! It was so droll! She promised to go and see her new mate's prefab with its own bathroom – no more sharing wiv uvver fam'lees ... and their own garden gate. Council had put nice wire fences round each one and the prefabs were to last for ten years! By that time, they hoped to build proper brick structure homes – a home for the *'eroes of our times!* Little did they know it but some of them were still standing some forty-years later!

'Went up ter the council man I did – yerse I did! An' I sez ter 'im I sez, "Yer must be stark ravin' bonkers in yer bacon bonce iffen yer finks ter git me out of me dream 'ome in ten years' time ... then you'se got anuvver fink comin'. It's good fer anuvver fifty years," I sez ter 'im. Guffawed 'ee did – nearly wet 'is pants 'ee did. "My dear Lady," she mimicked. 'I sez ter 'im, "Don't yer 'dear lady' me I ain't a lady an' I nivver will be. But I knows me rights. Me 'usband fought fer a land fit fer 'eroes – 'ee did 'n' all – yerse ... an' 'im wounded free times ... fought wiv the Desert Rats 'ee did ... fought everywhere 'ee did 'n' scars ter prove it 'ee 'as! Youse wanna talk like that to me old man," I sez ter this geezer, "'e'll shut yer trap good 'n' proper. Where woz youse?" I sez ter 'im... "yer weren't called up were yer – or youse wouldn't be talkin' like this. 'Op it, mate, I sez" And yer know

194

wot, Tabby?' Tabby shook her head, doubled-up laughin! 'Yer nivver seed a bloke skeddadle orff so fast – bet 'ee did actually wet 'imself! Mebbe 'ee woz one of them call-up-dodgers! Me 'usband spits on 'em. Right 'n' orl I sez!'

Still gullible, but learning fast, Tabby spent a year working in the blouse factory. She reckoned on one year's hands-on experience and then to try something else. She felt it behove her to get as much experience as she could.

The wedding was planned for her seventeenth year – Jean felt Henry would agree to that. Some of his other girls had married young.

Jean herself had had a bun in the oven, married on her seventeenth birthday, the baby Gertie arrived a few weeks later! She never showed her marriage certificate to anybody – they'd put their ages as twenty-one!

In blissful innocence of ideals and goals, Freddy and Tabby kept some things close to their chests for fear of being ridiculed for aiming so high!

Freddy was now an apprentice jeweller and making the engagement and wedding rings himself. A very promising young man was the opinion of his employers.

Chronologically younger than Freddy, nevertheless Tabby approached maturity at an earlier age; *many girls did!* Nobody had come up with an explanation of girls maturing before boys. There wasn't much in the line of analysing or self-analysing – *it was just how it was!*

VE day, Victory over Europe and VJ day, Victory over Japan, had meant more weddings than at any time in history! Six years of their lives given to their King and Country – men and women were hell-bent on enjoying life once more. The women sadly appeared to outnumber the men – so many young boys lay peacefully at *rest* in foreign fields. Young boyish hopes and dreams consigned to ashes. Far, far away, from their homes and loved ones. The universal accord was *we could never repay their sacrifice* – not in a million years.

'Enough tears to compete with Niagara Falls or the River Thames,' said Freddy's mother. She thanked God that Freddy had been too young for call-up before the end of the war. When his call-up did come, the MO deferred him – because of the damaged arm and leg from playing rugby. He'd been left with a slight limp, a pinched nerve in his left shoulder and his right arm was semi-stiff. He'd tackled a far bigger opponent than himself, hit a post and was unconscious for forty-eight hours. Luckily, no brain damage but it was the end of his rugby playing days. He was deferred, grade 3. As the years went by he did get better but by then there would be no more call-up.

Tabby'd been pleased – she couldn't bear the thought that he might have to go to Palestine for two years! Some of Freddy's relations were in Palestine.

Housing was a problem for people of all ages. It was the norm to get married and live in one room – a bed-sit in your parents, relatives, or neighbour's houses. People rushed to put their names down on council lists – some were still on the lists thirty years later! Priority was given to those with young children – the more babies you had, the more points you got, and you climbed the housing ladder quicker. There was gossip about blocks of flats being built but nobody could envisage it!

In Clapham Junction, the Braithewaites had relatives renting in the private sector, three or more storeys – with one toilet for several families. What the bathroom was like nobody knew, they'd not been privileged to observe for themselves. A cousin who had been a Desert Rat, came home to live in one of those houses in the basement, with one half of their window below ground level. A hero; there until he died on his sixty-second birthday, making an early morning cup of tea!

In a land fit for heroes! It left a bitter taste in many a mouth. In the East End of London there were private landlord houses – *condemned before the First World War*, with no bathrooms, and only outside toilets! Survived the blitz, the doodle-bugs, the buzz-bombs, the landmines and heavy bombing! A relative who lived in one of those streets vouchsafed that not a single occupier was killed or blown-up there! Her grandmother had lived in that particular street all her married life, brought her family up, and the men all returned safe from the war. Outside toilets were not unusual in the East End and elsewhere, right up to forty years or more after the war. But that was jumping ahead. Tabby didn't know that!

Some houses still had gaslight downstairs, in the kitchens and the bedrooms, with just the two downstairs rooms with electric light! A chamber pot was kept under the bed or a galvanised or enamel bucket in a corner of the bedroom. You had to be brave to go downstairs and out into the backyard after dark, to the outside loo, especially in *inclement* weather.

Jean's relative had such a house, and Jean hated the outside lavatory. If it rained heavily she had to ford the huge puddle of water in the sunken concrete between the backdoor and the lavatory. The WC they called it, and there was no Walter Raleigh to give you a hand with his cloak! The lavatories had no lighting at all! You took a torch with you, and wore your wellingtons!

The gas mantles were the bane of Jean's life as a child. She always managed to accidentally poke the match through the mantle and had to pop round the oil shop for a new one!

One day, feeling daring, Tabby related to Freddy about Ginger's passion for French kissing. His teeth gleamed like the Pearly Gates. 'D'ya want me to teach ya?'

They were walking, arms lovingly entwined, from the Odeon that particular night. They'd been to see the old groaner Bing Crosby's latest film: Freddy was a staunch fan. The street lights were lit, but there were dark alleyways where many a young swain, with ulterior motives, judiciously steered his amour. Freddy was no exception. He squeezed Tabby until she felt fit to burst. Giggling she related about Ginger and his

198

fanciful ambition to add her to his harem! 'But I didn't let him,' she said breathlessly. 'He didn't get nowhere with me, Freddy, cross me 'eart, 'opes ter die...!' Her words trailed off ... the blood was pounding in her ears, the boom, boom making her senses swim. Freddy held her tighter and tighter, her limbs were like jelly ... feeling herself drowning in oceans of love. Freddy's tongue was reaching, exploring, she was glad it was Freddy – not Ginger's initiation! Her carefully applied lipstick, in the ladies' lavatory at the Odeon during the interval was now but a memory. The fierce onslaught of Freddy's eager questing lips almost ate her. Ravenous he was! He stopped to come up for air. Tabby's heart was racing like a fast engine by now. His hot breath fanned her flaming cheeks, as he nuzzled her neck, her ears, wherever he could reach skin!

'I didn't give into 'im, I didn't; honest Freddy!'

'Soppy date, I know you didn't, he told me!'

Tabby felt poleaxed! She came back to earth so fast a bucket of water would have sizzled! 'He told you? Why should *he* tell *you?* I mean, I didn't know you knew Ginger?'

'Don't worry about Ginger, Tabby –he's not all that bad!'

Indignantly she wrenched herself free from his arms of steel, not without difficulty! 'Not all that bad – you don't know him!'

He laughed, cuddling her back into his tensile steeled arms. 'Feel a bit better now, love?'

She couldn't vent her ire on her Freddy, she permitted him to make a fuss, soothing her with little, gentle kisses.

It really was lovely to be cuddled, thought Tabby happily, until she remembered they'd been talking about Ginger and then Freddy had adroitly tried to change the subject. 'Well, let me tell you sumfink, 'ee is not a nice boy at all – he's horrible.'

'Tabby, stop and think! Can't you see he's got a man's body and feelings! But he's still only a boy! 'E's always looked older than his age; it's not his fault, nature has tried to turn him into a man before he's mentally ready or it! Yes! I do know Ginger – he played rugger before he got too fat. Great player he was. Didn't you know that love?'

She confessed she'd known he'd played rugby when he was younger and her mother always said 'Ginger's older than his age – he's a big boy,' and her father said, 'He ain't a boy – he's a man!' and Henry had shook his head saying, 'Makes no difference Jean – he looks like a man and he knows 'ow ter use 'is weapon. Anyway ... so there!' Sighing, Henry added, 'The boy's a man ... ask anybody at the pub ... 'ee doesn't go inter The King's Oak 'cos the guv'nor knows 'is age ... but any bloke'll tell yer – Ginger's a man! Iffen yer wants ter be a bit of a smart Alec, Jean, tell me he's a boy when 'e puts a bun in some girl's oven, tell me then!'

Freddy actually envied Ginger his feminine conquests, he wished he could persuade Tabby – he felt sure he could, but had hesitated – Jean had taken him aside one day, and asked him to take care because she was her youngest and none of her girls had buns in the oven before marriage. Prob'ly not for want of trying, thought Freddy, bemused but annoyed at Jean's insistence. For the life of him he couldn't see any hot-blooded bloke not wanting to try-it-on with the beautiful Braithewaite girls. A man would have to be made of stone not to! He made an attempt to mollify Tabby; she didn't usually get in such a flap. Obviously, Ginger's name was anathema to her.

'I know Ginger likes a bit of fluff, sweetheart, but, what man or boy doesn't? Look around you – there's far more girls than boys, three or more blokes after every girl! Change the subject! How would you like me to teach you French kissing?'

'What now? How do you know how to French kiss?'

'Me uncle of course, helped liberate Paris didn't he? Such beautiful girls – they were so grateful to be free they were giving it away, that's what he said – honest! Couldn't do enough to thank their saviours they couldn't. I'm not sure how he was there at the liberation – it was De Gaulle and his men who got there first! Anyway, he married his French girl – she's my aunt now. I never did tell you – remind me to sometime; lives in the Cotswolds.'

Tabby desperately tried to shush her giggling – why she was giggling she didn't quite know; it set Freddy off! Seemingly an inane thing to do – but then some kind of giggles were wholly appropriate to young lovers! And, afterwards, they would wonder what they'd been giggling for.

Tabby put in another ha'porth wanting to know if there was such a thing as English kissing or American kissing or even Italian kissing.

'Cor blimey, Tabby, why not be done with it

and call it international kissing, because if it wasn't it is now!'

Tabby's highly infectious giggling was, by now, threatening to choke her!

Freddy told her she was a minx. 'You tie a bloke into knots – fancy you thinking of that sort of thing! Come to think of it maybe there is a difference, but how the bloomin' hell should I know? I'll have to ask my uncle!'

'He's had plenty of flavours then?'

'Shush Tabby – give over, do, how should I know – wasn't out in foreign countries with him was I – how the heck should I know?'

Luckily her face was in the shadows, Freddy couldn't see her deeply flushed face: she was curious about this so-called French kissing. It had become all the rage since the outbreak of war. Some girls said it was more lustful kissing – others said it was awful – even others said it's a good giggle and great fun. But, it was unanimously agreed it depended on *who was* French kissing you.

Freddy, considering himself a man of action – wasted no further time, Tabby, caught unawares, found, to her astonishment the art of French kissing – Freddy's tongue skilfully prised apart her moist, sweet lips, as he darted it snakelike, down her throat. Tabby found herself reciprocating making Freddy so terribly hot and excited he was pushing his body hard and urgently, his feverishness almost overcoming her sense of preservation. Uttering sharp high-pitched gasps, she struggled in his vice-like grasp. She'd not known Freddy was so strong and determined. At

202

the sound of her shrieks the bedroom window of a house backing on to the alleyway flew open. An enraged man's voice bellowed 'Bloody cats! I'll throw me boot at yer! Yer randy moggies! I'll turn yer into cat's meat! *Stop yer caterwauling will yer?* I can't sleep for yer bloody row. The bloody war's over – 'n' we still can't git any ruddy peace cost of bloody cats! Yer orl ought ter 'ave been drownded at birth! Orl right Ethel – orl right love – wotcha mean I'm waking the bloody neighbours! 'Taint me! It's them bloody tomcats in that there alleyway. Must be after our Fluffy they must! Too bad – I brought her in an hour ago. Bloody randy tomcats! Need castrating them does – castrating I sez! I'll bloody castrate them iffen I catches them near our Fluffy! Cats! Worse than dogs in 'eat them are!'

Freddy and Tabby froze with bated breath … all along the terrace row, back windows were being flung open. Irate voices slanging each other… 'Wot the bloody 'ell – can't a bloke 'ave a goodnight's sleep? Iffen it ain't the air raids it's the bloody cats! Blinkin' toms! Castrate 'em orl I sez, yerse – castrate them orl!'

Above the general maelstrom, now well in its stride a woman's voice mockingly shouted 'Yer talkin' abaht yerseln, Tony? Yer a blinkin' tom ain't yer! At least them there cats knows wot it's orl abaht – they get more'n I do!' 'Yer shut yer mouf Lottie – yer didn't do so bad in the war!' 'Woz that my fault – youse weren't 'ere, woz yer?' 'No! Good job I wasn't, wasn't it? Be'ind the Maginot Line, wasn't I – fightin' fer the likes of youse ter 'ave yer oats in peace – wasn't I?'

203

Resembling a stone tableau, Tabby and Freddy clung to each other, his hand was over her mouth to stifle her giggles.

Crash! Bang! Wallop! More noise! Windows slammed, curtains were redrawn, one by one the lights went out, and the terraced homes settled down for the rest of the night – hopefully in peacefulness!

Mentally, Tabby welcomed the interruption to Freddy's forward love-making. Her mother had warned her not to go all the way!

'A decent bloke likes a *virgin wife*, lovey – no matter wot they sez ter tempt yer – they do yer know! Yerse! A bloke likes a virgin bride – yerse! Mark my words, lovey – yer goin' ter walk up that aisle of St Mary's in yer white dress with the Madonna lilies and London pride in yer bouquet! Youse'll look as pretty as a picture lovey, yerse yer will!'

For the life of her – Tabby honestly didn't know what a virgin was – what made her a virgin, and what didn't? Nobody had explained to her *in layman's language*, there were no books to explain it to her; none that she knew of. She didn't dare ask her sisters – they might ridicule her for being stupid!

Gertie had told Jean, 'Many brides are not virgins, Mum!'

'I know, I know, our Gertie, but it ain't right is it? Either youse a virgin or youse isn't – yer can't knowingly walk up that there aisle in white can yer – iffen yer ain't a virgin bride? Besides Tabbys' me last girl ter be married in white, in church. Two of me girls is 'aving register office

204

weddings. Nivver seems like real weddings, them don't, nah!'

Gertie sighed heavily. Jean was on her high horse again! She'd been just the same with the rest of her sisters. Two had married in registry office weddings. That rankled with Jean – Henry couldn't care less, 'As long as them's married respectably!'

'Youse means the registry office, Mum, not "register's"!'

'Cor, luv a duck, our Gertie – jist sez that, didn't I? The "register's" office!'

Gertie gave it up as a bad job! Unbeknown to Jean – Gertie did know that her mother was not a virgin when she married Henry. Her grand-mother had accidentally let the cat out of the bag – Jean's true age – and the gleeful Gertie only had to put two and two together to make four!

'Orl right, orl right, our Gertie – yer orlways 'as ter 'ave the last word! Tabby'll be me last daughter ter be married in church, wiv orl the trimmin's, in the sight of the Lord, Amen! Us Braithewaites'll show the six streets wot we can do now the war's been and gorn orl this time. The war's over!'

'The war's over!' Gertie was beginning to hate that overused phrase! It had outlived its usefulness, the novelty had worn off and it was hackneyed. Sighing, she thought how lovely it would be to wipe the slate clean from all those tedious worn out phrases.

Her husband had demurred. It was his con-sidered opinion, 'We've got ter keep using them, lovey, we mustn't nivver fergit wot it was orl abaht, 'n' we mustn't let our children or their children fergit either! It's our sacred duty, my girl! To all those lads and lasses in those graves in Europe and the Far East. Nay love, nay lass, thee and I must nivver fergit em!'

Gertie's husband was a genial, bluff Yorkshire-man, as Yorkshire as Yorkshire pudding, Jean had commented upon first meeting him. Gertie'd met him at the Palais and ended up teaching him the foxtrot. He appeared to have two left feet – eventually he overcame that and mastered the waltz, quick-step and palais glide. He'd never gone back to Yorkshire – Gertie the apple of her parents' eyes wouldn't leave her mother.

The talk now at 48 Grantie Road was 'the wedding this...' and the 'wedding that...' the empty whisky bottle was nearly full of thrupenny bits with everyone turning their pockets and purses out on Friday nights! More was added from the kitty whenever they played Pontoon or Penny-in-the-kitty.

Jean was determined this was going to be the wedding of all weddings. Cheerfully she brought home a National Savings Stamp book and badgered the family to purchase five bob's worth of stamps every week. Henry paid the deposit on the catering at the Civic Centre: it was to be a full spread, sit-down meal at 48! The Civic Centre Catering provided the waitresses.

So many neighbours and friends vowed to be at the church that Jean became anxious there might not be enough room! Gertie allayed her fears, changed the subject slightly – to flowers.

'I've started paying orff at the florists, Mum ...

fer the bride's and bridesmaids' flowers and the carnation buttonholes.'

'Oh! Ain't that nice of yer, our Gertie, I loves yer! Make sure it's a sheaf – not one of them round ones!'

Having already discussed it with Tabby, Gertie explained there would be a sheaf of Madonna lilies, London pride and lily of the valley: the bridesmaids were having mixed carnations.

Gertie was married in 1945 after the end of the VE day. All the world was getting married then! The churches and registry offices could barely cope. History would show that in 1945 there were some 40,000 weddings! Those who wanted church weddings were lucky if they could get them! It was sad, but, they gritted their teeth and smiled, they'd been doing that for six years: they made the best of it! Some promised themselves they'd have a church blessing on their Silver Wedding Anniversaries.

''Ave anuvver cuppa, Gertie, like some more stew? Yer've got ter feed the baby inside yer – yer know!'

'Don't I know it!' wailed Gertie in mock horror!

'I'm twice as big as when I 'ad our little Johnny.' Her eyes welled up tearfully, through a complication at birth – she'd lost little Johnny. She hadn't seen him –they wouldn't let her – but he was still in her heart – her Johnny!

'Look at the size of this stinker – 'ave yer ever seen a woman so big? I wish he'd drop ... little tinker, doesn't wanna come into this world – does he? Should've dropped him some time ago!

Can't say I blame 'im. Look at the state of the world! At the pictures the uvver night – I sat at the end of the row – couldn't squeeze into the uvver seats, I couldn't. The usherette were ever so nice she were. Warned everybody in our row not to try and squeeze past me or she'd 'ave their guts for garters iffen they did! Luckily we weren't at the sides, so people went out the uvver end! It were a right laugh I can tell yer, Mum! Yerse it were! A real comedienne she were – gave me a free ice cream in the interval – before the lights went up she rushed to the ice cream girl to get served first. Anyway! As I were jist abaht ter say, Mum, we saw the newsreel. Showing them there concentration camps they were ... I know we saw some of it after the war ... a long time ago now ... but this was worse, some captured newsfilm! Oh Mum, oh Mum!' Gertie burst into tears. 'All us women in the Odeon ... we woz screaming and crying and orl the men were shouting out "there ain't goin' ter be anuvver war as long as we live." They showed us the gas ovens and piles of bodies again. Oh Mum, I felt so terrible, *I wished I hadn't had that ice cream,* then the baby moved, and I got a stabbing pain! There were mile after mile of pathetic figures, some with jist their clothes, others wiv pitiful bundles – refugees they sez they were! Wot'll 'appen ter them orl Mum? Everybody's talkin' about it, orl the cinema's 're showin' it. British Gaumont News – Pathe News, orl showin' it...!'

Jean soothed her agitated daughter, warning her to think of the baby and telling her she had no right to go and see it! Weeping and almost incoherent, Gertie said they didn't know it was going to be shown. 'It were too horrible for words, Mum, it really were.' Her sodden hankie scrubbed at her water-filled eyes. ''Ow could any sane person do that to other human beings? Oh the bones, the bones.' She shuddered! 'At first … we … didn't … realise they woz 'uman bones … we thought they woz animal bones … then the cameras showed close-ups. Some of the women threw up and 'ad to leave the cinema. I wanted to, but I'd've been crushed as they rushed to the exits.'

'There there, lovey, don't upset yourseln – or the baby. Think of the baby, pet!' Jean held a cup of sweet tea to Gertie's trembling lips. 'Drink up, lovey, you've 'ad a shock! You must stay calm or you'll 'urt the baby. Yer don't wanna upset the baby do yer, lovey?'

Gertie sniffled and wiped her eyes slowly, melodramatically. 'Doctor MacFaddie sez this mornin' – the same thing ter me! I told 'im abaht the newsreel and he sez the world must see it – we must nivver fergit. That's wot 'ee sez ter me, *"It would be a gross betrayal of all those who suffered and died!"'*

'We'll 'ave no more talk of dyin' in this 'ere 'ouse Gertie. Come on, lovey, fergit it – yer bringin' a new life into the world, lovey, take care of yourself!'

Her daughter nodded slowly and heaved a heartfelt sorrowful sigh, as if all the world was on her shoulders. 'Doctor MacFaddie said if I don't drop the baby by tomorrow he'll git me straight into hospital and 'ave 'em bring me on!'

209

Soothingly Jean assured Gertie. 'It'll be all hunky-dory!' She walked Gertie home – a room in the house of a friend, who had a bit more spare room than at 48. 'The way yer waddling, Gertie, I can't see 'ow yer haven't dropped that bairn yet! It's right low is the bairn.'

'I ain't dropped it, Mum, but it's pressing on me bladder – iffen I don't git ter a lavatory I'm going ter leave a puddle outside yer neighbour's gate!'

Chapter Nine

Tabby's voice uttered a high pitched scream, Jean froze to the marrow – catching her breath in a short, sharp, drawn-out gasp.

'It's a *boy*, Mum ... it's a *boy!* Our Gertie's got a boy!'

'Praise the Lord!' breathed Jean fervently, devoutly crossing herself. She hadn't forgotten how to praise Him – she'd been a Sunday school teacher at the mission in Limehouse when she was barely fifteen. Not that she went to church very often now, but she most certainly believed in the Saviour and wouldn't have His name taken in vain in her house.

Tears cascading down her rosy cheeks – Tabby dropped the bombshell! 'And another *boy* ... and another *boy* ... *Triplets!* Mum! *All boys!* Our Gertie's got *three boys!*'

Struggling into her best coat, tears of happiness flowing like a waterfall, Jean could hardly believe such good news. Three babies – not one! All boys! They'd not long got back from leaving Gertie at the hospital where Matron had said, 'It'll be induced tomorrow after you've had a good night's rest.'

Self-evidently – the babies had arrived of their own accord, Jean snatched the telegram from Tabby's fluttering hands, her own weren't much steadier as she read the good news out aloud.

ALL BOYS STOP THREE OF THEM STOP
SISTER SAID SHE'S GOING TO LINE
THEM UP STOP ON THE LAWN STOP THE
WHOLE WARD HAS HAD BOYS STOP
LOVE GERTIE STOP.

'Oh, Tabby, the Lord Giveth and the Lord Taketh
– I mean the Lord Taketh … young Johnny, but
the Lord Giveth … three boys … all at once! Wait
'til yer Dad knows! Let's get back down the
hospital – I'll go potty if the buses are running
late again!'

'Can't take Benjie, Mum, 'ee's too young, they
won't let 'im in! He's still upstairs asleep, shall I
bring him down?'

'No. I'll ask Maisie. Nah, on second thoughts
you go and ask Maisie ter come and stay wiv him.
He'll be fretful iffen he duzzn't 'ave his afternoon
sleep. Leave him be, lovey. Blimey Tabby, I've got
three grandsons orl at once I 'ave an' all. Thank
you our Father in Heaven. Thank yer most
Gracious Lord. He must've known our Gertie
pined fer young Johnny an' he's given her three to
make up for it!' Quickly she crossed herself again
and kissed the plain crucifix which her grandmother had given her many years long gone. It
was a *plain cross* – Jean loved it – she couldn't
bear to see a figure on a cross. She said it
reminded her too much of our Lord's suffering.
The *Bible* said, 'Thou shalt not bow down to any
graven image' so Jean took that literally and
would *never* have a figure on the cross in her
house. 'A plain cross was good enough for our

212

Lord – so it's good enough for me!'

Tabby was back with Maisie before Jean had finished donning her headscarf! 'Three boys, Maisie! 'Ow abaht that eh? Come on Tabby bye-bye, Maisie.'

Scurrying to the bus stop, Jean was arrested in her stride. 'Mum, wot abaht the Dopeggy twins?'

'Oh Lord! I clean forgot them.' She rushed back to Maisie. 'The Dopeggy's 'll be 'ere later … takin' Benjie out for a while. Make sure they wash his face an' spruce 'im up a bit will yer, lovey?'

'Course I will Jean – now push orff or you'll miss yer bus. Give me love ter Gertie!'

To avoid confusion, Jean's three sets of twins, Dora and Peggy, Sally and Sue, and Ivy and Daisy, were given pet names within the family circle. They became the Dopeggy twins; the Sually twins; the Iveday twins.

Coaxing Jean to be faster, Tabby wondered what they'd call the triplets. 'Gosh, Mum! *Triplets!* Won't that make the neighbours sit up! Those fertile Braithewaites they'll be callin' us … yer a granmuvver three times, Mum! An' Dad's a granddad three times! Whoops! I'm an aunty.'

'Yeah, an' our little Benjie is an uncle three times and him still only a toddler himself. Uncle Benjie!' Jean guffawed heartily. Passing various neighbours she couldn't restrain herself any longer: 'It's a boy – *three* boys! Our Gertie's 'ad *triplets!* Got *free* grandsons we have! Got a telegram from the hospital – didn't we?'

Only one house had a telephone in all the six streets – and that was the private rent man.

213

'Slow down a bit, Mum, or you'll get a stitch! They ain't going ter run away, Mum – jist been borned, ain't they? Anuvver five minutes fer the bus. Triplets – wonder wot she'll call 'em, Mum?'

'Put yer best foot forward, Tabby. The bus might be early; bet it comes in a banana special about five buses one behind each other!'

Depending how heavy the traffic was in London the bus travelled from Ladbroke Grove down Oxford Street, via Regent street, down the Haymarket, through the City, through Poplar Plaistow, East Ham, Barking and to Dagenham, then it turned round and went back.

'We don't want that number, Mum. We ain't goin' ter the London Hospital – we're goin' the uvver way ter Romford.'

'Yeah! Yer right, love – orl of a doodah I am – yerse. Yer wouldn't fink I'd had fourteen of me own would yer?'

Their bus was in sight, just turning the corner, followed by five more – the *banana special*. Boarding the first one, they sat down thankfully. Looking back, Jean realised they should have known Gertie was having more than one baby. She'd doubled her bulk in the last month of pregnancy and could barely waddle: like an Emperor Penguin with its egg. But the midwife was adamant she could only hear one heart beat. And she'd only felt one baby. Gertie's extraordinary bulk was cheerfully laid at Jean's door! Her stews! Which Gertie had an abnormal craving for. Jean had supplied her with nourishing stew either at her house or she took some to her home. 'Yer can't beat a bowl of broth.' Gertie

214

obediently supped!

For a laugh, Jean teased Tabby, to while away the journey, telling her she might have twins or triplets.

'No fear!' said Tabby firmly.

'Yer nivver does know,' said her mother.

Tabby tried to take the bull by the horns explaining that her and Freddy planned on having two children, one of each, using the new fangled birth control methods.

Jean merely said, 'Yer'll 'ave wot God gives yer and be thankful!' She wasn't interested in birth control. Leave it to Mother Nature was her opinion, and that people shouldn't meddle with nature or play at God!

'How are youse avoiding more babies then, Mum, yer still young enuff ter 'ave 'em?'

'Mind yer own bleedin' business, our Tabby. Nice girls don't talk about things they know nuffink abaht!'

Jean refused to elaborate any further – it just wasn't nice to talk about such things until you were married; by which time it was too late!

Outside the hospital they purchased a couple of bunches of flowers from the barrow boy. He was doing a roarin' trade. The interior of the hospital smelt like hospitals always smell – polish and antiseptic and the odour of *baked metal bedpans* permeated from the sterilisers.

Jean spotted Gertie in the end ward. She looked radiantly beautiful, serene and peaceful like all new mothers do. Already an attractive young woman, she was positively blooming with her happy smile and air of complacency of a job well done. Her pretty bedjacket, knitted in a difficult lacy pattern by Jean, added to her lustre. It wasn't every day that one gave birth to triplets! Didn't Gertie know it! The nurses and mums on the ward were amazed. She'd no idea she was carrying triplets. She'd been expecting one and got three *Three bags full – Gertie* they were calling her: yes, three bags full!

'Here Gertie – some flowers fer yer, 'ow is yer gittin' on, lovey?'

With hugs and kisses, almost squashing the pretty fragrant blooms, they clung together, their tears of joy mingling poetically. Struggling to extricate herself from her mother and sister, Gertie's muffled words were almost unheard 'Give over – do, will youse two, what're we orl cryin' for? Supposed ter be a happy occasion, innit?'

The hovering young nurse extricated the flowers to put them in a vase – unrolling the wrapping paper to see if they were red and white blooms. 'No, okay, I'll leave you for five minutes, then we'll fetch the triplets in for your inspection. The Sister says they're gorgeous. Matron said it's been all boys this week and she's going to line the little buggers up on the lawn outside – *all* boys!'

Blushing prettily, the nurse hurried away. Tabby was intrigued, wanting to know what she meant about red and white flowers. Gertie explained it was a hospital superstition: red and white flowers meant blood and death!

This was a new one to Jean, hers had all been born at home and she'd been lucky and thankful for the few flowers she'd got, never mind the colours of them!

'Where's Dad, Mum?' Jean was deliberately vague, which never deceived Gertie in the least.

'He's somewhere, I'm not quite sure where! He'll be over the moon with his three grandsons!'

'And where's me little Benjie?'

'Yer wanna know a lot don't yer, our Gertie?'

Gertie said she felt it important for Benjie and her father to see the babies as soon as possible; anyway she was missing her little Benjie already. She'd seen him every day of his life since he was born she didn't want her brother to think she didn't love him any more.

Tabby intervened and explained he was too young to visit in hospital, it wasn't allowed.

Heads were turning in the ward. Matron in all her huge voluptuous glory, starched frilly, white cap perched proudly aloft; her deep blue dress covered by a crisp whiter-than-white, starched apron, with not a speck on it; and her wide black belt with its official fancy silver clasp – was sailing down the long room. Her apron crackling starchily, she was enormous, at least seventeen stone and no more than five feet two inches in height. Legs, like 'tree trunks' encased in regulation thick black lisle stockings held up her bulk with great aplomb. Her equally enormous bosom well-rounded, thrust up high, gave her an almost 'Rubenesque' appearance. She was obviously enjoying the sensation her entrance was causing in 'her domain'. 'Like a battleship she were, Henry,' said Jean, later that night.

Just as starched as Matron, the Sister followed in like manner; a few paces behind in deference to rank. Her frilly armbands on her upper arms were uniform with her cap, which defied gravity, being well anchored with Kirby grips.

Following their superiors, came the dainty little nurses – obviously probationers, they deemed it an honour to be in the presence of the dragon the esteemed and admirable hospital matron, *whose word was a law unto itself in her hospital,* and woe betide any person who upset the equilibrium of her vast domain. She was omnipotent was Matron, she knew it and she ran a tight ship. No visits one minute before visiting half-hour and no visitors left behind within seconds of the bell being rung! And no more than two visitors at any given time at a bedside.

And there were the triplets! All eyes craned to see them, carried by second-year nurses, they slept blissfully, unaware of the oooos and ahhhs which had greeted their appearance.

Jean was ecstatic, holding them each in turn – she broke down sobbing as if her heart would break.

'Come, come, my dear, why are you crying, have you no babies of your own?'

'Fourteen,' sniffed Jean into her saturated hankie – 'fourteen!'

Matron's countenance couldn't have been more surprised than if Jean had said she'd just come from the moon!

'Fourteen! You don't look old enough. *Fourteen!'*

'Thirteen girls and one boy – three sets of twins.'

Matron swung round – her eagle eyes fixing those of everybody in the ward. 'Did you hear

218

that? This lady has got *thirteen daughters* – and we haven't had a single one in the last seven days, have we?'

'No, Matron,' the patients duly chorused; they liked Matron, she was a bit of a wag with a droll dry wit.

The triplets were removed to the nursery once more and Gertie mentioned she'd chosen Edward for one of the triplets; but hadn't decided for the other two.

Her husband, who'd already been and gone back to work, had liked Edward and he wasn't really fussy about names – said she could choose what she liked.

Putting their three heads together, Gertie, Jean and Tabby came up with, Edward, 4lbs 8 ounces; Thomas a few ounces less and Peter at a mere 4lbs. 'Now we have three biblical names,' announced Jean contentedly!

'Don't yer mean two, Mum, Thomas and Peter?'

'Nah! Three in our family, Gertie. Thomas, Peter and little Benjamin. A Jewish woman told me Benjamin is in the *Bible* – I can't remember where and it means *son of my right hand.* Whether that's true or not I couldn't tell yer, bu that's wot she sez! Anyway I know for sure that Thomas the doubter is in the *Bible* and Peter – the Rock.'

''Cor blimey, Mum, youse do come up wiv fings in yer bacon bonce sometimes! Still iffen it makes yer happy!'

So, Edward, Thomas, Peter it was to be.

Jean reminded Gertie that, when she left hospital after the customary ten days, she was to be

219

sure to go and *be churched* first. 'Yer have ter go and thank the Lord fer being delivered from all that pain and all that – yer knows I orlways did, Gertie. Then the priest blesses yer.'

Gertie promised to adhere to *the churching of women* routine, even though she never went to church except for weddings, funerals and christenings. To Jean that meant no odds, all women should be churched before they take the baby out in public – babies in this case. 'I were churched eleven times I were – yer ask yer Dad!'

The ding-donging of the handbell clamoured down the ward. *'Visitors – out!* Or face the wrath of sister!'

'They're beautiful babies, lovey, yer be a good girl and get some rest – make the most of yer lyin' in and get yer strenff up – yer going ter be needin' it, lovey.

'Yer babies are a credit ter yer, Gertie, lovely colourin' thems got – like they've been on a holiday in the countryside; hardly a wrinkle on their little faces, my precious darlings.'

'Come on, Mum,' Tabby tugged her mother's sleeve, 'we've gotta go – ta-ta, Gertie, see yer tomorrer.'

Tabby was glad she was having a few days off this week. Because Gertie was two weeks over due, Jean wanted Tabby home with her 'just in case of complications'. If she'd dropped the baby at home she'd have had to help Jean, and there was little Benjie to think of. It was all right to leave him with someone for a few hours but not all day! Personally Tabby was of the opinion that it wouldn't have bothered Benjie – he loved

220

people to bits, whoever they were. A gregarious soul was how Freddy termed him! Another new word she'd just learned from Freddy – a bit of a mouthful!

Progress down the six streets was hampered with all the good wishes and proffered tots of sherry 'to warm the cockles of yer heart' or 'ter wet the baby's head' changed quickly to the plural – *babies!* Jean felt like the sherry was pouring from her ears. A nice glass of Guinness or milk stout wouldn't have gone amiss! The world and his wife wanted to know all about the triplets.

Yes! The Braithewaites had done it again. Given them something to natter about after her own three sets of twins!

Triplets this time round – her Gertie's babies – her beloved Gertie's babies. God bless them, one and all!

Chapter Ten

'It's a *fortune* – a bloody fortune! That's wot it is! I tell yer this, Jean – I wouldn't mind winning *that!* Nah! I wouldn't mind winnin' *that* on the bloody pools. Nah! I bloody well wouldn't...' spluttered Henry, venting his spleen on nobody in particular ... his emotions threatening to overcome him ... he was nearly incandescent with rage that *he* hadn't won the pools this week, nor any other week, come to that! And, he'd been doing the pools for bloody donkeys' years ... dreaming of what *he* would do with *his* winnings ... when he got the Big One Up! He shook his head dolefully, his eyes bulging in his fury. He was beside himself with his rage.

'So yer keep tellin' us – Henry! Wot're youse getting orl het up abaht? It ain't youse as been an' won it! Be different iffen youse had won it wouldn't it?'

Henry would not be placated. Henry would not shut up. No! Not Henry. When he got his teeth to grips with something, he hung on like a ferocious bulldog being baited in a pit. 'First dividend, woman – in the paper – look at it, woman, first dividend. There it is! In black and white. Yer c'n see it fer yerself, a bloody fortune!'

He thrust the day's newspaper under his wife's nose. Jean sighed heavily. Henry always allowed himself to get worked up like this whenever there was a jackpot on the football pools. She shoved the paper away forcibly, sighing loudly. 'Yer read it ter me, Henry – yer read it ter me.'

'*One thousand five hundred pounds* – blimey! I wouldn't have minded the five hundred quid! Could've bought a little cottage and a car wiv that I could an' all, yerse, I could've. Bloody 'ell!'

'Mind yer language Henry! Innocent little ears is in this room – ain't there, me precious babies?'

The triplets cooed harmoniously to their doting grandmother's delight. Couldn't do anything wrong in her eyes could they? They were toddling now and catching up with little Benjamin – their tiny uncle who could never see enough of them. As far as Benjie was concerned the triplets were *his* babies! Hadn't his big sister Gertie brought them home from the hospital – a long time ago – to be his playmates? He cuddled them if they cried and helped to feed them – but he didn't like their dirty nappies!

'Saucy little wee-wee-wee-ers, like youse was, Benjie,' smiled Jean, kissing her pride and joy – her only son – she never called him our son, it was always my Benjie, my son.

'Me Benjie not wet nappy – me wet me wee-wee in potty,' said Benjie sternly. More grown-up compared to the triplets, but still under school age and still the love of Gertie's life, she absolutely adored him – even though she could eat her own sons. All four boys were Gertie's babies – and she wouldn't have it any other way. Benjamin, Edward, Thomas and Peter ruled the roost round the Braithewaites' house!

The other Braithewaite grandchildren – so far –

were all girls! So, there was no lack of females to spoil the boys. They were sitting happily on the living room carpet square, playing with cars and aeroplanes which Henry had skilfully carved out of wood ... running them backwards and forwards on the polished lino surrounding the carpet square.

He was very good at whittling wood, was Henry. His father, long gone dead, had been a carpenter, so Henry had grown up with wood. He could tell you the name of any piece you cared to show him. He didn't think of his departed parents very often, they'd been very straight laced, dyed in the wool folk. But, gazing at young Peter, he was suddenly struck by his resemblance to his late father.

Jean had expected to have twice as many grandchildren by now. Expecting her married girls to have a bun in the oven every year or so – just like herself; but they hadn't! Even more amazing – none of them had fallen on their wedding night.

'Things is different now, Mum, us girls 've got a bit more sense; us don't 'ave ter 'ave babies, unless we really want them or iffen it's an accident.'

Jean couldn't quite keep up with her modern daughters who wanted to gad about after marriage. She lectured them sharply, 'God made women ter 'ave babies, new babies, new blood, that's wot keeps the world turnin' over.'

Daisy patiently explained that there were ways and means nowadays for modern girls not to be always *up the spout*. They didn't have to rely on their menfolk to take precautions, they could do that for themselves if they wanted to prevent a seed taking root. The modern generation had more choice: anyway, they liked going dancing and to the flicks about five times a week. When their husbands finished work at lunchtime Saturdays they went to watch West Ham – the Hammers – play at Upton Park or to play in friendly matches over the park – so the sisters went to afternoon matinees together or shopping up London – the West End. Or, they went cycling in the country, coming back with masses of bluebells 'on their last gasp' hanging forlornly from their panniers. Then there were the picnics, works outings, Beanos to Southend, Margate or Bournemouth. Sometimes they went on a week's holiday to Mr Billy Butlin's Holiday Camps – great communal fun! Jean's girls felt good to be alive and were making the most of their freedom. Life was for living … and *dirty nappies* were not always in their vision.

Miffed, to say the least, Jean reiterated she'd rather be a *stop-at-home mother*, a traditional one!

She was instantly jolted out of her self-righteousness by being reminded of her ambition to go to work in a factory – after the war ended. Soon after little Benjie'd been born in fact! But she had her answer *pat* blaming it on the euphoria after six long dark painful years of war, nappies, rationing, queuing, et al!

Her decision to remain at home was met with relief by Henry – more so by Gertie after having the triplets. For how would Gertie've managed the four children on her own? If Gertie'd had one

baby, then the plan to leave Benjie with Gertie –
for Jean to go out to work – would have been a
piece-of-cake. The plans of mice and men,
thought Henry! Jean was a very loving and caring
grandmother to *all* of her grandchildren. Even
Henry found himself not going to the Union so
often … he doted on the grandchildren, nearly as
much as Jean. Very much to his wife's surprise, he
couldn't see enough of the little tykes. Yerse!
Gertie'd done all right for herself – three babies
at one drop – pushing up her points on the
housing list – resulting in a brand new prefab
house (like a bungalow) a mere stone's throw
from the six streets. Being devoted to her mother,
that suited Gertie down to the ground – she
never wanted to live far from her mum.

Prefabs – prefabricated one-floor houses – were
jealously coveted in the days when young people
were living in one room (bedsit) with parents, in-
laws or friends – even with grandmothers! They
had their own large back and front gardens –
plenty of room to grow veg – smashing kitchens,
big enough to sit and eat in. Proper modern sink
units – not the old-fashioned Butler sinks. Their
own bathroom was even more of a luxury! Piping
hot water was laid on – no need to carry hot
water up the stairs in buckets, there were no
stairs! Yes, to be sure, the prefabs were very
popular – whole streets of them testified. You
were somebody if you got a council prefab!

Council flats, multi-storied and high-rise, were
slowly making way for rehousing the thousands
still without their own homes: the bombings had
smashed housing to smithereens. Inside the flats

were nice and, depending on how many storeys there were ... if they had communal lifts ... *if the lift was out of action* – a regular occurrence, then it was not much joy lugging a screaming baby and a heavy carriage pram, plus the equally heavy shopping up several flights of stairs; not for eight floors or double that! No wonder the mothers had back problems later on in life! It was every mother's nightmare – to be trapped in a lift with a baby and howling toddlers until the firemen were called to set you free. Then you still had to bump the pram and everything else back up the stairs – or down them! *Designed by men who didn't have to live in them* ... the washing lines were downstairs ... if it rained ... hard luck ... down bumped the pram with the baby and toddlers screaming ... by which time, your washing was soaking wet. It didn't help either ... if you were in the middle of feeding the baby ... then you had a screaming, hungry baby and a howling toddler! And the wet washing of course!

Obviously then, prefabs were very popular – with built-in refrigerator – now there was a luxury indeed! None of the people in the six streets had a fridge at the end of the war – to see one full of food in a friend's house was enough to set the green bug of envy into convulsions! A prefab was preferable to a high-rise flat, even though the rent of the flat was rather high – at two pounds a week, in sterling – they did have some benefits, with their sky-high views from huge picture windows, especially if you overlooked a park.

Edward had toddled over to his grandfather.

227

'Gan-Dad, wheel off car.'

Henry fixed it in a jiffy, smiling at his grandson, he was glad he was home more often these days; the boys were worth their weight in gold.

Gertie was pregnant again – hoping for a girl this time round. Henry had ferried her and Jean to the clinic in an old banger, recently acquired. The Braithewaites now had *wheels,* a new status in the working-class environment of the six streets.

The four boys didn't miss them – they were left in the capable hands of Aunty Maisie who was stuffing them with rich mock cream cakes. They loved Aunty Maisie – best of all they loved being *stuffed.*

Henry felt he was going places at last – he'd branched out as a wheeler-dealer in scrap iron and metal. Whatever he was – he was doing pretty well for himself – and acquiring a bit of *self-respect* now his Union visits had curtailed! Tabby was still living at home – her wages helped swell the family kitty. Henry felt proud that his wife hadn't *had* to go out to work – it made a bloke feel better that way. He was still old-fashioned enough to feel that a man should be able to support his own family. Henry was really worried about money – you could never have enough of it, in his esteemed opinion, but, yes, Henry was doing quite well. Their rent was now sixteen shillings a week for their three-bedroomed house, consisting of two big bedrooms; a boxroom; bathroom; living room; front room and very tiny kitchen. Their landlord was still the private owner – he hadn't actually said anything about selling the numerous properties he possessed in the six streets, but, if he did, then Henry secretly meant to buy it off him – if the price was right. Henry's palate for his *extra curricular activities* had become jaded with the increase and growth of his extended family – the grandchildren. He felt it behove him as their grandfather to set a good example.

So! Henry was happy! Happy to be with his wife! Happy to be with his grandchildren – twenty-four granddaughters and three grand-sons; and young Benjie – the light of his life. *His one and only wonderful son.*

Henry was feeling quite smug. He'd finished decorating the house from top to bottom. To Jean's astonishment – she hadn't known he was so clever – a right handyman was Henry, now! A mate had helped him to build a small glass outerhouse next to the kitchen. The working-class version of Victorian conservatories on a miniature scale! Or so they fondly imagined! It gave the Braithewaites more prestige! A car, and a conservatory – 4ft x 5ft! Henry loved sitting in it, watching the grandchildren playing on the handkerchief-sized lawn, where the air raid shelter had previously existed for six years.

He'd taken to wandering through the house to see what Jean was up to! She'd be in the kitchen, cheerfully stirring her latest concoction of stew. 'Oh! *There you are!*' he'd say, as if it was a revelation. Or she'd be upstairs, brushing her hair, or donning her make-up with the new fangled Pan-stik – which instantly browned a face with thick cream – very popular it hid blemishes expertly. And he'd say again, 'Oh!

There you are!' One day, after six 'Oh! There you ares' in a row, Jean had rounded on him. She was making the bed at the time, he wandered in and said, 'Oh! There you are! You're making the beds!'

'No! Henry. I'm not! I'm dancing the light fantastic! Henry will you please stop following me around like a yearling!'

Backing down the stairs muttering he said he *missed her company* and could he do anything for her? She was bemused at this new Henry and told him to put the kettle on for a cuppa cha and place the heavy tarpaulin over the cast-iron wringer outside, to keep the rain from rotting the heavy rollers.

Shaking her head, Jean wondered if Henry ought to go back to his extra curricular activities more often, again; at least it kept him from under her feet!

It fell to Tabby to explain to him that Jean did love him but felt he was spying on her! Henry's face registered shock.

'I wouldn't do that, love – I just *like* being around yer muvver! There's only you and Benjie at home now. It reminds me of when we only had our first three children … brings back memories it does, love. Yerse!'

'All right, Dad, why don't you and Mum go out togevver a bit more … you're still young, yer ain't ancient! Take Mum to the pub for the darts – she's good at it – could be in the ladies team she could.'

'She should be good, Tabby, taught her before youse lot were borned, I did.'

'There yer are then, Dad! Wotcha waitin' for? Gertie's husband sez he's taking Gertie for the ladies darts' team after the new baby is borned. It's a new ladies team – orl the pubs is havin' them now.'

'Lots of women won't go in the main bars, love – go to the ladies ones they do. All right, I'll do that – Jean never minded the main bar years ago – but the modern women don't seem to like going in the main bars ... I'll 'ave a word wiv yer muvver. 'And he did.

Jean thought it over for barely a few seconds. Obviously this new Henry was trying to get into her good books ... there was no denying it. He seemed to have eased off from *sowing his acres* – advancing years maybe? Whatever. Still only in his forties – but he'd been on the rampage, sowing wild oats for too many years – maybe his *carnal energy* had forsaken him ... maybe love-making with her was the most he could hope to achieve in this new-found Henry.

Most certainly he used up much energy on the house and garden, with the bright green lawn looking a picture – he'd given it a dose of weedkiller which seemed to work a remarkable transformation. He'd made a safe play area for the babies and toddlers – well away from the danger of the old-fashioned mangle, which Jean wouldn't get rid of. She liked to *iron* her sheets, well folded through its heavy rollers. It was just the job, she'd then hang them out on the line stretching the length of the garden on a nice windy day where they flapped and fluttered like a fully rigged sailing ship, in their crisp, bright

231

whiteness – which she achieved by judicious use of the little blue-bag which made the water turn blue but turned the sheets bright white!

The Braithewaites had needed a long clothes line, with their numbers; washing day at the round tin bath and the glass and wood rubbing board was a weekly marathon for Jean. A high pole at one end of the garden, a pulley on the house wall, up by the back bedroom window, and a long clothes prop were the manner of the day for women. When the rope slipped or broke, which it did, the girls had to rush upstairs, lean out of the window and pass the rope back through the pulley.

So he approached Jean and she good humouredly agreed to joining the ladies' darts team. Henry felt quite chuffed; things were beginning to brighten up in his little world, after all! Yes! All-in-all – Henry Braithewaite, you could safely say, apart from not having won the coveted pools jackpot, was feeling very mellow and happy. Until the week he read that the pools first dividend pay-out was a record win! Checking his pools by the radio – no bloody interruptions youse lot – he'd discovered he'd *nearly* won! He'd only needed that figure to be this figure and that figure to be that figure and he'd have won the jackpot! Damn! Perish the thought, so near, yet so far! Week after week it was the same – he never quite made it!

Jean'd laughed, 'Wot yerve nivver 'ad yer duzzn't miss, Henry!'

Glaring at her venting his spleen to whoever was within ear-shot, he'd stormed from the room shouting that he did miss it – missed winning the big one!

Unmollified by being reminded that millions of people felt the same as him – he'd looked in the Sunday newspaper the next day to read that it was the biggest ever pools win! This further exacerbated Henry's ire! All his life he'd dreamed of winning this big one on the pools … all his life! 'Hell and damnation, wot's a bloke ter do – year after year – yer pays yer pools money an' when it's nearly in yer grasp, yer lose it to some other lucky so and so!'

As he slammed out of the house – banging the door thunderously, it frightened the children, the triplets almost jumped out of their skins. Little Tommy went to Jean, putting his head in her lap. 'Grandad angry with Tommy, Grandma?' Cupping his anxious face in her warm hands she kissed him lovingly.

'Grandad not angry with Tommy darling – Grandad angry 'cos he nivver won a lot of money.' Satisfied with this, Tommy, his head still in her lap, closed his eyes and fell asleep.

A frightened Peter joined his triplet, dragging his favourite blanket behind him. He never went anywhere without it, and always slept with his little fingers fingering its satin bound edges until he fell fast asleep. Gertie'd stitched the satin ribbon which Jean had given her, which somebody had given to Jean from somebody else! Two little curly tousled heads rested comfortably in their grandmother's accommodating lap.

'Such bonny babies,' said Jean, smoothing her rough hand over their curls, soothingly.

Looking tenderly at them she thought again of the war years and the terrible loss of life at home and abroad: fifteen million soldiers dead; thirty-eight million civilians! All those who never made it back to Blighty. Once upon a time they too had been some loving mothers' babies – with their tiny heads fast asleep, like Tommy and Pete! Silently, Jean let a few tears slide down her anguished cheeks. It was a thought which never left her and always upset her even now! What awful wickedness there was in this world! She sighed very, very heavily; the thought was like a heavy ball and chain. She cuddled the children up onto her lap, her loving arms protectively enshrouding them – they slept peacefully, entwined as they'd probably have been in Gertie's womb. Jean looked at Edward; he appeared quite unconcerned now and carried on playing with his wooden toys and Jean's saucepan lids. Edward was a placid child, very warm and loving like his brothers no trouble at all.

Jean didn't know who worshipped them the most – herself or Benjie? Young Benjie was always telling them he was their uncle although neither he nor they were fully knowledgeable of what an uncle was but it conferred status on Benjie! Young Benjie'd heard somebody referring to the triplets and as Benjie being their uncle. His quick ears had earwigged, picked up the name and used it quite often. Jean earwigged him telling the triplets *'I love you because I'm your uncle!'* Edward, Thomas and Peter had beamingly repeated 'uncle' – Benjie or uncle was all the same to their little minds, they loved him to bits!

Their grandmother, Jean, was in her element with the triplets, indeed with all of her grandchildren – she'd had enough experience of her own. She'd quickly offered to look after the triplets all the time, but Gertie wanted to bring them up herself. She was adamant *they were her babies;* her mother was welcome to have them from time-to-time and help with them daily, which she did – but they were Gertie's babies.

Her mother had to admit it – Gertie now resembling an Earth Mother was an excellent mother – she'd had enough experience from her numerous siblings!

Life is full of shocks and surprises – Henry was to get another shock. He didn't yet know it. Tabby broke the news – Henry was shocked! Oh yes! Henry was shocked! He sat there, carved into stone!

'Say sumfink, Dad! Can't yer say sumfink? Aren't yer pleased? Everybody else is!'

A strangulated rattle emitted from Henry's throat. 'Give him time, love, give him time. Come on, Henry, say yer pleased fer Freddy!'

He looked daggers at his wife. 'Pleased!' The word was torn from his lips as he spat it out! 'Pleased! Yes! I'm *pleased* – bloody *pleased!* Ha! Ha! Ha! An' I've been trying fer the big one orl me bloody life! Oh! I'm pleased – bugger it!'

The front door already shaky on its hinges rattled and went thud! Henry'd gone – either to The King's Oak for solace or maybe to the Union?

Tabby's sigh was distinctively audible, she sat down heavily. 'I fought he'd be pleased wiv me good news, Mum?'

'He will be, lovey – once he gets over the shock … it's a very, very lot of money, Tabby – fer any man ter win – and Freddy only just a man! I don't know wot yer Freddy's wages is but you earn three pahnds a week, so that would be about umpteen years' wages fer youse! Must be like 'avin' a gift from the gods!'

'But it was sheer luck, Mum, honest! Freddy only joined the pool's syndicate a month ago. 'Cos we're savin' 'ard fer our marriage 'ee weren't sure at first if 'ee should waste 'is money each week. The other three blokes egged him on, their mate'd retired, they needed a fourth for their syndicate. Poor bloke I bet he's upset! Freddy sez they're orl goin' ter give that retired bloke a little bit of their winnings – 'cos 'ee only missed it by a week. Sez they're doin' it ter 'elp him out wiv 'is little bit of pension. Nice of 'em, ain't it, Mum?'

Jean grimaced thoughtfully and slowly, 'Yes love, very nice … the Old Age Pension isn't much. If the men didn't have their tobacco coupons at the back of their pension books, they wouldn't be able to afford their tobacco or cigarettes, either!'

Jean was thrilled for the young couple, especially when Tabby told her they were seeing about buying their own house. They'd decided to buy one outright from Freddy's winnings – a bit nearer to their wedding day. Fancy her Tabby, with a house bought and paid for (not yet) with *no mortgage* to worry about, and no rent either! No living in a grotty bedsit or somebody's spare room – or waiting for years on the council housing list unless there's a baby to give you extra points!

Her mother was correct, Henry swallowed his chagrin and the little green demon of envy was much subdued. He cheered up when Tabby told them Freddy was buying a house outright, so they wouldn't have a mortgage millstone round their young necks!

All-in-all, Henry came to terms with the pools win of young Freddy! He couldn't do otherwise, could he?

The money was to be left to accumulate interest in a building society deposit account. Tabby was not quite with-it as regards interest rates – she left that to Freddy.

House purchase turned out to be no joke, it wore their nerves to shreds looking round other people's homes as *possibles* until Tabby felt like an interloper … a few months of it, and they decided to call it a day for a while – their poor brains were becoming dizzy, making them punch drunk. They'd reached the point where they cheerfully could *not* have looked at another house for sale sign again! It was put on hold until nearer their wedding day.

Meanwhile they continued saving what they could – the whole of the vast Braithewaite family contributed their thrupenny bits every Friday night. So many empty jam jars became full of hexagonal heavy thrupenny bits. They were proudly displayed on a shelf for all to see!

Friday nights were impromptu piano nights with songs around the piano. Nearly everybody had a piano, if you walked down the six streets on Friday nights you would be spoilt for choice. Unless it was inclement weather, most front doors were wide open – you could invite yourself in. It made a great change from the pictures/movies/flicks, as they were called.

Most people had seen *The Man in Grey; Jamaica Inn, The Stars Look Down;* or, *For Whom The Bell Tolls;* certain persons had sat through four films twice over!

'On Mother Kelly's Doorstep' could be heard streets away! Or 'Don't Go Down in the Mine Dad'; and you could bet your bottom dollar (an Americanism) there would be at least one deep-throated voice belting out 'Old Man River' or the 'Mountains of Mourne'!

The wartime spirit was still alive and kicking in the six streets. The blackout had gone – good riddance – lights, glorious lights, streamed out on the pavements from open doors, vying with the twinkling stars in a friendly sky, free from the fear of flares, bombs and falling shrapnel. The boys were *home* – had been for some years now – all was right in the world again and there's never, never going to be another war, they chorused – and meant it!

Chapter Eleven

With the sap rising in his manly loins, young Freddy was becoming restless. Springtime – the time for young eager lovers; *in the Spring, a young man's fancies lightly turn to thoughts of love.* Freddy was no exception to the old adage!

Whether that was kosher or not Tabby was certain of one thing, it became increasingly difficult to prevent Freddy, as level-headed as he was, from taking advantage and going all the way! She did mention it to her mother who advised her to divert Freddy into some sort of physical activity – other than the one he seemed hell-bent on! *Letting off steam* Jean termed it. She didn't know much – if anything – about young men: she only knew about girls! So Tabby did not find her mother very open or forthcoming on the subject.

When she approached him about a hobby, he was perplexed: he already went to evening classes in bought ledger work and all that! He did exquisite marquetry, making beautiful pictures for their home. On top of all that, he took her to the movies at least three times a week in the 1/6d seats mainly – sometimes in the upstairs balcony seats for half-a-crown. (7½p; or 12½p). 'Didn't Tabby think he had enough hobbies for a young bloke?'

She wasn't sure how to answer that one – not wanting to get tangled up in *sex talk* which she

239

knew next to nothing about – too embarrassing, nice girls *didn't* was what Jean had drummed into her brain. What the word *didn't*, implied, to Tabby was still hazy and vague.

She persevered with getting Freddy's time and mind on healthy occupations to counteract the rising sap; actually Tabby wouldn't have known what the *sap* was – let alone the *rising*, if anybody had asked her. Like most girls of her age – except for the promiscuous, Tabby really was a little innocent abroad when it boiled down to plain sex!

Ballroom dancing was what she had in mind – to Freddy's astonishment. Though it was a possibility now that his limp was not so profound – he'd become used to it – and it was now a part of him.

Deciding it would be a good thing to be frank she told him so. 'I'm not worried about *Frank*, I'm Freddy, love!' She giggled artlessly. 'I mean talking frankly, you silly Billy.'

'Oh! Not content with me and Frank you now have a *Billy!*'

Her giggling made him tease her outrageously. Tabby wanted him to *burn up his surplus energy* and that was one way of doing it. She sugared the pill with her most winsome smile.

'Hello! Hello! What are you up to?' asked Freddy, suspiciously.

Wide-eyed, the picture of innocence, she gently mentioned she would like to learn ballroom dancing correctly, it was an interest in which they could share.

'My word, Tabby, you little minx. You don't just

knock. You *thump!* Next thing – you'll be wanting me back on the playing fields for rugby or football?'

Her warm eyes lit up like stars in their night-time glory, 'Yes! That an' all – you're leg is pretty good now!'

Sitting down abruptly, he put his elbows on the table, cupping his chin in his hands – his eyes never left her face ... unwaveringly, unmovingly. She gave him back stare-for-stare, until she had the grace to blush at her own obvious machinations. He'd seen right through her – she couldn't hoodwink her Freddy!

'What's all this about, Tabby, come on, do tell?' She shifted uneasily in her seat – she didn't want him to think she was trying to take over his life for him.

'It's just that we've got some way to go yet to our wedding day ... and...'

'I'm very well aware of *that* I can assure you! What about it? Come on, love, I'm not going to eat you, speak up.'

Coaxingly, her voice lowered an octave, she told him of her *fears* of what and where his ardour and passion might lead then to – regretfully!

He couldn't stop himself from laughing out loud at her delicacy of broaching the taboo subject. Blushingly she spoke haltingly, getting more and more embarrassed. How on earth do other girls speak about such delicate matters – her mind ran on...

Freddy did nothing to help her he was enjoying himself – thinking it would do Tabby good to *talk openly.*

241

She mentioned how they might rue it if they became careless and her mum and dad had warned her several times lately – as if they could read her thoughts!

Freddy thought that was rich coming from her father of all people – he'd sown his oats everywhere. Tabby had to laugh – that was one thing she did agree on.

'I won't rue it if it happens, Tabby, anyway, you know very well I would be terribly careful, you know I would, you do, yes you do. You're a spoilsport.'

Tabby felt she'd rather be a spoilsport than have what happened to Muriel Bloomsbury! Ginger'd told her he would be very careful – and, where was Muriel Bloomsbury now? In hospital having her first baby – barely gone fifteen – a shotgun wedding (put her age up) – Ginger's wife: Ginger barely eighteen, if that? They had no home of their own; his parents' house was awfully overcrowded – *so overcrowded even the dog was thinking of leaving home! The cat had already left!* The registrar was told Muriel was twenty and Ginger twenty-one! With the cat gone and the poor dog thinking about it, it was worse than a dog's life for Muriel now! Ginger didn't have a man's wage, a *proper wage,* and wouldn't until he really was twenty-one. And, to crown it all – Muriel's baby was *not* the first bairn which Ginger had fathered. Oh, no, no, no! But! Muriel was the first to prove it – she'd been a virgin. And, her father, a hulking twenty-five stone man, six feet, five inches tall with biceps as big as Belisha beacons (traffic crossing safety poles) on top of pole – a chest that would be the envy of an oak tree, had insisted on Ginger making an honest woman of his beloved daughter. Or else! Or else – Ginger looked at Muriel's dad – and was too scared to ask what the *or else meant!* With a bit of judicious arm-twisting – figuratively speaking – Ginger was persuaded to marry Muriel! Anyway he had to marry someone eventually, if he wanted – and he did – more nookie on a regular basis. After the war, the men and boys were after anything female – like bees round a honeypot they were! And they were men of the world now – and knew just as much, if not more, about French kissing amongst other things, earning more pounds, shilling and pence than Ginger – he, poor lad was no longer cock of the walk down the six streets.

Muriel was from the six streets, Ginger'd grown up alongside of her; she was decent looking, plenty of meat on her, and best of all, she actually liked *it!* Plenty of *it.* With so much strong competition around, Ginger didn't fancy going further afield when he had such a complaisant brood hen in his own backyard! And, she really had been a virgin, it was a feather in his cap – unsullied by any other male. So Ginger reasoned cheerfully to himself, Better the devil y'know than the devil y'don't!

Mothers of the six streets sighed with relief when Ginger made an honest woman of Muriel!

Freddy had willingly agreed to be Ginger's best man: he was glad to absorb Ginger's knowledge of women – he was too smart to let Ginger have any inkling that he'd not yet himself gone all the way with his Tabby! Sometimes discretion is the better part of valour, thought Freddy succinctly. Freddy was not stupid; in his heart he knew Tabby was right. It wouldn't be long now – he would be twenty-one and getting a man's wage – then the wedding could go ahead. With a house bought and paid for (not yet) they'd be able to have as many children as they liked – be able to afford to keep a wife and children in good style. If the truth was known, Freddy knew little more than Tabby as regards birth control but being a male didn't like to profess his ignorance. Apart from the French letter which the barber solicitously offered to sell him every time he went for a haircut – once a fortnight – and of which Freddy had accumulated a pile of them in his socks drawer – that was possibly the main source of birth control which his workmates knew about! 'Like eating a toffee with the wrapping paper on,' said his mates: Freddy had laughingly agreed, hoping to fool them into thinking he knew from experience!

Tabby's voice intruded on his thoughts. 'Freddy! The point is everybody knows we're getting married – everybody – but you still haven't asked me, in so many words, and I haven't got an engagement ring either.'

He mumbled, they were saving, going steady, it was an understood thing. 'Let's get engaged, Tabbs. Make it official and I promise to do whatever you want me to – okay?'

Her watermelon grin, similar to his own – split into two huge curves. They were baby-sitting Benjie – who was no longer a baby but a sturdy little fella. 'Huh-uh, Freddy, is that what you call a proposal? How about doing it properly?'

Calling her a cheeky Cockney baggage he dropped to one knee. 'Miss Tabitha Braithewaite, wilt thou do me the honour of taking my hand in the sacred nuptials of marriage – to be my wife – I will love and treasure you, I will go ballroom dancing classes with you … and … and anything else I'm supposed to have said and haven't! There! If that doesn't dampen my physical ardour I don't know what will?'

'A bucket of water!' laughed Gertie. She'd let herself in with the string key.

Having the grace to blush, Freddy stumbled back onto his chair, his face passing through various shades of beetroot. They'd been so engrossed they hadn't heard Gertie's entry. She'd put her finger on her lips, shushing the triplets to be silent – with their forefingers on their own lips they'd tiptoed after Gertie, thinking it was one of their favourite games of *Be Quiet* and hadn't made an audible murmur or sound.

'Gerrhravitt! Don't let me stop the young lovers – I'll go put the kettle on – where's Benjie?'

Speechless – Freddy jerked his head towards the ceiling.

'Bed early, eh? You're baby-sitting? *Mine* are still wide-awake.'

'Awake,' echoed the triplets solemnly. They were scrambling onto the laps of Freddy and Tabby – they loved cuddles and their Aunt and Uncle – they couldn't see enough of them. Grinning ruefully – succumbing to the all embracing cuddles of the triplets, Freddy said, 'You haven't

245

answered me, Tabby?'

Gertie shrieked from the kitchen, 'Go on, Tabby, put the poor bloke out of his misery!'

'All right then! All right! Of course I'll marry you – soppy date! Thanks fer asking me prop'ly – but we ain't got me a ring yet?'

He grinned triumphantly. 'What'd'ya fink I've got in this box then? Just get down for a minute, Tommy.' Tommy slid off his lap, his eyes never leaving the box which Freddy had produced from nowhere. Tommy liked presents! Freddy gave the unopened box to Tabby and kissed her lips lightly. That pleased Tommy, he loved kisses – he scrambled back onto Freddy's lap – hugging and kissing him.

'Tabby gorra p'esn't! Tommy get p'esn't, Freddy?'

'No, no, you little tinker, it's Aunty Tabby's turn today – a special present for Tabby. I'll get you some sweets later on.'

Clapping his hands Tommy beamingly said, 'Us have sweeties Mummy, from Freddy.'

'I earwigged yer, youse little terrors!' She put the tea tray on the table. 'I heard Freddy, you spoil my little men!'

'Don't mention it, I enjoy spoiling them – who wouldn't – three lusty young men! Why shouldn't they have sweets – the war's long gone, let 'em have nice things. It's Tabby I'm spoiling today, or rather at the moment.'

He was watching Tabby's face – opening the box slowly and dramatically. Gertie demanded she put her out of her agony and be a bit quicker!

'Wow! Tabbs – look at that!'

It was a solitary, many skilfully faceted diamond, on a gold built-up base. Sliding the ring onto her third finger of her left hand, she held it up to the light where it scintillated charmingly. She gasped, 'It fits perfectly – how did yer know me size?'

'Easy, I told 'im, didn't I Freddy?' said Gertie.

He nodded his head vigorously, enjoying the effect the ring was having on his long-time intended. It had been quite easy to get the size Gertie'd playfully suggested Tabby try her rings – one day, and then she told Freddy roughly the size of Tabby's finger.

'Made it meself, didn't I?'

'D'ya hear that Gertie – but then you would, wouldn't yer – you've got real earwigging ears, our Gertie, ain't yer? Oh yer are clever Freddy – ain't he boys?'

'Clever F'eddy,' echoed the triplets enthusiastically. Freddy stood up and made a mock debutante curtsy, pulling the knees of his trousers sideways like a skirt.

'I do declare, I'm all a-quiver.'

'Kivver!' echoed the triplets.

'Yerve gotta three little echoes 'ere Gertie. Who's been teaching them?'

'Yeah, I know Freddy, have ter be careful wot I sez now, dun I? You little imps of mischief.'

'Imps!' echoed the boys.

'See what I mean,' grinned Gertie, looking affectionately at her instant brood! 'Come on, boys, let's all have a cuppa.'

Freddy passed the cups of tea to each of the triplets. It was weak and milky and not too hot.

247

'Sugar, Tabby?'

'She's sweet enough, Gertie, she duzzn't need sugar!'

'Hah, hah, hah!' giggled Gertie mockingly. 'I'm sweeter'n Tabby! Me 'usb'nd tells me I gets sweeter – every day!'

'Mum-Mum sweeter,' echoed the triplets.

They didn't have a clue what it was all about – they just knew they were safe and comfortable in their grandparents' house, along with Mum-Mum and Tab-Ab and F'eddy. A nice cup of milky tea, the promise of some sweets – *all was right in their little world.*

'Mum'll be pleased, Tabby. Yeah – I knows youse been tergevver steady like, an' we're all savin' our thruppenny bits for yer – but yer didn't 'ave a ring did yer? 'S nice ter see a girl wiv an engagement ring. Makes it look right and proper – yer know – official like: what made yer choose a solitaire, Freddy?'

Frowning intently, his bushy eyebrows knitted together over the bridge of his well-chiselled nose – trying to appear blasé and sangfroid, like the cinema heroes. Freddy started to answer whereupon the three boys had a fit of the giggles. 'You little perishers, what're youse lot laughing at?'

'Burp!' Eddie's choke turned into another clearly audible chuckle and spluttering he innocently parodied, 'Can't tell 'arge from b'tter'!'

Freddy's eyebrows shot heavenwards. 'What did you just say, smarty pants?'

'The scallywag – it's all right, Freddy – keep yer

shirt on – it's one of their latest pet sayings …
going the rounds it is – can't tell marge from
butter. I jist told yer, didn't I, they're right little
echoes are my boys. Yerse!'

Splaying her fingers, Tabby was admiring her
ring. 'Diamonds are a girl's best friend. Mae
West'll tell yer that.'

Freddy retorted that if she didn't tell her then
the triplets would echo it. 'Come up and see me
sometime!' parodied Freddy. He was a bit of a
mimic, a bit of a card, when he wanted to be.
'Come up and see me etchings!'

Gertie gazed at Tabby then back to Freddy.
'Yeah! Youse two've got the same smiles – water-
melon grins … they say married people grows ter
look alike … youse two ain't even married yet! 'S
funny ain't it?'

The triplets sharp earwigging made Peter
mumble into his cup 'funny!'

Tabby'd always wanted a solitaire, it symbolised
a first marriage. Freddy had mockingly asked
how many marriages *she* was planning on?

To which she'd wittily breathed, 'Yer nivver
knows – yer nivver knows.'

'She's right, Freddy. Yerse – a girl nivver knows,
look at Mrs Gadworthy of the six streets, she's
been married *four* times already! And she's *only* in
her early thirties! 'Ow's abaht that then fer
starters?'

Everybody knew Mrs Gadworthy: a fine, smart-
looking woman with shoulder-length black hair,
black as a raven's wing – worn à la Veronica Lake-
style – peek-a-boo, banned in the wartime munitions factory – hidden under a turbaned headscarf

249

for fear of getting it caught in the machinery. The Veronica Lake style was taboo officially, with the injunction carried out to the letter ... it was terrifically popular!

Tabby pointed out that Mrs Gadworthy had only married four times because she tragically lost three husbands in the war. The first one – her childhood love – she married just before he went to Dunkirk. He never came back; didn't even reach the beach – as he was wading ashore from the DUK landing craft the Germans machine-gunned him in the water. His best friend – himself badly wounded – survived; he was shipped home and he told Mrs Gadworthy. Eventually she married the best friend. Somehow – recovered from his wounds – he ended up in Burma of all places ... and he died out there. Her third husband was a sailor, who'd eagerly arrived home on a longed-for leave to find his whole family had died the night before in a heavy bombing raid. 'Nivver knew wot 'it 'em,' the ARP warden said trying to be comforting, 'They nivver suffered.' But he suffered poor man, wife, three children, father and mother – all gone in one fell swoop. *Millions like us, he'd said to himself* as he went back to sea. Mrs Gadworthy had met him in The King's Oak pub. Feeling sorry for him – she was a tender-hearted woman – she agreed to marry him *there and then* on his short leave. He was blown up in an oil tanker – went to join his dead family.

Her fourth husband – and last – a soldier who had been through the whole gamut of the war, even worked on the Japanese death railway. He badly needed the warmth and loving of a good woman. Mrs Gadworthy, having suffered so emotionally herself, supplied his needs and nursed him back to health. In turn, he was absolutely devoted to her and in her own words, *he spoilt her rotten.* After three husbands and three heart-breaking telegrams, she enjoyed being spoilt. She was a lovely woman who would help anyone.

Not knowing the full story, Freddy had been a bit taken back – after he did know, he was filled with the utmost admiration for her. 'She must be one helluva woman!'

Gertie'd sighed mournfully... 'Yeah! Like that film we saw, *Millions Like Us* made me cry buckets it did – orl the cinema woz crying! The girl's 'usband nivver came back in the film. It really was *Millions Like Us* for people ... us Braithewaites were lucky!'

Freddy had thought Mrs Gadworthy had been married and divorced three times – which puzzled him ... divorce was astronomically expensive, could be as much as fifteen thousand pounds some bloke had told him. And, adultery had to be proved by hiring a seedy looking detective to photograph the guilty couple in bed with each other – usually in a hotel at the nearest seaside!

Freddy unsure about the veracity of it nevertheless knew from mates that blokes never contemplated going into marriage lightly – it was a *one way trip* too difficult to extricate from if you married the wrong girl. Hence the importance of a real engagement ring to make it official. A girl

251

could take a bloke to court for breach of promise, and win! So, unless a girl backed out, there was no turning back decently for a bloke who reneged!

To the Braithewaites the advent of the ring said it all ... the icing on the cake ... the real engagement party was now set in motion. It was to be a real humdinger of a Cockney knees up. Everybody fell over themselves offering to make cakes, jellies, trifles, blow up balloons and do anything else they could think of! Tabby was the very last of the Braithewaite girls to have an engagement ring. Oh! The happiness and palaver which ensued: Freddy felt half sorry for not leaving the ring until nearer the wedding date; if he'd known there was going to be all this fuss. Keeping his voice low he said as much to Tabby. She wanted to know why he was whispering. He gestured to the triplets happily playing Spitfires wheeling, dodging imaginary planes – making appropriate noises until Gertie persuaded them to be a little more quiet.

'Don't want three little Sir Echoes telling everybody what we say, do we, *little pitchers have big ears.*'

Hardly had Tabby got the ring on her finger than Gertie was making all sorts of plans.

'Whoa!' said Tabby.

'Yeah whoa!' said Freddy.

But Gertie was well away. 'The four boys will make smashing page boys, Tabbs.' She chucked Tommy under his chin – she loved his wheezing drawn-out chuckles – he was a card was Tommy, must be the influence of Freddy. Peter and

Edward joined Tommy, they too loved under the chin chuckling. Everything was a game to the triplets: they loved life – had a zest for it and life loved them back equally. Gertie couldn't help a smidgen of thought of the babies killed in the war, the young lads sacrificed – the futility the hopeless dogma, of man's inhumanity to man. Seen all the horrific newsreels she had, during the war and after, her heart – gentle kind, girl that she undoubtedly was – was pierced with sorrow at the thoughts of the agony of their poor mothers and fathers. *She prayed fervently every night that her children and Benjie would never have to be sacrificed to war.* In her opinion it was wrong to say they'd *given* their lives – an age old myth! They hadn't given them they'd had them *taken* away from them by the powers that be, who were still alive and prospering whilst they rotted in their unknown graves. Her mother would always softly murmur, *'He was somebody's beloved baby once upon a time.'*

It used to move Gertie to tears; now with her lovely boys, Edward, Thomas and Peter she felt it all the more; and for Benjie too. Nightly she prayed, along with billions of other mothers the world over 'Dear Lord God, save our boys from the horrors of war and sacrifice, amen.'

Gertie thought of how small the triplets had been at birth and just look at their sturdiness now! Jean's nourishing stews had had a magical effect – the boys, and young Benjie were strong, well built, robust, rosy cheeked and as manly-looking as young boys could be.

Benjie would be starting school soon. Henry

called the four boys his angelic cherubs; Jean wickedly said they're little horrors! She was only joking, but Henry told her to pull the other leg, they were their little angels which made Gertie guffaw!

'They might be when they come home to you, Dad, or when they're all bathed and ready for bed, but my goodness, you should see their energy! Horniman's tea and Bovril might be their tipple but I don't know what petrol they're using – it certainly gets each of them firing on all cylinders!'

Benjie was a gorgeous loving child; very reliably he kept an eagle eye on the triplets – even though he was not much older than them! He was their uncle and Benjie took his duties seriously. Right from birth he'd been surrounded by love – oodles of it – more after the war because he was a brand new baby, a boy, and they were no longer scared of bombings; no longer tired from shift work. Those years had been and gone – they were history; memories were indelible, and would always be retained deep inside them ... some things must never be forgotten!

'The boys'll make smashing page boys,' Gertie repeated herself extra loudly.

'Heard yer the first time, didn't we, Freddy?'

'What Oh! Yeah, yeah what was that, Tabbs?'

'Cor blimey, wake up, will yer? I jist said we 'eard Gertie saying the boys'll make smashing page boys, wake up, Freddy boy!'

'Sorry, sorry, yeah – I'll leave it to the women!'

The front door opened and shut, it was Jean and Henry. The triplets catapulted themselves with Jean falling to the floor laughing fit to bust, amidst a flurry of plump little legs and arms and smothered in wet kisses!

'Mind Grandma's nylons boys, whoops! Only bought 'em yesterday – better take 'em off before they ruins 'em! Before these scallywags ladder them; my last pair were in and out of the invisible menders so often it was a wonder they still held together! As a matter of fact they gave up the ghost not long after the last time!'

The daredevil little Thomas ran his hot chubby hand on Jean's leg. 'G'anma – nice leg, Tommy like. Fee-Pee (Peter) feel G'anma nice leg.' With six hands running the length of her leg Jean struggled to her feet shakily. 'Whoa, no you don't yer little perishers, blimey, 'ow did we manage wivout nylons, they're heavenly to wear?'

'*'Eavenly,*' echoed the triplets.

'*Blimey,*' echoed Tommy for the finale!

'Watch yer language, Mum! Little pitchers have big ears; Freddy just told us that one.'

'Cocoa powder or gravy browning and a black pencil for the seams,' said Sally entering the room with Benjie in her arms. He was getting a hefty lump and it was as much as she could do to stagger in with him. As she'd let herself in with the string key she'd bumped into Benjie – woken by the commotion – descending the stairs two at a time! He jumped the last few into her open arms, as she whirled him around like a dancing dervish he smothered her pan-sticked face with his special brand of kisses.

'Cor blimey mate, any 'eavier an' I won't be able ter lift youse at all!'

255

As usual, Sally had a bag of chocolates for the boys to share, which Benjie distributed fairly and then they lined up to kiss Aunty Sally thank you.

'Nylons!' exclaimed Jean. 'The buggers ladder quickly but at least they provide work for the invisible menders at the dry cleaning shop.'

Devil-may-care little Thomas gazed at his beloved grandmother thoughtfully, his mouth full of chocolate.

'*Uggers,*'he echoed loudly, his semi-open mouth releasing a stream of chocolate goo to dribble down over his chin. More loudly, '*Uggers!*'

Gertie frantically signalled 'watch your language!' Jean laughed she thought it funny! Gertie wasn't amused. 'They echo everything, Mum!'

'That goes fer youse too, Henry.'

'Me!' He looked at his wife askance. 'I nivver sed a bloody word!'

'*Uddy-erd!*' said Peter.

'*Uddy-erd!*, said Edward.

'*Uddy-erd!*' said Thomas.

'*Bloody word!*' said Benjamin.

'That's enough, youse little monkeys, we'd better mind our language, Henry, in future, Gertie's right.'

'Likes nanas,' said Thomas.

'Monkey likes nanas,' said Edward.

'Boys like monkey nanas,' said Peter.

'The triplets like bananas like monkeys,' said Benjie, lugubriously.

'That's enough, Benjie, don't encourage the triplets, you're their uncle!'

Benjie eyed his mother thoughtfully. Like Brer

Rabbit he said nowt, but continued chewing his chocolate. The triplets instinctively gathered in a closed huddle round him. It was not often Benjie was ticked off and they closed rank with him, en masse.

'Well, I'll be doggoned, look at that … in cahoots the little b…! Sorry! Nearly said it agin didn't I?'

'Watch it, Mum, watch it!' Sally sat down heavily with a thankful sigh; announcing her good news, she was nearly five months pregnant! She didn't seem overjoyed! She was to have been one of Tabby's older bridesmaids.

'*Our* wedding!' said Freddy, 'I'm the bride-groom, don't forget, can't have a wedding without me!'

'What are you on about, Freddy?' asked Jean.

'Oh don't mind me – I'm only the other half of the bride and groom bit. Just joking, don't mind me!'

Tabby burst out laughing. 'He's right – he is the other half of the bride and groom bit 'n' everyone who mentions the wedding says Tabby's wedding!'

'Oh, Freddy! Here give us a kiss. I'm your new sister-in-law to be!' Sally hauled herself to her feet and gave him a smacking kiss and warm hearty hug.

He was enjoying himself hugely, he adored the Braithewaite family; a fair-minded tolerant, kindly, bunch as they undoubtedly were.

Hastening to allay Sally's fears about her bridesmaid's frock, Tabby ingenuously told her the skirt and bodice of Sally's dress could be

257

stitched together *after* her baby was born, she might be a trifle bigger!

'If she's anyfink like I was wiv the triplets, she *will* be bigger,' announced Gertie, unhelpfully. Sally's face dropped, she didn't fancy being as big as Gertie before or after her pregnancy! And, she certainly hoped she wasn't in line for twins or triplets – one would be enough for her and her husband. There was only just enough room for the crib in their bedsit! She couldn't see how she could jump the housing queue, like Gertie'd done; the council list was a mile long! Everyone was having babies to jump the list!

Jean hugged Sally, 'Never mind, lovey, always brings a crust wiv 'em, bairns do – you'll see.'

Henry had just got back with some Brown Ale from the off-licence on the corner of the six streets. Jean sent him straight back for some Milk Stout for Sally. 'It'll 'elp wiv 'er breast milk.'

Henry was bemused and jokingly asked who was the mother-to-be?'

'Don't youse look at me like that, Henry … you … whoops! Sorry!' Her hand clamped swiftly over her mouth. The triplets beaming angelically clapped in delight – they knew Grandma had *nearly* said a naughty word.

'For sure, it ain't me, Henry – don't fergit you've started going to the Union three times a week lately!'

He had the grace to actually blush! He went hurriedly from the room: Jean called after him, 'And don't leave yer bike in the passageway, Henry – the babies might fall over it, or it might fall on them – iffen it does, youse'll be glad ter go to the Union *seven* nights a week – I can tell yer!'

'Oh, Mum! Don't be so 'ard on him. He has been trying this past six months!'

'He'll 'ave ter try a bit harder then, won't 'ee? I ain't as daft as I look, our Gertie, I can tell youse – orl of youse!'

Tactfully, they let the matter drop.

Freddy, glad to have a breather, volunteered to take the bike down to the shed at the bottom of the garden.

What a family, he smiled to himself. He would soon be one of them!

Oh the hullabaloo in the Braithewaite's house – eager hands stripped the front room and living room bare – piling some of it upstairs and the armchairs and heavy stuff put out on the microscopic lawn – fortunately it didn't look like rain! Thomas's earwigging had picked up piled higgledy-piggledy-upstairs and he babbled to all who would listen, 'My *black hen* is upstairs in Grandma's room!'

'No it isn't Tommy – Grandma hasn't got hens in the houses they're outside in Granddad's chicken coops. In the hen house!'

Tommy wasn't to be put off. 'Yes, black hen higgledy-piggledy lays eggs for gen'men – Mummy tell Grandma – black hen upstairs with furn'cha'.'

'Ah bless his little 'eart – 'ee means the nursery rhyme, Mum! Yer taught him it last week.'

'Oh yeah! Ain't 'ee sweet, I taught that to all youse girls and ter Benjie, didn't I Benjie?'

'Mummy did,' he said politely.

'Oh, Tommy, you are a proper card.'

'Tommy not got cards – Grandad got cards.'

Jean laughingly threw her arms upwards, 'I give up – the black hen's outside now go and look at him, love.'

Everything was so chock-a-block upstairs there was no room for guests' coats and bags. Somebody … had the good idea of putting them in the bath.

Jean blanched and hurriedly removed them – her guests wouldn't appreciate sopping wet coats – *the triplets loved turning on the taps!*

One of the son-in-laws, Derek, volunteered to stand guard at the bottom of the stairs after they had eaten their party food. He wanted to have a chat with Henry, now would be as good a time as any.

Doris and Peggy had made the engagement cake, icing it professionally – they'd been to evening classes to learn. 'It's a real one this time,' said Doris.

Poor Gertie's cake had been an austerity one – made of cardboard. Underneath the mock icing and cardboard was a little sponge flan! She was lucky to get that – as a gift in exchange, because they had laying hens.

The Sually twins worked in a bakery and turned up with some fantastic little fancy cakes and Jean's favourite bread – bagels … like little bread horseshoes.

'Wotcha, Aunty Maisie, wanna 'ave some cucumber sandwiches – or the mustard and cress ones?'

'Blimey, Ivy, a bit small ain't they? Are yer

feedin' the sparrers?'

'Mind yer tongue, Aunty Maisie – little ears are earwigging – our Gertie's warned us!'

'Oh, I get ya – the triplets, saucy little b...! Nearly said it – I'll 'ave ter put a zip on me mouf!'

Ivy giggled infectiously, 'Nah! stoopid! This is 'ow the toffs make their sandwiches – cuts orl the crusts off and cuts the bread slices into four pieces an' yer gets these little triangles. Cute ain't they?'

'Iffen yer sez so, Ivy, iffen yer sez so,' Maisie sniffed sarcastically. 'Bet they don't go far! I jist ate one triangle in one mouthful!'

Benjie sidled up, 'Greedy guts,' he said very politely! Poor Maisie was shaken rigid, it wasn't exactly a nice thing for a child to utter to an adult.

Ivy doubled up. 'Out of the mouths of babes and sucklings, Aunty Maisie!'

Maisie vacated her seat in a huff, to go and spend a penny. She didn't reckon on the heavy armchair wedged in the bathroom door. She managed to squeeze by to the lavatory but couldn't close the door.

Downstairs the three sets of twins were vocalising in good harmony; not quite the Andrew Sisters, on the radio, but good enough. The neighbours weren't complaining – most of them were cheek by jowl with the Braithewaite household, so it would seem. The overflow was propping up the walls. The benches round the rooms covered with thick grey army blankets were groaning under the combined weight, assaulting them.

261

Maisie having had a good pee tripped, literally, down the stairs; she'd caught her high heel or *tripped over a matchstick* to land safely in Derek's strong arms! 'Oh! You are nice – I'll have ter do it again later – make sure yer catch me agin!'

Derek grinned. 'Yer might break yer bleedin' neck next time, Maisie!'

'Language, language! The triplets might be earwigging, cheers old cock! Fanks!'

A party to remember: Tabby's and Freddy's engagement party: it was all *Let's Be Merrry And Bright;* the songs were never-ending; drinks flowed freely; there were so many whip-rounds amongst the men – it seemed as if they'd emptied the off-licence: crate after crate of beers and lemonades. The shorts were plentiful, but not plentiful enough – so there was another whip-round!

Jean was on her second rendering of *Sally* – part of Gracie Field's repertoire. Maisie, not to be outdone, warbled *Just A Rose In A Garden Of Weeds.* The songs, like the drinks, were never ending – a good old-fashioned party! Henry briefly wondered how the floorboards were taking the combined battering of umpteen heavy bodies, shoeless, in *Knees Up Mother Brown.*

He wandered out to the staircase to chat to his son-in-law. He liked Derek, had a good head on his shoulders in Henry's 'umble opinion.

'Got Mr Atlee, didn't we, Derek? Seems a nice bloke. Blimey, the landslide in '45, bet even Labour didn't fink they'd do so well, but they did – yerse! Still the grass weren't so green on the uvver side, in some respects, Derek. But youse gotta give 'em their dues. My old Dad always sed yer gotta fink fer yerselves, iffen the working class don't fink fer theirselves they're dun fer. 'S fact, 's truth!'

'Good and bad in every party, Henry! All have something to offer. Like your old man said, we gotta think for ourselves. Nah! I ain't joined any particular party yet, been mulling it over in me mind I 'ave. Ain't a boy no longer – served me King and Country for twelve years I did, man and boy. Twelve years in the Royal Navy, I'm in me thirties 'n' sez to my Sally, I sez "When the baby's born we're gonna sit down together and see where we go from here ... I rather like the idea of becoming an MP."'

'Our sort don't go that high up the ladder, Del boy!'

'Oh yes they do, sir, begging your pardon, you being older 'n' me! What about Nye Bevan, Ernest Bevin and Keir Hardie and all them? Many others from working class have done well in Labour and Conservative and Liberal! The Liberals were a powerful party before the turn of the Century or somewhere around there – I'm not quite sure. Lots of good men in all three main parties like there is in all walks of life.'

'Youse've got yer 'ead screwed on all right, Del boy – I wish ya a lotta luck.'

'Thanks, I'm biding my time I am, likes to see what's what and when's when first before I dip my toe into the water.'

'Fancy you saying that – it were one of me old Dad's favourite sayings, "what's what and when's when"!'

263

'Yeah! Fancy that, Henry.' Derek downed a copious gulp of Brown Ale, smacked his lips loudly, and appreciatively. 'Like I said, even if yer workin' class like us we can pick and choose which party we belong to or sway towards – which ever direction of wind takes yer fancy ... pick and choose. That's what yer call *democracy*, Henry. Met a lot of blokes I did – in the war – you'd be surprised who favoured one party and who favoured another! Those you thought were Labour through and through, turned out to be Tory and vice versa right across the whole spectrum of politics: Liberals favoured changing to Labour and Conservative and Labour and Conservative favoured changing to Liberals! Quite opened my eyes, I can tell yer, Henry. That's what got me interested in the idea of becoming an MP. I'll say it again – yer don't have ter do something a certain way just because you're working class ... no, no, no! Freedom of choice, Henry – it's our prerogative, like I said, we're a democracy: I'm not telling you right now whether I favour Labour, Liberal or Conservative, I'm weighing up my options. Freedom of thought is what we've got, yerse we have. That's what we fought for – it's what me mates fought and died for – in their thousands and millions – that's a pretty powerful word, *millions!* Can mean one thing to one man, and another thing to the next man, mark my words, Henry!'

Henry felt this conversation was getting a bit too deep for him, he felt himself floundering in uncharted waters – his son-in-law certainly was a deep thinker, and he respected him for it; oh yes!

He hurriedly mumbled something about having to see a man about a dog.

''Bout a dog and a black higgledy-piggledy hen,' added a little voice behind him, startling Henry! They'd been that busy conversing they hadn't noticed young Thomas earwigging.

Henry laughed and ruffled his curly head. 'Come on then, little fella, Granddad going wee-wee, you coming?'

Tommy nodded his tousled, curly head in happy anticipation; his grandfather scooped him up onto one shoulder. 'Tommy get black piggledy-hen upstairs wiv Granddad.'

'Buggered if I know wot this little tyke is on abaht?'

'Buggered,' said Thomas sweetly.

Henry groaned loudly, regretfully, 'Oh no! You'd better not let Grandma hear you say *that*, Tommy, or there'll be some flack flying around! Come on, let's go wee-wee – I'm bustin' me boiler!'

Sally'd wandered out to get Derek's glass for a refill! He could hear Freddy belting out a medley of popular songs – not just the wartime favourites – but all the new songs sweeping the country. He'd picked up a few selections of sheet music as he'd passed the music shop – they weren't really needed!

'Shall I put the children to bed, Mum?'

'Nah love! They'll go soon enough when they're tired! Wait 'til they're ready and willing – won't be long by the looks of young Eddie, nearly asleep on his feet he is, the little lamb.' Jean quit dancing to pick up Eddie who was just about to curl up into a ball on the floor. As she cuddled him closely, dropping a kiss on his dampish head, he gave a sigh and was fast asleep.

Tommy and Peter followed suit a few minutes later – that just left Benjie, twirling and dancing in the ring to the encouragement of clapping hands and cries of, 'Good old Benjie, come on lovey, keep going.' He became slower ... and slower ... and ... he sank to the floor fast asleep!

Tucked up together in the bed in the boxroom which had been left clear for them, they never made a murmur all night long – but were up with the lark at daybreak!

Chapter Twelve

The two young lovers appeared to have the Midas touch, fascinated with their nest egg steadily growing in the Bank of Brennaby, Laughton. At first, it was a puzzle to know which bank to invest in. The whole of Freddy's share of the big pools win was placed into an investment account. Jean knowing nothing about banks had suggested one of the *major* banks. Freddy's family suggested a building society. Freddy and Tabby were torn between both ideas. Obviously only Tabby knew Freddy's plans to have his own business: bearing that in mind, he decided to invest in a bank because as a businessman, he might need the goodwill of a bank behind him some day! He didn't intend to have a mortgage and wouldn't require the immediate goodwill of a building society. As a businessman he would need a chequebook account which only the banks could provide.

Tabby knew nowt about real savings although she'd always managed to save a little each week in national savings stamps – instant cash for special things such as outings or emergencies.

Jean had often dreamed of what it would be like to have a real bank account, to be able to walk into the hallowed premises of a *real* bank. She thought, we can all dream. She'd been watching too many movies – the Hollywood Dream in its heyday.

267

The dreams which gave glamour to many dull lives of the *hoi polloi,* began from the moment one entered the portals of the cinemas – the picture palaces! Redolent of hauntingly fragrant scents, hazy smoke from countless cigarettes – even whiffs of heavy cigars. Usually the manager would be in the ornate entrance lobby in his penguin suit and bow tie puffing away at a Churchillian-sized cigar. Hovering, beamingly polite and unctuous, his feet sunk into the plush carpeted *foyer,* which it was grandly named. The tall, braided uniformed commissionaire, in his peaked captain's style hat; his impeccably white-gloved hands decorously opening the doors for you – the smart peroxide blonde (usually blonde) gum-chewing behind the glass grille of the sumptuously decorated booking office, situated in the foyer. Immaculate in thick heavy make-up, à la Hollywood style – either short, bouncy Jean Harlow-style curls or the ubiquitous Veronica Lake peek-a-boo.

All the young fellas tried to get off with the booking office girls. They very atmosphere of the foyer, with its life-sized photographs of famous film stars in titillating poses (female) or brooding heroes (male); the elaborate blown-up posters advertising forthcoming films, to whet your appetite for more. For 6d (2 ½p) in the front seats, 9d (about 4p) in the back rows – which the Romeos coveted!

Even more grandly – marking you out as special – you could ascend the thick, plush-carpeted stairs to the upper circle 1/6d or 2/6d (7½p or 12½p). With the usherettes, in their trim

268

uniforms lighting your pathway into the dark or semi-dark, bowels of the land of make-believe, as you stumbled after her (until your eyes adjusted to the gloominess). You stumbled up or down the gradients from one level to another, clutching your half of your tickets (which the girl at the cinema proper door had torn in half, before she would let you pass inside) following the beam of the usherette's torch; stumbling over people's legs and feet, saying excuse me, sorry, when you squeezed yourselves past their upturned seats – destroying their enjoyment of the screen! The usherette's torch beam played on naughty couples doing what they shouldn't! It was a wonderful world inside a cinema, the nearest most people ever got to fitted carpets and glittering chandeliers. The cubicled lavatories were just like Hollywood. On a grand scale, the aroma of perfume was heady, wafting in the face as the door was pushed open. In there the soundtrack of the film was still audible, so you could keep up with the plot whilst have a nervous wee-wee. Making you wonder – not for the first time – why did *females* need to empty their bladders the very moment they sat down in their seat? Up would go the seats to noisy mutterings from people disturbed as you squeezed past yet again!

An enigma which no man had been able to solve – let alone the woman! Their bladders never provided the answer any more than their brains did!

In-between films, the filmy curtains slid back for local advertisements: one of Tabby's favourites was 'It won't be a stylish marriage – unless

269

Horn's supply the carriage', referring to a local car hire company, with pictures of their showroom nearby.

During the interval, the lights were brighter, making everybody blink owlishly – if you were quick, you could reach the ice cream lady before the queue became horrendous, to purchase a paper covered ice bricket; you even licked the paper clean – it had a flavour of its own! You could buy crisps, with the little blue bag of salt which you had to fumble for when the lights lowered again, making people's heads turn to see who was making the noise!

All the world was at your local cinema – you knew just about everybody – during the intermissions you craned your head this way and that to wave to them!

Many a blind-date romance began in a cinema – usually the friend-of-a-friend or a mate of a mate! If you were under age you couldn't get in by yourself for certain 'A' films – you had to ask someone to take you in! You gave the adult your picture money and walked cockily in with them. They got the tickets, handed them over for tearing apart – you said thanks and dashed off into seats near the front of the screen. Even Jean had taken children in; everybody did it – children were not frightened to ask any strange man or woman to *take us in please*. It was the way it was, the status quo! Occasionally the manager had a twinge of conscience or the doorman knew your age – and you'd be turned away pronto! Never mind, wait a bit, have another try, and slip past them. *It always worked!* You would even see the film twice round! Get your money's worth.

Everybody's dream world; like hoping to become a rich film star, hoping to win the Pools; hoping to win at the racetrack. People lived on hope, it'd kept them going in the war – *hope!*

Tabby had known about Freddy's ambition for their own house; it was now within his means. She hadn't taken much notice of his talk of his own business. She'd laid that at the perennial door of hope – but she knew now, and he'd sworn her to secrecy.

Not that much older than Tabby – actually – he was older in his mind; once a girl had a baby she was a woman but a man was not a man until twenty-one! Wiser heads had puzzled over that anomaly! Tabby asked Jean to explain it more succinctly.

'Lovey, there's much in this world duzzn't make sense. It doesn't matter lawfully for a woman when she's married – she's 'er 'usband's chattel! Even her body duzzn't belong to 'er, it belongs to 'im! Duzzn't matter how old she is – she can't even sign fer 'er own operation, no matter how urgent – *they've gotta get the 'usband's signature.* Only he can sign, her body belongs to 'im. In uvver words, she belongs ter 'er 'usband, lock, stock, and barrel, as the saying goes! A married woman can't sign fer fings on the never-never – only 'er 'usband can sign; even if she's the one working ter pay fer the furniture It's 'is – everything is the 'usband's.'

'Wot abaht the tallymen – earning their living on the knocker? You don't tell Dad abaht him?

271

Wot's the difference?'

The tallymen sold luxury items to women at their front doors – things women would like to buy but couldn't afford on the housekeeping money. The tallyman gave a woman a payment card, and he collected a shilling or sixpence a week from her. He was usually a middleman con-artist who sleekly added on a few bob to make himself a nice extra bit of profit.

The women got their extras for the home or for themselves or their kiddies; the men either turned a blind eye or were none the wiser, merely thinking what clever wives they'd got, handling the housekeeping money! What the eye didn't see the heart didn't grieve over was the women's maxim. Your friends or neighbours would always pay your tallyman for you if you had to go somewhere or other.

Not long after the engagement party, which had been a rip-roaring success a tallyman had knocked on Jean's door. A new bloke, selling an array of cooking dishes and serving dishes, made of a new kind of strong heatproof glass, Pyrex. Jean's eyes popped; quickly she called Tabby to look at them – urging her to buy them on the knocker for her forthcoming marriage. 'Nice, modern – look nice in your kitchen when yer gits yer 'ouse Tabby. She's buying 'er own 'ouse yer see – she's me daughter like – fiancé is buying it outright!'

The tallyman knew when he was on to a good thing, his eyes popped with excitement. 'Hang on, missus, there's a lot more of a selection than this lot, mixing bowls an' all!'

Tabby bit her lips reflectively, she was sorely tempted, but Freddy didn't like her touching their stamp savings for non-essentials. She'd never seen Pyrex dishes close up before. They were the bees knees, she knew she had to have them. 'Wot shall I do, Mum?'

Her mother didn't hesitate. 'Youse 'ave 'em, lovey; yer gives me yer tanner a week – I'll pay 'im – the tallyman – an' nobody's any the wiser. Right?'

'That's right, missus. There yer are, lovey, listen to yer muvver is wot I says, oh yerse! If yer makes it a bob a week on top of the tanner, I'll give yer this set of mixing bowls free!' Tabby couldn't believe her luck.

'That's the way us workin' class women do fings, lovey – we ain't nuffink but chattels orl right, but we knows a bargain when we sees one. Okay, mate, she'll have the lot!'

The tallyman, who'd got out of bed the wrong way, made a mental note to do a repeat performance – he couldn't believe his luck, the whole caboodle sold in one go! So, young Tabby got her dream dishes!

Not that she didn't feel guilty keeping it secret from Freddy; she most certainly did! It seemed a bit underhand but she had to agree with her mother about not stoking-up fires unnecessarily – she could mention them when she'd finished paying for them.

He was a friendly bloke the tallyman; Jean offered him a cuppa, he accepted with alacrity – anyfink free was his motto! A quite engaging, witty little bloke, from a family of fifteen children

273

with no twins or triplets in his family! They lost a few in the war! He'd been a rag-and-bone man – a 'totter' but was aspiring to loftier heights, on the knocker, it was just the next step up the ladder for him. He was fed up exchanging goldfish for old rags – then he met a bloke who'd been on the knocker for twenty years and – for an undisclosed sum of money – he'd taught him and some other geezers the tricks of the trade. 'It's the politeness and the 'umbleness that win the housewives over, and that's the gospel truth, missus.' The geezer had got a gammy leg, to supplement his meagre income, he was ready to impart his knowledge and trade wrinkles for a decently greased palm.

This new tallyman was a mine of information, even if he did take four cups of Horniman's and a half dozen precious biscuits: Jean made a mental note to buy *loose broken ones* in future!

Departed – one happy tallyman!

'Yer a lucky girl, Tabby, to own such pretty things at your age.'

She nodded her head and pointed out that she didn't yet own them, they didn't know the bloke, they could be stolen!

Her mother blithely told her it was the way of the world – her three bob rise would help pay for the goods and to quit worrying.

Doing well now was Tabby; oh yes! She'd left the factory – after an enjoyable working life and good camaraderie; got herself a better job now, in an office, near the Old Bailey – hadn't she? It was exciting travelling into the vast, busy, frenetic metropolis. She had a choice of stations, she either got out at Blackfriars or St Paul's – just a few minutes quick walk took her from there to the office.

She went shopping in her lunch hour at Ludgate Hill – just under the bridge was Fleet Street, with its pubs enjoying a brisk trade from the media; all the main papers seemed to be in Fleet Street. Journalists, copywriters, printers and the whole caboodle rubbed shoulders in Fleet Street. At Ludgate she found it exciting, purchasing from the colourful array of stalls on the bomb-site: pastel-coloured nylon stockings at twelve shillings a pair! Pink and pale lavender with matching see-through nylon gloves completed her wardrobe – travelling on the underground was not exactly clean, the nylon gloves washed and dried easily. It was almost *de rigeur* to wear gloves and hats to work; all part of the new sophisticated image of working up London.

Tabby was not enamoured with the office habit of smoking! One lunchtime she swopped her luncheon vouchers, provided by the company she worked for, to get a nice crusty thick ham roll from the Italian delicatessen (a tiny sandwich shop) and a distinctive flat box of Du Maurier cigarettes. She thought, maybe it was the image to smoke and look suave! Passing the cigarette box round the office and trying one herself she gave it up immediately – it was a mug's game, the taste of cigarettes, any cigarettes, was not her cup-of-tea! Anyway, it would be expensive – it was the norm to pass cigarettes round the office, a waste of good money.

Embarrassed, she weakly concurred with her

275

office mates that they were a great cigarette and looked smashing in their distinctive box, and they certainly smelt good. But she was never going to try another cigarette of any kind – ever. And she never did.

Tabby felt she was learning something new every day of her life, and she was. She was amused when a woman wearing a smart brown uniform dress entered the office. Taking some cleaning things from her brown bag proceeded to wipe and sterilise the mouthpieces of all the telephones. The cleaning of telephones was unknown to Tabby, she was vastly intrigued and couldn't wait to get home to tell her mother.

'Ain't that marvellous,' repeated Jean. 'I'd nivver 'ave known if yer hadn't told me. We live and learn!'

'Different generation, Mum, like in Tennyson's *Morte d'Arthur* he said something like this, "The old order changeth – yielding place to new."'

'Who's he, lovey, did 'ee really sez that?'

She looked to see if her mother was joking – she wasn't.

''As 'ee been 'ere to our house, can't say I r'collect 'im, lovey?'

'Yes, Mum! He's been to our house, I brought him home when I went to the library: Lord Alfred Tennyson.'

Not paying much attention – her mind was on the forthcoming nuptials – wool-gathering … 'I must have been out wiv Benjie then – when yer brought 'im home. Why didn't yer tell me? A Lord an' orl! Youse goin' up in the world, Tabby, love, yerse!'

Tabby pealed with laughter. 'Oh my! Mum! Yer not listenin' prop'ly! I didn't bring Tennyson home with me – literally. I brought him home – a library book! He's been dead donkeys' years! Oh Mum, oh Mum!'

Jean was convulsed, the joke was on her – she rarely took offence. Scrubbing the tears off her face she said 'Oh Tabby– youse'll be the deaf of me wiv yer book larnin'! Fancy me thinking a writer had come to our house ... wot a clever clogs yer are, my Tabby. Wot a laugh – it's a scream, wait'll I tell Maisie.'

She was off again, screaming it was so funny, so funny.

Jean wondered if Henry knew who Tennyson was – did he hear poetry in his house when he was young?

Fancy her Mum thinking she'd brought an academic home – well a poet then! On second thoughts, she had brought a literary circle home from the library with her everlasting passion for books.

'Dead and alive – I've brought 'em 'ome, Mum! Some 'is dead and some 'is still alive.'

Jean said she'd call 'im Mr Tennyson as it was polite to say Mr – even if he was a Lord in her humble opinion. Eh lovey, wait'll I tell Maisie! Yeah! Maisie'll find it a scream...' She was off again, laughing at her own denseness! 'Bet Maisie duzzn't know Mr Tennyson!'

'Wouldn't be so sure, Mum, her 'usband was a good scholar – very good at English he was, yer know. Aunty Maisie told me he learnt poetry at school ... she said one of 'is favourites is the

277

Daffodils by Wordsworth... "I wandered lonely as a cloud ... o'er hill and vale ... when all at once I saw a cloud ... a host of golden daffodils ... beside the lakes beneath the trees ... fluttering and dancing in the breeze...'"

'Oh, now, listen ter that. Ain't that beautiful? Makes yer fink yer can look outa yer window and see it like a picture. Yer a good girl, lovey, I'm larnin' a lot from youse. Maisie ain't ever told me her 'usband knew poetry 'n' she's been me bosom pal all these years – well I never did!'

''Cos some men fink it's not manly to know poetry, which is daft, poetry opens up the window of the soul – that's wot my Freddy sez.'

'And does Freddy know poetry?'

'Of course 'ee duz ... his sister quotes it in her sleep, so 'ee sez! Sez she's orlways spoutin' Tennyson, Walter de la Mare and William Blake.'

'At the missionary on Sundays, lovey, we used to sing sumfink by Blake ... er .. let me fink. I've got it:' Jean hummed then sang pleasingly and softly, 'Little Lamb who made thee – Dost Thou Know Who Made Thee, For he calls himself a Lamb ... that was when I lived up Limehouse. Me muvver loved going ter the missionary, I went wiv her. Born at Bancroft Road hospital, Mile End Old Town, she were. Very poor, but 'appy they all woz.' She let her thoughts drift backwards... 'Yeah ... poor but 'appy.'

'Orl the young men from that way, were *cannon fodder* in the Great War ... didn't stand a chance did they? "Over the top wiv the bleedin' lot of yer – or I'll shoot youse orl on the spot." That's wot they sez to 'em! Over the top they went to certain deaf from the machines gunners waitin' fer 'em!'

Jean burst into tears '…'n' every one of them some poor muvver's baby boy!'

'Oh Mum! Now yer gettin' maudlin jist when we woz 'avin' a good laugh. I understand though, let's 'ope the Second War will have been the last!'

'Yer duzzn't really understand until youse've had babies of yer own! *Nah it won't be the last war,* Tabby … men are fighters by nature … orlways 'ave been … orlways will be. Poor sods!'

'Changing the subject, can I put my bits 'n' pieces in the bottom of your wardrobe – nobody else goes there. Don't want people to see me bottom drawer yet, do I?'

'Yeah! Course you can! Silly nit wit you'll have yer own 'ome soon, got 'is Pools winnings invested – ain't he, your Freddy? It's a decent 'ome youse'll have; both of youse workin' – yer should be quite well-off, lovey. A better start in life than yer sisters. 'T'ain't their fault, 'twas the bloomin' war – didn't give 'em a chance ter save did it. No incentive – might've orl been blown ter smithereens! The men away fightin' only got about 8/6 (42½p) a day – I fink so, anyway, not sure rightly, but sumfink like that; leastways I fink that's what Ivy's bloke were gettin' as a Corporal!' Jean sighed heavily – it seemed like the war was forever flowing through the front door, permeating the inside and out again by the back door. No matter how much you tried to push it to the back of your mind it crept to the front again! Them that saved before the war – never 'ad a chance ter spend it – poor blighters – their mortal remains somewhere in a foreign field! Even the blokes deferred from the armed forces niver got much chance ter save, did they? Nah! Workin' shifts round the clock they were – ruddy government pushed Income Tax up to ten bob in the pound (50p) – half of every quid (one pound) which they earned! Said they'd get it back after the war – nobody ain't got a penny back yet – called post-war credits they is ... won't get no interest either iffen they do get it back one day. Henry's still waitin' fer 'is – so's everybody else – look how many years since the war ended and the Government still won't cough up! Looks like they're all in for a long wait!' (Little did Jean but know it – it was a very, very long wait.)

''Allo, 'allo, wot's this orl abaht?' she untangled Tabby's arms from her neck, 'Who's gettin' maudlin now?'

'You're a good Mum and I love yer to bits. I ain't clever like you seems ter fink, Mum, I'm jist *well-read!* Like yer said, we can't all be the same ... that's wot makes the world go round. Yer a smashin' muvver! Given the world fourteen lovely children you have 'n' all – we've got the triplets and Sally's baby on its way; and the other babies. Youse and Dad've done well, Mum, fanks.'

Jean blushed – praise from Tabby was quite rare. She told her that, 'Kind words butter no parsnips'. Her own grandmother had said that many times. She was a one for sayings, 'Empty vessels make most noise'; 'all that glistens ain't gold'. Her favourite was 'The Love of Money is the Root of all Evil'.

Miss Brink told her students many times, 'We

280

can't all be scholars; we all have hidden talents; we should never look down on anyone because they're not academic scholars. Some people were cleverer with their hands – craftsmen, especially in the old days before machinery and factories. They were brilliantly clever at making things by hand. Most of them couldn't read or write; it was frowned-on for the workin' class. *But they had good brains,* made beautiful furniture and other things; weaved their own cloth.'

Tabby and her classmates never forgot that – Miss Brink didn't let them!

Jean smiled, her Tabby was quite what Henry termed philosophical! 'I'm proud of you, Tabby, I wants yer to know that, lovey. You're a sweet kid even if I say so meself. 'S not long now to yer weddin' day … I shall miss yer, yerse, Benjie will 'n' orl. Lucky we've got Gertie nearby. Must count me blessings mustn't I?'

Tabby assured Jean she would visit her as often as possible, she wouldn't get rid of her tht quick! What would Benjie do without her – he'd miss his Ab-Ab – he still called her by that pet name.

'Mind you, Mum, he's got the triplets now – so I don't think he'll miss Ab-Ab all that much. He thinks the triplets are his! Keeps reminding them *"I'm yer Uncle Benjie – don't yer fergit it"*, bless him. Makes me roll up wiv laughter when he says that, it really does! Gertie sez the same thing … it's a right laugh!'

Tabby thought the time to her Wedding Day couldn't go fast enough; it was becoming harder to fend off Freddy's amorous advances, he kept hinting broadly about going all the way, now. Luckily Freddy discovered some latent hidden talents, craftwise, and busied himself making some decent furniture for their future home. They had enough of a nest egg to buy furniture but they didn't quite fancy some of the utility stuff which was still knocking around. An uncle of his had been killed – not literally, but so badly wounded with his hands and legs blown off. Mercifully he passed over recently; he was an older brother of Freddy's father. A good fifteen years older; he'd never married. Unlocking the shed at the bottom of his garden – the *hut* – they found it was chock-a-block full of well-seasoned wood; pine, oak, lime and yew – an amazing discovery. The uncle had been a skilled carpenter and joiner who made things for pleasure and gave them away. Two sheds actually – one the full width of the large garden and another tucked away in a corner. His tools were a treasure trove. Another surprise – he'd gone to war as a skilled linguist on Secret Services and that was as much as they learnt! Even Freddy's father, his own younger brother, never knew his hidden talents! The hobby was a cover-up! Pottering around in the *hut* Freddy discovered he'd inherited some of his uncle's talents. The smaller hut had every tool he would ever require. Tabby found this an unlooked-for blessing – kept him more occupied from trying to tease her into capitulation which she dared not – her mother'd never have forgiven her if she'd fallen for a baby before the great day. Her mother was determined that her last daughter would go up the aisle of the church a virgin or else!

Chapter Thirteen

To her surprise she found Freddy was a better dancer than herself, Tabby had wondered if his gammy leg would hinder him; true, it had seemed to have improved over the years. Once out on the dance floor, the slight lameness became negligible as Freddy took to dancing like a duck to water. He appeared somewhat surprised himself – he had what was termed a natural classical ability to be found only in the best of ballroom dancers. Once he learned the basic steps and absorbed the tempo he was well away; quite in his element so to speak. The very first lesson would have belied such an ability – he had tripped over his own feet, stumbled and generally seemed to have two left feet! The second lesson, he was a trifle improved – even the instructors felt there was *hope* for such a clodhopper. Unbeknown to Tabby, or the instructors, Freddy secretly practised with his sister! Come the third lesson at the dance hall – and away went Freddy. Foxtrot, waltz, quickstep – slow, slow, quick-quick-slow: even the Tango didn't beat Freddy. For the instructors, it was a delight to watch him take to the floor with Tabby. They made a beautiful couple and the instructors mentally wondered if they should put them in for the dancing competitions. It was early days so they bided their time.

After Henry heard of Freddy's prowess he was heard to remark quite proudly, 'My Tabby's fiancé seems to have the gift of the gods ... can turn his hand to anything he can – and his feet!'

'Time and tide wait for no man,' as Jean had predicted, and the wedding date loomed ever nearer.

Being so young, a week seemed like a month, and a month like a year, with a year looming ahead like eternity. The prospective bride became doubly nervous with the dates being crossed-off on the calendar.

Anxiously her fluttering mind stirred up the little grey cells – for she had no real idea of what being married meant, or would mean. If it was a failure – perish the thought, she scrambled the little grey cells on that one! It would mean being tied, possibly for ever to a man one was incompatible with. There was *no* easy way out of an unsuitable marriage: it was for countless mismatched couples legally irrevocable! Apart from costing money which most of the working class could only dream about; the climate and mores of their social order were a terrific barrier – not only would it be severely frowned upon, looked askance at, but could, in fact, cut one off socially! There were, as in everything, exceptions to the rule, but that was the consensus prevailing. Society did not look kindly upon a woman who did not honour her marriage vows, which were considered sacrosanct. For men, it was a different story – it always had been! Unfair, but true, which Gertie took pains to inform Tabby – Jean wouldn't tell her anything really – as the eldest sister, Gertie, therefore, felt it behoved her to have a talk with her little sister!

'Tabby, listen careful, love! The vows which you take in church are sacrosanct. Your husband will expect and demand that you obey them, never mind what *he* does in the future! It literally means where you promise to love, honour and obey, once you have uttered that phrase you are your husband's chattel! You don't belong to your-self – every part of you belongs to your husband!'

'Blimey Gertie! 'Ow many more people are going to keep walloping me wiv this "chattels!" business? It's enuff ter put a girl orff marrying fer life!' In her nervousness, Tabby who'd gradually moved away from her natural Cockney vernacu-lar culled from her family and their social circles, spoke it quite thickly which made Gertie lift an eyebrow.

In vain, Tabby had reiterated to all the wet-blankets times are changing. Everyone merely laughed resignedly, 'Pie in the sky,' Tabby.'

Gertie smiled gently, the bride was becoming unsettled – she knew from overhearing Freddy chatting to her husband last week that Tabby was still very much a virgin!

'Until the laws are changed for women that's the way it is. Divorce, as we've told you before, is on a par with being shunned for having an illegitimate baby – a bastard – a horrible word to use for a poor innocent baby and often a sadly duped woman.'

'But that is terrible, realy anachronistically terrible. This ain't the Dark Ages, Gertie!'

''Cor blimey, Tabby, that was a mouf-ful …

285

"ana … what"?'

'Anachronistically – means going backwards in time, more or less!'

'Yeah! Cor! Wait till I tell that one to me 'usband. I'll tell him he is "ana…"?'

'He's anachronistic.'

'And when the hell was the "Dark Ages"?'

'After the Romans were recalled to Rome – they'd been here a few hundred years; ruled us, didn't they: then Rome recalled her legions to save herself from the barbarians! The Romans ruled far and wide; they were essentially con-querors of other lands. Built wonderful roads, we still use them, that's how we got the saying "all roads lead to Rome". And Colchester was theirs! I can't remember it all – Freddy told me all that, loves history, does Freddy!'

'Now we're getting away from marriage to history, lovey, still it's interesting; I honestly didn't know what the Dark Ages woz! They must have married our peoples, blimey, must've been terrible fer them ter break up their homes and family life to go back to live in Rome?'

'Yeah! Suppose it must've been, mustn't it? I ain't worried about marrying Freddy; it's all this chattels business I don't like. Like yer sez, it's the law and I'll have ter do wot the law sez! But, I tell yer this much, our Gertie, I don't like it – no I flamin' well don't! And as fer what you calls them that horrible word, bastards – well I already knew that, didn't I, every girl knows that, but we duzzn't talk abaht it! I'm a free thinker, me, likes ter make up me own mind on important matters I do. Freddy sez that's wot 'e admires in me, see!

He sez change can only be effected by Parliament, 'n' it won't 'appen overnight, it'll take years and years; could take twenty to thirty years to change, so my Freddy sez!'

'And until then – women are mere chattels,' stated Gertie philosophically. 'Yer'll have ter talk to Sally's 'usband, Derek. Finkin' of becoming an MP 'ee is. Finks jist like youse 'ee duz, sez women shouldn't be chattels any more. I'll tell him when I see him that our Tabby sez it's ana...!'

'Anachronistic!' giggled Tabby. 'I'll support 'im iffen 'ee becomes an MP see if I duzzn't!'

'Yeah! Well, yer do that, lovey, yerse, yer do that.'

'The mills of God grind slowly ... presently we're all interested in stability and becoming prosperous ... 's goin' ter take a long time, I can feel it in me bones, I can. We're tryin' ter make it a land fit fer heroes, don't forget! Time will tell, just 'ave ter do our best, be decent ter uvvers; go along with the flow to the best of our abilities.'

'My word!' said Gertie admiringly. 'Youse do fink deep, duzzn't yer, lovey. Youse sounds jist like Sally's 'usband, Derek. Now, there's a talker iffen there woz one! Talk the hind legs off a donkey 'ee would, for sure. Yerse! Wot 'ee sez makes good sense though!'

'Along wiv the ebb and flow – is wot my Freddy sez, along wiv the ebb and flow!'

'Freddy's right.' Henry strolled into the living room carrying his daily bottle of Brown Ale, which he always picked up as he passed the off-licence at The King's Oak pub. 'Young Freddy's got an old head on young shoulders: knows 'ow ter speak 'is mind. I likes a bloke – knows 'ow ter speak 'is own mind. Good lad young Freddy. Even though the war's been over some time now, peoples is still in a semi-state of shock; 'ave ter pick up the bits 'n' pieces again 'n' start fresh, like!'

'I know, 'oo yerve been talking ter, Dad, it's Sally's Derek! Our Gertie's jist been talkin' like 'im 'n' all! What else does Derek say?'

''Ee tells the troof, dun 'ee? Might take a coupla generations ter erase the effects of the horrors of the war. Peoples 've been scarred terribly. The whole world, barring America, seems ter 'ave been bombed – folks 've lorst their familiar surroundings, ain't they? Stands ter reason, dunnit? Still *millions of refugees,* the pitiful flotsam and jetsam of 'em who've lorst their identities and their own countries – lorst their 'omes, their loved ones, everyfink. Some of 'em may never recover their memories or their sanity! Iffen yer digs too deep into yer soul abaht those peoples it might be more 'n' yer own mind can assimilate.'

Her mouth wide open in surprise to hear her old dad talking like that, she shut it with a gulp and nodded to Gertie, who was just as spellbound!

'Yerse, girls, yer mind can only take so much – we orl 'ave ter find our ways, step by step.' Henry ruffled his youngest daughter's curls. 'I've got a brain of me own, lovey, maybe I duzzn't use it enuff but it's orl up 'ere under me cap!'

'Sorry, Dad, I just didn't fink; me and Gertie

288

woz jist chattin' abaht women being chattels when they gets married!'

'Don't let that put yer orff marriage, Tabby. I ain't yet met a married woman 'oo can't twist fings round fer her own benefit.'

'Dad!' Gertie expostulated, with a wry grimace.

''S troof, innit?'

'Maybe, maybe not ... I don't always get me own way wiv *my* 'usband!'

'Wanna bet on it?' laughed Henry, pouring his ale carefully into a large glass. 'Spoke to yer 'usband the uvver night at the darts match, sez 'is little woman twists 'im round her little finger!'

Gertie had the grace to blush. 'Well, some of us married women ain't as clever as Tabby at reading 'n' writing an' orl that but we still finks abaht fings youse knows like...!'

Downing his pint, and smacking his lips with gusto, Henry wiped his mouth with the back of his hairy hand. 'But youse orl goes round the mulberry bush 'n' back again before youse gets down ter the nitty gritty.'

'Iffen yer sez so, yeah! Wot's wrong wiv that? We puts our families first – our priority – got our priorities right we has! Youse knows, cooking, cleaning, feeding, queuing for rations – not everyfink is off rations yet, no it bloomin' well ain't! By the time we've shopped, seen ter the babies, scrubbed the nappies on the rubbing board; rushing back in wiv 'em every time it rains; tryin' ter get 'em dry; coping wiv screamin' hungry babies; staggering out to the line wiv heavy carpets ter beat the livin' daylights out of 'em; gettin' 'em off the line, struggling back in wiv 'em; tripping over the cat … I could go on for ever!'

Henry threw his hands out palms forward, 'Orl right, girl, orl right. I knows wot yer does, don't I? Got the picture, ain't we Tabby?'

Biting her bottom lip hesitantly Tabby nodded her head. Gertie made marriage sound like something from Charles Dickens!

'Iffen yerve got schoolchildren 'n' them's too young ter go on their own, youse get ter juggle feeding babies and going backwards and forwards to school! Don't fergit the washing, ironing, mending, knitting, darning socks; the lino ter be polished on 'ands and knees. The stairs ter be brushed; the door knocker cleaned wiv brasso, and the doorstep. Coping wiv teething babies, sleepless nights: can't switch off can we? Still 'ave ter carry on don't we? 'Ave a nice hot meal ready fer yer 'usband in the evening … who expects ter come 'ome to a nice clean quiet 'ome, expecting the bathed, perfumed, sweet young girl he married – ready fer a bit of nookie *every night!* When all yer feels like doin' is layin' yer 'ead on yer pillow and kissin' the world goodbye fer a solid ten hours sleep! No sooner 'ave yer shuts yer bloomin' eyes, than the babies, or baby is wailing fer its two hourly feed or feeds! Seem ter 'ave an inbuilt clock, they really duz. They lets out a high-pitched scream; yer 'usband stuffs 'is 'ead under the pillow, and that's yer night's sleep down the pan!'

'An' I bets yer wouldn't 'ave it any different, Gertie,' Henry winked at Tabby.

'Nah! Course I wouldn't, would I? Likes bein'

married wiv babies I do, but I tells the troof don't I, Dad?'

'No use askin' 'im, never around when youse lot woz babies; niver saw a dirty nappy did 'ee?' Jean entered and flopped into her favourite armchair.

'Mebbe, when me children are grown up and leave 'ome we'll be able ter make sumfink of ourselves – somehow?'

Jean snorted derisively, 'That's wot youse finks! Youse'll 'ave yer grandchildren to occupy yer time.'

'Hello, Mum, sit still, I'll make a fresh pot of tea, left the triplets with their dad I 'ave – betcha they're pesterin' the life out of 'im, do 'im good!'

Peering round the room, Jean cocked her head, listening intently. 'Where's Benjie? Can't 'ear 'im.'

'Left him wiv the triplets, didn't I! 'Elpin' ter look after them 'ee sez, bless 'is little cotton sox: he's a little angel, Mum, 'ee realy is.'

'Knows that, don't I, Gertie? Had a placid muvver didn't he? By the time my Benjie entered this world for better or worse, I woz an *experienced muvver*, wozzn't I? A placid muvver makes a placid baby is wot my old granmuvver orlways sez.'

'I 'elped youse bring Benjie up, Mum,' said Tabby.

Jean nodded, smilingly. Pointing out that Benjie had never woken her at night, always slept the whole night through. 'Don't let that fool youse, Tabby, the rest of youse lot had me up all hours, I can tell youse; yerse!'

291

Tabby grimaced thoughtfully, and Gertie hastened to explain that she was just initiating Tabby into some of the rituals of a married woman's life. Whereupon Jean just laughed cheerfully saying that after the first month it would become a natural way of life, just like breathing in fact, natural instinct! Gertie chuckled, making her mother reflect on how alike she and Gertie were, almost like sisters; the age gap was so short, she'd had Gertie when she was young.

'We don't bring home, or rather – we didn't bring home all those eligible authors and poets from the library, like you, did we Mum?'

'Yer meanz Lord Tennyson?' cackled Jean.

Henry'd had enuff of women's talk. Making a fast exit, he muttered something about a darts match and he'd have his supper when he got home. 'Put it in the oven will yer, Jean, lass?'

'Don't yer get ter blamin' me iffen it's orl dried up then.'

But Henry was already out of earshot; the door slammed behind him, putting Jean's teeth on edge. She swore the door would fall off its hinges one of these days – just a few more slams!

With thirteen daughters, talk had never been Henry's cup of tea – he was a ladies' man when it came to sowing his oats; that apart, he was more of a man's man. Who could blame him when up against the feminine wiles and machinations of the fairer sex. Always out-talked, out-smarted, out-voted; he knew very well when to make himself scarce!

'There ain't much me and Gertie duzzn't say to

292

each uvver, is there Gertie?' said Jean, nodding her head maddeningly slowly, knowledgeably at Tabby.

'Knows abaht the Pyrex! Oh yerse I duz!' Gertie looked at Tabby mischievously. 'Knows a lot I duz, yerse, knows a lot I duz!'

'Yer jist sed it, twice, Mum's told yer.' Gertie's head was bobbing like a Chinese doll!

'Yer won't tell Dad or Freddy, will yer?'

Gertie looked horrified, and asked what sort of sister she took her for. 'Ow d'yer finks I got this here dress I'm wearing? From a tallyman – on the knocker of course. Stoopid! … 'n' the fake-fur suits fer the triplets? And me new set of sheets? Off the knocker wasn't they, orl of 'em. Youse ain't the only one, lovey. Mum takes care of the tallyman fer orl of us. All the women do it, don't they, Mum?'

'Well, I'll be blowed, I'm borned in this 'ouse, lived 'ere orl me young life, ain't I? I never knew Mum used the tallyman, I'll be blowed.'

'Yer might be blowed 'n' all mightn't she, Mum?' She gave her mother a saucy wink.

'Keep yer mouf clean, Gertie, child ain't wed yet. Let 'er stay innocent until 'er time comes.'

She didn't have a clue what her mother and Gertie meant, though judging by the wink, it was something salacious. Blushing she murmured about powdering her nose which they knew she never did, she escaped to the cool confines of the tiled bathroom, pressing her hot cheeks against the cold white tiles. But she didn't get off the hook so easily. She couldn't stay in the bathroom for ever; resignedly she went back down, knowing full well they were in a bantering mood!

'Little pitchers have big ears that's wot we women sez, lovey: men at work, children at school – right on cue – the tallyman calls. Pretty smart set-up?'

Tabby wondered if the husbands guessed? Apparently not, they just thought the wife or the missus was clever and saved from the house-keeping! Least said, soonest mended was what the wives thought!

'Too occupied wiv their own thoughts, ain't they, Gertie? Go ter work when it's dark in winter 'n' come 'ome when it's dark: working a com-pulsory five-and-a-half day week, Monday ter Saturday midday; they're blue-collar workers – that's wot they calls men who works wiv their 'ands! In the factories or uvver jobs suchlike. On their half-days they goes ter football, at the Hammers ground in West Ham … or elsewhere, or plays themselves. Football's the number one topic in our streets! Then they go greyhound racing; the dogs; do the pools; place horse racing bets with a bookie's runner standing on the corner, by the fish shop – with a wary eye out for a zealous copper! Saturday mornings we pack the younger kids off to the Saturday morning picture clubs; Sunday afternoon, after dinner, we packs 'em off to the Sunday pictures ter let the men 'ave a lie-in wiv their wives in the afternoon.'

'Yeah!' said Gertie dreamily, 'Yeah…!'

'In the evening fer tea we 'as winkles, cockles, whelks, mussels – wot we gets orff the barrer boys Sunday mornin' when they pulls their barrers up 'n' down the six streets. Dad reads his papers of

294

a Sunday mornin', then the men goes to The King's Oak fer a quick one!'

Tabby was slightly puzzled, why were they taking pains to tell her all this; *she already knew it off by heart* – it'd been her life too, for as long as she could remember!

Jean and Gertie reiterated they were only trying to point out that life after marriage followed a prescribed ritual in the six streets. Tabby then pointed out *she* would *not* be living in the six streets! So who was to say that her and Freddy would follow such an habitual way of life!

Jean admitted she had a point or two, but it was the prescribed manner for almost all working-class peoples of their social status!

'Yer dad let's Tabby read the Sunday papers after he's read 'em orl! He niver used ter let youse uvver girls read them until you went out to work; he knows Tabby is a good reader so he let Tabby read them – youse were privileged, Tabby, yerse, yer woz!'

Mockingly Tabby curtsied, 'Fanks, Mum, am I supposed to curtsy to me dad jist 'cos 'ee lets me read the Sunday papers? Only cost a few coppers each they do. Anyways, 'ee duzzn't read them properly! He jist skims through them muttering a few words on each page, then he turns over to another page!'

'No need ter be sarcastic, lovey, jist 'cos yer can read well, yer farver left school at twelve! Youse could go into any 'ouse in the six streets 'n' youse'll find all the uvver farvers doin' the same as my Henry. Only bits they really read are the melodramatic bits, the salacious bits and the sports pages! Makes 'em feel important it does, to the rest of the family – ter be seen reading the Sundays – whether or not they understands wot they're reading! Youse've gotta give 'em some respect ain't yer? We wimmin ain't goin' ter disillusion them, is we? Got a lot ter larn ain't she, Gertie? Had her nose in her books and the world's passed her by!'

'Yeah! But don't worry, Tabby, times are changin' fer wimmin, slowly I know, but they 'is changin'!'

'I'll believe that when I sees it!' said Jean firmly.

'Don't look so worried, little sister, t'ain't as bad as we've made it sound! Jist givin' youse a few tips and wrinkles from our vast experience, eh Mum?'

Jean nodded sagely.

That was Tabitha Braithewaite's initiation into the ways and rituals of the working class of her social sphere. She wasn't stupid, she knew what was going on around her, but, certain things were never actually spelled out to young women. You were either a child or a woman; there was no official or semi-official in-between status. You wore ankle socks until the day you left school; the following day you never wore them again, except perhaps for roller skating or long bicycle rides into the countryside. Stockings and make-up did not have the approval of fathers until one left school.

A deep, heartfelt, prolonged, audible sigh escaped from Gertie. 'I was jist thinkin' can't be much fun fer a man can it? To 'ave ter go away and fight and kill people, even if you don't want to? What some of 'em went through the war years must have been their worst nightmares come true! No wonder most of 'em didn't even want ter go on holidays ter the seaside; after demob they were jist happy ter be 'ome wiv their loved ones for them there really is no place like 'ome!'

'That's understandable, I woz tellin' my Freddy about that and he told me about his uncles ... I mean the uncle who woz on secret war work; doesn't like eating out any more – can't stand seein' strangers watchin' 'im, 'ee prefers to eat at home. That ain't the uncle who left all that wood; it's anuvver one, still alive he is!'

Jean measuredly poured herself another cup of the fresh piping hot tea which she'd made. Thoughtfully she stirred its golden amber colour, swirling it around the cup, savouring the hot heady fragrance. There was nothing like a good pot of tea.

'That's a strange fing ter say innit? I suppose, in a way, 'ee could be right, six years of eating away from 'ome in strange places! D'yer know where 'ee were posted?'

'Oh Mum! How the heck would I know that? Won't even tell his own bruvver, Freddy's dad. Said 'ee can't say, 'cos he signed the secrecy act like 'is uvver bruvver!'

'Wot difference does that make now; war's been over fer years?'

'Honestly Mum. I don't know. He told Freddy that the secrecy act which he signed – means everything will go to his grave with him! Never be able to tell a soul, that's what he said. Won't even tell Freddy, he won't; and he thinks the world of

Freddy. If anyone starts probing or quizzing him – he just walks out of the room.'

'Changing the subject – me and Gertie ain't exactly stoopid yer knows; ain't clever like youse – ain't got yer brains – but we don't do so bad, do we, Gertie? The radio's on all day, we gain lots of knowledge from some of the programmes. We join in Housewives' Choice for a good morning sing-song, as we does our 'ousework – yer bacon-bonce takes it orl in, an' yer stores it away in yer belfry. Listens ter classical music we do 'n' all! We gets more knowledge than lots of them white-collar toffs up the City. Yerse!'

'S'right Mum! Sometime. I get ter thinkin' an' I thinks ter meself I duz – if there hadn't been a war – I might 'ave made "sumfink" of merself, eh Mum?'

Jean nodded encouragingly.

'But I'm only a woman!' Gertie finished lamely.

Shocked, Tabby's tongue tripped over the words, *Only* – she drew herself up to her full height – 'yer not jist only a woman … even if…' she giggled – 'yer your 'usband's chattel! Youse both 'ave got brains. Mum's brought up fourteen children all still alive! You've got triplets! 'Ow many women d'you know wiv triplets? I don't know any young woman wiv triplets. Yer looks after them good and proper. Let me tell yer sumfink, that's an *achievement,* yer keep them beautifully. I knows yer me big sister, Gertie, but I'm not stoopid! I'm a woman, ain't I? Miss Brink, me teacher, she told me a long time ago, "Women have got good brains, *many* are better than *some* men – with brain power! Look at the

first woman doctor – Elisabeth Black – that was
her name, I think. All that male prejudice against
a woman becoming a qualified doctor – and she
did! Look at Marie Stopes who founded the birth
control clinic in 1921! She wrote verses and plays
and she wrote a manual *Married Love* in 1918.
How about that than? It helped thousands of
women to avoid babies and backstreet abortions
with knitting needles stuck up 'em. What about
Florence Nightingale – eh? She and her nurses
saved more men than any general could – no
matter how tactical he was. Elizabeth Barret-
Browning wrote poetry; Beatrix Potter with her
little books for little hands. Why the list is almost
endless with women's achievements; there'll be
more as time goes by, mark my words. What
about Nancy Astor, the first woman MP?'

'Gosh! How did I give birth to such a little
rebel woman as you, lovey? I loves yer and youse
is probably right, times is changing. *Yer dad still
thinks women came out of the ark!* Here, I'll put the
kettle on again. Like a wee drop in yourn, Gertie?
It's in the sideboard, right-hand door, half a
bottle. Fetch it will yer lovey – I won't be a tick.'

'It's been great fun talking ain't it? It's … er …
what's the word … illum…?'

'Illuminating.'

'Yeah! That's it, spot on, illuminating. You make
me and Mum fink a bit harder! D'yer mates fink
like you?'

'Yes and no, Gertie! Depends. Some never gets
their noses beyond romance books; can't say I
blame 'em; romantic escapism – *one of the perks of
life innit?* Keeps 'em happy. Gives 'em a good

299

read, dunnit? Yeah! There is uvvers, like me – read similar books, think deeply, yer know – they like the classics of Jane Austen and Emily Brontë and the new women authors that are gradually springing up!'

'Miss Tabitha Braithewaite, for a very young woman I daringly salute you from the bottom of me heart. Hopes any girls I 'ave will be cast in the same mould as youse. A wonderful thing!'

'Fanks, I ain't that clever, 'n' I ain't experienced like youse and Mum. Keeps me eyes open and earwigging as well as me nose in books. Finks iffen we have daughters they will be cleverer than us. Stands ter reason dunnit, the way of the world. What's that phrase that Yank used: *"It's the way the cookie crumbles"!'*

'Yer can say that agin – here, a nice hot pot of Hornimans.' Jean sat down sighing contentedly. It did make a nice change to have intelligent talk! A change from babies, nappies and shopping!

Tabby pointed out the *importance* of a woman having self-esteem, admitting they're a person in their own right, an individual: not a piece of cod on a fishmonger's slab.

'Oh daughter! Youse'll be the deaf of me – youse will!' Jean rubbed away the tears of laughter rolling down onto her nose. 'I'd put youse against Churchill in the 'Ouse of Commons any day. Maybe men unite ter keep women as chattels? Your Freddy's gonna 'ave an 'andful wiv youse, lovey. Fink I better warn 'im! Drink yer tea, d'ya wanna wee drop 'n' all? It won't 'urt yer in yer tea.'

The wee drop turned into *several* wee drops

with the fat brown earthenware teapot being filled a few times more; Gertie'd brought a small twist of tea with her. The yellow cable woolly tea cosy kept the pot hot. Jean liked a good strong cuppa; Henry didn't like the tea cosy, 'Makes it stewed,' he said.

'I knows one fing, we orl comes from Adam's Rib – larnt that at Sunday school I did 'n' orl; we orl did, yer granmuvver made sure of that! Clean dresses, hair tied wiv ribbons; eh, we looked bonny in them days! It ain't so long ago – but feels like a lifetime! I made youse lot go, didn't I! Yerve got ter larn abaht God and Jesus 'n' the Holy Ghost, the free 'n' one – and the *Bible* somewhere 'n' the best place to larn is in God's house, the church, innit?'

Nobody said a word, Jean was on one of her pet subjects.

'I means ter say, I duz, we ain't orl going ter be equal. He made men and women different to com–'

'Complement one another,' said Tabby, dutifully.

'That's the word, complement – iffen he'd wanted men and women ter be the same he'd 'ave made us the same, wouldn't 'ee? Wouldn't've 'ad ter take a rib from poor old Adam ter make inter a woman would 'ee? Complement each uvver, we do, the man on the radio sed that word; means we sort of suit fine, it don't mean compliments, it's spelt wiv an "e" after the "l"! I looked it up in the dictionary which Tabby borrowed the uvver day, from Freddy.'

'Miss Brink told me that 'n' all! She's a lovely

teacher, Miss Brink. I enjoyed my lessons wiv her; she made everything seem interesting, got a lot ter thank 'er for I have!'

'Oh, Tabby, don't start talking about the sweetheart she lost in the war. Let the dead rest in peace; it's the best way. The war's been and gone long ago now!'

'Youse do think 'ard then, Gertie?'

'Course I do, don't I, Mum? Learnt a lot from me 'usband, older'n me ain't 'ee – away in the fightin' 'ee were fer six years, hardens a man, so 'ee sez. Sed they orl grew up overnight in the armed forces! Yer either did that or yer went AWOL – or did wot a few poor silly blokes did, committed suicide, didn't they? Couldn't face orl the 'ardship and the drill and thought of having ter go overseas to kill people! Orl right, Mum, must be the wee drops making me a bit maudlin! I'll 'ave anuvver wee drop iffen yer don't mind? Told me 'usband I'm thinkin' of goin' ter night school! Reckons it's a good idea, but wot abaht the triplets, if he's asked ter work overtime? Needs the overtime to pay fer their shoes: we gets 'em those wide ones; good quality, called Doggy Toes! They ain't cheap at three pairs a time. Tommy kicked the toes out of his uvver pair in two weeks. Our Benjie's teaching 'em ter play football! Sez he's going ter get them ter play fer the Hammers up Upton Park, 'n' 'ee's goin' ter be their manager! Bless 'im! He duz love the triplets, took him shopping wiv us we did the other day and he told everybody "I'm their uncle, they belong to me."'

'Young Eddie's jist as bad, toddles along

scuffling his toes on the pavements. If I've told the little tyke once I've told him a million times! Got a mind of his own 'ee 'as, just smiles 'is sweet smile and sez, *"Told yer millions"'* Me next door neighbour sez if I go ter night school her 'usband will give her permission ter go wiv me.'

Delightedly Tabby urged her to go to English and Business Studies: she reckoned it was fantastic Gertie's husband didn't object. She would no longer be a mere chattel – well … unofficially – it was a beginning, she promptly offered to babysit if Gertie's husband was on overtime. 'My Freddy sez education is the best route for the workin' class. "Stepping stones to success in life and fulfilment of self!" Wasn't that a great thing ter say? He's a luverlee bloke, my Freddy.'

Gertie cleared the table. 'Your Freddy is goin' places, lovey, mark my word, even me dad sed that, didn't 'ee, Mum?'

Jean nodded in agreement, and pointed out that Freddy was getting a bargain with their Tabby. She'd be a wife any man could feel proud of, especially if Freddy goes up the ladder. She reckoned Tabby would be just a rung behind him. The Braithewaites were on their way up – the whole family; Derek would become an MP, she could feel it in her waters, Henry agreed.

'It's a grand feeling ter know me daughters 'ave got good 'usbands wiv … wot's that new-fangled word yer used Tabby, the uvver day?'

'High aspirations, Mum!'

'Yeah. High wotsists – wot Tabby jist sed. Henry sed he can see us sitting in the Strangers' Gallery – or is it the Visitors' – anyway, where

303

they sits ter listen ter Parliament debating – listening to our son-in-law down there on the back benches! Eh! That'd be sumfink, wouldn't it?'

Freddy had checked with the bank, their nest egg was doing very well – better than he'd even dreamed. His lump sum share of the Pools win had been invested in an assured high interest rate account. He told Tabby, 'Takes money to make money, love.' The bank manager told him money always goes to money.

'Let's set the date for our wedding day, love, I don't think I can hold out any longer!' Not being able to think of any valid reason not to set the date she acquiesced. At least then, she wouldn't have to keep Freddy from going all the way to preserve her *hallowed* virginity on her mother's insistence! Daily it became a struggle to *prevent* him ... she was running out of excuses and didn't like arguing with him; she loved him too much for that. A few weeks prior to the set wedding date – provided the vicar could marry them on that preferred date (chosen because she wouldn't have her periods on her honeymoon) – Freddy would reach the magical age of twenty-one and be a man with a man's wage. (They still hadn't let on about Freddy's ambition for their own business.) The date was set between them – mutually. It was a toss-up who was the most excited, Tabby or Freddy. He knew one thing, it would be a physical release which his body could hardly, barely, thrillingly wait for! Trying to appear blasé, underneath Freddy was all nerves.

In their social circle marriage was a serious step, a matter of life and death so to speak – that's how it seemed … an irrevocable step in life! Marriage was 'until death us do part, according to God's Holy Will'.

He hadn't wanted a shotgun wedding any more than Tabby did – look at poor Ginger! Mind you, *poor young Ginger* seemed a very happy fulfilled man! Marriage appeared to agree wholeheartedly with him, his bride being as carnal-minded as her obviously carnal-minded husband – a well-matched pair! Freddy's father would have been furious if Freddy had dared to compromise Tabby! Being married, that would be something else he wouldn't have to worry about! His family were a tall family they were amused by Tabby's height and referred to her amongst themselves as *the little one,* meant warmly, not derogatorily. His mother rammed it into his brain 'don't you get that little one up the spout, my son: you ain't too big fer me to thump you one. She's a nice, clean, good girl who any mother-in-law would be proud to have.'

Secretly Freddy was grateful for Tabby's mental strength and keeping him at arms length when it came to carnality, for want of a better word to describe his lust and agonising desire! He'd no desire to father an illegitimate child, any more than Tabby – the word 'bastard' was a terrible burden to place on an innocent child's life which would stick for ever! *To be born out of wedlock* was a terrifying phrase. Society at large did not look kindly on bastards whether they were upper-class, middle-class or lower-class: it was a moot point whether such a child could legally inherit. No! he couldn't do that to a child of his own loins: if it had happened it was true they could have rushed a marriage – but the stigma would be there – all their social circle would know, it would be obvious on the child's birth certificate, for ever; and *for ever is a long time!* During the war, his younger sister had been evacuated and the locals shouted out dirty evacuee bastards – it wasn't true, of course; his sister was as legitimate as himself – but names stuck! Anyway, his good name was a necessity for his goal of becoming a successful businessman.

He'd discussed his ideals and aspirations with his friendly, cheerful bank manager. Any bank manager would be friendly and cheerful with a client who deposited a huge Pools' win into his bank! They'd gone out for a meal together, a two-hour lunch! Concrete, interesting and viable possibilities had been discussed and mulled over during hearty appetisers. Partaking of a well-made steak and kidney pudding and two vegetables with treacle tart and yellow custard cloyingly departing down their gullets, Mr Chirley remarked, 'It's a change from the war-time staple of rabbit pie, a nice tasty change.'

Mr Chirley did not habitually wine-and-dine his clients but money, good money, tended to sway one advantageously; he could smell out a good thing, a man of aspirations and means, a mile away. He was quite capable in his judicious summing up of young Freddy. A good young bloke – aiming high. Good, decent prospective wife (he'd met her) with similar aspirations and a mind of her own, hmm, hmm! Mentally he rubbed his hands with undisguised glee – oh joy – oh money, money, money for his bank! The private owners would be so pleased, maybe he'd get a big walloping rise? The possibility was there – then he'd be able to purchase the beach hut at the seaside which his crabbed-face wife kept insisting on as a necessity for the image of a successful bank manager – then he'd get some peace and quiet from her wittering tongue!

The auditor's report to the bank's owners a few years ago, when another Pools' winner deposited his winnings had been great joy for Mr Chirley: he'd bought the black Ford car which Mrs Chirley had also deemed necessary for a husband in his exalted position. Such joy, the day he'd driven it home! Mrs Chirley had, unthinkably, permitted – yes permitted – him to enjoy himself in bed that night. A carrot which alas, he was not permitted to inveigle himself of too often; true she'd been cold-as-ice and her body stiff as a board – but the blessed relief of the shooting of his life sparks had stayed with him these many years. Dare he hope she would be so accommodating again if he bought the beach hut? His nightly wet dreams in his single twin bed and his self-masturbation every morning before he shaved were his only present form of relief!

Privy now to young Freddy's plan of setting himself up in business, Mr Chirley beatifically offered him a cigar – one of his manifold sins that dared not be smoked at home.

Setting on *the wedding date* proper would bring everything into line, nicely, thought Freddy; he mentioned it to Mr Chirley. Deep in his heart-of-hearts, Mr Chirley, underneath his habitual crusty exterior, as benefited a bank manager was a soppy romantic, he liked young Freddy immensely. He was more than keen to help and advise such a smart forward-thinking, promising bloke with terms of advice about his fortune and the interest accumulated on the added interest. He could feel it in his very bones, young Freddy was going up the ladder of success and enterprise. Mr Chirley had been in the army and had risen through the ranks of the Royal Fusiliers' Regiment. After demob, he'd returned to the bank where he'd worked, man and boy, before the war. His present exalted position was owed not just to his banking nous ability and climbing, but due partly to another factor which stood him in good stead and helped him most quickly. He'd been in the same regiment, indeed he'd fought with, the son of the owners of the bank, their only son. Such celestial luck which astrologers liked to bandy around was now Mr Chirley's honeypot! Mr Chirley had actually saved the life of Tigger – the pet name for Mr Adolphus Gustave Gluckstein who had been adopted when a six-week-old baby by the present owners of the bank. Owners for all of thirty years, the bank retained its old name for continuity and neatness! The Glucksteins could not do enough to help Mr Chirley – well within moderation. Gus gave chapter and verse to Mr Chirley's bravery in the face of enemy fire – and the long and the short of it was Mr Chirley was awarded the MBE! True, Mrs Chirley had snobbishly felt he deserved higher than that, but Mr Chirley was more than satisfied, he'd just done his duty.

As the bank manager, where he'd humbly started his career as a mere clerk, Mr Chirley was now a most respected gentleman. Needless to say, at the Hammers' home matches he was just one of the lads in his cap and West Ham football scarf. He didn't quite think the woolly hat went with his new image so he compromised with the cap. And his ear-shattering football rattle, which he rattled vigorously in-between singing along with the crowds, 'I'm forever blowin' bubbles, Pretty bubbles in the air, They rise so high, nearly reach the sky, Just like my dreams they fade and die.'

As is well documented, Mr Chirley was a softie underneath his outward mien. He had a way with young persons, his army training stood him in good stead; they liked him and trusted him with their money. The reputation of his bank was nonpareil, it was no lowering of his exalted status for Mr Chirley to take young Freddy out to lunch; quite the opposite. They'd met on the football terraces; afterwards they'd enjoyed a convivial round or two at the nearest pub – the Red Lion with like-minded men and youths.

The day he espied young Freddy enter the hallowed portals of his bank he'd told his chief clerk, Tebbit, 'He's going a long way is Mr Frederick Debnon, yes, a long way, a fine young man.'

'What about his fiancée, sir?'

'Charming little slip of a thing, wish I was ten years younger! Can't be barely five feet tall!'

'Is she of good standing, sir?'

'Oh, I forgot, from up North aren't you, Tebbit? You don't know the Braithewaites; fine family, very large – thirteen girls and one boy. Good, clean, honest folk, well respected family in this area.

'Miss Tabitha is head and shoulders above them: quite a knowledgeable young lass. I know her older sister Gertie, the eldest, I was brought up round here, you know, oh yes. Don't speak in the vernacular do I –goes with the job not to! You should hear me at a Hammers' home match! Tabitha is what my dad used to call a blue-stocking, a bit of a bookworm, have you not spoken to her?'

'Can't say that I have, sir, she merely pays her money in each month to the counter clerk. Seems a quiet person, never opens her mouth to anyone!'

'A good thing, reticence in a woman! A very good sign, yes indeed, she'll make a good businesswoman.'

Tebbit looked startled, 'If you say so sir, if you say so!'

'I do, Tebbit, I emphatically do!'

'It's a smart house with smart rooms, whatever the word smart means in this context? But, oh, I don't know, really! It doesn't seem ter 'ave a family feeling abaht it. No, it don't!'

He sighed annoyingly, getting tensed – very tensed. They'd been out looking for houses for months! Tabby had her needle stuck in the same groove! None of them seemed a friendly family house! In vain, Freddy had rooted out more properties for her to look over – properties many young women would give their eye teeth for. But not Tabitha Braithewaite! He was absolutely, thoroughly fed up! Feeling more and more like an interloper with each house they viewed.

Elbows bent, resting on the table, her face cupped in her pink fingernailed hands, Tabby looked quizzingly at him. She really did love him, she adored him, she didn't want to argue with him, he was such a lovely bloke, an audible sigh escaped her pink lips.

'All right, Freddy! I promise! Next house we look at, I will make a decision. Can we give it a bit of a rest for about one month. I'm sick of looking at people's twee homes where you can hardly swing a cat round let alone bring up a family. We've got a few more months before our wedding day.'

'But … but… Tabby! The whole house may need decorating; we might not have enough time to get it finished!'

'So what? Got plenty of spondulicks in the bank, ain't we? We can afford professional decorators. People did before the war, Mum told me. Done by professionals it would be money well spent.'

'By whom? D'ya know a good decorator? Seems to me it's the age of DIY.'

'Sally's brother-in-law, of course. Professional ain't he … set himself up in his own business after being demobbed from National Service. Doing well he is, in great demand from the gentry – their homes knocked around by the bombings and all that – can't wait to get hold of good decorators! Pays him over the top they do – up front, youse ask Sally! Billy jumped on the bandwagon – he's making money hand-over-fist ever since. Works a sixteen-hour day, seven days a week – he duz! You liked the way our Sally's flat was decorated, didn't yer? Billy did that. Wasn't' Derek, he duzzn't know one end of the paint-brush from anuvver, let alone paint the walls! Told you they'd bought that flat, didn't I?' Not waiting for a reply she added in the same breath, 'Would have taken them too long ter qualify fer a council place!'

'I'm not with you, Tabby. Start again. Yeah, I know about Billy and his decorating business – you didn't tell me. Yeah I did think Derek decorated the flat. So it was Billy, was it?'

'His brothers and sisters are all married, only his Mum and Dad are in the house, Derek did tell me the council said they'd got enough room and didn't qualify at the moment – others more needful than them! Not a priority are they? *Don't qualify!* Makes me laugh! Six years fighting for his King and Country and he don't qualify! *Land fit for heroes;* don't wanna know him and the other poor sods now they're out of uniform, do they? Before you start, I know what you're going to say, millions like him – but good Lord, it ain't justice! It's an injustice,' she said softly putting her soft warm arms round him and hugging tightly. 'I know, so does Derek, he ain't bitter abaht it. That's why he wants to become an MP. Says, "The best way to right wrongs in a democracy is to *hit through the ballot box,*" that's what Derek intends to do!

'Fortunately he left some money in a bank, when he went overseas; even more fortunately, the bank never suffered a direct hit during the war. Just a good shakin'. The interest accumulated, enough for a deposit on the flat, and some furniture.'

'He has talked about becoming an MP down at The King's Oak; I just thought it was the beer talking! Y'know, men's talk – pie in the sky!'

'Well, my dear Mr Debnon, it ain't, he really wants to be an MP. Come on, Freddy, cheer up – we're going places too – or me name ain't the future Mrs Tabitha Debnon!'

'We are, we most certainly are! All right, kitten, ask Derek, or ask Billy, about decorating prices and all that. Tell him we want the best, nothing's going to be too good for you, kitten! I'm beginning to lose track of all your brother-in-laws, it's a wonder anybody can – *I'll have twelve sister-in-laws and twelve brother-in-laws* all on the same day! My mind boggles!'

'Nope! Don't let it worry ya! Even Mum and Dad's minds boggle – they've given up trying to work out who's who!'

Crushing her to his chest he felt the plumpness of her body, her mother's stews were fattening her up for 'Thanksgiving'! He wasn't complaining, all the more to hold. He liked a bit of flesh on a woman, especially when she was his.

Chapter Fourteen

Excitement reigned supreme in the Braithewaite household: the forthcoming wedding occupied almost all of Jean's waking thoughts. So determined was she that the remaining and youngest Braithewaite girl would be seen off in style.

There was to be no hand-me-down wedding dress, worn by countless other brides; no, not for her Tabby. It had been necessary for some of her older daughters due to coupons and other necessities. The only borrowed item of Tabby's bridal ensemble would be the handsome, Valenciennes lace found in an old forgotten trunk of Jean's own mother. How her mother came by such a rare, expensive piece of lace was quite beyond her comprehension. It might have been the lace on her great-grandmother's dress, judging by an old badly-faded, sepia portrait at the bottom of the trunk.

As for the trunk and its other contents – languishing undisturbed for aeons underneath a pile of old junk in her late mother's loft – well, that was quite a surprise! Luckily, Henry had decided to root around in every nook and cranny before turning the rented house back to the private landlord. He'd not held out much hope of discovering anything of monetary value but, as he so rightly said, 'Yer niver do know wiv old folks.

Puts fings away and fergits orl abaht them.'

When he uncovered the massive trunk with its strong lock he let out such a whoop of joy; Jean could have been forgiven for thinking of him as Long John Silver and a booty of pieces-of-eight!

Henry'd had to smash the lock, which had taken some doing; when the contents were revealed – not pieces of eight nor even pounds, shillings and pennies – he'd been so disappointed to find it full of nothing but old clothes and bits 'n' pieces – not even some decent silver cutlery or candlesticks! 'Every working bloke's dream is ter find an old trunk full of money or silver; wot does Henry Braithewaite get – nothing but old toot.'

He felt quite bitter did Henry – somehow he never seemed to be able to put his mitts on a fortune – couldn't even win the top dividend on the Pools could he. 'It jist isn't fair!'

'If me old Mum was alive now I betcha she'd have forgotten orl abaht this trunk!'

'Wot was there to remember about it?' asked Henry. 'A pile of old clothes 'n' bits 'n' pieces – no good to anyone, is it?'

But Jean disagreed, it was a great find. Vaguely she recalled her mother telling her a story to do with certain persons who'd worked for the gentry in the big houses at Forest Gate – in the old days when it was *de rigeur* to employ at least one servant and a cook. Such gentry were one step down in the pecking order of the gentility proper.

Unlike some people they'd set great value on their retainers; valued their servants and were good Masters and Mistresses. Insomuch they often gave or left to them, possessions of their own in gratitude for their loyalty. A little bit above the crumbs from under the table. Hence the forgotten trunk – which Jean thought of as a box of delights. The historical value of the contents of the truck in terms of antiquity did not, at first, enter their minds. Henry's, because he was so disappointed, *'Not even a brass farthing!'* Jean's, because her memory of the story was so vague, and her mind immediately jumped to how she could utilise the materials and lace for her beloved younger daughter's wedding of the year!

It was only when Tabby'd brought some books home on historical costumes from the library, were they more fully enlightened to their treasure trove.

Nothing then would do for Tabby but to urge her father to break the lock on the old trunk in their loft where it had been deposited after removal from Grandmother's loft. Somehow, after first breaking it open he'd managed to fasten it so securely it had become jammed! It has been a great stroke of luck at the time, for, if they'd not removed it from Grandma's loft after the funeral it would never have seen the light of day – the house was flattened a few weeks later by a doodlebug and the trunk would have been blown to smithereens, along with the house which vanished into thin air, leaving a pile of rubble!

The opening of the box – *for the second time* – had put the cat amongst the pigeons as far as Gertie and the other girls were concerned. They wailed that Jean should have remembered all the old dresses, which they could have utilised for themselves! Make-do-and-mend and the coupons system had been no joke! *All those years.*

'I did tells yer orl, it were nuffink but rubbish,' said Henry. 'Youse didn't 'ave ter believe me, did yer?'

His daughters were not amused because he hadn't exactly spelled out what sort of rubbish it was – even his wife hadn't given it another thought! Had she done so, she now realised what it would have meant to the girls – with austerity during and after the war. In 1941 alone, the ration of clothing coupons was about sixty-six per man, woman and child. As for nice materials availability, you could whistle for it – if you were lucky – or depend on the black market! And all those years Grandmother had the secret trunk in her loft. Jean's mother had died of a heart attack after a particularly heavy bombing raid – it had missed her house that time, but flattened those at the end of her street. Henry'd got some lads to help him and they'd stripped the house of everything moveable.

In the dark loft, by torchlight they'd literally had to fight their way through enormous cobwebs. The story of the trunk had been handed down since that day but it was just a story, they never thought anything more about it. Not after Henry's disappointment!

Even little Benjie knew about a *trunk*. His little mind pictured it as belonging to Captain Hook because Tabby was always telling him fantastic stories.

As she'd grown older Tabby thought of poor Miss Havisham sitting in her bridal finery with her bridal banquet all laid out, being nibbled by rats from *Great Expectations*. She ventured to mention it half-heartedly to her mother who couldn't see the harm in having a decent rummage in the trunk. They had electricity in their loft, so it would be easier to view the contents, and the library book on costumes had set Jean's mind to thinking certain thoughts!

Wonder of wonders – there was a wedding dress. A sumptuous gown, neatly, carefully, folded and laid in brown tissue paper, of some unknown sort – which crumbled as they slowly unwrapped the gown. *What a wedding dress.* To Tabby's disappointment it wouldn't go anywhere near her now well-rounded figure; Jean's legendary stews had worked their miracle on the once painfully thin child. It had an eighteen-inch waist span, with not enough surplus material for it to be let out enough for Tabby!

'Sorry, lovey, handspan waists they used to have in them days: took pride in them, me mum told me many times, her mum told her! *With the aid of grim corsets!* You're a twenty-six-inch waist lovey and your great-grandmother must have been very short, no more than four feet eight inches, if she wore this for her wedding?'

Removing a tarnished silver frame from underneath the dress or gown, to give it the correct nomenclature, Tabby had a good look at the dull, sepia photograph. 'Yeah, she was very, very, tiny.'

'Mum, look, here she is wearing the dress, standing beside her husband. Didn't your mum tell you her father – your grandfather – was at least six feet, three inches tall? Oh, doesn't she look sweet, wiv her little waist, looks like a doll, standing beside 'im, wiv his mutton chop whiskers. Nice looking, weren't he? What happened to him, Mum?'

Jean shook her head in bewilderment – 'If only we'd opened the trunk before me mum died, if only?'

Whistling softly through his teeth, Henry sat down very abruptly. '"If ifs and ans were pots 'n' pans – there'd be no need fer tinkers," that's wot me old dad used ter say. A little word *if* wiv a big meaning!'

'Orl this lovely material,' murmured Jean tragically, 'orl upstairs in her loft, then ours! Us havin' ter clothe ourselves with coupon rationing! Sixteen coupons fer a man's pair of trousers, no sorry, eight fer the trousers, thirteen fer a jacket, five fer a waistcoat ... let's fink ... er ... um ... three fer a pair of socks, one fer two hankies or a tie ... eleven fer a woman's dress, fourteen fer a coat! Orl this wasting away upstairs!'

Indignantly, Tabby rounded on her, pointing out it wasn't wasted; it was historical, possibly worth a lot of money; they'd better not touch anyfing else.

Henry had a few quiet words with his wife, and it was agreed, unanimously, that the trunk was for Tabby – her wedding present! Tabby was over the moon – her first real antique.

The costume team demurred, they felt it should go to a suitable museum for the benefit of the nation. Jean said no! It had been in her family all these long years and it should stay in the family – for after the Lord, family was more important than others, in her humble opinion! Anyway, what the nation hadn't seen wouldn't be missed!

So the trunk was Tabby's – for ever!

The wedding veil was not to go to the museum – to their heartfelt dismay; no matter how much forceful pressure they applied, Jean was adamant and obdurate. It was for Tabby – a family heirloom! Henry told the team they were wastin' their breff – once his wife made up her mind she wouldn't budge.

So they stood back whilst Jean made up her mind about everything. She pounced on a large box, the last thing to be removed from the trunk; her eyes almost disappeared behind her eyebrows when the lid of the box was carefully removed. It was crammed chock full of trimmings of all sorts; scintillating diamonds of beads and beadwork in all shapes and sizes. More lace, colourful ribbons in various widths. 'Oh, my giddy aunt, oh my giddy aunt!'

'Who was your giddy aunt, Mrs Braithewaite?' asked one the team.

'Just a sayin' we 'ave love, jist a sayin'! Look at these ribbons and kid gloves, ohhh! Ter fink it might have orl been blown ter smithereens!'

Jean's jaw dropped, she was utterly gobsmacked!

She told her daughter she was goin' ter be the best-dressed bride of the six streets or she wasn't her mother. 'Jist leave it ter me an' Maisie, yerse!'

Tabby'd been thinking of purchasing her

wedding finery; Freddy was all for it – they could afford the best. But now Jean was adamant that herself and friend Maisie were full of ideas and, being skilful needle women Tabby would have the best of the best different from all other brides!

Before their respective marriages both Jean and her friend had been in the *rag trade* – but not in factories, in *haute couture*, the *crème de la crème of skilled needle women*. They'd started very young – a mere fourteen years of age; both had married young, had their families young – nevertheless they were still capable of turning out class and elegance when they put their minds to it. Once a skilled needle woman always a skilled needle woman. Like riding a bike – one never forgot. Maisie had worked privately in Forest Gate for a Jewish family who were quite well-to-do. The matriarch adored her gowns smothered in bugle beads, pearls, sequins etcetera. No hardship for Maisie, such work was her forte – the elegant, lavishly decorated gown she produced for her boss to wear at her eldest son's Bar Mitzvah was a stunning creation of different shades of beads and sparkling diamanté, with a semi-train sweeping grandly from the rear. Predominantly pink in colour, the subtle shading effects which Maisie created so painstakingly, with the tiny seed pearls and bugle beads, gave the appearance of wave after wave of different pink-toning which was a joy to look upon. Her employer was absolutely ecstatic. 'My dear, you have surpassed yourself this time – I just can't wait for my son's special event, his Bar Mitzvah. It's the highlight of the calendar of every Jewish mother with a son – it will be a knockout with this gown. My dear it is simply fabulous, fabulous; I cannot wait to see the effect it will have when I float into the celebration room!'

But she did have to wait, and, as predicted, the gown was a knockout with her friends begging her to loan such a valuable needle woman to them for their sons' Bar Mitzvahs. She discouraged them all, insisting that Maisie was her discovery and her jewel and she had no desire to share her! A wonderful compliment to Maisie which left certain well-to-do women in tears. Maisie only had one pair of hands – such intricate work, as hers undoubtedly was, did not leave her enough time to oblige any desperate women who cajoled for her services.

Jean also worked for a Jewish family at Forest Gate; there was a friendly rivalry between the two households. Jean was an excellent cutter and seamstress. It was not uncommon for Jean and Maisie to work in tandem on a particular gown for their respective employers, pooling and using their expertise to good advantage. Jean had not worked privately as long as Maisie (because she married young) but she was the better dressmaker.

'It's all *in the cut*,' she would tell her daughters. 'You get a good cut and you can do anything with a garment because it will fit and hang well, yerse it's orl in the cut. The cut is the foundation stone of any well-made garment. Orl of a skilled needle woman's knowledge can't make up for a bad cut.'

Her daughters, whilst liking sewing, had never

become anywhere near as skilled as Jean and Maisie who'd trained whilst young. Cut their teeth on sewing they had!

Jean and Maisie had both been extra horrified at the Holocaust; their affection for their employers was genuine, they had an empathy with them. A good Jewish woman is a friend for life they'd both reiterated.

After they'd had their first babies, their employers didn't want to lose them, they'd gone home laden down with lavish baby clothes and other gifts beyond their own pockets. Many a tasty feast, wrapped in a pristine white cloth, had been taken home to be shared with their husbands. It had, finally been quite a wrench for them to give up their jobs at Forest Gate. In the end they still made clothes – or adapted other ones for them … working mainly from *home* right up to the outbreak of war. Jean had become terribly fond of *rollmops, bagels* and *fresh salmon!*

Tabby's wedding dress was to be the needle women's finale. Using a Blackie pattern chosen by Tabby herself, and to be adapted with Maisie's skill of beadwork et al, Jean had carefully cut the heavy brocade – obtained on the black market – no questions asked – via Ginger's uncle, the black marketeer! It was a beautiful figured brocade – best quality. Maisie was going to follow the outline of some of the patterned cloth with seed pearls and bugle beads and diamante from the attic box.

The Braithewaite girls longed to see the pattern; they longed to see the brocade. Alas, their mother wouldn't even let them have one peep at it. Only Maisie, Tabby and Jean were permitted to see anything – their mother was doggedly determined in that respect; she considered it unlucky for others to see a wedding dress before the great day. To which purpose, the creation, from its birth and the trimmings, was kept locked in Jean's wardrobe. The least sound, whilst they were working in the boxroom and whoosh – a sheet was hastily thrown over everything!

Gertie pleaded in vain: 'Go on, Mum, we don't know if Tabby's hairstyle will go with the wedding dress. Let's have a little peak, go on, Mum, I won't tell anybody.'

Tabby whooped, 'Ohhh, Gertie! You can never keep secrets, can she, Mum?'

'Nah! She can't! Yer knows yer can't Gertie – don't you dare show her, Tabby, or orl the six streets'll know by tomorrow! It's unlucky.'

Bowled over – Gertie had the grace to blush! Anyway, as far as Tabby was concerned she was wearing the same hairstyle as always – loose, long and wavy. Freddy loved it like that and her mother told her it would look wonderful with her dress.

Undaunted by such truthful allegations Gertie attempted to glean information by using another tactic.

Laughing fit to burst Tabby asked what Benjie'd told her.

'Benjie! My dear sweet little brother – the apple of me eye – 'ee jist gives me 'is angelic smile and sez black velvet – 'is mummy told him ter say that! Bribed him with chocolate 'n' orl she has. It's not fair, Mum, go on be a sport, yer can tell me!'

Jean's sides were aching from laughing now – she'd done a good sccrct scrvice job on Benjie and the triplets – she knew Gertie could never, never keep her mouth shut any more than she could stop breathing. Along with her earwigging skill it was one of her assets, depending which way you looked at it. If you wanted something to get round the six streets – tell Gertie.

'I've madc a toile of the boys' outfits – I tell you this much, I wouldn't be surprised if they upstage the bride, an' that'll take some doing, I can tell yer, once me and Maisie've finished her gown! It's a cracker, is her gown. The boys'll look smashing – like the archangel Gabriel! I 'opes my little Benjie duzzn't put on any more weight.'

Gertie sniffed, she felt quite miffed, with her nose put out of joint! 'That's yer own fault, Mum, yer orlways overfeeding him and the triplets, jis 'cos yer had ter go wivout in the war. Dad's jist as bad – 'ee orlways gives Benjie some of his own dinner – dotes on 'im 'ee does. Stands ter reason I suppose – 'is only son.'

'Can I borrow your antique brooch, Gertie – you know, "Something old, something new, something borrowed, something blue"?'

''Course yer can – stoopid! I fought yer sed yer wearin' yer pearls, is it a high neck dress?'

Tabby shook her head smilingly – if Gertie thought to catch her like that she had another think coming!

Wheedingly, hopefully, in a last attempt to break the barriers Gertie mentioned she thought the Valenciennes lace veil was the something old bit!

'Ain't tellin' yer nuffin', are we, Mum? Orl the six streets'd know by breakfast time tomorrow! Youse'll orl jist 'ave ter wait 'til me wedding day.' So Gertie gave up! In the face of such opposition how could she do but otherwise.

As the great day loomed ever nearer, Tabby began to wish it all over and done with. The strain of keeping Freddy at arm's length; looking at properties – yes, they'd started that palaver again – was driving both of them round the bend. Freddy ominously muttered if he never saw another property again it would be too soon. They'd been to talk to the vicar at the rectory – or was it the vicarage? Her mind was getting muddled up with so many things to think about: They'd had a long spiritual talk with the *dog-collar* which Freddy naughtily called him! He couldn't, for the life of him, see how an un-married priest knew and understood about being married. And he was well under thirty!

Tabby vaguely mentioned he'd probably *larnt* in theology school or wherever they went to learn how to become a dog-collar or maybe God had told him – part of a priest's calling. For Freddy's part, he still felt quite strongly that a bachelor dog-collar wasn't the most suitable person to discuss marriage with – especially the personal side. Having said that, however, Freddy had to admit the dog-collar was a decent likeable fellow. 'But actuality and theory are two different things, Tabby.'

She marvelled, yet again, at her young fiancé's astuteness and his usage of good grammar. She'd have to remember to tell her Mum that – *actu-*

ality and *theory;* her Freddy certainly knew his onions.

That day – after the visit to the dog collar – they must have visited a hundred houses; her head was splitting, she felt sick. When Freddy said one more to see she could have sunk to the ground. Here they were on their way to inspect the last possible family home, *suitable for a young couple.* And it was a shop! Presumably it was a large roomy family flat over a shop? She didn't fancy the idea of a flat in which to bring up a large family – she expected to have a large brood – her sisters were very fertile! True, she'd privately considered family planning, the modern way of having children; Freddy wasn't interested. He turned out to be like all men – didn't relish taking precautions. She'd vainly tried to win him over.

'That's what all men say, lovey, until the band of gold is on yer finger. Then it's a different story – yer theirs, body 'n' soul, fer the price of a dog's licence: *seven-and-sixpence* is all it costs 'em! Yer his chattel, 'n' yer promise in front of the vicar ter love, honour, and obey. And they keeps yer to it – yerse! Got one-track minds, men have, lovey. And it ain't the race track 'eiver! I guess the good Lord knows wot He's doing to encourage procreation for perpetuating the human race. Especially since the war. Got ter replace orl the poor souls who died, ain't He?'

'Mum! Yer niver sed a truer word in all yer born days! Babies! They're everywhere. I do love 'em but yer can't go out shopping on a weekday wiv aht bein' surrounded by babies! Remember when I had some time off work? Went ter Green Lanes 'n' then East Ham, didn't I? What did I see? Babies! Seems like they've sprang up overnight like mushrooms!

'Yer don't see men! They're either at work or sleeping 'cos they're on shift work. It's babies, babies and more babies! With their proud mums – who're almost always heavily pregnant! And the baby in the pram sometimes no more than nine months old!'

'I jist told youse, lovey, it's the Lord's way of repopulating 'n' who're we ter tell Him different? Youse luvs the triplets and Benjie, 'n' yer uvver nieces and nephews. Youse should be used ter babies by now!'

The Gospel truth, which Tabby was well aware of. It was strange most of the babies were boys! You had to keep your eyes peeled to spot a pram with a pink coverlet. The Lord was balancing out the sexes again – *repasturing His acres.*

So here they were, her and Freddy, at the nearest railway station to the last vacant possession property on the long list. Her headache had become so acute she thought she might faint any moment. Freddy failed to notice her discomfort, he was excited and enthusiastic about this particular property. She sighed heavily, smiled and carried on like a Trojan – she didn't want to spoil Freddy's euphoria. Undoubtedly this property must have something more going for it than the others they'd turned down.

Her mother always conceded that life was full of surprises – from Freddy's happy chattering this house was meant to be a surprise. She hoped

328

it was a good one.

Departing from the steam train, they stood watching the man with his little green flag as the train chug-chugged-chugged, gathering speed until it was but a speck in the far distance, highlighted by the clear blue sky on this beautiful, sunny day. Leaving the station, they both sniffed the balmy air appreciatively – they were in the country. Such a refreshingly clean area with grass, trees and not a flat in sight.

Taking their time – there was no immediate hurry – it was utterly calm and peaceful, strolling hand-in-hand like lovers the world over, Tabby's headache left her – whoosh! Greatly relieved she determined to enjoy herself – even if she didn't like the property. Who could fail to feel uplifted in this verdant environment, as they strolled further from the station, under the arch of trees meeting trees from either side of the lane from the station. The twittering of birds was something new. They stood stock-still listening to several, trilling their hearts out in perfect harmony. The sun shone on their faces, as they left the welcoming shade of the trees, to approach a proper tarmac road. This road, bordered by hedgerows of blackthorn, offered up the pleasure of seeing busy birds flying in and out of the welcoming hedgerow. Tabby began to hum softly, a spirit of contentment was sneakily stealing over her senses and little grey cells. Slipping her arm into Freddy's, she squeezed tightly against him. He looked downwards at her serene happy face and knew the heady enchantment had overtaken her, as it had himself. The strain had faded from

Freddy's face too – it was *luverlee* to be young, in love, out buying their first home. The road meandered slightly until it approached a small hamlet. Past the little Post Office, then a grocer's shop, and a butcher's shop, a small newsagent's, a chemist shop, a teeny-weeny hardware shop, to an empty haberdashery shop situated right next to a chocolate-box cottage with bottle pane windows and an abundance of outside wooden beams. Past that could be seen acres of green fields; a cluster of cottages and a reasonably-sized church with a cockerel weathercock standing proud at the pinnacle of its spire.

Tabby pinched herself. No she wasn't dreaming – Freddy had stopped right outside the haberdashery shop and the cottage attached! It was two cottages actually, made into one large spacious home. Her heart began pounding like a sledgehammer; her breath came in short sharp gasps. This was *it*, she knew it! Freddy grinned at her, his watermelon smile rivalling her own: he didn't need to ask her if she liked what she saw – it registered clearly on her loving face. She stepped back a few steps to have a better view of the whole; her squeal of delight startled a furry, marmalade cat, who'd been innocently lounging on one of the outside window ledges. He yawned prodigiously, stretched himself daintily, leapt lightly off the cill and stood waiting expectantly.

The roofs were thatched – real thatched roofs. She'd often dreamed of a chocolate-box cottage after seeing one on a box of chocolates – long empty which Jean had saved from before the war; it was too pretty to throw away.

Freddy must have remembered Tabby showing him the chocolate box lid months ago! Her eyes, with their butterfly lashes, gazed upwards, yes it was as blue as in the chocolate-box picture – not a cloud in sight. It was a good omen! Whirling suddenly, startling both Freddy and the cat, she threw her arms around his neck in gratitude. Raining kisses on his face as he lowered his head and shoulders to hug her back. Fleetingly he wondered what people would think; he needn't have worried, not a soul was in sight – it was lunch time.

'I'm sorry I was miserable earlier on – I'd a headache, it's gone now thank goodness; I thought you meant a flat over a shop – I had no idea...' Her voice trailed away.

'Stoopid! I knew you thought it was going to be a flat over a shop. D'ya think I didn't know – can read you like a book I can, my precious. Wanted to surprise you, didn't I?'

He opened the front door with a key from his inside pocket, and it creaked alarmingly on its unoiled hinges, setting his teeth on edge. 'Shall I carry you over the threshold, sweetheart?' He made to lift her, ducking his head under the low lintel – he didn't want a duck's egg bump on his wedding day.

Tabby demurred saying as she hadn't yet got the gold band on her finger, it might be bad luck! They entered the interior, the happy motes of sunlight streaming through the unwashed windows; specks of dust danced in them, making the cottage come alive. It was a perfect home, it even had a large old-fashioned inglenook fireplace with delft pottery tiles in the traditional blue surrounding it. Heavy oak beams – Freddy's head was but a few inches from them – a little winding staircase, three fair-sized bedrooms, and an attic room under the eaves. Gazing around, almost dumbstruck, a thought entered her mind, it was double-fronted outside, so where were the other upstairs rooms?

'You're quick-witted love.' He took her hot little hand in his huge paw and led her slowly down the stairs. In the living room he crossed over to a door which she'd thought was a walk-in cupboard. He opened it with a melodramatic flourish bowing obsequiously – and lo and behold, there was the empty next door haberdashery!

She gasped, her clenched fist in front of her mouth. Tears of delight tumbled in rivulets of stinging tears cascading down her face, she was oblivious to them... 'Oh Freddy, oh Freddy – you're the most dearest darling in the whole wide world!'

'Hey hey, sweetheart, mop up the Niagara Falls, will you? No more tears today, this is a happy day – I take it you like this house – it meets with Miss Tabitha Braithewaite's unequivocal approval – this time?'

'Like it? Like it! Ohhh! I love it – stoopid! I'm crying because I'm happy, stoopid! I just know we're going to be happy here, I can feel it in my bones!' Her face dropped, she whispered tremulously, 'Supposing we can't afford it, Freddy? Ohhh! I'll die if we can't. Please say we can afford it – please, Freddy, please, please.'

Looking grave, he shook his head solemnly, putting his hand into his jacket pocket: he was wearing his brown Harris Tweed hacking jacket today, the one she liked him in best of all! Tabby stood like a statue, scarcely daring to breathe – oh – it was agonising!

Slowly, very slowly, pausing for effect, he murmured, 'I went to the bank, they gave me the figures.' He shook his head once more. She bit her finger to stifle her lips from interrupting him. Please God, she silently and earnestly prayed swiftly, please God, I'm keeping my promise to you to be a virgin when I walk up the aisle in your house – please don't let me down, please make Freddy say yes!

Methodically he removed a sheet of paper from the entrancing envelope, as Tabby looked on mesmerised.

Tremblingly, acutely nervously, her fingers opened out the all-important sheet of paper, thinking, this can't be real, we must be able to afford it – it's our dream home – off the box lid I've loved all my life, I'll die if we can't afford it.

'Ohhh! Ohhh! You are awful, Freddy Debnon, how could you, but I love you' – all said in one breath – 'we *have* got enough money, stoopid! This is the deeds to the cottage and the shop. Oh Freddy, I love you! How could you torment me like that? You've bought it all – lock, stock and barrel! How could you let me think … you rogue, ohhh – you are awful, Freddy, now where's my hankie, I'm going to cry.'

'Here, have mine. I hope we're not going to have the Niagara Falls every time you're happy, sweetheart? If you are there won't be much room in this cottage, we'll be flooded out! I'll have to make sure you're happy all our life.' Mopping her streaming eyes and nose – which had decided it was too good an opportunity not to take part – she giggled, choked and gulped air down the wrong way! He thumped her between her shoulder blades.

'Ouch, that hurt.'

'It's nothing to what you'll get my girl, if you don't stop your floods – Niagara must be drained dry by now. How about you know what *now* Tabby? Nobody need never know. We're in our own home!'

'What d'ya mean? Oh no! *Oh no!* Freddy you promised me!' She waggled an indignant forefinger in his face. 'I don't like people who break promises, you *can't* trust them! Not until we're properly married in the House of the Lord, married in His eyes. I promised Mum, she'd kill me if I wasn't a virgin on me wedding day! I'm being a virgin bride if it kills me!'

Freddy lugubriously retorted, it might not kill her – but it was definitely killing *him!* A man – a hot blooded man – had only so much patience and willpower. 'All right, all right, sweetheart, don't go getting upset. I'm only teasing you' (not really, he thought resignedly). 'Oh blimey there you go again – Niagara Falls! Now what?'

She laughed amidst the flow of unchecked tears. 'Ohhh! Freddy, you are awful you really are stoopid!'

'But you love me,' said Freddie disarmingly. He dropped a kiss lightly on her nose. 'Hmm! Salty

– I like sweet things!'

She scrubbed her cheeks furiously with his hankie – sopping wet now and went to hand it back.

'You can keep it!' he said magnanimously. 'But you'll have to give me one of your coupons so I can get some more. Do we still need coupons for handkerchiefs?'

'Dunno, ain't bought any for ages. Ivy works in a laundry now – she's in charge. She brings home all the missing, lost hankies – we squabble over who's going ter 'ave the prettiest ones. It's the Fully-Finished Laundry yer see. Me mum still won't trust her sheets to it though – prefers to rub-a-dub-dub in the small tin barf. Said she's used to it 'n' doesn't want her things mixed up wiv uvver people's fings. Daft really innit, would save her a lot of work, the laundry van picks up the washing at people's front doors 'n' brings it all back, nicely cleaned and ironed and wrapped up in pale green paper.'

'Yeah! Daft innit.'

'Is this cottage or rather cottages and the shop really 'n' truly *ours?* I know I jist saw the deeds, but...'

'*Stoopid!* How many more times must I tell you – *yes!* It's ours – well actually it's in my name only, Mr Chirley sez that's the usual way of doing business!'

Sniffling loudly she uttered the dread phrase, 'Because I'm only my husband's *chattel!*'

He guffawed, 'Technically speaking, you ain't my chattel until the band is on your third finger of your left hand my little Niagara Falls, but, yes

– Mr Chirley – the bank manager, that's what he said to me – in different wording. It was he who told me about this being on the market with vacant possession: I asked him how he knew about it. Said the owner had banked with him for over thirty years, since he was a boy, as a matter of fact; he died and the family told him they were selling up with vacant possession. So, I wangled some time off work, tootled down here, had a good dekko, went straight to Mr Chirley at the bank for a banker's draft and paid for it, lock, stock and barrel. No mortgage, every blessed part of the whole is *ours.*'

Her legs suddenly felt all wobbly – she sank to the floor, cuddling the purring marmalade cat, who, to all intents and purposes, had adopted them as his new owners. Actually he did come with the cottage – the fishmonger had been feeding him. He hunkered down beside her, revelling in the happiness he'd been able to give his future bride – an unmortgaged home. Every woman's dream. Soon she would be all his and the prettiest bride of the six streets. It couldn't come soon enough, the sap was stirring in his loins, he felt fit to burst all over!

'Chattel or no chattel – yer knows wot yer trouble is, Freddy?' said Tabby, reverting to vernacular again. 'You breathe!' She collapsed – sobbing as if her heart would break. Freddy couldn't make it out? Now, what had he done wrong? There was no understanding women. That old cowboy in the film had been right. 'Wimmin is queer critters!'

First Tabby had a headache, then she hadn't!

Then she's been given a beautiful cottage and shop, all fully paid up. Her dreams of the chocolate box lid. Then what does she do? Floods the place out with tears. He pulled her to her feet, cuddling her tightly – a good hug was always beneficial – so he'd found! Maybe that would stop the copious flow of tears? But no! Her sobbing grew louder and louder ... the tears never-ending. He wondered where the tap was for the flow from her beautiful eyes, normally sparkling, were now all watery and bubbly, the tears cascading scaldingly; flood after flood. Was there to be no end to them? He murmured into the top of her hair, 'There, there, sweetheart, if you really don't like it – I can sell it back again.'

'Don't you dare ever, ever, ever, sell our beautiful dream home! I'm crying because I'm happy, stoopid!' She wailed louder and louder, the sound echoing around the empty house.

Freddy's eyebrows knitted together comically. 'If you're crying because you are happy – what do you do when you're sad?'

'Cry of course, stoopid! Only different tears!'

'My word! My, my, my! Are there different tears for different occasions?'

'Of course there are – stoopid! These are happy loving tears, you can have pleased tears; angry tears; surprised tears...'

He gently laid his huge palm over her salty tremulous lips. 'All right, sweetheart – I've got the picture, you've convinced me – now put a sock in it, eh!'

She mumbled softly, 'Pinch me, Freddy, tell me I'm not dreaming.'

Removing his hand from her lips he pressed his eager searching ones against them, bruising her mouth in the intensity of his emotions which were ominously threatening to brim over – he knew he wouldn't be able to keep himself in check if they did. Then he pinched her sharply!

'Ouch!' she screamed shrilly. *'That hurt!'*

Falling about laughing Freddy reminded her she had told him to pinch her.

'Not that hard. I hope nobody heard me? You're being a bully now Freddy, but I do love you and I'm terribly proud of you – 'n' – I bet I have a bruise tomorrow!'

Tabby couldn't get home fast enough to tell her mother about her *chocolate box lid* cottages and shop; or should she call it *cottage*. It had been two, but it was *one* now? Maybe she'd be on safer ground to say the singular, or folks might get confused! She'd be quite a way from them – well – not far by train and it was a good regular service – but she'd miss her mum and Benjie and Gertie and the triplets whom she saw every day of her life. Waiting for the train, Freddy gave her the *icing on the cake!* The telephone was already wired in at the shop and he'd arranged for her mother and Gertie to have their own telephones installed before the wedding day – as a gift from him and Tabby. Sally and Derek already had a telephone; a budding MP needed one. Freddy reckoned the rest of the Braithewaite girls would get phones once they knew their mum was on the phone. They'd all be able to keep in touch.

The thought of the collective phone bills made

him mentally shudder! He'd got everything worked out; he would move into the cottage that weekend, Tabby would be able to speak to him via the phone from her mother's house – her phone was being installed tomorrow – a surprise! Jean had often said she'd like a telephone to keep in touch with her family and friends. More and more people were having telephones; like a rash, as one got one another followed suit. Tabby was pleased, she knew Benjie would by over-the-moon with joy. He had a toy play phone and was always phoning imaginary friends. What the triplets would make of a real phone was anyone's guess: they copied their Uncle Benjie in everything!

Freddy'd spoken to Billy about the decorating and he and his boy (apprentice) were going to bed-down at the cottage and decorate as fast as they could. Tabby was to choose the colours and the stencils – she wanted stencilled borders on the walls. She felt it was the *best* kind of decoration for a *chocolate box cottage*.

Freddy and his father had made the furniture – his father, very hopefully made a cot! *That* was to be a special surprise for Tabby!

She'd already *ticked* him off for not keeping her in the *picture* about the cottage and shop. Turned out that her mother already knew! She'd shown him the old chocolate box lid, which Tabby had loved since a baby.

'When she was five,' said Jean, 'she looked at the picture and said seriously to us, "Mummy – when I'm a big grown girl I'm going to live in a house like that!" We used to laugh and tell her it

339

was only a dream, but it was a dream which she tucked away amongst the little grey cells – what she calls her brain – and she never forgot her dream.'

'You should have told me, Freddy, you told my Mum! 'T'ain't fair!'

He just laughed pleasantly and reiterated it was a man's prerogative to provide for his bride as and how he liked – or could?

She'd huffily tossed her head scornfully, 'That'll change one day, men won't always get away with it. It wouldn't go on for ever – women would get their *rights* some day, they would no longer be mere chattels!'

Freddy didn't argue the toss, he said he hoped they did, but until then *he* would be the man of the house.

A slow ruminative, naughty smile slid across her face. 'We'll see about *that!*'

He thought his beautiful bride-to-be was a really *spunky little lass* and was glad she was marrying him. He couldn't, for the life of him, think of any other female who'd attracted him like Tabby.

'Thanks Freddy ... yer knows I loves ya stoopid ... but I won't be a pushover to appease masculine ego. Got a mind of my own, I have.'

'Thanks for warning me – sweetheart mine – how about a little' – he winked suggestively – 'you know what – consummation?'

She disappeared like a whirlwind, leaving him roaring with laughter.

Chapter Fifteen

Jean hollered up the stairs. 'Tabby! Tabby! It's your turn fer a barf. Come on, lovey, afore the hot water boils over in the copper!'

Her daughter dutifully padded three-quarters of the way down the carpeted staircase, avoiding the brass stair rods with her bare feet. Jean handed her a bucket of hot water.

'Ohhh! That's hot, Mum – the 'andle I mean. Crumbs 'n' custard!'

'Jist told yer, didn't I? Hurry up, there's a good girl! There ain't enuff room to swing a cat in our kitchen – the quicker yer empty the copper the quicker yer gets out from under me feet.'

Tabby poured bucket after bucket of hot water into the bath. There was a back boiler in wintertime – but the boiler was insufficient in summertime.* Running the icy cold tap onto the hot water, she crumbled a few perfumed *Bonsoir bath cubes* into the bath, and added a few drops of *Evening In Paris* perfume from its little dark blue glass container. She was making sure that she would be very fragrant, deliciously fragrant, today of all days. She lay supine, revelling in the

*The bath upstairs was a normal bath in a bathroom. The bath for washing clothes was a round tin bath. Bathrooms only had hot water in winter from back boilers of fires downstairs, but not in summer time.

luxury of a nice hot bath thinking of the one Billy 'n' his boy had installed in the cottage. He was a Jack-of-all-trades was Billy; not just a mere decorator. He'd fitted the white bathroom suite and the white wall tiles. She thought it fab! Freddy disparagingly muttered, 'Reminds me of a mortuary slab,' which was daft as he'd never seen a mortuary slab. The frilly pink gingham curtains were set off prettily by the white bathroom furniture. She'd chosen the pink floral linoleum from the Co-Op in East Ham: always had a good supply they did.

Freddy had an aunt who'd been a GI bride and was now safely ensconced in the United States of America. In 1946, along with thousands of other brides and numerous offspring, she'd sailed off to *Valhalla* – the *promised land.* It was for many, but, alas, not for others – once the bubble burst and reality took over. Her departing vision of Britain had been of a country in the grips of austerity until, in time it would, and did, arise Phoenix-like from the ashes. Meanwhile her standard of living was sky high – she'd delighted in sending her nephew a whole bale of thick fluffy pink towels and facecloths, the like of which nobody born since 1939 had ever seen – or remembered!

Freddy, the Heavens be praised, had the foresight to have an immersion fitted to the boiler so they would have piping hot water upstairs and downstairs. 'In my lady's chamber,' parodied Freddy, 'summer and winter?'

Females cinched their waists with wide belts made of a thickened *web* kind of elastic that hooked together with big metal clasps. To make waists look even smaller, some girls wore *waspies* underneath their blouse or dress, around their waists. Dresses ballooned fantastically-feminine with the aid of froth after froth of tulle half-slips. High heels were *de rigueur*, the higher the better; see-through nylon gloves, lots of heavy make-up; plucked eyebrows and small frivolous hats – they were absolutely one hundred percent feminine with a capital *F*. To see a bevy of such well-dressed girls swaying along together on their stiletto shoes and having a high old giggle was enough to turn any man's head.

Jean thought they looked smashing. They did! Absolutely no doubt about that! After wartime austerity and drabness, the butterflies – *the girls* – made it spring in Park Lane – wherever you looked. Putting smiles onto faces which had passed through horror and come out on top.

It was the eve of the *big day* the nuptials of Tabby and Freddy. She was still very young, only seventeen – many of her sisters had married at the same age.

Benjie was going to be hit the hardest: he adored his sister, she'd been ever present in his life from the day he'd been born. She told him he could stay with her as often as he liked to give Mum a break. Jean, quick off the mark, retorted, she'd be at the cottage having the break with Benjie – she wasn't going to be left out, no fear.

Though loved undoubtedly by all her children, Jean was especially closest to her eldest and youngest. It was, for sure, to be a *terrific wrench* for Jean and Gertie when Tabby left the house to become a bride with a home of her own.

As Freddy had predicted, the entire Braithe-waite clan was now on the telephone. You couldn't get to the phone before Benjie – at the first ring he was off like an arrow from a bow! Jean had stopped counting how many times a day her phone rang. Benjie would gabble away to his sisters, until Jean threatened to have the phone cut off if he didn't let her speak to them! Benjie would *huff and puff* and say his dear Freddy had the phone put on for Benjie!

'Yer a little tinker, Benjie, wait until youse grows up, then youse can 'ave yer own telephone.'

Not in the least disconcerted, Benjie told his mother, 'It's Benjie's phone; me new bruvver give it ter me, I'll let youse use it, Mum, 'cos I loves ya!'

'Cheeky little monkey, wait 'til yer Dad gets 'ome.'

'He'll bring me a bar of chocolate,' replied Benjie, unruffled. 'Daddy loves Benjie – *everybody loves Benjie* – I'm an uncle, I am!'

Jean told Gertie, 'And d'ya knows what Gertie – the little tinker's right, his Dad will fetch 'im a bar of chocolate... 'ee duz ... every Friday night. Benjie can twist 'im round 'is little finger!'

Gertie said it was nothing new, she'd know that since the day Benjie'd been born. Her dad did the same to Peter, Edward and Thomas – he called in at her prefab on Friday nights on his way home. The triplets clambered up to the window to look for his bicycle coming down the road. 'You'd laugh, Mum – when Dad knocks at the door, Thomas gets all excited and shouts,

344

"Mum, Mum, there's a *body* at the door!" and I say "Is there a body at the door?" and they all yell, "Yeah! There's a *body* at the door – it's Grandad!'"

Jean was all het up on the wedding eve, Tabby fervently hoped she didn't get one orf her migraines on the wedding day! She'd warned Tabby, 'Only soft drinks ternight, lovey, keep off the spirits.' She hoped Jean would take her own advice! Neither were drinkers but Jean did like a drop of Guinness and a wee tot of whisky in her tea.

There hadn't been any need to worry after all – the excitement of the wedding was enough to get the women and girls partying before the party even started.

Wallowing in her Bonsoir perfumed bath, she'd been soaking for twenty minutes. Tabby's mind was on the morrow and her beautiful wedding dress – locked in her mother's wardrobe, and the bridesmaids' and the pageboys', and Gertie hadn't had a glimpse of them – *to her utter chagrin.* No matter how many sweets she gave the boys, they never told her the colour!

Benjie, Edward, Peter and Thomas were so excited, Jean didn't think they'd sleep that night. But they did. Benjie was sleeping with the triplets – it would be too noisy at Tabby's hen party.

Frances, Lucy, Sophie and Miranda were the tiny bridesmaids; the first two were Dora's twins, the latter Peggy's twins. Yes, the Dopeggy twins had twin girls themselves. Spitting images of their twin mothers, even Jean couldn't tell the little ones apart!

Sally, the matron of honour, had fortunately given birth prematurely three weeks before the wedding. Jean had left the bodice unattached to the skirt until Jacqueline was born – her downy hair and round little face with its apple cheeks bringing great joy. Benjie importantly announced he was Jackie's uncle. Having made allowances for Sally's sizing it'd been no problem to attach the skirt and bodice: the dress fitted perfectly to Sally's utmost relief. It was such a joy to wear something different from a maternity smock for nine months!

The only problem would be in feeding little Jackie. With the help of the *dog-collar* the service had been set in-between Jackie's feeding times.

Her daughters began to arrive now; Jean hugged them all, she loved each and everyone of them to bits. Heavily pregnant, each of them, including Gertie who was pregnant again. The Braithewaites were a fertile bunch to say the least! The Lord was making sure of repopulating the world. To date seven of her daughters had been told they were carrying *more* than one baby … the rest were not sure yet. Henry was amused, wondering how they would all fit in for parties and family gatherings. Jean had firmly replied, 'The Lord will provide.' If that wasn't a good cause for thanksgiving and *rejoicing* in the Lord's goodness to her family, what was? Her only regret – her own mother had not lived to see all these new Braithewaites. Every night Jean prayed, using the Psalm as taught her by her mother, at her knee…

I will lift up mine eyes.
Unto the hills
From whence cometh
My help...

It had always been a great silent comfort to her:
Tabby was having it in her wedding service – in
memory of Jean's mother, at Jean's request.

The *dog-collar* had been pleased, he liked the
Psalm which Jean also favoured.

Praise the Lord
All ye nations,
Praise Him all
Ye people...

Such a dithering and dathering – the hen party
was in full swing. Jean fervently prayed none of
her pregnant daughters would drop their babies
prematurely at the actual wedding – nor at the
reception, come to that.

The bath water was cooling, Tabby was startled
from her languorous reverie – she could hear
thcm partying downstairs, and the bride was still
in her bath!

Somebody banged on the door and shouted,
'There's a queue of pregnant women downstairs
waiting to come up and relieve their bladders!'

Jean herself was outside the door now, 'Come
on, lovey, you've been ages in there.'

'Sorry, Mum,' she kissed her. 'Just making the
most of me last night at home.'

'Come down in her dressing gown then – got

some good news ter tell youse all I have, come on. And for goodness sake don't cry *because* yer 'appy, lovey! We wants yer ter look yer best termorrow.'

'Promise, Mum,' smiled Tabby staunchly. 'I don't fink I'll sleep a wink ternight, don't fink any of us will!'

Her bulky daughters gathered around her like a mother hen with her brood, Jean gave them the good news. The antique clothes and other antique items from the trunk had been sold for a six figure sum. Jean and Henry now had more money than they had ever dreamed of in their whole lives – apart from the Pools of course: Henry was still dreaming about *them!*

Such a gaggle of chatter and voices shrieking to be heard had Jean clapping her hands to her ears.

'Shut yer moufs, the lot of youse. Blimey, what a racket youse all makes. Yer farver's down the pub celebrating the good news wiv yer 'usbands and 'is cronies. Now *ternight* is Tabby's night and *termorrow* is Tabby's day, an' don't youse lot fergit it and don't even one of yer *think* of dropping her baby ternight or termorrow, 'cos it's jist not on. So youse'd better warn yer little tykes inside yer bellies ter 'ave a good kip until after termorrow then they can come when they like ... we'll be ready for them!'

'But, Mum, where's the letter, yer niver told me?'

Jean produced the letter, waving it under her nose and whipped it away again. 'Before yer go up them stairs, Tabby, I want yer orl to 'ear wot I've got ter tell yer. About the good fortune!'

Umpteen eyes focussed on their mother – waiting expectantly (excuse the pun). 'I ain't told yer Dad yet, what I'm going ter do wiv me fortune, it's mine, not 'is – chattel or no chattel – it woz me muvver's trunk of fings, so there! 'ee can put that in his pipe and smoke it.'

''Ee don't smoke a pipe, Mum,' said Gertie.

'Trust youse ter come up wiv sumfink, Gertie – jist a sayin' innit?'

Jean cleared her throat noisily. 'It's me own money, it woz me muvver's inheritance but she didn't know it poor old soul. Shame that woz, she could've dun wiv a few extra bob when she were alive. Well girls! That's neever 'ere nor there; I'm telling youse orl, 'cos yous're my girls 'n' I luvs ya orl ter bits. I'll tell Henry – yer farver – tomorrow *after* the wedding ceremony 'n' none of youse lot *will breeve* a word, and that includes you Gertie – keep yer mouf shut until our Tabby 'ere 'as got her gold band on her third finger of her left 'and. Then, I've dun me duty to orl me daughters, *orl blessed thirteen of youse,* an' I luvs yer orl! I'll tell yer farver when he's orl merry 'n' bright … 'ee knows I've got sumfink … quite a bit … but 'ee fink's it's a few 'undred. I rang up the auctioneers they told me "It's an *astronomical* sum of money realised, Mrs Braithewaite, bigger than the last big Pools win!" Are youse listening girls, any of youse remember 'ow much the last big Pools win was?'

Dora spoke softly, 'I do, it was £75,00!' There was an almighty gasp from several throats, eyes fixed themselves on Dora.

'Seventy five thousand pounds!' they mur-

349

mured to one another. Not a person moved, their eyes glued back to their mother – for once Gertie was silenced.

'Wot I'm trying ter tell youse is there were some fings in the trunk which none of the museums 'ad the good fortune to possess – trinkets I fought they woz. Shows yer 'ow much yer muvver knows dun it? The auctioneer said people were bidding over the phones, from orl over the world! Now … it ain't £75,000 – thirteen pairs of ears listened intently – 'this is big money, girls, big money. It's … it's £95,00 after the auctioneer's take their cut!'

Not a sound could be heard. Nobody moved a muscle.

'Okay, girls, you can talk now! Listen though – orl of youse girls is getting a fair share of this money it ain't goin' on the dogs, or the 'orses! I luvs yer orl, yer knows it, so I won't keep tellin' yers. I'm proud of yer orl, an' me grandchildren. There's so many of youse, even Benjie, bless him, can't remember how many times he's an uncle! Wot I'm goin' ter do is this … I've spoken to Mr Chirley of Brennan Laughton today, and he's goin' ter invest the money fer us, but the best bit is, I can afford ter put a bit of money on a 'ouse fer each of yer – except Tabby, she's got 'ers already – but she'll 'ave a share too.' She pinched Tabby's cheek playfully.

'I'll pay ya removals and give youse a lot ter spend ter furnishing yer houses – and yer pick wot yer wants, send me the bills and Mr Chirley will deal wiv it for me. Now, girls, 'ow duz that strike youse?'

350

There was a stunned silence, broken by Daisy starting to cry. 'Oh Mum, oh Mum, what would we do without you … where will we all live?' she sniffled. 'We've *gotta* stay tergevver as a family – it's important fer our children's sake. You've told us often enuff that families should live tergevver – well not tergevver but near each uvver; we orl gets on well tergevver, don't we?'

'Yeah! Yer right, Daisy, Mum orlways sez "blood is ficker'n water", eh Mum?'

''S r ight, Gertie, 's right!'

'Tabby were sayin' there's some nice properties up the road from her … ain't there, Tabby?'

'Yes, yes, there is … a small select housing estate, just outside our village, within walking distance of my cottage!'

'In that case, we'll orl pop down ter Tabby's when she gets back from her honeymoon in Folkestone – and we'll 'ave a dekko at the show house … then a cuppa at Tabby's cottage. Okay, Tabby?'

'That's no problem, we've got a shop as well – the door from the cottage opens into it from the living room.'

Stunned silence, eyes swivelled now to Tabby. 'A shop?' asked Sally. 'A *real* shop?'

'Yeah! We were going ter surprise youse in a few weeks wiv our house-warming but Mum's jumped the gun wiv 'er news an' plans, so I might as well tell youse now. Freddy bought it all – for *cash!*'

'*Cash!*' Uttered several voices unbelievingly.

'Yeah! Mr Chirley safely invested Freddy's Pools win, yer remember 'ee 'ad a share of a syndicate win – *money makes money*, apparently – so Freddy paid cash … we've still got money ter spare, we saved from our wages too. We *don't* 'ave ter worry about a mortgage, we'll orlways 'ave a roof over our 'eads.

'Freddy's goin' ter give orl of youse and 'is family a lump sum of money – 'ee luvs yer orl to bits – sez the Braithewaites are the loveliest family 'e's ever met.'

Margo, heavily pregnant spoke up. 'Mum, *if* I don't drop this baby now from shock, I'll drop it in church tomorrow – don't think I can take any more surprises tonight. No matter how pleasant.'

'Here' – Jean passed her smelling salts under Margo's nose – 'feelin' a bit better now?'

'Yeah, faintly, glass of water, someone please.' Her baby moved suddenly, she could feel it pressing on her bladder and she shifted herself from side to side to ease the pain of the jolt. 'I'll be glad when this baby comes, I feel I'm carrying an elephant, not one little baby – a proper Dumbo!'

Alert, Gertie asked if she was sure she was only having *one* baby, 'cos that's how she felt with the triplets.

'I'm not sure – don't youse go putting the mockers on me Gertie, I ain't prepared fer more than *one* baby! Doctor sez it's a healthy lively baby.'

'Better not let Benjie hear youse calling it Dumbo – 'eel call it Dumbo orl its life.'

'He wouldn't dare.'

'Oh wouldn't he?' laughed Gertie. 'Benjie's quite a wag, ain't 'ee, Mum?'

'Yer right 'n' orl, go an' sit down Margo – better orl of youse pregnant ter sit down. I'm warnin' youse agin – don't drop yer babies at the wedding tomorrow, tell 'em ter stay put 'cos their granmuvver sez she ain't ready for 'em yet.'

Hysterical laughter and giggles – her brood went to sit down again *What a mother!*

'Come on, girls, look at orl yer faces, stained wiv tears – and yer mascara – yer looks like yous've come from fightin' Sugar Ray Robinson. Let's be 'avin' yer, powder yer noses – put yer lipsticks on this is supposed ter be a 'appy 'ome an' a 'appy occasion, 'n' I don't want the photographer ter fink uvver wise.

'Back upstairs, Tabby, go on, go an' get dressed – yer don't look respectable! Yer hair's in rats' tails and yer dressing gown's sopping wet, the photographer will be 'ere in a minute. So! Come on, upstairs wiv yer 'n' look lively.'

'But...'

'But me no "buts", lovey, up them bleedin' stairs now! Youse got uvver fings ter fink of – yer'll be a married woman termorrow, make the most of ternight!'

She needn't have worried, the poor bloke was virtually struck dumb, so many daughters and nearly all heavily pregnant – and *his* wife was pregnant too. She wouldn't believe him, wouldn't have believed it himself if he hadn't seen with his own eyes! His mind boggled thinking of them waddling into the church tomorrow. At least the *bride* wasn't pregnant, or if she was she didn't show it.

Brr-nnn-g! The phone shattered their over-

353

excited nerves. Who could it be? They didn't want any more shocks tonight – especially not Margo! It was Freddy's aunt from America – would somebody hurry and pick her up at Heathrow Airport, she'd managed to catch a flight *via Reykjavik* in Iceland! She was tired, fed up, wanted a bath, a nice soft bed and a whiskey and coke.

Margo rang her husband who was playing cards with Daisy's husband, babysitting. They'd planned to go to Freddy's stag night but the baby-sitter was very late.

Josh promised to go and pick her up and take her to the hen party! He didn't know what she looked like...? 'Hold a piece of paper up with her name on it – *she'll find you*, Josh.'

It was Jean's turn to sit down after the photographer had gone. She was beginning to feel she'd had enough news to last her a lifetime!

Maisie was warbling away, she'd downed several sweet Martinis. 'Who were you with last night...' Jean hoped the unborn babies were enjoying the hen party.

It was a hen night to remember, Maisie wore an old-fashioned bloomers swimming costume complete with mob cap. She had some good news of her own. Her husband had got a transfer near to Tabby's village!

Jean was happy, the reception was at her house, a fitting finale for the Braithewaites – the family home, before they moved away from the six streets for ever. It was cosier and friendlier having wedding receptions at home. Freddy had wanted to splash out on a hall; Jean and Henry had talked him round! He compromised when Henry agreed to let Freddy foot the bill for the reception: caterers from the Civic Centre; the wedding cake; the material for the wedding clothes; and the wallop. Henry and Jean hadn't to spend a penny on their daughter's wedding. He even paid for the bridal bouquet and the bridesmaids' bouquets and the buttonholes. Tabby paid for the mothers' corsages – orchids, pink ones.

At his stag night, Freddy was terribly keyed-up; he'd be glad when it was just him and Tabby – he didn't think the rising sap in his loins could wait much longer, he'd burst!

The soft mellow tones of the organ playing Handel's 'Water Music' changed to the magnificent 'Here Comes the Bride', Tabby and her father had arrived on time for the nuptials. The mighty organ reached a crescendo as Tabby entered the church doors – veiled, but smiling serenely, she walked slowly down to where Freddy was nervously waiting for her with his best man. The congregation gasped. Tabby was not wearing puritanical virgin white! She'd pleaded with her mother and won! Jean had actually cut and altered her great-grandmother's wedding dress of pale old gold, she'd married it with a new bodice from the figured taffeta, which Maisie had skilfully stitched all over with gold bugle beads and diamante, following the shapes of the flowers of the new brocade. The skirt draped beautifully with a long heavy folded train trailing for yards and yards behind Tabby. It rippled and rippled pleasingly; the whole effect was of undulating movement mesmerising the onlookers. In her hands she carried a sheaf of Madonna lilies, lily of the valley and pink and white rosebuds, with trailing golden ribbons and maindenhair fern.

Behind her, on impeccable behaviour, followed the tiny bridesmaids dressed like Nell Gwyn, complete with baskets of oranges and nosegays, with many hued ribbons fluttering from the baskets, trailing down the fronts of their dresses as they held the baskets in both hands. On their heads they wore circlets of pink rosebuds.

Following them came the pageboys, Benjie and the triplets, Thomas, Edward, and Peter in the blue uniforms of Nelson's midshipmen. Benjie was in dark ruby red velvet with a spotless white frilled blouse, his King Charles style hat, sumptuously ostriched-feathered held firmly under one arm. Jean had coaxed his long curls into ringlets – no wonder he hadn't had a haircut recently and certainly not before the wedding. Gertie could have kicked herself; she might have known – she should have guessed. Her heart missed a beat; she gazed proudly at her little terrors – they couldn't have appeared more angelic if they'd tried. They were a credit to their mother – and her mother – she'd schooled them well, *with bribery.*

Sally, the matron of honour, Rubenesque from new-found motherhood, resembled the famous portrait of Mrs Siddons, but she was in pale lavender, head-to-toe, carrying a satin covered *Bible* with white ribbons, a small, miniature nosegay on the end of them.

Jean'd promised her youngest daughter that her wedding would be the best ever of the six streets and it surely was. The five yards of heavy old gold train, the fantastically beautiful Valenciennes wedding veil – there couldn't possibly be any comparison with anybody else's wedding. Even the *dog-collar*, who'd married more people than he'd had hot dinners, was not immune to *this* bride's outfit.

Before getting into the car to go to the church, Jean had kissed Tabby, 'This is what life is all about, lovey, *family;* you jist can't beat it – blood's thicker'n water.' She'd cried buckets, helping to dress Tabby in her wedding finery; Maisie cried with her. All their hard work had worked a miracle – nobody would ever see such a splendid wedding gown as this one. With its leg'o'mutton sleeves, finished at the long cuffs with the tiniest of buttons (removed from the original bodice), tiny seed pearls meticulously stitched all over the cuffs by Maisie: so close together the whole cuff seemed made of seed pearls; Maisie had *surpassed* herself. The close-fitted, new bodice, pin tucked and beaded with beads from a forgotten age. Her pearls were round her neck, and Gertie's antique brooch pinned to one shoulder. The whole effect was opulence but with a dignity and beauty – beauty sadly lacking in the dark war years.

The *non accurate* historical content of the wedding dress, bridesmaids dresses and pageboys' outfits didn't matter one jot – the whole effect was of stunning beauty; a fabulous turnout. Jean and Maisie glowed with pride at their own fantastic needlework. It had been a hard slog, but worth it!

The hen night had gone down a treat, and apparently so had the stag night! Nobody was more surprised than Freddy when Josh stopped outside The King's Oak and took Freddy's American aunt in to see her nephew!

In the wee small hours – in bed – for what was left of the hen night – Henry had whispered to Jean, 'We're lucky us Braithewaites, old girl!'

'Not so much of the old girl bit if you don't mind, 'Enry with an "H"! It ain't hundreds yer know!'

'Ain't it?'

'Ninety-five thousand smackers, Henry, so–'

'Cor blimey,' said Henry. He rolled over and was fast asleep! He'd imbibed heavily at The King's Oak!

Freddy gently folded back the veil from his bride's face, he was so choked he thought he would burst into tears himself.

'You may kiss the bride now,' said the Dog-Collar. He didn't need telling twice; his hungry sensuous lips pressed firmly to Tabby's rosebud mouth; as they stepped forward to sign the register the organ broke out into 'Love Divine All Love's Excelling'.

Then they were floating back down the aisle, nodding right and left, grinning their identical water-melon smiles; past the smiling faces as the choir broke into 'Hallelujah Sing to Jesus, His the sceptre His the throne...'

Out into the sunlight with not a cloud to be seen in the sky, *enough blue to make a sailor a pair of trousers* was what Jean always said; meaning it would be a beautiful day, it was, heavenly beautiful!

Their hearts were full of love. Tabby was thinking ... I was a real *virgin* bride – even if I am in *old gold* ... thank you Lord for keeping me from temptation, I know I'll never regret it.

Freddy was thinking, I'll be glad when this is all over, I can't even remember if I posted my football Pools coupon. I think it's on Mum's mantelpiece. Supposing it's a winner?

The Lord God looked down from Heaven, smiled *beatifically* on the happy young couple and whispered softly, ever so softly, 'If that's all you're worrying about young man – then you're a lucky fellow. It's a time for peace now – peace and future generations!'

'Henry, that was Tabby on the phone, you're a grandfather – again.'

'Loverlee – boy or girl?'

'Two of one and one of the other.'

Henry choked on his tea. 'Blimey, Jean, not *another* set of triplets!'

'Afraid so!'

'Blimey, Jean, blimey.'

'Mind yer language 'Enry wiv an "H", Braithewaite!'

'How many we got now – blowed if I can remember?'

'Fifty-three wiv this lot, eights sets of triplets:

359

twenty-six girls – how many boys, Henry?'
'Don't ask me, love, I'm lost!'
'Me too, Henry. Fertile girls the Braithewaites!'

Author's Note

To give an idea of weekly wages, pensions and the cost of houses, here are some examples (in decimal money):

Wages
1941-44: a skilled man earned £5; an unskilled man earned £4.
1945-50: a skilled man earned £6.50; an unskilled man earned £5.
1951-60: a skilled man earned £11; an unskilled man earned £7.

Pensions

1931-40: old age pensions became available for men at 65 and women at 60. Previously it was 25p at 70 years of age. In 1936 the pension was 50p.
1941-1944: the old age pension was 50p.
1945-50: a single man's pension was £1.30; a married man's pension was £2.10.

Houses

1931-40: average house price - £750 (£650 in the provinces)
1941-44: average house price - £800
1945-50: average house price - £2,200
1951-60: average house price - £2,750

The above will give the reader some indication of the vast fortune in terms of money which Jean, the mother in this novel, obtains from some of the contents of the old trunk in the attic.

Violet Frederick Foot
Norfolk, 2000

The publishers hope that this book has given you enjoyable reading. Large Print Books are especially designed to be as easy to see and hold as possible. If you wish a complete list of our books please ask at your local library or write directly to:

Magna Large Print Books
Magna House, Long Preston,
Skipton, North Yorkshire.
BD23 4ND

This Large Print Book for the partially
sighted, who cannot read normal print, is
published under the auspices of

THE ULVERSCROFT FOUNDATION

Other MAGNA Titles
In Large Print

ANNE BAKER
Merseyside Girls

JESSICA BLAIR
The Long Way Home

W. J. BURLEY
The House Of Care

MEG HUTCHINSON
No Place For A Woman

JOAN JONKER
Many A Tear Has To Fall

LYNDA PAGE
All Or Nothing

NICHOLAS RHEA
Constable Over The Bridge

MARGARET THORNTON
Beyond The Sunset